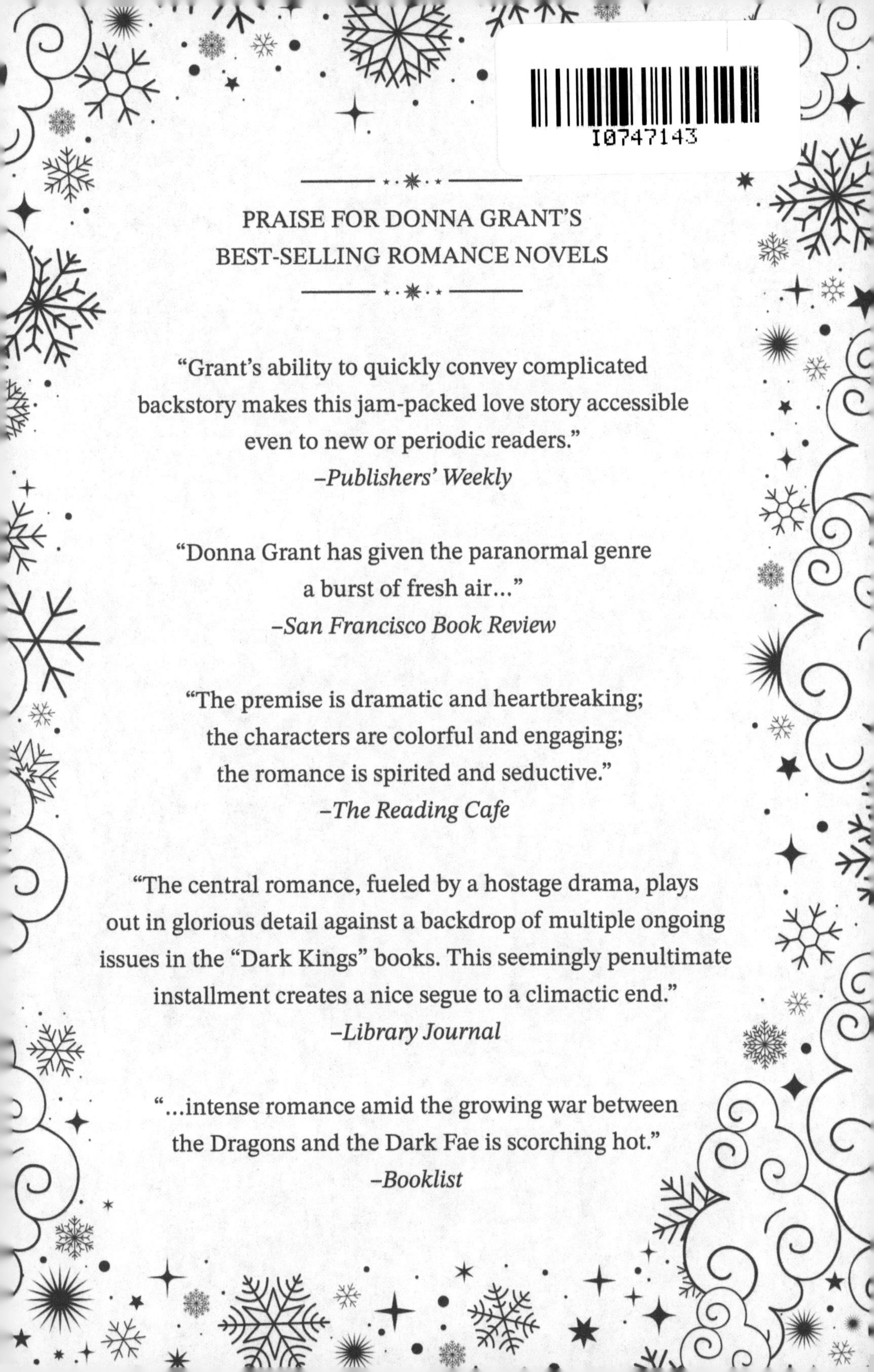

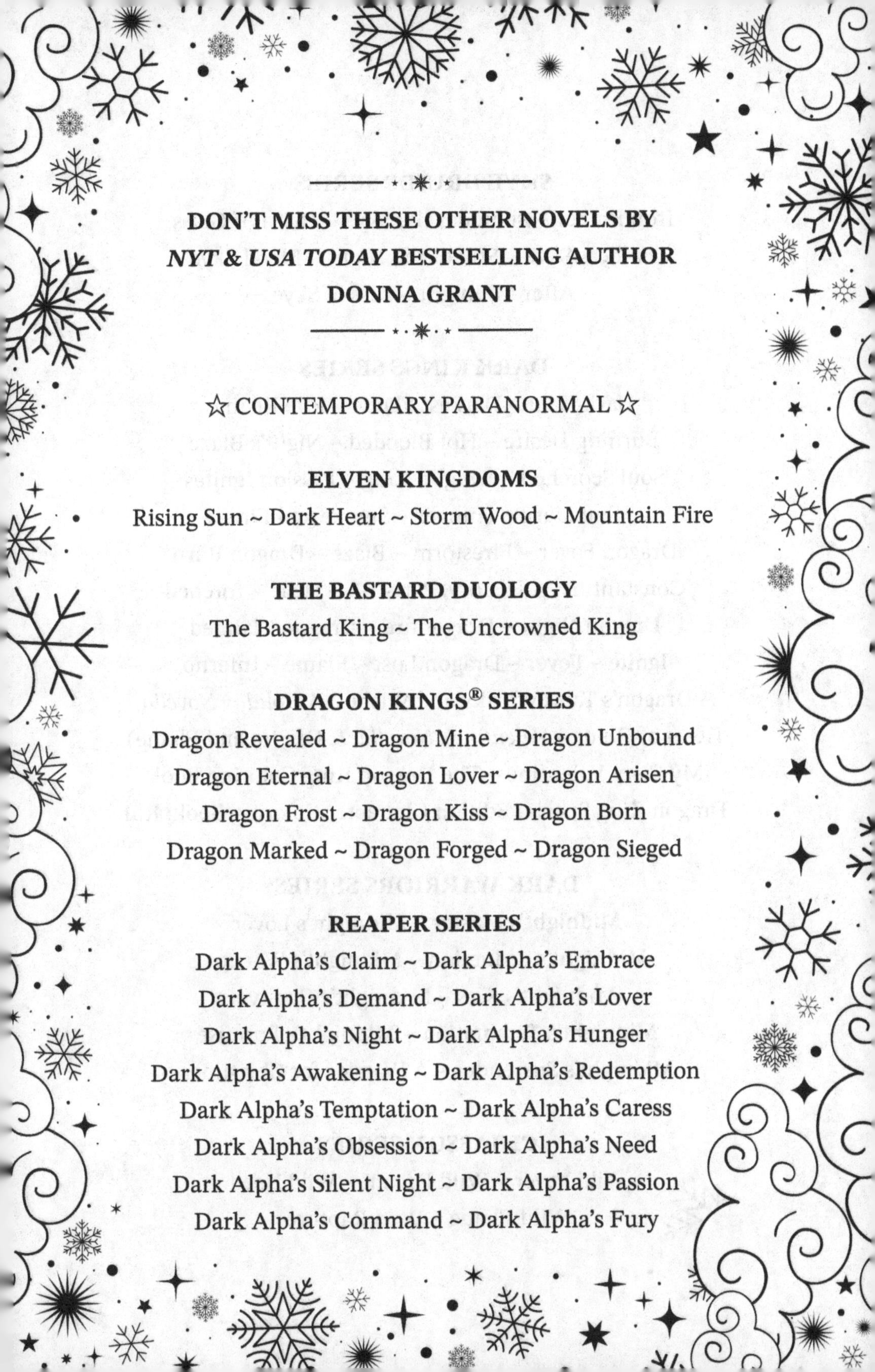

DON'T MISS THESE OTHER NOVELS BY
NYT & *USA TODAY* BESTSELLING AUTHOR
DONNA GRANT

☆ CONTEMPORARY PARANORMAL ☆

ELVEN KINGDOMS
Rising Sun ~ Dark Heart ~ Storm Wood ~ Mountain Fire

THE BASTARD DUOLOGY
The Bastard King ~ The Uncrowned King

DRAGON KINGS® SERIES
Dragon Revealed ~ Dragon Mine ~ Dragon Unbound
Dragon Eternal ~ Dragon Lover ~ Dragon Arisen
Dragon Frost ~ Dragon Kiss ~ Dragon Born
Dragon Marked ~ Dragon Forged ~ Dragon Sieged

REAPER SERIES
Dark Alpha's Claim ~ Dark Alpha's Embrace
Dark Alpha's Demand ~ Dark Alpha's Lover
Dark Alpha's Night ~ Dark Alpha's Hunger
Dark Alpha's Awakening ~ Dark Alpha's Redemption
Dark Alpha's Temptation ~ Dark Alpha's Caress
Dark Alpha's Obsession ~ Dark Alpha's Need
Dark Alpha's Silent Night ~ Dark Alpha's Passion
Dark Alpha's Command ~ Dark Alpha's Fury

LARUE SERIES

Moon Kissed ~ Moon Thrall

Moon Struck ~ Moon Bound

WICKED TREASURES

Seized by Passion ~ Enticed by Ecstasy

Captured by Desire

Books 1-3: Wicked Treasures Box Set

☆₊˚.⋆☾⋆⁺₊✧

☆ HISTORICAL PARANORMAL ☆

THE KINDRED SERIES

Everkin ~ Eversong ~ Everwylde

Everbound ~ Evernight ~ Everspell

KINDRED: THE FATED SERIES

Rage ~ Ruin ~ Reign

DARK SWORD SERIES

Dangerous Highlander ~ Forbidden Highlander

Wicked Highlander ~ Untamed Highlander

Shadow Highlander ~ Darkest Highlander

ROGUES OF SCOTLAND SERIES

The Craving ~ The Hunger

The Tempted ~ The Seduced

Books 1-4: Rogues of Scotland Box Set

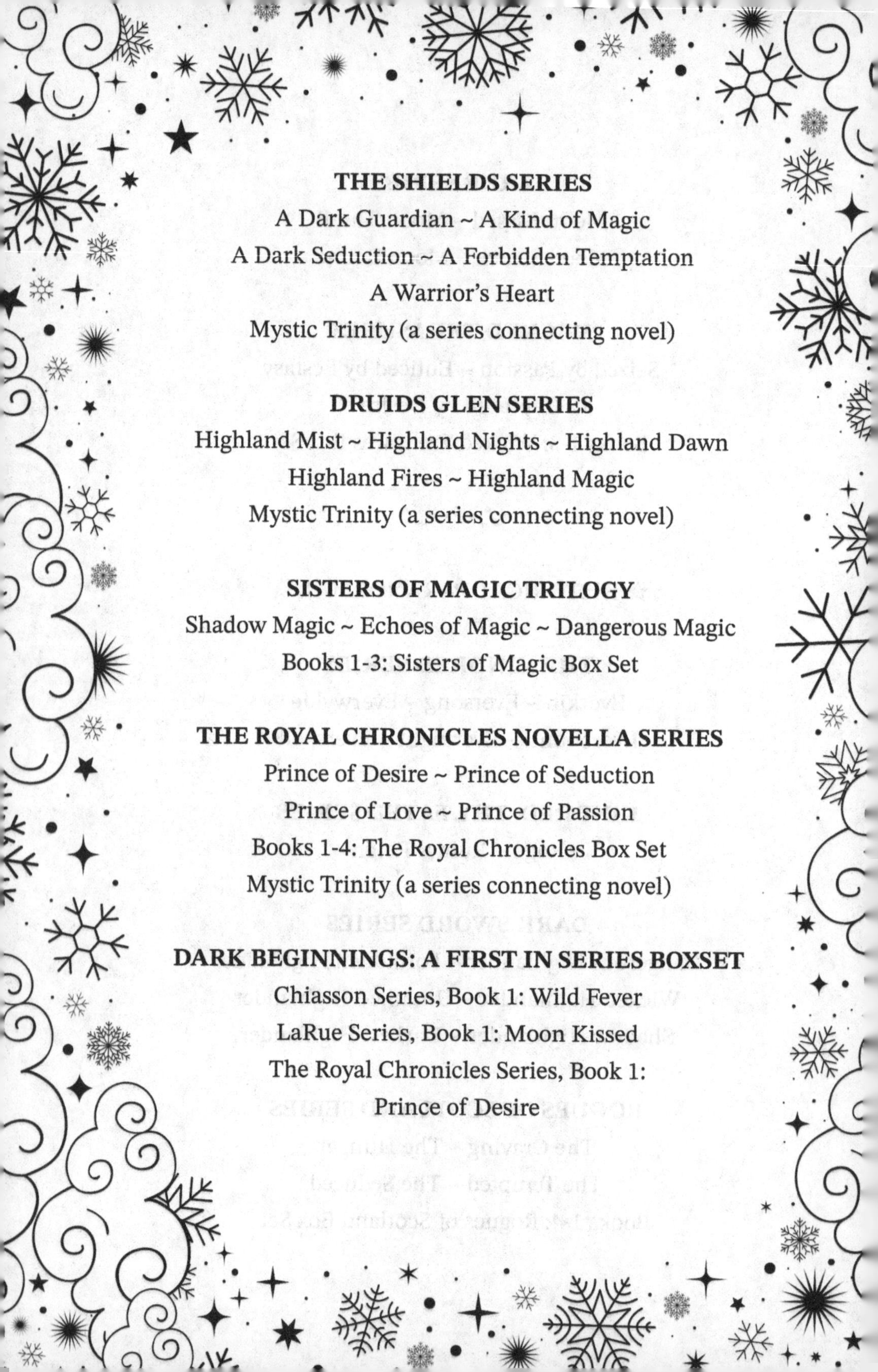

THE SHIELDS SERIES

A Dark Guardian ~ A Kind of Magic

A Dark Seduction ~ A Forbidden Temptation

A Warrior's Heart

Mystic Trinity (a series connecting novel)

DRUIDS GLEN SERIES

Highland Mist ~ Highland Nights ~ Highland Dawn

Highland Fires ~ Highland Magic

Mystic Trinity (a series connecting novel)

SISTERS OF MAGIC TRILOGY

Shadow Magic ~ Echoes of Magic ~ Dangerous Magic

Books 1-3: Sisters of Magic Box Set

THE ROYAL CHRONICLES NOVELLA SERIES

Prince of Desire ~ Prince of Seduction

Prince of Love ~ Prince of Passion

Books 1-4: The Royal Chronicles Box Set

Mystic Trinity (a series connecting novel)

DARK BEGINNINGS: A FIRST IN SERIES BOXSET

Chiasson Series, Book 1: Wild Fever

LaRue Series, Book 1: Moon Kissed

The Royal Chronicles Series, Book 1:

Prince of Desire

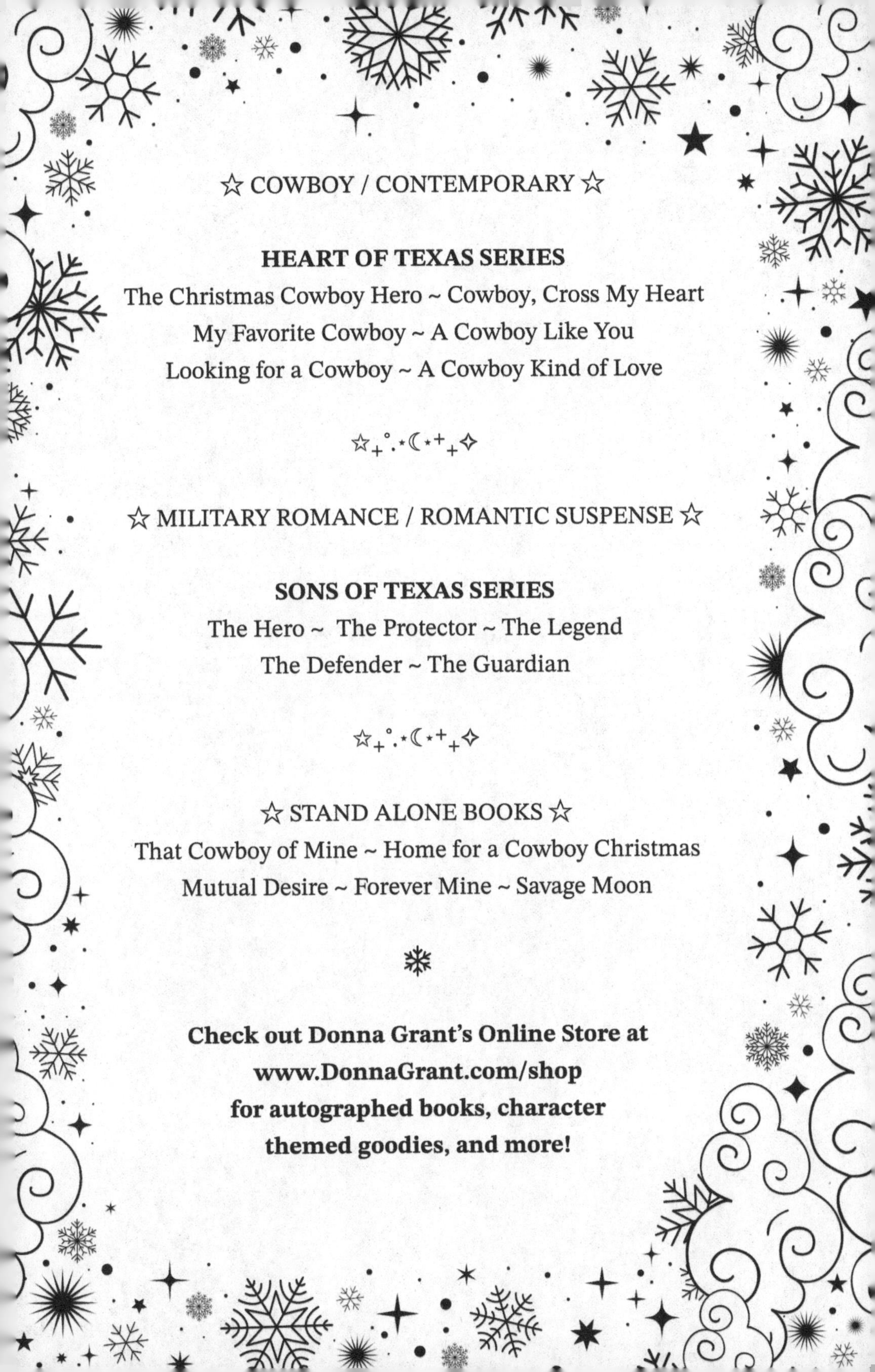

☆ COWBOY / CONTEMPORARY ☆

HEART OF TEXAS SERIES
The Christmas Cowboy Hero ~ Cowboy, Cross My Heart
My Favorite Cowboy ~ A Cowboy Like You
Looking for a Cowboy ~ A Cowboy Kind of Love

☆ MILITARY ROMANCE / ROMANTIC SUSPENSE ☆

SONS OF TEXAS SERIES
The Hero ~ The Protector ~ The Legend
The Defender ~ The Guardian

☆ STAND ALONE BOOKS ☆
That Cowboy of Mine ~ Home for a Cowboy Christmas
Mutual Desire ~ Forever Mine ~ Savage Moon

**Check out Donna Grant's Online Store at
www.DonnaGrant.com/shop
for autographed books, character
themed goodies, and more!**

MOUNTAIN FIRE

ELVEN KINGDOMS
BOOK FOUR

NEW YORK TIMES & USA TODAY BESTSELLING AUTHOR
DONNA GRANT

Human Land
Dragon Land
Sheerish
Dragon Land
Orgale
Belanore
Giant's Mountains
Ferdon Woods
Flamefall
Stonemore
Corral Plateau
Silver Falls
Iron Hall
Cairnkeep
Ravala Canyon
Ever-Reaching River
Dangerous Peaks
Rupora
Argares
Zora
Highvale

7 RACES OF ELVES

SUN ELVES (GOLD ELVES)
– recognized by their golden complexions.
Known for their levelheadedness, think things through.
Have long memories. Maintain a love of
freedom and personal expression.

Skin: golden brown
Eyes: amber, copper, gold
Hair: golden blond, tawny
Ability: Readers
Magic Color: yellow/golden

MOON ELVES (AKA SILVER ELVES)
– Isolated race who prefer only themselves.
Moon elf society values individual
accomplishment and rights.

Skin: very fair, silver tint
Eyes: various shades of blue (icy blue)
Hair: blue, silvery white
Magic Color: silver

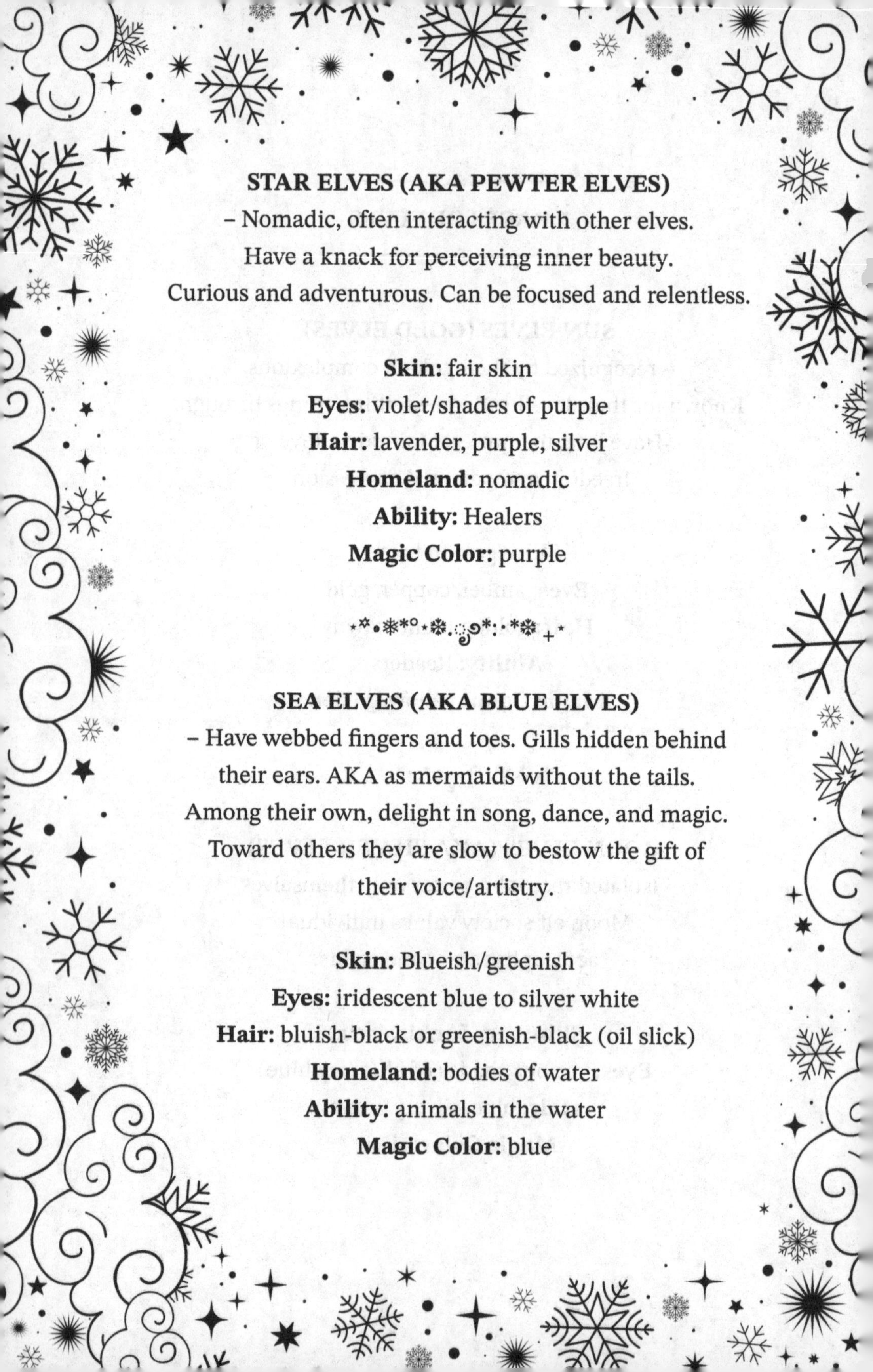

STAR ELVES (AKA PEWTER ELVES)

– Nomadic, often interacting with other elves.
Have a knack for perceiving inner beauty.
Curious and adventurous. Can be focused and relentless.

Skin: fair skin
Eyes: violet/shades of purple
Hair: lavender, purple, silver
Homeland: nomadic
Ability: Healers
Magic Color: purple

☆•❄°•❄•:*°*•*❄ + *

SEA ELVES (AKA BLUE ELVES)

– Have webbed fingers and toes. Gills hidden behind
their ears. AKA as mermaids without the tails.
Among their own, delight in song, dance, and magic.
Toward others they are slow to bestow the gift of
their voice/artistry.

Skin: Blueish/greenish
Eyes: iridescent blue to silver white
Hair: bluish-black or greenish-black (oil slick)
Homeland: bodies of water
Ability: animals in the water
Magic Color: blue

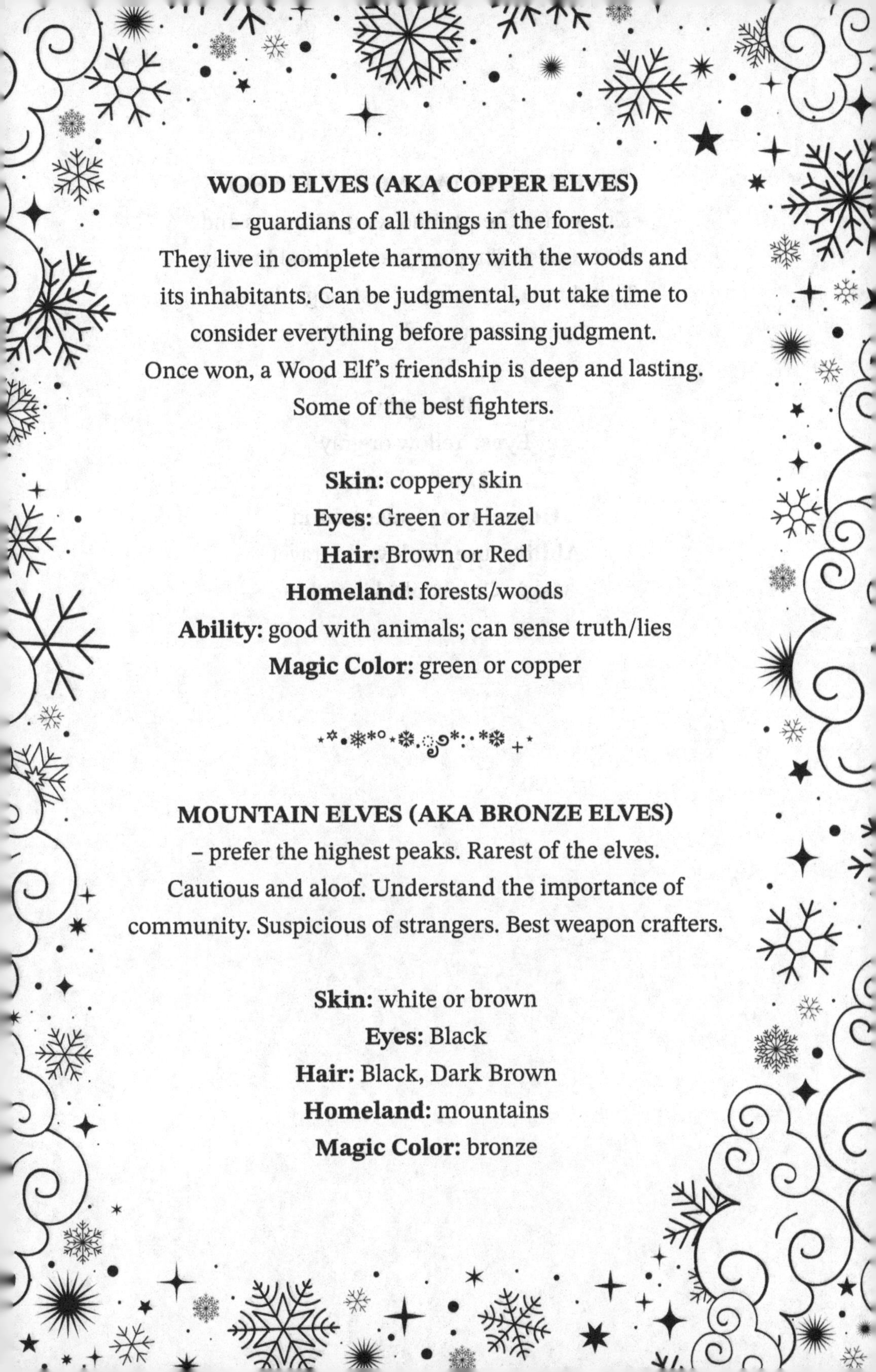

WOOD ELVES (AKA COPPER ELVES)

– guardians of all things in the forest.
They live in complete harmony with the woods and its inhabitants. Can be judgmental, but take time to consider everything before passing judgment.
Once won, a Wood Elf's friendship is deep and lasting.
Some of the best fighters.

Skin: coppery skin
Eyes: Green or Hazel
Hair: Brown or Red
Homeland: forests/woods
Ability: good with animals; can sense truth/lies
Magic Color: green or copper

❄•❋°*❀.꧁ꙮ*.•*❀ +*

MOUNTAIN ELVES (AKA BRONZE ELVES)

– prefer the highest peaks. Rarest of the elves.
Cautious and aloof. Understand the importance of community. Suspicious of strangers. Best weapon crafters.

Skin: white or brown
Eyes: Black
Hair: Black, Dark Brown
Homeland: mountains
Magic Color: bronze

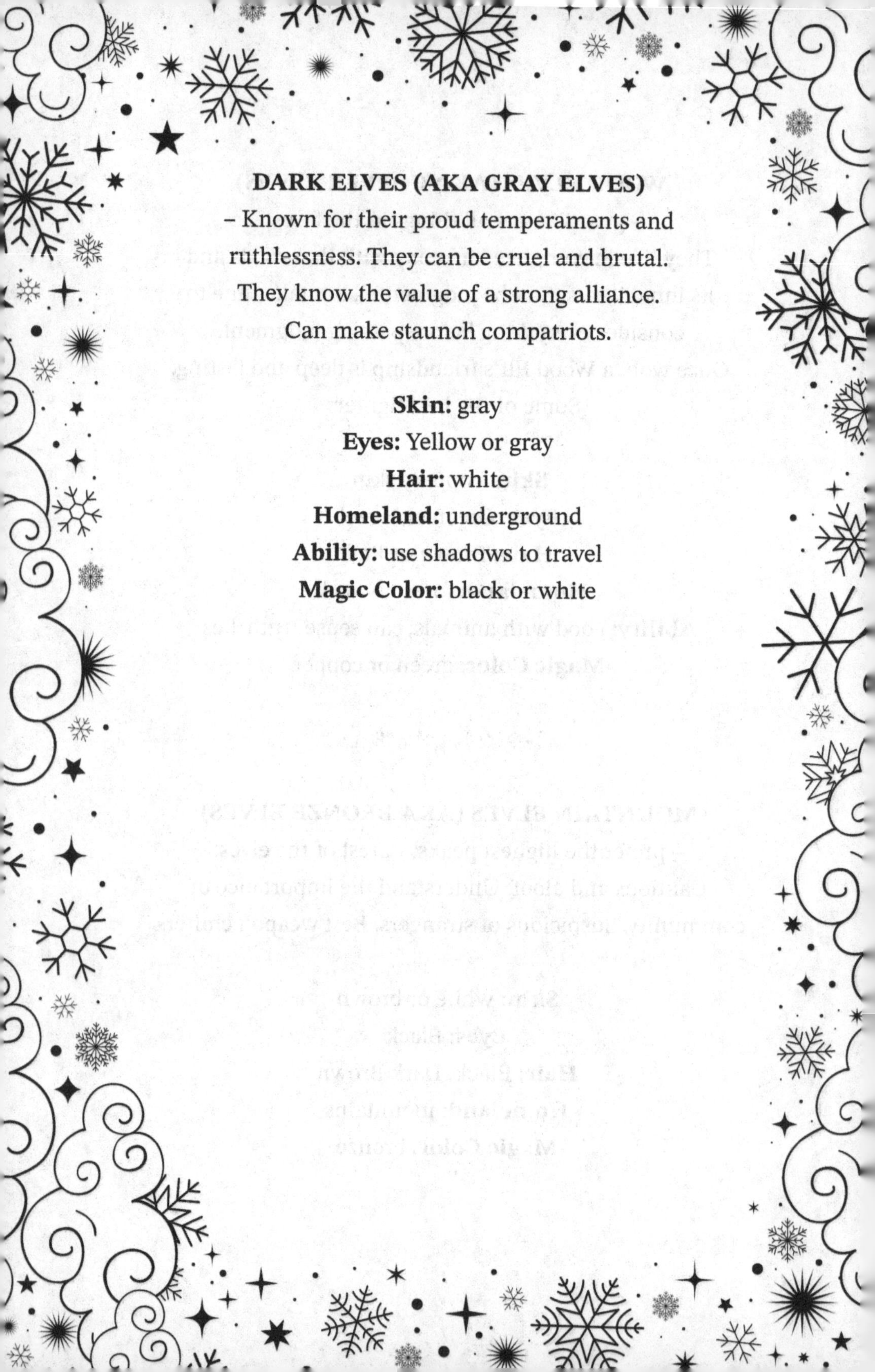

DARK ELVES (AKA GRAY ELVES)

– Known for their proud temperaments and ruthlessness. They can be cruel and brutal. They know the value of a strong alliance. Can make staunch compatriots.

Skin: gray
Eyes: Yellow or gray
Hair: white
Homeland: underground
Ability: use shadows to travel
Magic Color: black or white

MOUNTAIN FIRE

ELVEN KINGDOMS
BOOK FOUR

1

Belanore
Winter

The first rays of sunlight broke over the city like bright, glittering fingers of the gods sweeping aside the darkness. Inej shivered and pulled the worn shawl that had belonged to her mother tighter around her shoulders as she watched the city out the window. She had been sitting on the edge of the narrow, thin mattress she called a bed for the last hour, waiting for dawn.

She drew in a long breath and grabbed her bag as she stood. Her eyes scanned the living quarters that had been her home for the past four years. It wasn't much. In fact, it could barely be called a residence. The walls were cracked and looked as if they might buckle at any moment. Her only lock was the chair she wedged against the door. Many might turn their noses up at the state of it, but it had been hers.

It had taken minutes to pack up her meager belongings into the bag. Now, as she looked about the space, she wondered where the past years had gone. She had fallen into a rut without even knowing it. Or maybe she had known.

She had a mundane life, cleaning the homes of the wealthy while scraping together enough coin to keep a roof over her head and food in her belly. Sometimes, she went without a meal, just to ensure she had a place to lay her head. Too many years without had made her cherish her teeny flat all the more. And she had sworn never to be without a home again.

Yet, here she was, walking away from all of it.

A part of her fought against the idea of leaving. To venture not just out of the city but into an unknown region. To do something she would normally never do. All her life, she had fought to have a home, food, and clothing. There was no assurance she would make it to her destination. Even less, that she would complete her mission.

If she did succeed, if she did return, then she would figure things out then. No use worrying about any of it now.

Inej turned to the window once more. A ball of red-orange rose higher, banishing the last vestiges of fog and darkness. Every night, she had gone to bed looking up at the stars. Every morning before heading out to work, she had gazed outside. Not at the people, but at the sky. Not to dream of a life that was out of her grasp—she was much too practical for that. Instead, she looked at the beauty above her. Whether it was raining or the sky was clear, day or night, it didn't matter.

She didn't have friends. She wasn't the sort to open herself up to such associations, but Krata hadn't seemed to notice. The petite girl, with her bright blue eyes and sunlit hair, seemed to be made of joy itself.

The opposite of Inej in every way.

No matter Inej's tone, no matter her words, Krata's smile never wavered. Nor did her insistence on them being friends. Krata only ever saw the good in others, and for some reason, that included Inej. She thought Krata a pest, someone who just couldn't take the hint that they weren't wanted.

Inej had no choice but to tolerate her since they worked the same cleaning job. Krata talked endlessly, spinning wild stories out of thin air. Never caring that Inej never commented. And somewhere along the way, Inej began to enjoy the stories and the way Krata always waited so they could walk to work together. Then, one day, Krata wasn't on the street corner.

Unease gripped Inej as she walked to work alone, and it only grew when Krata never showed. When a second day passed without Krata, Inej went to check on her. But Krata never answered the door. The third day without her, and Inej began to fear the worst. Still, she searched the city, asking others if they had seen Krata. Their answers were all the same: nay. Inej had no choice but to acknowledge that Krata—the girl she had refused to befriend, yet had—had vanished like so many others.

Krata had been kind and good-natured. She deserved better. And fate had seen to it that Inej could get vengeance on her behalf. It was a poor apology for Inej being so horrible to her when Krata was around, but it was something she could give. And she did it willingly.

She looped the handle of the bag over her shoulder and walked out of her flat without a backward glance. The city's streets were already teeming with people, and poverty was everywhere she looked. Yet it was also an area where others were the most giving to those in need.

Belanore was one of two cities in Shecrish. It was situated to the north, while Rannora sat to the south. Inej meandered through the streets heading east, in the opposite direction she usually walked to work. She rarely ventured out of the city into the rainwood. Now, she intended to not only leave the city but also head to the mountains. But she wasn't going in blind. She had a map.

Her heart knocked wildly against her ribs with every step. It felt wrong, strange, not to show up for her job. Though now that she thought about being a human who intended to go up against an elf, perhaps that was why she was so anxious. It was insane to contemplate such an act, yet she refused to change her mind.

The closer she got to the edge of the city, the more apprehensive she became. She could turn back, go home. But she would always wonder what might have happened had she kept walking. So, she continued on. She hadn't done anything for anyone after her mum died. Krata forcing friendship on her made Inej realize just what she had been missing.

She couldn't turn back time and be a better person. The only thing she could do was get payback. And maybe, if she were lucky and the gods favored her, she would stop future abductions.

The alley narrowed as Inej cut between buildings. She turned the corner and drew up short at the sight of the Star Elf casually using the wall to hold himself up. He had one foot propped against the stone as he folded a small piece of paper, turning it around in his fingers. The top portion of his long, silver hair was gathered at the back of his head.

He didn't look up as he asked, "Heading out on a journey?"

Inej glanced behind her to make sure no one else was there.

Then, she eyed the elf. He wasn't blocking the way exactly, but she would have to pass him to get where she needed to go. Elves controlled Shecrish because they had magic, and they far outnumbered the humans. She had seen them be cruel far more than she had witnessed their kindness. It was why she made a habit of never underestimating them. Or giving them a reason to turn on her.

"I am," she eventually answered.

"You packed light."

She frowned, confusion and disquiet building within her. He spoke as if he knew her, but she had never seen him before. She studied the stretch of space she'd need to use to slip past him. Even if she inched along the opposite wall, he could easily grab her. It might be better to turn around and find another way.

"I'm no threat," he said. "To you," he added, almost like an afterthought.

This was getting stranger and stranger. "I never said you were."

Dark purple eyes briefly met hers, the color intense and bold. "Your body language says otherwise."

"Who are you?"

He shrugged one wide shoulder. "I have many names."

"Give me one." She regretted the command the moment it was out of her mouth. Despite his relaxed appearance, the Star Elf reminded her of a coiled viper waiting to strike.

He chuckled as he dropped his foot to the ground and turned so that only one shoulder made contact with the building. "Names aren't as important as many think."

"Will you let me pass?"

"Of course. I never intended to stop you," he replied, his expression still amused.

She wasn't sure if he enjoyed toying with her or not. The more time she stood with him, the longer it would take for her to reach her destination. She wasn't sure why she decided to walk past him, but she did. To her astonishment, he straightened and pressed himself flat against the façade to give her more room.

"Good luck," he said when she drew even with him.

She found herself looking into his purple gaze for a heartbeat too long, then jerked her eyes away. She waited until she got to the end of the alley before allowing herself to look over her shoulder. But the elf was gone.

Inej turned in a circle, making sure he hadn't snuck up behind her somehow. There was no trace of him, however. It was almost as if he hadn't been there at all. She shook off her paranoia and continued on her journey.

The entire plateau was one huge rainwood. Belanore, like its sister to the south, Rannora, had been hacked out of the forest. It was easy to forget that as long as she was within the bustling metropolis, but the closer she got to the outskirts of the city, the more visible the woods became. Mammoth trees stood like daunting sentries around the perimeter, as if waiting for the time they could reclaim the land once more.

She usually saw the rainwood from the tower near the city center. It didn't seem as imposing as it did when standing within it. Perhaps that was why she preferred to remain in the city. It was a world she knew well, from the dangerous animals who attempted to prey on her to where she could hide. The rainwood was a different jungle altogether. She knew little of the plants she should stay away from, and even less about the various animals that could kill her if she wasn't paying attention.

Inej hesitated at the edge of the rainwood and stared into the dense foliage. Anything could be waiting to devour her just steps inside. But there was a looming threat all over Shecrish, and it wasn't going away. It, in her opinion, was far more dangerous than anything the rainwood or the Dangerous Peaks held.

She squared her shoulders and stepped into the forest. The air changed instantly. Gone was the dirty, slightly heavy city air. In its place was air thick with sticky heat and rich with the scents of earth and green things. She tied the ends of her shawl together as she wove her way through the vegetation. She glanced at the sky every now and again to make sure she kept her bearing. The intersecting canopy made it difficult, but she found a way.

The map was secure in her bag, tucked between the food she'd scrounged together and the box that held her revenge. She put her hand on the outside of the bag where it rested against her hip. She kept her pace quick, her ears open, and her gaze vigilant. A few times, she heard voices and hid until they were gone. When she came to one of the many roads dissecting the rainwood, she hurried across and blended into the underbrush once more. She ate as she walked to make up the time she'd spent talking with the Star Elf. It wasn't until she spotted the mountains looming ahead through the trees that she paused to tear off another portion of bread.

As she chewed, she allowed herself a sigh of relief for getting through the rainwood unscathed. One obstacle down. But the next hurdle was even more intimidating. She leveled her gaze on the formidable mountains, their white peaks disappearing into the thick clouds.

She dusted off her hands when she finished the bread and headed toward the foothills. They looked easy enough to traverse at a distance, but the closer she got, the taller and steeper they became. She forged ahead, no matter the cost. She put her foot on the first rock and started the climb.

Inej didn't look back. Only one other knew where she was going. Whether she succeeded or not, no one would know her name, which was how she wanted it. She wasn't doing this for glory or recognition. She was doing this because Krata had broken through decades of barriers and made her feel something again.

2

Navara

The twin crescent moons hung like beacons in the dark sky, drawing Manu's gaze from his position atop the mountain. Snow flurries teasingly swirled around him in their mischievous dance. A few caught on his lashes. He lifted his face to the moons and closed his eyes.

While standing in the cold and ice atop the towering mountaintop, he allowed himself to forget his obligations, promises, and the hundreds counting on him to keep them safe. He could even forget that evil crept like a plague across the land, moving ever closer to his doorstep. But only for a moment. That second of freedom, however, gave him the ability to keep going.

Manu opened his eyes and scanned the snow-covered mountain. It was harsh terrain, even for someone like him, who had been raised in such brutal conditions. The weather kept other elves—and humans—away. The majority of those who dared to venture into the Dangerous Peaks were never seen again.

He saved those he came across. Yasmin had been one of those. He'd never imagined that years after saving the human, they would be thrown back together, or that he would join the Defense Intelligence Agency and a Dark Elf to fight the malevolence that had been moving in the shadows for too long.

A biting wind whipped up around him, pulling him from his thoughts. Manu tucked his gloved hands into the pockets of his fur coat. The high collar that fastened together protected his lower face from the frigid climate, but there was no escaping the bone-chilling cold altogether. The snow reflected the dim light of the moons, allowing him to see everything.

Movement to his right caught his attention. He scanned the next mountain slope and spotted something moving amid the dense cluster of evergreen limbs laden with snow. A moment later, he saw the wolvite. Manu tensed at the sight of the creature's creamy coat, and his suspicions were confirmed when he saw the missing top portion of the animal's left ear. The wolvite swung its head toward Manu and stood still as stone.

He had tangled with the beast before and barely come away with his life. It hadn't fared much better—Manu was the one who'd damaged the animal's ear. While their encounter had left them both severely wounded, the wolvite could've killed him but hadn't. For some reason, Manu had also held back. They'd both walked away, and from then on, gave each other a wide berth.

Long, forlorn howls erupted a short distance away. He had long suspected that the wolvite was the leader of his pack. It wasn't long before others trotted out of the trees to join the male. He counted ten of their white coats. And they all stared at him. Just when Manu thought they intended to come after him, the leader trotted away, and the others followed.

Manu released a breath, but he didn't relax. The moment he let his guard down was the moment one of a hundred different animals could end his life—if the weather didn't get him first. What would happen to his people then? That thought had been weighing more heavily upon him since he agreed to hide the children Yasmin and Ravi had claimed as theirs.

The couple had been compelled to get the kids out of Rannora after a bounty was placed on them across Shecrish—all because they had finally shuttered the Shaldorn Stronghold. That was how the entire mess had begun. As a child, Yasmin had been tricked by a Moon Elf named Gita to go into the mountains. Once they reached Shaldorn, Yasmin had been enslaved, only to endure years of torture. But she managed to do what no one else had done before: she'd escaped.

Manu had found her on the brink of death, nursed her back to health, and brought her out of the mountains to the edge of the rainwood. He hadn't expected to ever see her again. Yet, somehow, the leader of the DIA, Durga, learned of Yasmin's time at Shaldorn and forced her to take Ravi to the stronghold so he could stop the sale of a device intended to be used against the dragons across the border.

But Yasmin and Ravi weren't working alone. A Dark Elf named Dain—going against the Counter Corruption Division and acting on his own—had put one of his agents, Arya, undercover. When things went badly, Manu and Dain joined the trio to help win the day. It had come at great cost, though. The Masters—those responsible for erecting Shaldorn *and* all the kidnappings—wanted all of them gone. Their names had been leaked, and they were all being hunted. Everyone but Manu.

He considered himself lucky since the others were in hiding. It didn't stop them from continually attacking the Masters, though. Manu wanted to help more, but so far, nothing else had come to the Peaks. He wasn't sure how much longer he could say that, though.

The mountains used to be isolated, but since Shaldorn, more and more elves risked traveling into the area. He came across small bands of mercenaries at least once a week. They were usually too intent on surviving the unforgiving weather to notice him or anyone else. So, he let them wander deeper into the Peaks, knowing they would die either from the weather or an animal attack. Since they were there looking for his friends, he didn't lose any sleep over it.

But the mercenaries kept coming. More and more of them. During Dain's last visit, he had said the bounty on him and the others had gone up. And worse, the children had been added to the list. It was a ruse to draw out Ravi and Yasmin, which was why Manu had the young. The only reason Yaz and Ravi were able to keep fighting was because they knew the children were safe.

But how much longer could Manu ensure that? How long did he have before a mercenary found their way to his home?

He rubbed his eyes and blinked against the cold. The flurries turned to sleet as the wind changed and began to howl. Tiny shards of ice pelted the exposed skin of his face. Because it was expected, he had taken up the mantle of leadership after his father's death. Who would step in if something happened to him? He hadn't taken a wife, nor had he chosen any of the infants brought to Navara for his own. He had considered it once, but he hadn't been ready for the additional responsibility. It was enough that he had his entire tribe to look after.

Besides, with as much time as he spent out patrolling, the baby would be watched and cared for more by others than by him. How was that fair to anyone involved? Yet now, he wondered if he should have taken an heir. If he died without one, the line would be broken.

At least, the line they counted.

He had watched animals give birth, but elves and humans on Zora couldn't reproduce. No one knew where the infants came from or who brought them—and, honestly, few questioned it. It was just how things were. It was by that quirk of fate that Manu had landed in his father's arms. Any child could have been given to the leader and his wife, but it had been him.

Manu perused the mountains, taking in the valleys, slopes, and peaks. Years of guard duty had trained his eyes to see farther, look deeper. If he weren't looking, he probably would've missed the lone figure picking their way down the slope, hunched against the icy storm. Their clumsy, gangly steps told him the individual was an outsider. They probably wouldn't make it through the night.

He took one last look at the sky studded with billions of tiny pinpricks of light. His friendship with Ravi and Yaz had given him new information, including that the Dragon Kings hadn't vanished as everyone had thought. They had been on another world. But they were back. Was one of the stars above him their world? Or perhaps one was where he had been taken from as a baby.

All his thoughts about that and who would lead after him made his mind turn to questions he hadn't had before. Like, had he been born, or was he created? Had he been taken from his mother, or had she given him up? Had he been wanted? Cared for? Loved? Was he missed?

Those weren't thoughts that should be going through his head when there were so many other things for him to worry about. Manu took one last look at the figure on the slope before turning and making his way back to Navara. The entrance to the city within the mountain was well hidden, making it nearly impossible to find by anyone other than his tribe.

Dain and Arya were the only two Dark Elves he allowed to travel by shadows into Navara, and that had taken drops of their blood as well as special magic that had drained him for days afterward.

Manu broke into a run, vaulting over boulders and leaping down the slope before bounding back up again. He cleared several peaks until he slid sideways down an incline to the edge of a valley. He stood and made his way to the base of the next mountain. His steps slowed when he reached the wall of rock.

He removed his glove and flexed his cold hand before pressing it against the stone. A heartbeat later, twin bronze beams of light no larger than his pinky nail ran up from the ground before taking right angles and intersecting at the top to outline the door. The moment the lights touched, the rock shimmered and faded, allowing him entry. It returned to its solid form after he'd stepped inside.

The tunnel quickly widened to a pathway as he walked deeper into the mountain. Another ten steps, and the path diverged to a dozen others that would take him anywhere he wanted to go within the hollowed rock. Manu took a track to the left, crossing one of the many bridges over the river that ran through the mountain on his way toward his home.

At first glance, things looked as they had for generations, but all he had to do was look deeper to see the unrest that had settled over his people. The Masters' reach had stretched even to them. Few might know the Masters by name, but all knew the malevolence was growing.

And though he hated to admit it, some citizens were against him sheltering the humans, even if they were children. It troubled him that there were those who would happily toss the young out and not think twice about it. A month ago, he would've sworn none in his tribe would act with such callousness, but times had changed. Which was why no one outside of those in the manor and Jalall, his closest friend, knew they were there. There was prejudice against humans across Shecrish—even in the Dangerous Peaks.

He hurried home so he could have a moment to himself before returning to his duties. Once he was in his quarters, he shut the door and locked it with his magic before leaning his hands against the wood and dropping his chin to his chest.

The future had never been more uncertain than it was at that moment, and he feared it would only get worse. He straightened and unfastened his coat to shrug out of it before hanging it on a hook. It had been almost a week since he'd heard from Dain. Their group was growing larger thanks to new allies, but, unfortunately, that meant more bounties. Thankfully, a new location to the south along the coast had been found for them to live.

Manu went to the sink and turned the spigots before splashing water on his face. He looked at himself in the mirror as he dried off and noticed the lines around his eyes that hadn't been there the year before. He wasn't getting any younger, and it was his responsibility to think of the future of Navara.

Except there wasn't any time for that now. He'd let it go for too long and had put everyone in an untenable situation.

3

The howl of the wind made Inej want to scream in protest, and she would have, except her jaw was locked from clenching her teeth to stop them from chattering. Her jacket was so thin, it was almost like not having anything covering her at all, but a layer, no matter how threadbare, was better than nothing.

She tripped over one of the thousands of rocks hidden beneath the inches of snow, and because she had her arms wrapped around herself for warmth and wasn't able to get a hand out quickly enough to catch herself, she twisted as she fell and hissed in pain the moment the snow met her cheek. She did her best not to touch it with her bare hands as she climbed to her feet. Her thoughts drifted to the conversation that had changed her life.

"Where is the blonde who is always smiling?"

Inej stopped dusting at the sound of the Moon Elf's voice directly behind her. She slowly turned to face the beautiful female. Gita never had a single strand of blue hair out of place. Her eyes, an icy blue that could cut right through someone, never missed anything. And right now, they were locked on her.

"I don't know," Inej answered.

One dark blue brow arched before the elf's eyes narrowed. "You think she was taken."

Taken. It made it sound as if Krata had been whisked away for a lavish holiday instead of snatched from the streets or even her bed. Of course, an elf would put a spin on it since their kind were only just now being abducted.

"I fear she has been." Inej kept her voice even, refusing to allow the tremor of fear to be heard.

Gita smoothed a hand down her gown, the cerulean color making her fair, silvery skin appear luminescent. "That is all anyone can talk about. Some of my acquaintances have also gone missing. It's dreadful."

Inej shouldn't be happy that the elves were also being kidnapped, but now that they were, perhaps something would be done. "Does anyone know who is doing this?"

"There are suspicions," Gita said as she turned and walked regally to the sofa. She sat and leaned against the arm, tucking her legs against her. "But these people are dangerous."

Inej knew she should get back to work, but she had to know more. Gita rarely spoke to them, and if there was a chance she could get something out of the elf, then she was going to do just that. "Are the elves going to do anything?"

Gita visibly winced. "That's where things get problematic."

"What do you mean?"

"The group is in the Dangerous Peaks."

Inej looked out the window. The tower was one of the tallest in the city, allowing her to see over the towering trees of the rainwood to *the distant mountain. Few ventured there. The icy slopes were home to the Mountain Elves, a solitary race that rarely left their villages. Most went their entire lives without seeing a Mountain Elf.*

"It's an inhospitable place," Gita continued. "Especially to my elves."

Inej frowned as she slid her gaze back to her. "Why?"

"There is a sickness that takes us. It strikes without warning and kills just as quickly."

"In other words, it keeps you out. Doesn't it affect the Mountain Elves?"

Gita reached for a teacup and gracefully lifted it to her lips. "They become immune to it as babies. But for elves who don't live there…"

She trailed off, letting Inej finish the thought. "Surely, someone can do something."

Gita's lips parted, her face glowing with excitement, before she hastily looked away and took another drink.

"What? What is it?" Inej pressed.

"I don't want to get you involved. It's too risky."

Inej took a step closer, tightening her hand on the dusting cloth. "You have a plan," she guessed.

"I never should have said anything."

"Please," Inej begged. "I need to know. I believe my friend was abducted. I want…nay, I need to do something."

Gita's pale blue eyes met hers and studied her for a long moment. "I don't know," she said hesitantly.

"I can help. Let me help," Inej implored.

The elf tapped her lip thoughtfully. "You're human, so you wouldn't be affected by the virus."

"Exactly." Inej tried to contain her excitement. She knew in her

gut that this was what she was supposed to do. Now, she just had to convince her employer. "I'm a quick study, and I'm adaptable. I can be whatever you need."

Gita looked her over slowly as if taking her measure. "You just might be what we need."

Inej stumbled again, returning to the present. She caught herself and tucked her fingers under her armpits. She should've insisted that Gita give her proper clothing to endure the unstable weather of the Dangerous Peaks, but she had been too eager to strike back at those who had taken Krata. She had been so blinded by her anger and thirst for vengeance that she could quite possibly be walking to her own death. She would laugh, but the effort would take more energy than she dared expend.

The problem was, she didn't know how to quit. So, she kept walking. She hadn't dared to stop, even for the night, because she knew that if she lay down to rest, she wouldn't get up. It had never entered her mind that she would lose the sun behind the ever-present, ash gray clouds, or that she would barely be able to lift her face against the violent gusts of wind.

She tried to keep walking in a straight line, but that was impossible when crossing areas where rocks, cliffs, and water caused her to constantly alter her path. She only had a bit of bread left, and only because it had been so frozen she hadn't been able to eat it earlier. At least water was still available—not that she wanted to drink something cold.

Maybe she was going crazy. Between the cold and seeing nothing but white, it wouldn't surprise her if she was losing her grip on reality.

"Maybe I never had a grasp on reality," she mumbled.

That made her chuckle and then frown. She was dying, and

there was nothing she could do. She was too far from the rainwood to make it back, and likely too far from the mountain city to find her target.

One foot forward. Then the other. Another and another step. Inej didn't know when she had stopped feeling her toes. When she tried to rub her leaking nose against her shoulder, the pain it caused made her eyes water. And her fingers weren't faring any better.

She had never known these kinds of bitter temperatures. The winters in the city couldn't prepare anyone for this level of agony. Even if she had layers of clothing, she would still be cold. Maybe Mountain Elves didn't exist. Because how could anyone survive in this climate?

When Inej next dared to look up, she saw she had reached the opposite slope. She looked back at the valley behind her. When had she crossed it? And when had the sleet stopped? She shrugged and continued. The beginning of the incline was easy, leading her into a false reprieve. Before she knew it, though, she was facing a wall of rock. She looked up and grimaced. There was no way she could get up that.

She found an easier path to the left and altered her course. Still, she had to use her hands to climb up. She crested the summit just as sunlight came from behind the mountain. Inej cupped her hands around her mouth and blew warm air into them, but she could barely feel it. Whatever energy she had left was gone. She was too frozen to go even one more step.

Watching a sunrise from a mountaintop wasn't a bad way to die. She closed her eyes and lifted her face to the sun, seeking its warmth. For a moment, the wind paused its incessant assault. She dared to open her eyes and gasped at the sight before her: a land of white that sparkled when the light hit it. Bits of dark green from the trees poked through the snow as if teasing her with color. The gray clouds broke apart, revealing a clear sky so vivid a blue that she wasn't sure the color had a name.

And all around her, the mountains rose like towering walls, separating the rainwood from…she didn't know what, but there had to be something past the Peaks. Or maybe it was nothing but the end of the world. The Peaks were a land someone could get lost in, a place you could disappear into. Now, she understood why no one ever saw the Mountain Elves. Why would anyone leave such a beautiful—albeit hostile and bitter—place?

She dropped to her knees and stayed in the moment, even as her mind screamed for her to get moving. When the clouds returned, she fumbled in her bag for the map to see if she was heading in the right direction. Inej gripped the paper as tightly as her numb digits allowed. No sooner had she unfolded it and held it up than the wind snatched it from her hand. She jumped up, stretching her arm out for it without thinking where she was. Her foot met nothing but air. She windmilled her arms, searching for something, anything, to grab onto. Then she was tumbling down the mountain.

The first two impacts of her body were against thick snow. Still, it was hard enough to knock the wind from her. But the third collision was her back near her left shoulder against a rock, making her cry out in pain. The wind quickly swallowed the sound as she dropped straight down. Her brain barely registered the plunge before she impacted the snow and continued to roll down the slope.

The world spun so fast she couldn't tell where she was going or where she had been. All she could do was hold her arms against her so she didn't injure them. Just when she thought she might be okay, her leg slammed into something solid. Pain ripped through her, and a scream tore from her lips. The impact slowed her descent, but she didn't dare attempt to stop herself from rolling. Instead, she waited until she finally came to a stop.

Inej didn't move for several minutes. The only reason she knew she was alive was the agony shooting through her body in time with the beating of her heart. Just when she had begun to admire the beauty of the mountains, it had shown her what it thought of her invading its space.

She rolled onto her back, clenching her lips tightly when her leg throbbed excruciatingly. She turned her head to look at the slope and gasped at the cliff she had plummeted from. It was a miracle she had survived the fall. But then, to also get down the rest of the mountain covered in trees and only hit one? Though she might have hit more. Everything hurt, but it was difficult to determine which of the many impacts had caused the damage.

Inej closed her eyes, her heart rate beginning to slow and her breathing evening out. She was so tired. It wasn't snowing or sleeting now. What would a few minutes of rest hurt? She was already falling asleep when she told herself she needed to rest her leg before she tried to stand.

She woke with a start, unsure of what had pulled her from her slumber. She strained her ears to listen, even as her gaze darted around. Water gurgled gently to her right. Above her, the clouds sat heavily as if waiting to dump fresh snow atop her. There was no sign of the sun behind the thick layer of clouds. She had no way of knowing how long she had slept. It could have been minutes or hours.

Her fingers curled into a fist, seeking warmth. She winced at the discomfort, but it was nothing compared to when she sat up and debilitating pain shot up her leg. She swallowed a scream and held her shaking hands over her left leg. With tears distorting her vision, she carefully touched her knee and shin. Even that little movement sent a rush of agony through her so thick it made her nauseous.

The growl behind her made her heart skip a beat. All thoughts of emptying her stomach vanished. She slowly turned her head and spotted the enormous animal. It had a thick, cream-colored coat and yellow eyes that stared right at her. The beast pulled back its lip, showing her rows of pointed teeth in its long snout. Then, more of the animals walked menacingly out of the forest to surround her.

So, this was how she would die.

The dog-like animal flicked its ears as if listening. One of the others turned its head. Then the rest looked to the side. There was a loud bellow as something launched from the trees. The beasts scattered, then rushed toward the intruder.

Inej watched as something in gray fur fought the beasts. If she had been able to run, she would've immediately gotten up. While running wasn't an option, she wasn't going to stay. She looked around to make sure none of the animals were near her and crawled away, dragging her injured leg behind her. She clawed at the ground, her fingers sinking into the thick snow as she fought to put distance between herself and the animals intent on eating her.

Yelps and growls sounded behind her. She glanced back and saw four individuals standing on two legs and covered in thick, gray fur, fending off the creatures. She bit her tongue against the pain in her leg and kept pulling herself away, right until she encountered the stream cutting through the valley. She either had to cross it or turn around, and since she couldn't stand, she couldn't do either.

She pulled herself to the edge and looked at her reflection in the water. All it would take was one look for them to know she was human. Brown hair, brown eyes, brown skin, and curved ears. Nothing remotely elvish.

Inej thought of the vials and looked for her bag. Miraculously, it was still looped across her body. She pulled it from her side and feverishly dug inside it for the box. When she pulled it out, her heart sank when she saw the smashed lid. She glanced back at the fight and saw elven features before daring to open the box. Out of the seven vials, only one was still intact. She grabbed it before dumping the box into the water and watching it sink. Clutching the vial in her palm, tension filled her when she realized the growls and whines had ceased. Footsteps crunched in the snow as the individuals approached.

"You're safe now. The wolvites are gone."

The voice was deep and smooth. Commanding, and yet gentle. Inej had never heard anything so seductive in all her days. She turned her head toward him and found herself staring into eyes as black as midnight fringed with thick lashes.

"We should go," one of the others said.

Inej watched the man who had spoken turn his head to the side. The first things she saw were the fresh scratches and blood on his cheek and brow. Then she saw his pointed ears through the long, dark brown locks of hair that fell across his face. Shock went through her as she realized she was with the elusive Mountain Elves.

The man looked at her leg before returning his gaze to her face. "I can offer assistance."

"Manu," hissed one of the others.

Her heart hammered in her chest, shock reverberating through her as the name settled into her.

"The one you seek is named Manu," Gita said.

"Manu," Inej repeated, testing the name. "What does he look like?"

The elf shrugged. "He looks like any other. What I do know is that he's the leader of a group of Mountain Elves. We know the area where they live, but not a specific location. If you head there, he'll find you."

And he had. It was surely a sign then that she had made the right choice in coming to the mountains.

Manu ignored his companion, his dark eyes holding hers. "If you stay out here, the wolvites will return. The choice is yours." He held out his hand and waited.

Inej didn't hesitate to reach for him.

4

Manu squatted beside the female, her hand still in his grasp. She was shivering, her face reddened by the frigid temperature and fierce wind. As inadequately dressed as she was, he was surprised she was alive at all. He took off his coat and wrapped it around her, finding himself sinking into her soulful brown eyes that glowed like amber caught in sunlight.

"We have to move," Jalall urged.

Manu glanced at his friend and captain. Jalall was right. They needed to get back to Navara, but there was no way he could move the woman with her leg in its current condition. He blew out a breath and looked at her limb once more. He wanted to see how badly it was damaged, but in the end, it didn't matter.

He reached into the bag he kept tied to his belt and drew out the green leather pouch. As he pinched some of the magical herbs between his fingers, Jalall held out a flask. Manu nodded his thanks and dropped the herbs inside. As he returned the pouch to his bag, Jalall swirled the herbs into the water and handed the container to the woman.

She hesitated, her wary gaze looking Jalall over slowly. Manu watched their silent exchange. From an early age, Jalall had caught the attention of others. Sometimes, he used it to his advantage, but it often landed him in trouble. So, it didn't surprise Manu that the human might find him appealing.

"It's water and healing herbs," Manu told her.

Her head swung back to him. A small frown puckered her brow before she grabbed the flask and drank deeply. The longer he watched her, the more amazed he was that she was still alive. Her clothes were worn, her boots thin. She wasn't wearing gloves or even a scarf to cover her neck and face, nor did she have a head covering. Her dark braid was crusted with ice and snow, as were her eyebrows.

Manu met Jalall's gaze and nodded. They couldn't wait for the herbs to take effect before moving. The wolvites could return at any time. Jalall put a hand behind her back as bronze magic snaked from his palm into her. The female went limp, the empty water flask falling from her hand as Manu caught her against him.

"Let's go," he said, gathering her into his arms.

Jalall straightened, his lips pursed. "You won't be able to move as fast as usual."

"Good thing I have you three with me," Manu replied with a grin as he got to his feet.

Jalall shook his head and ordered the other two guards to spread out as they began their journey home. Manu adjusted the woman. She was as light as a feather—too light. He glanced at the sky, hoping the snow would wait until they reached the mountain.

He leapt over the stream with ease, but the landing jarred the woman. Even in sleep, she groaned in pain.

"Are you sure this is wise?" Jalall asked.

"I am."

"She's human."

He looked at his friend. "She's a person in need of help. We're not lowlanders, old friend. We have the means to assist. That means, it's not just our duty to do it, but it's also an obligation."

Jalall began the climb up the mountain slope. "I know."

"Do you?" Manu asked crossly.

His friend halted and slowly turned to him. "I've been watching your back since we were barely walking. I will continue to follow you until I take my last breath. I just wanted to warn you."

"Shall I leave her, then? Drop her right here and let the wolvites have her?"

"Manu—"

"I'm serious. Should I? Is that what you would do if I wasn't here?"

Jalall looked away and sighed.

"Because I remember when we found Aman barely clinging to life six years ago. Now, he's one of your lieutenants." Manu turned his head to look at Aman, who had already reached the top of the peak and stood waiting for them. "It's okay to bring in strange elves, but not humans?"

"Aye. Fuck," Jalall bit out as he glared at Manu. "Is that what you want to hear? We have enough trouble with the Masters and the human children. We don't need her."

There was such a deep-rooted fear of humans among the Mountain Elves, and Manu had no idea where it had come from.

Their race rarely interacted with other elves, and there was even less interaction with humans.

Manu grunted. "This place has isolated us from the other elven races. It means we're slow to hear what is happening in the lowlands. But we *do* hear. Everything that's happening with the Masters has been done by elves. Yet it is those you would welcome into our home instead of humans, who are being subjugated simply because they don't have magic. Imagine if the positions were reversed."

Jalall sighed again as he shook his head, his anger gone. "You've always had an idea of what the world should be, old friend. I hate to be the one to keep reminding you that it won't ever be like you hope it will."

"Not as long as kindness is ignored."

Jalall slapped him on the back and grinned. "Do you always have to be right?"

"Only when it counts," he replied with a laugh.

There was no more talk as they made their way to Navara. The wolvites didn't follow, but Manu knew they were there. If Aman hadn't seen the female and gone to investigate, she would likely be dead now.

Jalall was the first to walk into Navara. Manu was next, with the other guards behind him. Unfortunately, their arrival didn't go unnoticed. Elves stopped to stare, whispering and pointing at the woman. They couldn't see her, but that didn't stop the news of their arrival from spreading like lightning through the city. Jalall gave him an I-told-you-so look but didn't say anything more. He wouldn't. His friend kept that for when they couldn't be overheard.

Manu never wanted someone who always agreed with him. It

was why he'd installed Jalall as captain. Because he didn't hesitate to voice his opinion. It also helped that Jalall had his ear to the ground and knew the happenings within the city.

As they headed deeper into Navara, Jalall dropped back to walk beside him and whispered, "We could bring her to my place."

More and more elves came to look at the woman Manu had in his arms. He could've brought his coat up to cover more of her face or unbraided her hair to keep her rounded ear hidden, but that would've only delayed the inevitable. Besides, he wasn't the kind to hide things. He opted for honesty with his people.

Yet he saw the prejudice in their faces, and he hated it. He kept the children secluded in his home, but even they were getting restless. The woman just needed a few days to recover, and then she would be gone. She would never even see them. Just in case.

"All right," Manu agreed.

Jalall turned from their path and headed toward his house. Once inside, Manu followed his friend to a spare room. Jalall pulled back the covers so Manu could lower the woman onto the bed. He glanced at her face as he did and saw that the magical herbs had already worked to repair her blistered skin.

"Do you want your coat?" Jalall asked.

Manu shook his head as he gently straightened her injured leg, then removed her shoes. "Leave her to rest for now."

"She's looking better already."

Jalall covered the woman, and the two of them walked out.

"How is she alive?"

"You mean because of the state of her clothes or lack thereof?" Manu asked when they reached the front parlor.

Jalall shrugged out of his coat and tossed it over a chair as he scratched his cheek. "Exactly. She should've succumbed days ago if she came from the lowlands."

"Where else *could* she have come from?"

"Brought here by a Dark Elf, perhaps."

Manu sighed as he dropped into a chair. "We can't rule out that possibility. She might be running from the Masters. We won't know until she wakes, and we ask."

"You assume she'll speak the truth."

"I try to never assume anything. Her body is in rough shape."

Jalall nodded. "You should rest here, too, for a bit. You go out there, you'll be stopped by others demanding answers."

It was tempting, but all that would do was delay the inevitable. "I'd rather face this now. Maybe I can stop the spread of some of the rumors."

"Shall I join you? I can post guards outside the door," Jalall offered.

"I can handle it. Have some food. I can hear your belly rumbling from here."

Jalall's laugh followed him out the door. Two steps out, and Manu wished he had remained with his friend. Just as Jalall had predicted, citizens swarmed him, demanding to know why a human was within the mountain.

Manu stopped and lifted a hand, waiting for them to quiet. "We came upon an injured individual surrounded by wolvites and rendered aid. It shouldn't matter if she's an elf or a human. We guard these mountains against threats, but it is also our responsibility to help those in need. The woman is resting and healing now. I know nothing about her and won't until she wakes."

"How long is she staying?" someone asked.

Manu shrugged. "That depends on her injuries. Now, please, everyone, go back to your day."

He didn't wait for them to disperse as he shouldered his way through the crowd toward his home. He opted to enter through the side entrance in hopes of going unnoticed. After he slipped inside, he hurried to the stairs and up to his room, softly closing the door behind him.

"Is it true?"

Manu jumped at the sound of Sameer's young voice. He turned and found all six of the children sitting on his bed, watching him. Their ages ranged from three to fourteen. As the eldest, Sameer had assumed the role of protector. While Manu didn't know the full story, he knew Yaz had found the boy dying in the street. Sameer's body was riddled with scars, and he wore a patch over the left eye he had lost in a beating by an elf. No one should have to endure such hardships, but especially not children.

Manu knew what they wanted to know, but still he asked, "Is what true?"

"That you found a human woman," Malini said.

As second eldest, Malini stood her ground against anyone who even thought about harming her siblings. The six had only had each other to rely on until Yasmin found them.

Manu looked longingly at his bed. Even if the children weren't here, he wouldn't have slept. There was too much to do. "Aye. She's resting and healing now."

Jaya, the youngest, sat perched on Sameer's lap, her dark eyes watching him thoughtfully. Despite her age, she had the eyes of someone who had lived decades longer.

"Who is she?" Malini demanded.

"That hasn't come up yet. The wolvites were about to attack

her, and she was already injured. We had to get out of there quickly. Once she wakes, I plan to get some answers," he told them.

Jaya slid from Sameer's lap and made her way over, arms outstretched. Manu picked her up, tucking her against his side. She gently touched his face. He turned to look in the mirror and saw the scratches.

"You've a wound on your back, too," Malini said.

Manu flashed a quick smile to Jaya and set her down. He pulled his herbs from his bag and dropped them into a glass before adding water and drinking.

"Do you think she's from the Masters?" Sameer finally asked the question all of them likely wanted to know.

The children knew the risks that Yasmin and Ravi took. All the adults tried to keep them from worrying, but there was nothing anyone could say that would alleviate those concerns until their family was reunited.

Manu set the cup down and faced the kids once more. "I don't know anything yet. What I do know is that humans don't come here unless driven. She might be running from something, but I haven't ruled out the possibility that she was brought here."

"What better way to find us than by sending in another human?" Malini said softly.

Manu walked to the bed and dropped to one knee in front of them. They should be playing and getting into trouble, but each of them knew the horrors of life on the streets in Rannora, of having an empty belly and no place to call home. Yaz had brought each of them into her world and protected them. None of that would ever erase the things they had seen or endured.

He held out a hand to Malini, who put her small one into his.

He held it for a moment before releasing her. "It's one of the many reasons the woman isn't here. We'll let her rest up and then help her get to where she's going. But that means all of you need to stay out of sight. If she is from the Masters, I don't want her to see any of you."

Sameer sat up straighter. "That won't happen."

"I promised Yaz and Ravi I'd protect you, and I'll do that for however long it's needed," Manu vowed.

Malini twisted her hands nervously in her lap. It was the only thing that gave away that she was anything but stoic. "What of Yaz and Ravi?"

"I've not heard anything since the last time Dain checked in," he said.

Jaya perked up at the mention of the Dark. "Dain?" she asked excitedly.

Sameer returned the youngster to his lap. "Dain isn't here now."

Jaya's lips puckered and turned down in a frown.

At that, Malini got to her feet, and the rest followed suit. "You need to get some rest."

Manu straightened and turned as they filed past him and out the door. He had worried how they would adjust to Navara, but they had adapted better than most. The two eldest usually did the talking, but that didn't mean Din, Hadi, and Surya, or even wee Jaya, weren't listening to every word.

He had always believed Navara the safest place in Shecrish. Times were changing, though, and he needed to be prepared.

5

Inej was slow to rouse, pulled softly from the comfort of sleep's warm embrace. She rubbed her cheek against something soft and turned onto her side, not yet ready to wake. Something poked her, making her grimace. She shifted, but nothing alleviated the discomfort.

She scooted back and lifted the covers to see what was jabbing her. It wasn't until she stared at the metal buckle that she became aware she wasn't in her bed. Her eyes traveled up the length of the buckle to the edge of the garment. Gray fur met her gaze. The last time she had seen that was when Manu had wrapped his coat around her. Her head whipped to the side, expecting to see him, but as she scanned the chamber, she found no evidence of another.

"He's cunning and dangerous," Gita told her. *"He'll present himself as your savior, and that will allow you to get close. You'll have to be careful since you are human."*

Nothing like being reminded that elves considered her kind less than. *Inej wisely held her tongue. Gita was giving her what she wanted, but she knew the elf would take it away in a heartbeat if Inej didn't follow as expected.*

"His people may not be aware of who he is, but trust me, he's the ringleader in all of this," Gita stated.

"How are you so sure?"

Gita's ice blue eyes sparkled. "Have you heard of the Defense Intelligence Agency?"

"You're a DIA agent?" Inej whispered in shock. Everyone knew of the organization, but she never imagined encountering one of their spies.

Gita put a finger to her lips. "Manu is responsible for my last assignment going sideways. It's why I'm hiding out here for a bit."

So, Inej wasn't the only one who craved payback. Now, she understood why Gita was so willing to share information. "I'll find Manu, but how am I to kill him? I don't think I'll get close enough to use a blade."

"Being human, you might. They wouldn't think twice about you carrying a weapon, though I doubt they'd let you keep it."

Gita got to her feet and walked to a cabinet. Inej watched as silver magic rolled from the elf's finger into a lock. A soft click filled the silence before the door swung open. A heartbeat later, Gita turned, holding a narrow box about six inches long.

"This will help," she said and lifted the lid before handing the case over.

Inej looked down at the vials of clear liquid nestled tightly inside so they didn't rub together. "What are these?"

"Poison."

Inej swallowed hard as she held out the hand that had held the vial so tightly, but her palm was empty. Her stomach dropped, cold and hollow. The one weapon she'd been entrusted with was gone, and the crushing weight of her failure closed in. She yanked the covers up in desperation, rummaging through them on the off chance the vial had fallen from her grasp.

Her fingers brushed something near the pillow. Her hand closed around the vial. The relief surged so swiftly it made her dizzy. She brought her hand to her chest and cradled the poison in both hands.

She sat with her eyes closed, holding it for several moments before daring to open her eyes once more. She had tangled herself in Manu's coat and the covers in her mad search, and only just remembered her leg injury. Tentatively, she moved her limb and was surprised when there was only a hint of an ache, almost like an afterthought. She had never taken magical herbs before, as they had always been too expensive. If she got sick or injured, she dealt with it herself because going to a human who practiced medicine was tantamount to suicide.

Inej slipped her legs out of the blankets, then perched on the edge of the bed and looked around her. The opulent covers were a rich sapphire blue that reminded her of the sky at dusk. More sapphire cloth was draped behind and above the bed canopy. A large, oval, rust, blue, and beige floral motif rug with intricate borders and a central medallion sat at the foot of the bed.

A set of rust-colored chairs with cobalt accents rested against the wall next to a short table. There was a tall, wooden wardrobe against another wall. And those walls? They were stone—with no windows. However, there were several hanging lights that would no doubt brighten the room. They were dimmed, allowing her to see without blinding her.

She had wanted to find Manu, and the gods had delivered him

straight to her. They hadn't put her in prison. Unless this was just to get her to let her guard down. Only a fool would trust her, and Manu wasn't a fool. They would be watching her, just as she intended to watch them.

Her gaze swung to the door. There was only one way to find out if it was locked. She rose, testing out her leg. Once she knew she could stand, she hid the vial under the mattress. Manu's coat slipped from her shoulders as she took the first step. She removed it and draped it over the back of a chair before walking across the plush rug to the door. She steeled herself as she wrapped her fingers around the knob and turned. To her surprise, it unlatched. She slowly pulled it open a crack and peered outside.

When no one yelled at her to get back inside, she dared to widen the opening a little more and stared into an empty hallway. Distant voices to the left reached her. She heard someone laugh, and then more conversation, but she couldn't make out the words. Inej poked her head out before stepping into the hall.

"You're up. Good."

Startled, she whirled around at the deep voice to find one of the men who had rescued her. He had a face that would stop most in their tracks. He was tall with a warrior's build. His dark brown hair was kept short on the sides, while the top was longer and shoved to the side. He had an easy smile and dark, compelling eyes. If it had been said, she couldn't remember his name. He was the one who had handed her the water. Someone in charge of all aspects of his life.

He held up a stack of folded clothes. "I was about to deliver these to you. I thought you might want to bathe and change before you eat. Unless you'd rather eat now?"

She was famished, but she usually was.

The elf's smile remained in place. "I'm Jalall, and you're a guest in my home."

A guest? That was unexpected.

"And you are?" he prompted.

She licked her lips. "Inej."

"Are you strong enough to follow me a short distance?"

"I believe so," she replied.

He dipped his head and walked past her. His boots didn't make a sound on the stone floor. No wonder she hadn't heard him approach. She would have to be more vigilant. Inej fell into step behind him. The stone was cold beneath the thin stockings covering her feet. Thankfully, they only went across the hall. Her mouth went slack when she entered the bathing suite.

A rectangular rock tub sat against the far wall and sank into the floor with about a six-inch rise around three sides. A sizable arch had been cut out of the wall, with a decorative edge around it. Sitting along the bottom of the arch were various-sized lit candles. There were two small arches on either side positioned lower near the water with more candles. The ceiling above the tub was arched with lights ringing the top to give the appearance of sunlight. To her left, a rock had been hewn into a pedestal with a round sink balanced on top. Mixed in were more richly colored rugs, decorative lights, and plants.

"Take your time," Jalall said.

She turned to say thank you, but he had already closed the door behind him. Inej locked it, though it was more for her peace of mind. Nothing would keep an elf out if they wanted in. He might act nice, but she didn't trust anyone. She hurried out of her clothes and moved to the tub. Ribbons of steam rose from the surface as if beckoning her to enter.

Inej dipped her toe into the water to test the temperature. It was hot but not scalding. And after nearly being frozen, she was ready to be enveloped by the heat. She stepped into the water and sat. Her muscles immediately eased, and she sighed. She quickly unbraided her hair and then reclined against the back.

She might not know how she'd gotten to Jalall's or what was next, but she had found Manu. Now, it was just a matter of getting close and delivering the poison. She had made it over the mountains and survived a fall and nearly being mauled by wolvites. She could finish this mission.

Her grumbling belly drove her to finish her bath. She felt renewed by the time she rose to dry off. Then, she turned to the clothes Jalall had set on a stool when they entered. There were a few options to choose from. She sorted through the different items and found a pair of wide-legged pants in deep red. The matching scoop-neck tunic skimmed her curves and fell past her hips with a deep slit on each side. The sleeves were too long, but she was able to push them up to her elbows. A little more digging in the clothes, and she located some socks. They were her only option since her shoes were gone, and she didn't want to walk on the cold stone. She then found a comb to run through the long strands of her hair.

With one final look at herself, she unlocked the door and stepped into the hall. There was no sign of Jalall. She was wondering where to go when a pretty elf came out of her room with linens wadded in her arms. She barely spared Inej a glance as she passed.

"Ready to eat?"

She jerked at Jalall's voice behind her and bit back her terse reply. She hated being startled, but she had to remind herself that he wasn't doing it on purpose. Probably. She forced her face into something that resembled a polite smile. "I am."

"Follow me." He walked a few steps before he glanced at her over his shoulder. "I'm glad to see that I was able to find you something that fit."

"As I have no coin, I can work off the payment."

Jalall shot her a frown as he turned the corner. "Excuse me?"

She realized he might have taken her offer to mean sex, and while he was nice to look at, the only elf she was willing to let into her bed was Manu. And only to complete her mission. She stayed away from elves as a rule. "I meant I'm capable of work. I can clean, and I'm willing to learn any other skill."

"There's plenty of time to talk about that later."

Inej entered the room to find food already set out on the table. He motioned to the chair on his left, and she took it. She forgot about finding a way to pay off her debt as her senses were overwhelmed by the varied and delicious smells that descended upon her. Her mouth watered as she looked at the different dishes.

"I'm informal," Jalall said. "Which is my way of telling you that no one will serve us. Take what you want."

She looked at him, trying to judge if he was serious.

He chuckled and reached for a spoon to scoop some food onto his plate. She accepted the bowl when he passed it to her. One by one, she took a sample of everything, and then she looked down at her plate. It all looked so good, she wasn't sure where to start. Finally, she just dove in.

The first bite was divine, and every bite after only got better. She forgot about Jalall, Manu, and even her mission as she ate until she was full.

She pushed away her empty plate and sat back. That's when

she became aware of Jalall's dark gaze on her. "I'm sure you have questions."

"I do. And I'm not the only one."

As if on cue, there was movement near the doorway. Inej looked up and into Manu's eyes. Her heart missed a beat at the size of him. Out on the mountain, she hadn't realized how tall he was, or how wide his shoulders were. His very presence filled the room, making it difficult for her to breathe. The expression on his rugged face gave nothing away. His black eyes held hers as he crossed to the table and sat.

She slowly drank in the sight of him, from his thick brows that slashed over deep-set eyes to his strong nose and wide forehead. Then lower to his pleasing mouth and strong jaw. His shoulder-length hair was the kind of dark brown that looked almost black in low light. The long strands were shoved away from his face as if he'd just run his fingers through the length.

He didn't look like a monster, but no matter how nice his outward appearance, she knew the blackness of his soul.

6

The Below

No matter how many times he walked into the world of the Dark Elves hundreds of feet below the surface, it never got easier. Water dripped somewhere off to his left. The air was particularly damp in this section of the compound, but that would change in sixteen steps.

One had counted his steps after his first visit, where he had run into walls because there were no lights. The Dark didn't need them to see, unlike the rest of the elven races. Then again, Dark Elves didn't fare well in sunlight.

Thirteen, fourteen, fifteen, sixteen. He drew in a deep breath as the humidity of the tunnel gave way to drier air when he entered the next room. One turned at a thirty-degree angle and walked forward another nine steps. There, he came to a door and rapped his knuckles twice. A high-pitched grating sound emanated from the opposite side as the metal bolt slid across the wooden door planks.

The only way he knew the door opened was the soft stirring of the air around his face. No one greeted him, nor did anyone appear. He strode into a small antechamber that led into one of the thousand corridors crisscrossing each level of the compound.

He counted twelve steps before he took a sharp left and entered a hallway. His hands fisted at his sides. He hated that the Dark refused to light the way. They watched to see when he would give in and use his magic to help him see. He hadn't. And he wouldn't. He did have his pride, after all.

The hall was long but straight. And silent as a tomb. One knew from his time exploring that five corridors branched off, with ten doorways. Some of those doors led to rooms, but a few led to stairways that were shortcuts to other areas of the compound. Despite his many hours exploring, he had yet to see every inch of the building—and he wasn't sure he ever would. He had the Masters' ears, and they trusted him to do their bidding, but that didn't mean he had been granted full access.

At least, not yet.

He bit back a grin and finished counting to fifty-three, where he came to a stop and flexed his hands. One wasn't so quick to knock on this door. It would be foolish for him to proceed too eagerly. He took the time to clear his mind of all thoughts except for the reason he had been summoned. Once he'd safeguarded his mind, he visualized a barrier around his body. It wouldn't stop him from being hurt if the Masters didn't like what he had to say, but it would save his life. He sat with both for several seconds, letting his armor settle into place. Then, he knocked.

A full minute passed before the door opened. This time, a faint, red-orange light radiated from small flames flickering inside glass domes hanging on the stone walls, fifteen feet apart in the massive circular room. He didn't spare a glance at the Dark who stood at the door. Instead, he focused on the spotlight illuminating the center of the room.

He didn't need to count these steps, but he did anyway. Nineteen from the door to the center. When he reached it, he stood still as stone, not even reaching up to scratch the itch on the side of his nose. This room was one of the most dangerous in all of Shecrish. Just because he worked for the Masters didn't ensure he would leave a meeting with them alive.

One kept his gaze forward and waited for the Masters to speak. They sat high above him, completely in shadow. No one knew exactly how many Masters there were, but he had counted ten distinct voices in his previous visits to the room. Some accents were easy to pinpoint, like the three Dark and two Wood Elves. The Sun Elf had attempted—badly—to disguise her voice. The two Star Elves didn't bother to alter theirs. Neither did the two Moon Elves.

Those voices, their inflections, the word choices, and even the tempos were ingrained in his mind. He intended to learn their identities. And he was close to figuring out the Sun Elf. Very close, indeed.

"What is your update?" demanded a deep voice from his left.

This Dark Elf always spoke first, making it appear as if he led the group. Perhaps he did, but One would never presume until he had confirmation. One swung his head in the direction of the voice and lifted his gaze. He couldn't make out the silhouette of the figure. The Masters used the shadows effortlessly, but no one could stay in the dark forever.

"It's as you anticipated. Gita took matters into her own hands." He had actually been the one to predict her action, but it wouldn't do to point that out.

A snort came from his right. Then a female Moon Elf said, "I told you she would find a way. She's an asset we should've used instead of locking away."

There was no debate or argument between them. At least, not verbally. One got the impression that *much* happened he couldn't see. He would find out someday, once he claimed his seat among the Masters. But right now, he had to deal with Gita. She had been in charge of the Shaldorn Stronghold, and for years, he, along with Two and Three, had been her right hands.

But then Ravi and Yasmin came along and disrupted everything. Gita's perfect run came to an end, and the Masters had tucked her away in Belanore until they could figure out what to do with her. She had then become his problem as she fought against the confines of her rooms and her need to exact revenge.

"What did she do, exactly?" a male Wood Elf asked.

One inwardly bristled at being the one to deliver the news, especially since he had been tasked to keep Gita under control. In order to do that, he would've had to stay by her side every minute of every day, and that was impossible with his many other duties. As well as his extracurricular activities. That didn't absolve him of failing to restrict her, however.

He swallowed and forced his body to relax before he answered. "She learned one of the humans she employed was taken. Gita then manipulated the other female to go after a Mountain Elf."

There was a beat of silence, shock rocking through those in the room. He understood since he had been just as staggered when he found out.

"You're telling us this human is going into the Dangerous Peaks in search of the Mountain Elves?"

Awareness tingled through One at the sound of the new voice. The female had the unmistakable accent of a Sea Elf. He had wondered how long it would take the Masters to get one of them on board. Not all the Masters spoke, so it could be that she had been there from day one and he just hadn't known. Still, it was a new voice to add to the other ten.

He turned around to look in the female's direction, fruitlessly peering into the shadows for a glimpse of her. "I am, indeed."

"Why?" the Sea Elf demanded.

One needed to choose his next words carefully. He wove many lies and was several people. Keeping it all straight was a matter of life and death. He knew Manu had helped Ravi and Yasmin, but he didn't know how Gita had learned of it—a mistake he would have to spend the next few days correcting. "Gita believes Mountain Elves helped the others take down Shaldorn."

The truth. At least part of it. He hoped it would be enough.

"Then the human has doomed himself. Even if he survives the weather, he'll never get into any of their domains."

"*She,*" One corrected. "And she actually survived and was found by the Mountain Elves."

The Dark leader's voice boomed through the chamber, "Explain!"

Words had always come easily to One. He knew what to say to someone to get exactly what he wanted. Sometimes, it was information. Other times, it was action. Occasionally, it was simply a reaction.

He had a plan for everyone. He'd long been tempted to end Gita's life, but it hadn't been time yet. He had made a rare mistake in assuming she would adhere to the Masters' plan. Gita had gone behind his back, but he wouldn't allow the Masters to know that. Sure, some might think her resourceful, but many would believe him inept. What One had to do was find out who had told Gita about Manu.

"We all know that while humans can kill us, they are too timid to try. Gita never expected the human to be able to kill any of the Mountain Elves, but she knows that some help those stranded in the Peaks. So, she'll get close and learn what she can," One explained after he faced the male.

Once more, the female Moon Elf preened. "Look what Gita can do, even confined. We should release her and allow her to take care of our problems."

The Masters had big problems in the way of three substantial hits, one on top of the other. First, Shaldorn was shut down. Then, Arya deceived them into believing she would join their ranks, and, once freed, escaped with Jai, taking a Sea Elf prisoner with them. The latest strike had been when an undercover agent liberated several prisoners from the very compound he stood in.

The Masters had moved freely about in the shadows for decades as they built their empire. And the more they grew, the more fear spread about them. Few knew their name as the Masters, but that was changing. Anyone who went against them was dealt with swiftly and violently. Those responsible for the current incidents had yet to be caught. And that wasn't good for the Masters.

"Our decision regarding Gita stands for now. Let's see what happens with the Mountain Elves before we revisit what to do with her," the Dark stated. "Because, lest anyone forget, she is the reason we lost Shaldorn."

Not to mention a hefty sum of profits.

"Return immediately with any updates," the male ordered One.

He bowed his head at the command and walked out of the spotlight, moving back into the shadows to begin his long walk out of the compound where he'd eventually make his way Above. He usually took the opportunity to wander when called to the Masters, but he headed topside immediately this time.

Gita's bold scheme went against his plans. He could have been more persuasive with Inej when he spoke with her, but something had held him back. In the end, he'd decided to let things play out. The human was clever and capable. Would it be enough for her to get close to Manu? He wasn't so sure.

He could send an anonymous warning to the Mountain Elves. It might stop Gita's plot, but it wouldn't help his. Inej and Manu were no longer his concern. He could adjust to whatever happened in the mountains. The real issue now was Gita.

One should've taken care of her weeks ago. Too much interest was focused on her now for him to remove her. But the moment he got the chance...

7

Navara

Manu hadn't been prepared for the sight of the human. The face he had seen crusted with ice and blistered red with cold was gone. In its place was a woman of uncommon beauty. Her cascade of hair was a river of the deepest brown that caught the light like polished obsidian. It spilled down her back in endless waves, wild and soft. He wanted to sink his hands into the strands and never let go.

Her brown skin glowed from the healing herbs as if kissed by the sun. There was a smattering of freckles across her nose that only added to her allure. Thick brows arched ever so slightly over her large eyes. Just like the first time he'd looked into them, he found himself drowning in the warm pools. Yet he recognized her wariness, as well as the walls she had erected around herself. Her plump lips drew his gaze, and he wondered what that mouth would look like smiling.

"We just finished eating," Jalall said, breaking into his musings. "There's plenty, if you're hungry."

Manu waved off his friend. "I've already eaten."

"Sit. I'll get us some tea," Jalall urged as he got to his feet.

Manu took the seat opposite the woman. "I'm pleased to see you're feeling better."

"I owe you a debt of thanks," she replied.

Her voice was smooth and sultrier than it had any right to be. It went through him, skimming along his skin and sinking into his blood. He shifted to adjust his thickening cock. He had been too long without a bed partner if he was responding so blatantly. "How much did Jalall tell you?

"Not much," she replied.

"My name is Manu, and I lead here. Jalall is captain of the army. We brought you to our city so you could recover."

She lifted a cup to her lips and drank before saying, "I'm Inej."

Manu tested the name on his tongue, both eager to say it but also hesitant—as if once released, he would be forever altered.

"The herbs worked remarkably well on her," Jalall said as he returned with a tray bearing a teapot and three cups.

Manu let his gaze run over Inej again. "I can see that."

"I've never had healing herbs before," she confessed.

Jalall's brows rose as he set the tray on the corner of the table, holding it with one hand as he passed out the cups. "Have you never been ill or hurt before?"

"They're far too expensive." Inej shrugged as if it were no big deal. But it was.

Manu took the teapot and rose to fill Inej's cup before pouring some for Jalall and then himself. "If you don't mind me asking, what were you doing in the Peaks?"

"What does anyone, especially a human, come out here for?" she asked.

Jalall sank into his seat after setting the tray aside. "There's nothing out here."

"You're here," she answered.

Unease slithered up Manu's spine. "These mountains are unforgiving, even to those of us who have spent our lives among them. For others, they're a death sentence, of which you were nearly one of those statistics."

She lowered her gaze to her cup. "Nearly." Her eyes lifted to meet his. "But I'm still alive."

"Barely," Jalall stated. "Even if the wolvites hadn't found you, you wouldn't have been able to travel with a broken leg. You would've frozen to death."

"And yet, I sit healed and warm at your table."

Manu felt Jalall's gaze on him, but he didn't look away from Inej. "As I said, we brought you here to recover. And thanks to the herbs, you have. Tell us where you were headed, and we'll escort you there."

A quick frown furrowed her brow, but she quickly erased it. "Do you know what's going on in the rainwood?"

"People are being taken by the droves. Aye, we know," Jalall stated.

She looked between them. "I came here to escape that."

"Before today, how many Mountain Elves have you seen?" Manu asked.

"None," she admitted.

He brought the cup to his lips and drank. "We like our solitude."

"I'm not asking for a handout," she said defensively. "I can pull my weight."

Jalall sat back in his chair, holding his tea in one hand. "What makes you think this place is safe?"

"It's isolated. I also doubt any of your people have been taken." When they didn't respond, her lips flattened. "You're right, I would have died out there if you hadn't found me. But the gods brought you to me for a reason."

Manu hated to admit that she was right. If only he knew what that reason might be. If Yaz and Ravi's children weren't here, he would probably allow her to remain. But he refused to jeopardize their lives for anyone—even a human as beautiful and intriguing as Inej.

"Perhaps the gods did intervene," Manu told her. "However, my priority is keeping my people safe."

Her eyes widened in surprise. "You think I would harm them? I'm a human."

"So you say," Jalall said. "There is magic about that can transform a human into an elf, or an elf into a human."

"I assure you, I'm human," she replied with a note of bitterness. "I pose no threat to anyone here."

Manu shook his head. "Be that as it may, you will be leaving. Just to be sure you're healed, we'll give you another dose of the herbs tonight. By morning, any lasting effects will be gone."

"Morning?" she asked softly, her confusion visible on her wrinkled brow.

Jalall set his cup on the table. "As Manu said, we will see you to your destination."

"I don't have a destination. I ran," she said.

Her desperation was palpable. Manu knew that sending her back out into the mountains would be signing her death warrant, but he couldn't leave her here. "We can take you back to the rainwood."

"So I can be kidnapped with the rest and suffer some unknown fate?" She shook her head. "I'd rather die in the cold."

"I'm sorry," Manu said. And he was. More than she could know. It wasn't in his nature to turn from those in need, but he had no choice.

Inej calmly pushed back her chair and stood. "Me, too. If you will excuse me, I'll return to my quarters."

Jalall nodded. Manu tried to keep his eyes from her as she walked past, but his gaze was drawn to her hair. He watched the ends sweep against her hips, and an image of her in his arms, her hair wrapped around his fist, flashed in his mind. He blinked and shoved it aside, even as his gaze lingered on her shapely body. All too soon, she walked out of sight.

Manu turned around and found Jalall watching him silently. He winced, hoping his friend hadn't noticed his interest.

"You know..." Jalall began.

Manu cut his gaze to him. "Don't."

"She was eyeing you as much as you were her."

"I told you not to."

Jalall grunted as he leaned forward to pour more tea. "She is attractive."

"And leaving."

"Not until morning. How long has it been since you've bedded someone?"

Manu dropped his head back against the chair and stared up at the ceiling. "I really don't want to have this conversation."

"Again, you mean?" Jalall asked with amusement. "How can

an elf such as you, who has the pick of anyone in the city, sleep alone?"

"I don't always sleep alone."

Jalall made a frustrated sound at the back of his throat. "If you were going to wed Tahmine, you would've done it already. She's an all-too-willing bed partner who believes you will eventually take her as your wife. You need to put her out of her misery."

"I've told her repeatedly that we're not marrying."

"Yet, she still comes to your bed."

Manu ran a hand down his face. "Aye. *She* comes to *me*. Not the other way around." Though he was considering going to her tonight to relieve his aching body.

"And you let her. Stop stringing her along, my friend. Do you want a wife?"

"I don't know."

Jalall grunted. "I think you should find a wife. If it isn't someone among our people, the other Mountain tribes would love to offer up one of their women for a match."

"What about you? You need a wife."

"I'm not ready."

Manu couldn't believe he had let his friend drag him into this conversation again. "Me having a wife has nothing to do with who will succeed me."

Jalall rolled his dark eyes. "We both know you don't need a wife for that. The new infants brought to Navara are always offered to you first. You've never taken one as yours."

"I'm not ready," he threw Jalall's words back at him.

"You're going to keep saying that, and then one day, you won't have a chance to teach a child what they need to know to lead."

Manu looked into his best friend's eyes and said the words he had been mulling over for the last few weeks. "Then you'll succeed me."

"Don't you fucking dare," Jalall said, his voice low with anger. "I have no wish for such responsibility."

"You're the only one who knows what to do."

Jalall threw up his hands. "Then take one of the children!"

Manu's plan hadn't gone over well, but he'd known it wouldn't. He never should've said anything. Now, Jalall would push even harder for him to accept one of the infants as his. The problem was, Manu couldn't choose one child over another.

Worse, what if he chose wrong?

"What do you think about Inej?" Manu asked, needing to change the conversation.

Thankfully, Jalall went along with it, his fury evaporating. "I think she's hiding something."

"I got that, too. Any idea what?"

"Nothing yet. I searched her discarded clothes and bag, but there was nothing to find."

Manu drummed his fingers on the table. "She was visibly upset about leaving."

"If we can believe her story."

"We should make sure she wasn't followed."

Jalall nodded slowly. "I'll alert the guards on duty tonight and send a couple of teams to scout tomorrow morning."

"We won't be able to stay hidden for long. More and more of the Masters' thugs are coming into the mountains."

"They don't know your name. You aren't on the list with Dain and the others. You're safe."

Manu twisted his lips. "I thought so, but is that false hope?"

"If anyone comes, they'll have to get through me first."

"If they discover I was involved with taking down Shaldorn, the best thing I can do is leave Navara to keep the city safe."

Jalall's brows snapped together. "You can't leave. Our people need you."

"Do they? I'm not so sure. I brought the Masters' ire by helping Ravi and Yasmin."

Jalall shoved aside his tea so hard that the liquid sloshed over the sides. "You did the right thing. I only wish I had been there to help. I have an idea. If your name gets out, I'll leave and tell everyone I'm you. That way, the city will be left alone, and you can remain as ruler."

Manu got to his feet. "That plan is shite."

"It's solid," Jalall said as he stood. "And you know it."

"Nay, I don't. You're staying, and that's the end of it."

Jalall didn't back down. "Only if you do. If you leave, so will I. Then what happens to Navara?"

Manu should've seen that coming. He shook his head and sighed as he looked away. "I know taking a stand against the Masters was the right thing to do, but I thought—hoped—they would never venture into the mountains."

"So did Ravi and Yasmin, or they wouldn't have sent the kids here." Jalall slapped him on the back. "We've been vigilant. We'll continue to be cautious. And we won't let strangers in."

"You mean no more strangers," Manu said with a grin as he looked at his friend.

Jalall chuckled. "Inej is right, though. She's no threat to us."

"If she's human."

"It won't matter. Because she'll be gone in the morning."

Manu was suddenly exhausted. He wanted to find his bed and sleep for a week, but there was still too much to do before he could get any rest. "If she doesn't give us a direction, we'll take her to the lowlands."

"She'll just return to the mountains."

"Then that's on her. We'll have done what's right." Hopefully.

Jalall nodded solemnly. "Go home, my friend. Find someone other than Tahmine to take to your bed and then get some sleep."

"I'd really love it if you stopped worrying about my sex life."

"And miss out on teasing you? I don't think so," Jalall said with a laugh.

Manu wore a smile as they walked to the side door. He looked over his shoulder once in case he caught a glimpse of Inej, but there was no sign of her. He waved goodbye to Jalall and headed home. He was halfway there when he spotted Tahmine. She stood waiting for him by the bridge. He should send her home, but his body craved release. Manu paused beside her. She smiled up at him, her dark eyes searching his.

"You know there can't be more than this between us," he told her, remembering Jalall's words.

She looked down and took his hand into hers before lifting her gaze to his once more. "I know."

8

Inej was plastered against the door, her ear to the wood, listening, and though she could hear Manu and Jalall talking, she couldn't make out any of the words. She sighed and gave up. They were talking about her. She was sure of it. But *what* was being said was harder to determine.

The vial of poison lay under the mattress where she had left it. It was the first thing she had rushed to find upon entering. Thankfully, it hadn't been discovered when the linens were changed. That didn't help her current situation, though. Sure, she had the poison, but what good did it do if they sent her away and she was unable to use it?

She would be escorted out of the city in a few hours. She had nowhere to go. While she could return to Belanore or even travel to Rannora, she had come to rid Shecrish of Manu. She had to remain. Somehow, someway.

She walked to the bed and sat on the edge. Manu was nothing like she had pictured. The fact that he, as well as Jalall, had been kind took her aback. They kidnapped humans from all over the plateau. It stood to reason they would bring her to their home under the guise of helping her, but to send her on her way afterward? That didn't make sense.

Unless...this wasn't Manu's base of operations. Perhaps no one here knew about his duplicity. Maybe he could maintain the illusion of a benevolent leader to his people while he destroyed lives elsewhere. He didn't intend to send her away. He would pretend to take her, but intended to do with her as he had done with Krata and however many others he had abducted. If that happened, she would never get close enough to kill him—at least not with the poison. She had no weapons, and the chances of her finding one outside the mountain were unlikely. That meant she needed to remain where she was.

But how? Being so close to someone who had so little regard for someone's life was unnerving, especially after being such a hero and saving her. Just thinking about it made her sick to her stomach.

She had decided to end Manu's life when she took the mission. Her anger got her to agree. Yet she had never killed anyone before. Agreeing to it and doing it weren't remotely the same. Now that she had met him, spoken to him, it seemed an impossible feat. The subtle plan of pouring the poison into his glass seemed too easy. What she wanted to do was launch herself across the table and hit him while demanding to know where Krata was.

Then there was Jalall. They were very close, which meant he had to be in on it, too. If she succeeded in snuffing out Manu's life, would Jalall take his place? It was something to consider. Perhaps she could remove both of them before she was discovered. None of that would matter if she couldn't find a way to stay put, however.

A soft knock sounded on the door. Her head jerked toward it as she jumped to her feet, her heart hammering.

"Inej?" Jalall's voice called through the panel.

Her feet were wooden blocks as she made her way to the door, fully aware of how precarious her position was as a human among elves. They could take her tonight, and no one would be the wiser.

Or maybe everyone in the city knew and simply wouldn't care.

She slowly opened the door to see the Mountain Elf standing in the middle of the hall. It was a courtesy she hadn't expected, and it was disconcerting.

"Your herbs," he said, holding up a glass.

She stuck her arm out and accepted the water and herbs, all the while waiting for him to shove open the door or yank her out. He did neither.

"The house is locked, but you are free to roam the inside," Jalall told her. "My door is at the end of the hall, should you need anything."

"I've not known an elf to be so fearful of a human."

He pointed to his left. "The kitchen is that way, should you get hungry. Help yourself to whatever you find."

Her jab to see his reaction fell flat. Of course, he wasn't afraid of her. He had magic, where she had none. She was the scared one, and they both knew it. She was locked in the house because they didn't want her to get out.

"Sleep well," he replied before walking away.

Inej closed the door and flipped the lock. She carried the water back to the bed. They were freely giving her something—twice now—that cost more than she made in a year. She might feel fine, but why not take the opportunity to ensure that she was completely healed from her trek and fall?

She quickly drained the water. This time, she was more aware of the slightly bitter taste. The elves' magic, as well as their easy access to the enchanted herbs and even the Star Elves who could heal others, made them a far more advanced race than hers. She wondered if humans had outnumbered them at one time, and the elves had used their power to subjugate them. Not that it mattered. Nothing would topple the elves.

Her encounters with them had always been brief. Even working for Gita, she and Krata didn't interact with her outside of a few words. It wasn't until Krata's disappearance that things had changed. Inej hadn't wanted to talk about it. It had been Gita who had coerced it out of her. And Inej was glad she had because then she had gotten the answers she needed.

And found a purpose.

The elves were too afraid of Manu to do anything, but she could. Inej didn't want to be a hero. She wasn't doing this for fame or glory. She was doing it for a girl who had befriended her and stayed around, even when Inej hadn't wanted her.

There was no bringing Krata back—or any of the others who had been taken. It was bad enough that humans lived in fear of the discrimination and racism that ran rampant every day. Now, there was the added threat of being snatched and taken to who knew where, with who knew what being done to them. It was too much.

Inej removed her clothes, laying them out at the end of the bed. She turned off all the lights except the small lamp beside the bed. Only then did she slip naked between the sheets. The mattress was soft, cradling her as if it had been designed specifically for her. She had never slept on anything so luxurious. She turned onto her side, her head cushioned by a plump pillow.

Her eyes grew heavy. Finally, she gave in and allowed them to close. Her thoughts, however, didn't turn off. An image of Manu as he knelt beside her in the snow filled her mind. If she hadn't known who he was, she would have been grateful for his help. After all, what kind of elf showed one side of himself to others while giving in to a darker side in private? A monster, that's who.

A monster she had to get close to. One who needed to trust her so she could find a way into his life. That could happen in many ways, but there was one true way to get him to lower his guard, and that was in bed.

Inej had never used sex against someone before. She'd never needed to. When her body yearned for release, burned for that kind of connection, she went looking for the right man. One who wanted a single night. Someone who wouldn't ask too many questions. A person who would erase all her thoughts for a short time until they went their separate ways.

Those men weren't easy to find. Sometimes, she would search for days before finding one. But when she did, it was worth it.

That wouldn't be how it was with Manu. He might hold some of the attributes she enjoyed, but his true identity marred anything she might find enjoyable. She could fake it, though. Females of all races had been doing that since the dawn of time. It would be worth giving him access to her body if she could end his reign of terror.

In an odd twist, the memory of him gently holding her hand returned. She gave herself a mental shake to dislodge it. He was good at pretending, and she could never allow herself to forget that. The moment he was able, he would do with her what he had done to countless other humans. So, no matter how deeply she feared him, she had to do this.

She rolled onto her back and stared at the canopy, wondering what Manu was doing at that moment. Had he left the city to go find others to abduct? There were rumors that those taken were killed. Others said they were enslaved. It didn't matter what was being done. The elves were disrupting the people's lives.

But elves had begun to vanish, too. Did that make what Manu did even worse if he were going after his own kind? She wanted to feel sorry for the elves who had been kidnapped, but she could only dredge up a little pity. It was about time the elves felt some of what the humans did on a daily basis.

9

anu's mood was grim as he dusted snow from his body and entered the mountain. It was an hour until dawn, but he had no intention of returning to his bed. He might have satiated his body, but he couldn't relax in his room once Tahmine fell asleep. He probably should have woken her so she could return to her own bed, but he hadn't. Instead, he had gone for a walk outside, and it was a good thing he had.

His strides were long as he hurried to the guard center. Manu opened the door to find the next elves readying themselves to relieve their counterparts. "A whiteout is coming," he warned.

The atmosphere quickly shifted to one of concern as word spread. The weather was always volatile in the Peaks, but the whiteouts were particularly hazardous. It didn't matter how well someone thought they knew the mountains. They were no match for the vicious storms.

Everyone knew what to do when a whiteout was barreling

down on them. Soldiers were already making their way through the city, so everyone could prepare. As long as they stayed inside, they would be fine. He jogged to Jalall's and banged on the door.

His friend answered quickly, blinking away his sleep as he buckled his pants. "What happened?"

"Whiteout," Manu said and turned to head back out.

Jalall caught up with him in moments, his coat already in place. "How many are outside?"

"I don't know."

"How long until the storm hits?"

Manu quickened his steps. "I give it twenty minutes, if we're lucky."

"Fuck," Jalall murmured. Then he began barking orders to the soldiers.

They endured whiteouts far too frequently not to be prepared. If anyone got stuck outside, the rule was to take cover and wait for the storm to pass. Everyone knew it, yet every so often, someone thought they could get back before it hit.

By the time he and Jalall made it back outside, the guards who had been on duty were rushing toward them.

"Have you seen anyone?" Manu asked.

Three of the four shook their heads and headed inside. The fourth lingered, her breath billowing past her lips from her run through the snow. "I saw a figure headed our way. They looked to be coming from Sachin's territory."

"They're too far away. They'll never make it," Jalall said.

Manu looked up at the mountain before him.

"They'll know what to do," Jalall added.

Manu checked the sky.

Jalall grabbed his arm. "Don't do it."

"I'll be back," Manu said as he pulled out of his friend's grip and ran toward the slope.

In three leaps, he was at the top. He turned in the direction of the tribe nearest them and scanned the mountains looking for movement. The animals had already taken shelter. If there was any kind of activity, it would be an individual.

Manu heard Jalall shout his name. He glanced over his shoulder to see his friend scrambling up the side of the mountain. Manu looked west, where the storm was barreling toward them. It was moving quicker than he had initially believed. He wished anyone still out here luck. They would need it.

He jumped down the slope, sliding on his side along the snow about thirty feet before jumping again. He landed beside Jalall.

"I thought for sure you were going," his friend said.

Manu turned his head away from the biting wind. "I didn't see anyone."

They jogged back to the city's entrance. Manu lingered, unable to shake the feeling that someone was still out there.

"They know what to do," Jalall shouted over the rising wind.

Manu nodded and followed Jalall into the mountain. The door slid closed behind him, sounding loud as it cut off the howling of the wind. He pulled off his gloves and removed his hat, stuffing both into the pockets of his coat.

There was nothing left to do now but wait it out. Manu wouldn't be able to rest until he knew that every member of his tribe was accounted for. Jalall had already dispatched soldiers to begin going door to door to see if anyone was missing.

"I thought I sent you home last night," Jalall said as he walked up. "What were you doing out?"

Manu walked to the bridge that overlooked the city. Lights

were flickering on in windows as citizens were roused from their beds. "I did go home." He paused before he said, "With Tahmine."

"Ah. Now, I understand why you were outside. It is perfectly acceptable to ask someone to return home."

"Maybe for you."

Jalall sighed loudly. "Shall I wake her?"

"I don't wish to embarrass her. Besides, she'll hear the commotion soon enough." At least Manu hoped she would. The kids. Fuck. "I need to check on the children."

"Go. I have this covered."

Manu sprinted home and entered to find servants already moving about. He tossed his coat onto a table at the entrance to his house and took the stairs three at a time to the next level. He paused beside the boys' room first. They each had their own room, but they always ended up sleeping together. Same with the girls. He silently opened the boys' door and peered inside.

Sameer's head lifted from the pillow. A moment later, he slipped from under the covers and came over.

"I'm just checking to make sure everyone is here. A whiteout is moving in," Manu whispered.

Sameer rubbed his eyes and frowned. "What's that?"

"Conditions that make it impossible to tell the difference between the snow-covered ground and the sky, as they both look the same."

"What do we need to do?"

Manu smiled to ease the boy's sudden distress. "Nothing other than stay put. Are Din and Hadi with you?"

"Of course."

"Good. Go back to bed."

He closed the door and moved across the hall to the girls'

room. He counted all three of them sleeping soundly. Manu quietly shut the door so as not to disturb them, then looked down the long hall. With a sigh, he walked to his chambers.

When he stepped inside, Tahmine was already up and dressed. She glanced his way as she braided her hair. "I woke to find you gone. Again."

He tried not to get angry at her irritated tone. Maybe Jalall was right, and it would be better if he cut things off. But he didn't have the time or the inclination for an argument at the moment. "A whiteout is coming."

Her anger dissipated instantly as she finished tying off the ends of her hair and faced him. "Who's missing?"

"No one yet."

"Good." She walked past him and out of the room.

While there was nothing to do but wait out the storm, measures were taken for those who discovered that one of their loved ones was outside. Tahmine was headed to the group of women who saw to that. He looked at the bed. He had been happy to bring her to his room. Sex had always been satisfying between them, but he was doing her a disservice by continuing to string her along. It didn't matter how many times he told her that nothing could come of them as a couple. He saw the same disappointment on her face every morning after. Whatever contentment their time together brought got wiped away.

Manu left his home and walked the streets. Most went about their business as usual. He glanced toward Jalall's place and saw a figure in the window. His steps slowed to a halt as he met Inej's gaze. The moment he headed in her direction, she backed away from the pane.

He walked inside, his head swiveling to the left where she

stood. For a moment, they simply stared at each other. She stood serenely, a question in her eyes. And he braced himself, wondering what her reaction would be.

"It appears you'll be staying with us for a while longer. A whiteout will be here shortly," he said.

She arched a brow. "A whiteout?"

"A type of storm that no one goes out in."

Her gaze darted out the window. "I see."

"You're safe inside."

"I gathered as much." Her brown gaze returned to him.

He wasn't sure why he remained, or even why he had spoken to her at all.

"Is there anything I can do to help?"

Manu was surprised by her offer. "There's nothing anyone can do now, other than wait it out."

"Of course."

Still, he didn't move. What was it about the human that made him keep returning to her? She was guarded, cagey, even. But then again, she was a human in a city of elves. And as far as she knew, the only human in Navara. He was beginning to wonder if she was afraid of anything. Because what kind of woman walked into the Dangerous Peaks without proper clothing or even a direction?

"How long do these whiteouts last?" she asked, interrupting the awkward silence.

He shrugged. "Depends. Some are gone within an hour, others last much, much longer."

Their conversation ended when Jalall ran up. He looked between them before telling Manu, "We have one missing."

Dread curled icy fingers around his spine. "Who?"

"Milad."

Manu clenched his jaw. Milad had spent his life in the army, only retiring a few months ago. "That's not great news, but he knows what to do."

"Is everything okay here?" Jalall asked.

"I was merely informing Inej of what was happening."

Jalall slid his gaze to her. After a long moment, he turned to Manu. "I know you haven't eaten. Come, let's get you some food."

"I can get some at home."

"Come on," Jalall called over his shoulder as he walked away.

Manu closed the door and motioned for Inej to walk ahead of him. "You must eat, as well."

She hesitated for a fraction of a moment. She hadn't been comfortable the night before. Was it him? Jalall? Or the combination of them both? Surely, she knew she was safe. If they had meant her harm, they wouldn't have saved her from the wolvites or brought her to Navara.

His gaze lowered to the sway of her hips as she walked. She exuded seduction as if she had been born to it. It was subtle, refined. Her allure was tantalizing in ways that deeply affected him. And his body reacted just as it had the night before.

He jerked his gaze away from her. What was wrong with him? More importantly, what was it about this human that inflamed his blood so?

Jalall moved about the kitchen, pulling food out of the cold box for them to eat, but the only thing Manu wanted was Inej. He moved to the opposite side of the room to put some distance between them. But it wasn't far enough. His gaze moved to her again and again. Thankfully, she didn't appear to notice. But Jalall did. His friend's frown said everything.

Manu wasn't hungry, but he ate to keep up his strength. Jalall filled the silence, talking about inane things that would entertain Inej but give little away about their tribe. It was a gift Manu didn't have, so he didn't interrupt. For her part, Inej seemed interested. She was hard to read—harder than most. It made him wonder about her arrival, even as he fantasized about stripping her out of her clothes. He was in a bad situation. The sooner Inej went on her way, the better.

Her gaze suddenly lifted to his, and he found himself drowning in the dark pools of her eyes once more. He didn't want to look away. Ever.

"Manu, come on."

Jalall's voice broke into his thoughts, yanking him into the present. He looked at his friend to find him at the door of the kitchen, frowning. Manu didn't know what he had missed, but he glanced at Inej one last time and followed Jalall out.

10

A strange disquiet settled over the house once Manu and Jalall left. Some relished the idea of being idle, but it had always grated on Inej. She preferred to have something to occupy herself. Otherwise, she would sink into her thoughts—and that was never a good place to be.

She packed away what little food was left and then wandered the house yet again. The pounding on the door that morning had woken her from a deep sleep, no doubt thanks to the herbs. By the time she dressed and walked out of her room, Jalall was gone. She had caught a glimpse of him and Manu hurrying away from the window. Others dashed about, their faces tight with apprehension.

Inej walked back to the front of the home, pressed her cheek to the glass, and looked up. She couldn't see the top of the mountain, but the fact that it had been hollowed didn't sit well with her. What kept it from caving in on itself? What if the wind from the storm blew hard enough that boulders fell and crashed into the city?

She eyed the rocky roof over her. How sturdy was it? The idea of being crushed caused her chest to seize with a newfound fear. She needed to see the sky, to have the sun on her face. She took a step back. She couldn't stay here.

Inej whirled around, only to find her feet frozen in place. Where did she think she could go? She knew nothing of the city. She didn't know the size of it or how to get out. Were there guards who might stop her? What about exits? Surely, they must have more than one.

What if she did get out? What then? She'd barely survived the first time she braved the mountains, and she'd had a map. She had nothing now. Not to mention, she hadn't done what she came to do.

She dragged in a ragged breath and tried to think of anything other than an imaginary rock falling on her. But her mind wouldn't let it go. If she didn't find something to do, she would give in to her fear.

Inej raced through the house, glancing into rooms as she ran down the hall until she found herself in the kitchen. She was a decent cook, but she was a better baker. Turning in a slow circle, she looked over the spacious room and its many cupboards. Then she started opening them, one by one.

She found flour, sugar, and eggs and set them out on the table. There was a basket of small red fruit. She sniffed, taking in the sweet, aromatic smell before popping one onto her tongue. An explosion of flavor filled her mouth from the juicy berry. Both sweet and tart, it left a distinct tang as she swallowed.

Immediately, she ate another as she searched for bowls and baking dishes. The kiln was different than those in Belanore, but she eventually figured it out. Then she wound her hair into a knot at the base of her neck and turned her focus to crafting the pastry.

Inej hummed as she got lost in the work. She forgot about the storm, the tension building within the city, the threat of being crushed, and even her very reason for being there. Her fingers kneaded the dough as she effortlessly worked it into shape, before allowing it to rise. Then she turned her attention to the berries, eating more as she tested them with herbs until she found a combination she liked.

The first batch was soon baking, the smell filling the kitchen and making her smile. She got the second batch ready and turned to set them aside when she found herself looking at Manu. She startled at his presence and jumped, nearly spilling the tarts. His hand darted out and caught the edge of the tray before it tipped.

"The storm has passed," he said.

She searched his face, wondering why he had come. Or maybe he was just checking to make sure she hadn't run off. "That's good."

"You have flour on your cheek."

Inej reached up and rubbed first one cheek and then the other with the back of her hand.

Manu stepped back. "It smells good in here."

"I don't like sitting idle," she said as she set the tray aside and checked on the baking tarts.

She pulled them out of the kiln to cool. When she turned around, Manu was gone. Inej shrugged and set aside the hot tray as she put in the second batch to bake. She had convinced herself she'd imagined Manu's visit when Jalall walked in, brows raised.

"He wasn't lying," Jalall murmured.

Inej looked at the mess she had made. "I'll clean everything up."

"If those taste as good as they look, I don't even care." He flashed her a wide smile.

If she didn't know Manu's secret, she might think he and Jalall were friendly. But she *did* know the truth. Being on the receiving end of their deception left her cold. She wanted to shrink away and retreat, but she couldn't. Not when so many lives depended on her.

Inej forced her facial muscles to relax and her lips to curve into a smile when Jalall's hand hovered over the pastries. "Be careful. They're still cooling."

His face fell. "Save one for me and Manu. We're headed out to look for our people who got stuck in the storm."

He was gone before she could reply. She finished the baking and took her time cleaning. She was considering another soak in the tub when a loud commotion reached her. She ran to the front windows and looked out to see a crowd gathering.

Without thought, Inej reached for the door handle. It turned easily beneath her hand. It wasn't until the door swung open that she realized what she had done. She debated whether to remain inside, but she was curious about what was going on. She stepped out onto the stoop and watched as elves hurried to the left.

The tension she'd sensed earlier was gone. The mountain itself even felt different. She lifted her gaze and peered up. There were homes built halfway up the interior with roads crisscrossing from one side to the other. Light filtered in from an opening near the top, to enormous mirrors that caught the beams and directed them to the next mirror and the next to light up the city almost as if they were outside.

She heard the trickle of water and spotted a river winding through the city. She followed it to the right, where water tumbled softly from stones up the mountain to spill into the stream. More plants, like those in Jalall's bathroom, dotted the city and climbed the walls.

Inej's lips parted in shock when she turned to get a look at Jalall's house. It was a stunning display of columns and arched windows that had been carved out of the rock. She realized she was in some kind of residential area by the other houses sitting close by, and she wondered which one was Manu's.

The noise of the growing crowd tugged her attention from the architecture. She turned toward the rising voices and found herself pulled toward them. When one of the elves shot her a dark look, Inej remembered that her hair was up. She hastily released it to cover her rounded ears—not that it would do much good. She looked far different from any Mountain Elf.

She stayed toward the back of the gathering crowd and stood on some steps to see over everybody's heads. They were fixated on something far in the front. A shocked murmur rolled through the gathering. Inej rose up on her tiptoes and strained to see.

A woman's voice broke as she yelled, "Milad?!"

The heartbreaking sound brought a frown to Inej. She bit her lip as she leaned one way and then the other, hoping to see something, but she was too far in the back to make out anything. She studied the expressions of those around her to get some idea of what was going on. There were several tense moments of silence before someone released another mournful wail.

"Manu found them," someone in front of Inej said.

Suddenly, the crowd's anxious mood changed to one of relief.

It was just as she had predicted. Manu had fooled his people into believing he was some kind of hero.

A sudden shout silenced the assembly. Even Inej stilled, hoping to hear something. She picked up voices toward the front, and she thought she heard Manu speaking. She tilted her ear toward the sound, but the voices were soon drowned out by a murmur growing louder through the crowd.

"What's going on?" someone asked.

Another answered, "Jalall went back out after someone."

"Who? All our people have been found," a third asked.

No response came, leaving her to wait like everyone else. Inej lowered her heels to the ground to give her feet a rest. She glanced over her shoulder toward Jalall's house as the crowd began to disperse. It was close enough that she could dart back inside without too many people noticing her. With elves leaving, she was able to get a glimpse of the front, where she saw three elves being helped away. They must have been the ones who had been caught outside.

She wasn't ready to return to the house, so Inej remained on the steps, watching and taking in more of the city. It wasn't as big as Belanore, but it was impressive, nonetheless—if she could get past the worry of having the mountain cave in on her. Would this place be her tomb? It was better than being eaten by wolvites or freezing to death, she supposed. Barely.

Her head swung back around when she heard Jalall shout. She jumped from the steps and slipped between others to get closer so she could see. Inej climbed onto an ornate rock and saw a Mountain Elf stumbling inside with Manu following a couple of steps behind.

Elves rushed to the newcomer. Manu issued orders to some of

the guards before he walked to Jalall, where they spoke quietly. Then, the two males headed her way. She stayed on her perch but squatted so she wasn't so noticeable. Manu and Jalall never saw her as they passed.

Inej wondered about her decision to linger outside. What would they do to her when they found her gone? It wasn't as if she could get far. She sighed and jumped to the ground, intending to follow them as everyone returned to their lives. The threat was over. At least, for now.

She didn't get two steps before a deep, gravelly voice behind her said, "Step aside, human. You did your part. It's time for mine."

A male elf shouldered past her. The cold look in his eyes when he looked back at her sent warning bells ringing in her head. She glanced down and saw the tip of a blade peeking from his hand as he strode forward.

Inej looked ahead to see where the elf was headed and spotted Manu and Jalall. They had their heads bent close as they spoke. She looked back at the elf with the weapon to see him adjust his course, headed directly for them. Anger churned in her gut as his words echoed in her head. It hit her then that Gita must have sent the elf because she didn't believe Inej could pull it off. If anyone was going to take Manu's life, it was going to be her.

Without another thought, Inej shouldered her way through the crowd after the Mountain Elf. He still wore his coat, covered in ice crystals, making him easy to pick out.

"Manu!" she shouted, but her voice was drowned out by the noise around her.

The Mountain Elf turned his head slightly, having heard her.

She wove through others and lengthened her strides into a run, but the elf managed to put considerable distance between them.

She pumped her arms, sprinting when she saw him nearing Manu. The male pulled back his arm, ready to thrust it forward and up, when she burst through a group and launched herself between the two. The Mountain Elf's eyes narrowed dangerously when she bumped into Manu, sending him stumbling forward.

"What the fuck?" Manu mumbled.

The Mountain Elf peeled back his lips in a snarl and whispered low enough that only she could hear, "Fool."

One moment, he stood in front of her. The next, he was wrestled to the ground by both Jalall and Manu in a blur of motion and force. Shouts erupted as onlookers recoiled, fear rippling outward as they backed away. Inej was breathing heavily from her mad dash to stop the elf. She couldn't believe she had done it. She glanced around for the weapon, only to find it embedded in her chest.

She stared down at it in confusion. Shouldn't she feel pain? Why wasn't there more blood? Her gaze lifted to Manu, but the world began to spin. She took a hesitant step just as her legs gave out.

Manu heard the splash as his magic held the elf. Jalall jumped up, and Manu lifted his head to see others looking into the water and pointing. Someone had fallen in. He made sure the soldiers had the assailant before racing toward the river and spotting Inej being carried away. Jalall was just ahead of him, and they dove into the river at the same time.

Jalall managed to grab her hand and pull her to a stop. Manu came up on her other side and helped to keep her above water. Her eyes were closed as blood spread. He saw the end of the dagger sticking out of her and exchanged a look with Jalall. Neither said a word as they swam ashore. Others were there to help them. Manu pulled himself out of the water as Jalall laid Inej on the ground.

"Herbs!" Jalall shouted.

Manu knelt beside her prone body as someone handed Jalall a bag of herbs. Manu held her head as his friend readied the herbs. He then opened her mouth while Jalall dribbled the water onto her tongue. When she wouldn't swallow, Manu shifted and massaged her throat until she finally swallowed.

"She needs more," he urged.

Jalall's face was tight with concentration. "I'm trying."

Manu couldn't believe she had gotten between him and a would-be assassin. She was the last person he would have thought would risk her life for his.

Her pulse was slowing beneath his fingers. "Hurry," he urged. "We're losing her."

"Take the dagger out," Jalall said.

Manu shook his head. "I don't know how deep it went or what organs the blade damaged. She could bleed out."

"We don't have a choice."

He met Jalall's gaze and grimaced. Then he grabbed a young lad near him and dragged him down beside them. "The minute I take the dagger out, press hard on the wound. Do you understand?" Manu asked him.

The boy nodded and held his hands out at the ready. Manu hesitated for only a heartbeat before wrapping his hand around the handle of the blade and pulling it out. Blood poured from the wound before the boy applied pressure. Manu tossed the blade aside and continued helping Jalall get the water down her throat.

The seconds stretched endlessly until they got two cups into her. Her pulse was still much too weak for his liking. There was no Healer in Navara at the moment, and Manu didn't know if the herbs would work in time. What if this had been one of the children? How would he explain to Yasmin and Ravi that he hadn't been prepared for every eventuality?

"She's cold."

Manu startled at the lad's voice. He blinked and realized that

Inej's skin was, indeed, chilly. He'd been so intent on her wound that he had forgotten about her being submerged in the icy water.

"We need to get her to my place," Jalall said as he slipped his arms beneath her neck and knees.

Manu covered the boy's hands with his. "Thank you, lad. We'll take it from here."

The youngster moved away as Manu and Jalall got to their feet and headed to the house. They carried Inej into the bedroom. Before Manu could yank back the covers, Chanda, their childhood friend who took care of Jalall's house, did it for him.

Once Jalall had Inej on the bed, they made quick work of cutting off her wet clothes and pulling the covers up around her. Manu kept his hand pressed against her wound to stop the flow of blood. Then, they waited.

Manu kneeled beside the bed, trying not to get the covers wet while keeping pressure on the injury as Jalall paced. Manu looked down at Inej and recalled how she had jumped in front of him just as he saw the weapon. "I want to question the assassin."

"He's being held." Jalall suddenly halted, his chest rising and falling rapidly. "That blade was meant for you."

"I know."

"If I had known—"

Manu shook his head. "Don't. You couldn't have. Had I seen him, I would've brought him in, too."

"What was she doing out of the house?" Jalall asked as he ran a hand through his damp hair and sank onto a stool.

"Seeing what was happening like everyone else."

Jalall grunted. "I told her to stay inside."

"If she hadn't been there, I could be the one lying on this bed."

"Don't even fucking joke about that."

Manu held his friend's gaze. "I'm not."

"A Mountain Elf tried to kill you. I can't wrap my head around it."

"I knew the Masters would come for me."

Jalall's lips twisted. "I thought it might come from another race. Not one of our kind."

Manu had known it would happen, but he had still been taken off guard. "There's only one reason for the attack. They know about my involvement now. More will come. And not just for me."

"He didn't even take off his coat," Jalall murmured.

"If I had been the one to find him instead of you, he likely would've attacked me there."

Jalall stared at the floor absently. "He wanted to get close to use the blade instead of his magic. Why?"

"To make sure he got the job done?" Manu shrugged. "It doesn't really matter. The bounty on us is high."

"Then we close off Navara," Jalall stated as he lifted his gaze to Manu.

"We cannot stay locked in the mountain forever."

"That doesn't mean we bring others back as we have before."

Manu shifted closer to Inej, hoping to ease the ache in his knees. "Agreed."

"I'll see that done now."

He watched Jalall stride from the room before he slid his gaze to Inej. The long strands of her wet hair were clumped in thick sections and spread across the pillow. "You saved my life," he whispered.

Forty-six minutes passed before color returned to her face. Only then did Manu lift the covers to check her wound, careful not to look at her exposed body. He pulled his hand away and smiled in relief when blood didn't well up.

He stood and stretched his back when Jalall slowly walked back into the room. Manu glanced at his friend. "She's healing."

"Good," Jalall murmured.

Manu frowned as he walked closer to him. "What's going on?"

"Your assassin is dead."

For a long moment, Manu didn't speak. "How?"

"He hanged himself."

"Did he? Or did one of our people help him along?"

Jalall shrugged. "Everyone swears they had no part in it, but many saw the attempt on you."

"And they might have taken matters into their own hands." Manu flattened his lips as he shook his head. It had been a long day already. "What are the odds that he would've told us anything?"

"Minimal. Still, he might have let something slip."

"We know who he works for, and we know why he was here."

Jalall threw him a drying cloth to wipe the remnants of blood from his hands. "You need to stay inside the city."

"I'm not going to be imprisoned."

"We can't take the chance of something happening to you."

Manu stared down at the dried bloodstains on his hands—blood from a human who had no loyalty to him. "Sooner or later, the Masters will get one of us. They have unending resources, and plenty of those ready and willing to take a life for coin or the sheer pleasure of it. If they get to me, they'll go for the children to draw out the others."

"Then we need a plan."

Manu fingered the edge of the drying cloth. "Closing off Navara only buys us a little time."

"Then we take what we can while we formulate a plot to go after them."

Manu laughed, thinking Jalall was jesting. It wasn't until he saw his friend's stern expression that he sobered. "I have a bounty on me for doing just that. Let's not add you to the list."

"They have no idea how many are in our tribe."

"You want to take our people and throw them into a war?"

Jalall dropped his arms as he straightened. "As you told me not so long ago, we're in a war, whether we admit it or not."

"I hate when you throw my words back at me." Manu pinched the bridge of his nose with his thumb and forefinger. "Our army is sizable, but we don't know if they turned just a few Mountain Elves or entire tribes."

"Then we find out. I'll go to Sachin and bring the assassin's body to them. I can see if he's one of theirs. Regardless, it should be easy enough to decipher where the leadership stands about the Masters, at the very least."

"I'll go with you."

Jalall pulled a face. "You need to stay for the children." He jerked his chin toward Inej. "What are you going to do with her?"

Manu ran a hand down his face as he studied her. "I owe her my life."

"She returned the favor after we saved her from the wolvites. You don't owe her anything."

"I don't know what to do about her yet."

Jalall grunted. "Send her on her way as you already decided. She could be one of them."

Manu swung his head to his friend. "You honestly think she nearly died to make me believe I can trust her?"

"Why not?"

"Would you go that far?"

"We both would, given the right circumstances."

Manu had to admit that he was right, but he still wasn't ready to make a final decision about her. "Are you heading to Sachin's today?"

"The sooner we get this taken care of, the better."

"Take four soldiers with you. The group will be small enough to appear innocuous but give you enough backup should you need it."

Jalall started at Inej. "Send her on her way, old friend."

"You have a week. If you aren't back, I'm coming for you."

12

Manu dropped into the chair and leaned forward, bracing his forearms on his knees. Inej hadn't stirred in hours. He kept seeing her dive in front of him in slow motion. He hadn't thought to look for the weapon as he shifted her out of the way and tackled the elf to the ground. Why hadn't he checked to make sure she wasn't injured?

He squeezed the bridge of his nose between his thumb and forefinger. He needed to convince a Star Elf to reside there permanently. At least for as long as the children called Navara home, in case one of them was gravely wounded.

He dropped his hand and found himself staring at her again. He should've checked for the weapon. At the very least, he should've made sure that Inej didn't fall into the water. Witnessing her injury had been harrowing. He couldn't imagine if it had been one of the kids. Dain might know a Healer who needed to hide out for a bit. It was one of the first things he'd ask, just as soon as the Dark visited again.

Manu surged to his feet and stalked across the room. He wasn't a pacer. He always thought it better to focus the tight, unused energy in other directions, but that wasn't as easy as it usually was now. His nerves were frayed, his muscles stiff. He wanted to burst from the city and run through the mountains.

He wanted to race after Jalall and confront Sachin himself.

He wanted to be able to question his would-be assassin.

And he wanted Inej to wake up.

But he couldn't have any of it. And sitting here thinking about all the things he couldn't do only caused more friction within his usually calm mind and body.

He cast yet another look toward the bed. Inej's hair was dry now, the covers pulled up to her chin. Twice, he had put his finger to her neck to check her pulse, even though he could see her chest rising. There was no need to touch her again. Why, then, did he yearn to do just that?

Suddenly, she drew in a deep breath and rolled her head to the side. He stared, silently urging her back to consciousness. She moved her leg beneath the mound of covers they had piled on her for warmth. Manu returned to the chair and sat, his body vibrating with impatience.

Minutes ticked by with nothing, and then, finally, her eyes opened. His breath caught in his chest as she stared at the canopy above her. Then her head turned toward him, and their gazes met. The air left him in a whoosh at the sight of her striking brown eyes.

"Welcome back to the land of the living," he said.

"I take it I almost didn't come back."

An image of her cold, still body lying on the bank of the river with blood gushing from her wound flashed in his head. "It was close." He cleared his throat. "Thank you, by the way."

"Where's the elf?" she asked hesitantly.

It never dawned on him until that moment that she might be frightened of the assassin coming after her. "Found hanging in the cells."

"He killed himself?"

Manu sighed. "It appears so."

She pulled her arm from under the blankets and started to sit up. The cover fell, and he averted his gaze as he got to his feet.

"Are you hungry?" he asked while heading to the door.

"A little."

He might not be looking at her anymore, but Inej's face was etched in his brain. He mentally pictured her sitting up, her tangle of dark hair falling around her. "There are clothes in the wardrobe for you."

Manu left before she responded. He had already spent more than enough time with her. Now that she was awake, he had work to get back to. Manu headed for the front door, intending to leave. He gripped the handle, but he didn't turn it.

He didn't know how long he stood there, debating what he should do versus what he wanted to do, when he heard her door open. His mind pressed him to leave, but he was already turning around. He took three steps and saw Inej standing in the hallway.

Her hair had been brushed and now cascaded over her right shoulder to hang past the swell of her breast. She wore a long-sleeved tunic gown of deep brown that gently hugged her curves and was embellished with bronze and gold embroidery at the hem, wrists, and the soft V neckline.

His gut twisted when she touched where the dagger had entered her chest. The pain was gone, and she was alive, but nothing could erase the memories of how the event had unfolded. After a moment, she swung her head toward the kitchen. Just when he thought she would head in that direction, she looked his way.

Manu walked toward her, compelled by some unknown force he couldn't ignore to be near her. She didn't retreat or look away. Instead, she held his gaze until he stopped beside her. Her attention was a mix of boldness and caution. And he had an idea why.

Inej had asked to stay at Navara, and he had refused. Now, he was contemplating allowing her to remain. She would never get near the children, and her movements would be monitored, just in case. He wanted to trust her because she had saved his life, but there were too many variables for him to consider—and too many counting on him for protection—for him to freely give it.

"Do you still wish to remain?" he asked.

Her brow puckered with a small frown. "I do."

Manu slowly released a breath. "I'm going to grant it. Don't make me regret the decision."

13

She was staying. Inej couldn't believe her luck. All because she had refused to allow someone else to take Manu's life.

"You won't," she promised, speaking the lie easily.

Was it really a falsehood when he would be dead and unable to regret anything?

His black eyes searched hers for a long minute. "I hope not."

She wondered what he saw when he looked at her. She wasn't sure she had hidden her apprehension earlier when she woke to find him there. For a heartbeat, she had been sure he was there to arrest her—or worse. She hadn't dared to ask if he or someone else had questioned the assassin. If he was allowing her to remain, that meant either the elf hadn't told them anything, or they hadn't been able to question him.

"I ask that you remain in this house until I return. I'll take you for a tour of the city then," Manu told her.

"Of course."

He stood there for a moment before turning on his heel and

leaving out the front door. Inej leaned forward to watch him. A smile pulled at her lips as she walked into the kitchen. She had found another obstacle in her way and triumphed over it.

"You would be wise not to get any designs on him," Chanda said.

Inej hadn't formally met the elf, but Chanda made no attempt to hide her disdain for Inej. "I have no such intentions."

"Sure."

Inej frowned at the elf, not liking the curt tone or the flippant response. "I'm serious."

"Look," Chanda said, turning to face Inej, her dark brown eyes flashing with anger. "Manu isn't just our ruler, he's handsome, strong, kind, and unattached. There are few who wouldn't wish to be with him."

"Are you one of them?"

Chanda rolled her eyes. "I am not. I've known Manu and Jalall my entire life. They're like my brothers."

"But there is someone you know who *does* want Manu."

The elf's lips parted, but she must have thought better about replying because she turned away instead.

Inej decided it would be best to let the topic drop as she searched for food. She was prepared to get close to Manu however she needed to. If that meant sleeping with him, then she would do it. If she were into elves—which she never had been—and she went on looks alone—which she usually did—she would've already called him to her bed.

But this wasn't a quick night of fun. It was about life and death. Freedom and ending evil.

Inej sat in Jalall's library, staring at the books for the last several minutes. She had been drawn to the room the moment she saw it. Two walls of stone cut into symmetrical shelves lined with books. The smooth, stone floor was covered with rugs layered over each other in different styles, colors, and sizes. Then there were chunky, plush cushions spread along the floor of the far wall with pillows scattered on them. Her eyes had lifted to the ceiling, where hundreds of tiny lights hugged the stone, giving the area a soft ambiance.

She chose a book and settled onto the cushions. After what she had been through, she deserved a day off. But she couldn't concentrate on the story. Her gaze drifted across the rugs, and in a heartbeat, she was back in Gita's home.

"You might find yourself falling for his lies."

Inej laughed as she shifted in the chair. "I'm not that susceptible."

"He's a powerful elf."

"I've never needed a man—or elf—before. I'm not going to start now."

Gita smirked. "I take it you've never been in love."

"Love is merely a label others wish to place on emotions that rise and fade as often as the sun to make themselves feel better."

"You really are the perfect one to send after him," Gita replied smugly. "If you complete this, there just might be a job for you at the DIA."

Excitement bloomed in her chest, but Inej was quick to tamp it down. "Since when does the DIA hire humans?"

"You're going undercover. Do you think you're the first human covert agent we've had?"

She hadn't considered it at all, actually. This was something she was most certainly interested in, but she didn't want to show too much enthusiasm. That kind of job could change her entire life. "Good point. What do I do when I complete the mission?"

"Get yourself back here."

Her gut clenched nervously. "You make it sound easy."

"It won't be." Gita laughed and poured herself some wine. "You'll have to find a way out of the city. I've heard the Mountain Elves live inside a mountain. I'm sure it'll be guarded. My advice is to get out before anyone finds Manu." She turned and walked back to the sofa. "Then you need to run as fast as you can."

"And if I can't get out or run fast enough? I take it that I'm on my own."

"I'm afraid so. That's one of the drawbacks of being undercover. You get a lot of intel upfront, then you're thrown into a mission and have to get yourself out."

Inej looked at the wineglass, wishing for some of the liquor herself. "How will you know if I succeed if I don't make it out?"

"Trust me, word will spread quickly enough. He's the one leading all the kidnappings. Take him out, and they'll stop."

"Just one elf? Are you sure?"

Gita waved a dismissive hand toward the box of vials. "If there are others, use the other poisons. I leave it up to your discretion. So? What do you say? Do you still want to do this?"

"Without a doubt."

The slam of a door jerked Inej out of her memories. She listened to see if it was Manu's or even Jalall's arrival, but she didn't hear boots heading toward her. In fact, she didn't hear anything. Perhaps Chanda had left to return home. After their encounter in the kitchen, the two had given each other a wide berth. Inej eventually returned her attention to the book, but this time, it wasn't Gita who invaded her thoughts. It was the assassin and the knife he'd plunged into the middle of her chest.

She snapped the book closed and gave up on trying to read.

"Not a good story?"

Her head turned toward the door, where Manu stood. Several strands of his deep brown hair had fallen over his forehead. He shoved them back with his fingers and leaned a shoulder against the jamb. The elf filled up any room he entered with his size, but also with his authority. There was a stillness about him that took her aback. As if he were weighing the room, her, and their conversation.

"I can't concentrate," she admitted and rose from the cushions.

"It's late, but I can still take you for the tour if you'd like."

She had lost all context of time being inside the mountain. "I didn't realize. I can ask Jalall."

"He's gone at the moment. Taking the prisoner back to his tribe."

And just like that, her anxiety returned. How many others knew about her? Gita hadn't said she had other agents about, and she should have at least warned Inej that someone else might be coming. How had he even known she was here? What had he said?

"You did your job. It's my turn."

He made it sound like all Inej had been needed for was to get into the city. And, gods, what if that was *exactly* what Gita had used her for?

"Inej?" Manu called.

She put the book back in its slot, refusing to think about how sexy her name sounded in that deep voice of his. "I was just thinking about the wolvites," she said to cover her silence.

"They won't bother Jalall's group. Too many individuals. The wolvites like to get their targets on their own."

She shivered as she remembered the rumbling growls. "If you say so."

"This might be a good time for the tour. There won't be that many about, which means you'll get to see more of Navara."

They walked from the library together. She waited as he used magic to lock the front door behind them. Then, he turned to the right.

"As captain, Jalall lives close to the city entrance, as well as the guardhouse."

"You have an army?"

He cut her a look as they began walking. "We do, indeed. So do the other tribes. Don't forget that Rannora and Belanore each have soldiers. And then there are the Asavori Rangers." Manu nodded toward where they were headed. "There are residential sections in both Rannora and Belanore, but here, it's mostly mixed together. You'll find shops next to homes."

"Navara is much bigger than I expected," she mused.

"We're one of the larger mountain tribes. Smaller tribes merged with us a few times in the past. We've had to build up," he said, pointing to the homes above them. "We have everything we need here."

She shot him a look. "Everything?"

"Water," he said, pointing to the gentle waterfall and the river. Then he pointed to the mirrors. "Lights." They walked past a building to an open area with large, raised plant beds. "We also grow our own food."

"You hunt?"

"Of course. Each household has its own larder. There is also one for the city as a whole."

They continued on the path as she looked at the different homes. All were as similar as they were different. Each individual family put their own touches on the stone edifices with colorful fabrics and lighting.

"Some homes are carved with pretty designs, and others aren't. Is that a choice?" she asked.

"All of them began without any embellishments. Those who have the skill to etch designs can be hired to adorn a home."

Inej knew the moment she spotted the enormous manor to the left across the river that it was Manu's. It sat near the waterfall, and she imagined there were breathtaking views. She listened as Manu pointed out different shops and told her what was sold where.

Finally, they reached the end, but they didn't cross the bridge. Instead, he took her up a flight of stairs to the next level. She paused near one of the thick-leaved plants that grew among the rocks. Some were small, others huge.

"That's called a thrie," he told her.

"How do you get it to grow?"

He pointed to one of the mirrors that directed light toward them. "The mirrors do most of the work, but we use a bit of magic learned from a Wood Elf many generations ago."

They continued walking. Inej noticed that the light in the mirrors began to fade, causing windows to illuminate in homes. Night gave the city a different look.

He pivoted to walk across a bridge. She started after him until she realized there were no handrails. One wrong step, and she could plunge to her death. Manu stopped and looked at her over his shoulder, waiting for her. There was no telling how long she had to remain in Navara, which meant she needed to learn to adapt to her new surroundings like she had so many times before.

Inej squared her shoulders and followed Manu. The bridge was actually wider than she initially thought. They could walk side by side, and there was room enough for two more people. That didn't mean she had any intention of getting near the edge, however.

"This level, as well as the two above us, are more homes, but you'll still find a few shops among them," he said.

"Are any hiring?"

He shrugged. "I'm sure they are. That isn't why I brought you up here."

"Oh?"

"Come," he urged and took her to yet another staircase.

14

With each step Manu took, climbing to his perch, tension melted from his body. The lanterns were few, which cast many of the steps in darkness. He checked on Inej as the stairs became steep and narrow. She kept up, though her breathing was labored. The trek might be long, but it was worth it—even if they got a little wet from the waterfall.

He sighed once he was at the top and used his magic to light the lantern hanging from a rock. Then he looked out across Navara. From this height, the city was stunning, no matter the time of day. The location wasn't a secret, but it also wasn't a spot that many visited. And it was one of the reasons he came.

"Oh," Inej murmured as she came to stand beside him.

Pride filled Manu. "This is Navara in all her glory."

"I can see everything. So many homes."

"The houses are easier to discern with the lights coming through the windows."

She stepped forward, the edge perilously near.

"Careful," he said, putting a hand out in front of her.

Inej looked down and immediately backed up. "I didn't realize I was that close."

"You can sit." He motioned to the boulder that had been carved into a bench.

The ends of her hair brushed lightly against his palm as she turned. He found himself reaching out for the glorious locks and quickly dropped his arm to his side. She lowered herself onto the rock and returned her attention to the city. He took in her profile, his gaze lingering on her long, slim neck before lowering to the outline of her breasts.

"Do you come up here often?"

Her question snapped him from his thoughts. "Not as often as I once did. My father used to come up here daily. This was a place we would talk."

"It's a sacred place for you."

He shrugged and sank onto the other end of the bench. It was the wrong thing since it brought him closer to her. Only a hand separated them now. "I suppose you could say that. I like to come up here for the view. And to clear my head."

"I imagine you have tremendous responsibilities."

"Anyone in my position does. Some carry them easier than others."

There was a brief pause before she asked, "Is it easy for you?"

"Nay." He finally looked at her again, only to discover her staring at him. The lantern hung over her, bathing her in a warm glow, as if it, too, were mesmerized by her presence. "I had hoped things would become less challenging the longer I remained in my role, but that hasn't been the case."

"You don't like the power?"

Manu glanced at the ground. No one had ever asked him that. "Every single individual living in Navara counts on me to keep them safe. The weight of that is…" He trailed off, unsure why he had started to tell her his deepest thoughts. He cleared his throat and changed the subject. She didn't care about his struggles. She only cared about her future, and rightly so. "We don't get visitors, be they elf or human. Mountain Elves are reclusive by nature, and it might take some time before the others warm to you."

"It won't be much different from Belanore, then."

Anger simmered within him on her behalf. "I don't tolerate any kind of discrimination. If it happens, let me know."

Inej turned her attention to the view. "That would paint an even bigger target on me. I can handle whatever happens."

"You shouldn't have to."

"It's just how things are."

Manu scratched the back of his neck. He wouldn't argue, but he would get the word out among his people. Just because racism was accepted in the lowlands, didn't mean he would tolerate it in Navara.

They sat in comfortable silence for a few minutes, watching and listening to the city. He cut his eyes to his home and spotted one of the younger children running past a window. Right behind him was Sameer, a big smile on the juvenile's face. But if he could see them, then so could Inej. Thankfully, her attention was directed the opposite way.

"I have no way to pay for lodgings," she suddenly said. "Or for the clothes given to me. At least, not yet."

"You will remain at Jalall's home until we can find you a place."

She swung her head to him. "I used to clean. I'm happy to do that again."

"We'll find you something. I'm surprised you've not asked for a position in a kitchen so you can bake."

"Those are generally difficult to come by."

He thought about the delicious pastries. "Is it something you would be interested in?"

She stared at him blankly for a long minute.

"Did I say something wrong?" he asked, confused.

"I'm trying to figure out if you're teasing me."

He grunted and leaned back against the wall. "I leave the jesting to Jalall since he has a better aptitude for it. You have a talent. But this is also me being selfish because I want more of those tarts."

"I..." She swallowed. "Aye, I would enjoy a position that allows me to bake."

"Good." He pushed to his feet. "I'm sure you would like some time to yourself. Shall we return?"

She rose and headed down the steps. Manu paused to extinguish the lantern before following her.

He unlocked Jalall's door and stepped inside first. Inej watched him close and lock the door behind her. "Return to doing whatever you wish," he told her.

"You're staying here?"

He didn't know if the surprise in her voice was one of delight or dread. "I am."

"I assumed you would've assigned someone else to watch me."

Manu walked past her toward Jalall's study. "Someone will relieve me later."

He saw her glide past as he shut the door. Manu ignored Jalall's desk and headed to the sofa instead. He dropped onto it and blew out a breath as he stared at the opposite wall, where a painting from Jalall's mother hung. The house was silent. He had no idea what Inej was doing, and now he wished he hadn't cut their night short.

There were at least a dozen guards he could've stationed in the house with her, but he hadn't. Nor did he intend to. Everything of importance was locked away, so she couldn't get to it. He remained because he couldn't seem to stay away from her.

The shadow in the far right corner moved, catching Manu's attention. He turned his head just as a Dark Elf stepped out. Dain was dressed in all black from his long coat with six vertical slits at the bottom and silver armor plating the shoulders, to the shirt beneath, where more armor extended over his chest and abdomen, to his trousers tucked into knee-high boots with more armor on the front.

Scars crisscrossed the Dark's face. One ran from his left temple through the brow and across his nose, and then over his right cheek. Another dissected his mouth from right to left. The deepest ran from the inside corner of Dain's left eye, diagonally down the left cheek to his jaw. He wasn't an elf you wanted as an enemy.

Manu looked into the yellow eyes of the Counter Corruption Division agent. "About time you showed up."

The Dark Elf snorted and walked to the desk. He pulled out the chair and lowered himself into it. His gray skin had a sallow tint—

the only sign that he had exerted a tremendous amount of magic getting to Navara.

Dain's white hair fell to the middle of his back, and he always left it loose. Another thing that he was never without were the two small, silver metal bands fastened around locks of hair on either side of his face.

"I went to your place," Dain finally said.

Manu glanced at the door. "Some things have happened."

"Aye. I saw the human. What's her story?"

"Her name is Inej. She claims to be trying to find somewhere safe."

A white brow rose on Dain's forehead. "Claims? You don't believe her?"

"I have no way of checking her story."

"But?" the Dark pressed.

"I was going to send her on her way after she recovered. Then, someone tried to kill me. She got between us and nearly died herself."

Dain's yellow eyes flashed as he sat up straight, his body rigid. "How did they learn about you?"

"I don't know," Manu said with a sigh.

"*Who* was it who tried to kill you?"

"A Mountain Elf from another tribe. Jalall went to deliver the body and see if he could uncover whether the tribe is working with the Masters, or if the attack was about something else."

Dain quirked a brow as he leaned back, though his body was still tense. "Do you have so many attempts on your life that you can be so dismissive?"

Manu briefly lifted his gaze to the ceiling. "You know I don't."

"We both know this was the Masters. I want to know how they learned about you."

"You and me both. The kids are safe, however."

Dain leaned on the arm of the chair. "I just came from speaking with them. Tell me what the real problem is?"

"We need a plan in case someone gets to me. I can't be the last line of defense for them."

"I had hoped you would be able to stay hidden," Dain said with a long sigh. "Navara was another escape for us if we needed it."

Manu shrugged. "It always will be. There are places within to hide."

"That's good to know. I hope it never comes to that, but we need options."

"For the children, too."

Dain drummed his fingers on the arm of the chair. "The only way those children will be safe is if they're not in Shecrish."

There was something about the way Dain said the words that made Manu study the Dark. "You want to use your relationship with the Dragon Kings for a favor, don't you?"

"I'm going to ask Esha for the favor. But aye, I am."

The Asavori Ranger was the mate of Kendrick, a Dragon King. It was a bold move, but if it worked, it would alleviate a lot of issues for everyone. "Have you spoken to Yaz and Ravi about it?"

"Not yet. I was hoping it wouldn't come to that, but I've always feared it would."

"The kids are stuck in my home. While they have the run of it, I don't want them seen by anyone but my staff. I want to trust my tribe, but fear makes people do things they normally wouldn't."

Dain nodded slowly. "And now there's Inej."

"I've already considered that she might have been sent here to find them."

"Or you."

Manu gave him a flat look. "Please."

"A human can kill an elf."

"She saved my life."

Dain sat forward, his face hard. "Don't forget who the Masters are, or the extremes they've gone to. Elves dismiss humans, which would make her a prime candidate to get close to you."

"If she wanted me dead, why get between me and the assassin?"

"There are many reasons. Just take heed."

Manu looked to the side as he considered the Dark's statement. Dain was used to assuming that everyone lied and deceived. Manu hadn't had to do that until recently, and it wasn't something he enjoyed.

"You don't want to believe she is anything more than what she says, and there's nothing wrong with that," Dain said. "Keep hoping she's exactly who she claims. But until you know for sure, be on guard."

They were wise words. Dain wasn't just a spy, he was also a warrior who had seen more than most. The scars on his face told a story, and Manu would bet that there were more on Dain's body. He was selective of those he got close to, but the Dark was also one of the most loyal individuals Manu had ever met.

He dipped his head. "I will. What about you? How are things going in the lowlands?"

"Quiet. Too quiet. Something is up."

"What do you mean quiet?"

Dain shifted, causing his coat to creak. "The kidnappings have almost stopped."

That should've been cause for celebration, but given Dain's choice of words, Manu knew it wasn't. "Are you sure we haven't scared them away?"

"No such luck, I'm afraid."

"You said the abductions have almost stopped. Regardless of why, that's good news."

Dain's lips compressed. "It is, but I'm afraid that what happens next will be worse."

"You have connections all over the plateau. Surely, you've discovered something about who the Masters are."

"Those who know won't breathe a word. And those who might know are too afraid to talk."

Manu sat forward. "We have to do something."

"What do you think we've been doing?" Dain said in a low voice vibrating with fury. He slowly rose to his feet. "Perhaps I should take you to the Below. Maybe a trip to the Mortham Compound is in order. We just pulled out Farah and Rohan."

Manu stood and stared across the expanse into the Dark's yellow eyes. "And how many years did I and my people handle those at Shaldorn before the DIA and CCD finally got involved?"

Dain's nostril flared before he spun away. He was silent for several moments before his shoulders rose and fell.

"You're stretched too thin," Manu said. "You can't keep going at this rate."

"There's no one else." Dain faced him again and shook his head. "My outburst was—"

"Don't think twice about it. We've all been there."

Dain looked at the door. "Watch your back. I'm going to talk to Esha. Someone coming after you has changed things."

"I'm fine."

"And you need to stay that way. I'll return as soon as I can."

Manu frowned as he took a step toward his friend. "You've not rested for long enough."

Shadows rose up around Dain quickly before they vanished with him.

15

The house was quiet when Inej left her room. Not being able to see the sky out a window to know the time disoriented her. Her bare feet didn't make a sound as she walked the house. The door to Jalall's office was still closed, but so was the entrance to his room. Manu could be in either.

Or he could've left.

Inej rubbed her eyes and headed for the front windows. She cracked the shutters and peered out into the city to see the first stirrings of light through the mirrors from the top of the mountain. A few lights were on in windows, but most remained dark. She suppressed a yawn and contemplated her current situation.

She hadn't gotten a chance to use the poison the night before. She might have lost her opportunity, especially if Manu sent someone else to guard her. She needed to be ready to deliver it at any time. That meant she needed to keep it with her.

The hairs on the back of her neck suddenly prickled with

awareness. She looked behind her and found the object of her loathing sitting in a chair, his onyx eyes soft as if he had been sleeping. His legs were stretched out before him and crossed at the ankles, while his hands were laced over his flat abdomen. His jaw was clean-shaven, and he wore fresh clothes.

"Early riser, I see," he said.

Her stomach quivered at the sound of his deep, sleep-roughened voice. This would be a lot easier if she didn't find him so damn alluring. He was the epitome of evil and had no right to affect her in such a way. Perhaps that was how he got close to those he kidnapped. They were compelled to go to him.

"I don't know the time," she admitted.

He used the arms of the chair to push to his feet. "We keep a clock similar to what they use in the Below."

"You've been there?" She regretted the question immediately.

"I have not," he said with a half-smile. "It's a comparison a friend made to me once."

Nice recovery, she thought.

He pointed to her right.

Inej looked over and, sitting on a shelf, was a device she hadn't noticed before. She walked closer to take a look. "How does it work?"

"It uses water," he explained as he moved to stand beside. "The container you're looking at is filled with water. There's a small hole that allows the water to drain at a constant rate. The metal bowls below it will sink as the water drains, indicating the passage of time. It's just past six in the morning."

She spotted the lines that showed the time. Now that she knew where to look, it was easy. "Interesting."

"There are smaller ones. I can have one brought to your room."

Inej turned her head to him. Was he being nice to make her lower her guard? Well, too bad. That wouldn't work on her. But she needed him to think it would. She curved her lips into a soft smile and hoped it reached her eyes. "I'd like that."

"I'll see it done then. I must go, but Chanda will be here shortly." He gave her a nod and walked to the door.

She turned to follow his progression and watched him leave. She quite liked having the house to herself without anyone watching over her. Inej leaned to the side and peered down the hall to the kitchen. When no sounds came from that direction, she held out her arms and twirled around with a smile.

It was the only celebration she would allow herself until Manu was dealt with. By the time she was dressed and her hair braided, she found Chanda in the kitchen. She almost turned around and left, but Inej would have to face the elf eventually.

"Good morning," Inej called out as she entered.

The elf shot her a look. "Maybe to you. I'm up an hour early to watch you so Manu can see to his duties."

"No one needs to watch over me. I have no intention of stealing anything."

"So you say," Chanda replied tartly.

Inej moved to block her path. The elf had to tilt her head back to meet Inej's gaze, and when anger blazed in Chanda's dark eyes, Inej held up her hands to indicate she wasn't a threat—though they both already knew that. "I admire your protectiveness for the people you care about. I don't wish to make any more work for you."

"Too late," Chanda stated.

Inej saw the ingredients sitting on the counter. "I can cook for myself. You shouldn't have to do that."

Chanda walked around her and then out of the room as she said, "Perfect. Clean up after yourself, too."

The sound of voices pulled Inej from the book she was reading. She made out Chanda's high-pitched vocals that went on for some time. The answering voice was low and soothing. Manu. Inej closed the cover and rose from the cushions. She was in the middle of sliding the book onto the shelf when her neck prickled again.

She dropped her arm and turned around. Manu stood in the doorway once more, almost as if he didn't want to enter the space. Some might take it to mean he didn't want to overcrowd her. She knew it was just a tactic to get her to lower her guard. The problem was that he moved too quietly. She would have to be more careful around him. It wouldn't do to have him sneaking up on her when she was trying to poison him.

"Are you busy?" he asked.

Inej hesitated as she thought about her encounter with Chanda earlier. "Is this about something I did?"

"What do you mean?" he asked, his brow furrowing.

"I could hear Chanda." And while Inej hadn't been able to make out the words, it didn't take much to guess the elf was venting about her.

"Ah. She's never taken to change well." He motioned with his head for her to follow.

Inej trailed him into the kitchen, and just when she expected there to be some kind of confrontation, he took her out the side door. Chanda didn't even look up from her position at the counter.

They were twenty steps from the house when Manu said, "Chanda is kind and good-natured, but also caring."

"I got that from her."

"Her husband died a few years ago, and she hasn't been the same since. Give her time. She'll come around."

Inej was doubtful of that. She certainly hadn't, if her past with Krata was any indication. Chanda wouldn't come around. But that was fine. Inej would just stay out of her way as much as possible for the short time she was here. Hopefully, she would be able to live somewhere else, and then it wouldn't be a problem.

Inej looked around at the Mountain Elves going about their days. Everyone in Navara could be as guilty as Manu. Or they could be completely innocent. She needed information, and if Chanda were any indication, it would be very hard to come by. The only ones willing to talk were Jalall and Manu, and since Jalall was absent for the moment, that left Manu. She didn't think he would willingly divulge his sins to a human. But she had to start somewhere.

"You said you don't get many visitors, so how do you know what's going on outside of the Peaks?" she asked.

Manu nodded a greeting to someone as they walked. "My father and those before him made it a point to remain in the know. Being reclusive is one thing. Being ignorant is unacceptable."

"Does that mean others from the rainwood visit?"

"We call it the lowlands. We have various ways of getting information. Sometimes, it's from those we encounter in the mountains. Other times, neighboring tribes hear things and pass them on to us."

Inej became aware of others stopping what they were doing to look at her curiously. She was uncomfortable with their blatant looks, and it was hard to keep her thoughts on track. He hadn't given her much at all. And she couldn't help but feel he was leaving something out.

Suddenly, Manu stopped and faced her. "I've allowed you to remain in Navara. That means you're under my protection, just as anyone else who lives here is. Do you understand?"

She stared into his eyes, getting sucked into the dark depths. He seemed earnest, as if it were important that she believe him. He continued to stare until she nodded. Only then did he continue walking.

They crossed the nearest bridge, and she found herself on the opposite side of the river. She had wondered about it from their perch the night before but walking along the path gave the area a different look now that she was here.

Every couple of steps, someone either called out a *hello* to Manu or stopped him to talk. He didn't refuse a single one. It made her look deeper at the residents of Navara. Was Manu that good of a deceiver that none of them knew who he actually was? Or was it that they knew and didn't care? The latter terrified her.

While everyone sought his attention, no one wanted hers. They were curious, and they stared, but they disregarded every smile or wave she gave. Manu had warned her. It was her nature to ignore everyone. After all, that was how she lived in Belanore. But she couldn't be herself there. She didn't just need to convince Manu that she was someone to trust who was escaping the horrors of the lowlands, she needed to convince everyone else, as well.

And to think she had thought this part would be the easiest.

She was trying to be someone she didn't know how to be. How did the DIA agents do it?

Inej tired of standing while Manu conversed with one elf after another. Unfortunately, none of the conversations were worthwhile to listen to either. She turned away and spent some time studying the city when a large hand touched her lower back. She barely stopped herself from jerking away. Her head swiveled to Manu as he gave her a slight nudge forward. Seconds later, they were on their way again.

"Sorry about that," he said.

She thought about their conversation the night before. "Your work never ends, does it?"

"Does anyone's?" he asked with a chuckle, his dark orbs sliding to hers for a heartbeat.

"I suppose not."

A short time later, he motioned to the side with his hand. "Here we are."

Inej walked into the brilliantly lit shop, overwhelmed by a combination of floral, fruit, and sugar scents. They instantly evoked a feeling of comfort and warmth. She gazed at the bright colors of the various candies in the display case and moved closer to get a better look while Manu spoke to a male elf behind the counter. She should've been paying attention to them, but she was busy picking out the different aromas.

Most everything was some form of sweet, and behind the array were a couple of pies. A lot of thought and care had been put into each candy. The pies, not so much.

"Let's sit," Manu said.

She followed him to one of the small tables and watched the steady flow of customers. Each one left with some candy, but no one ordered pie. Her view was suddenly blocked, and she looked up to see a middle-aged female beside their table. The elf set down two slices of pie and smiled at Manu before walking off, a slight limp in her gait.

"Try it," Manu urged her. "Tell me what you think."

Inej looked at the deep purple fruit in the pie before cutting into the too-thick crust with her fork. She lifted the bite and sniffed, drawing in the smell of batter and berries, before tasting it. The fruit was sweet and juicy, but there was too much sugar, which overwhelmed the fruit itself.

"Well?" Manu asked around a mouthful of pie.

"It's good."

He shot her a flat look. "There's no need to lie."

"It's not horrible. It just needs a few adjustments."

"This is the closest we get to any form of pastry. Daas's gift is the candy, though he tries with the pies. They're good, but they don't compare to what you created."

She lowered her fork, afraid to hear what his next words might be. She had stumbled into baking by accident at a job. It soon became something she loved, but when the cook returned, she had been forced back into cleaning.

"He has agreed to bring you on for a trial period."

Blood rushed in her ears. Inej stared at Manu. He was handing her a dream she hadn't dared allow herself to think about. Did he know that it was something she wanted more than anything? It all seemed too good to be true, and things like that simply didn't happen to her. "You've only tasted one tart."

"And it was very tasty. Even if that's the only thing you know how to bake, it will sell and sell well."

He stared at her as if waiting for her to say something. What did she say? He was dangling something she loved in front of her, and she couldn't figure out if he was being generous or cruel.

"Inej?" he asked softly.

His brow was furrowed. She saw every groove in his forehead. It looked like he was concerned. He had called her name. That meant he wanted an answer. Inside, she was screaming "*Aye!*," but she couldn't let it out. She couldn't let him know just how badly she wanted this.

anu had expected Inej's shock, but her reaction went beyond that. She hadn't been able to hide the flash of fear in her eyes. Her body had tensed in a visceral reaction that left him puzzled. She enjoyed baking. She was also good at it. He had never eaten anything so delicious, and he knew others would think the same. Not to mention, she had asked about working. It was the perfect solution.

Or so he had thought.

"The choice is yours," he told her. "If you'd rather have some other kind of work, then I'll—"

"Nay," she said hurriedly over him. "I want this."

"Good."

He glanced down and noticed her knuckles had turned white from holding the fork so tightly. He didn't know what her life had been like before she arrived in Navara, but he could guess. Dain and Jalall would tell him to be cautious, that it could all be an act. And some of it might be. But her reaction just now hadn't been.

If Inej was working with the Masters, then he had granted her access to his city and his people. He hoped she was all she said she was, but he wouldn't be the leader he was supposed to be if he freely accepted everything she said. It went beyond just the children he was in charge of. It went beyond even his tribe. This was about everyone in the Peaks.

The abductions hadn't reached the mountains yet, and he wouldn't be the one to give the kidnappers entry. He couldn't watch Inej every hour of the day, and if she had come under false pretenses, the only way that would come out was if she thought herself accepted. Hence why she would be working with Daas. Not only had Daas been close to Manu's father, but Manu trusted him to keep an eye on her.

Everyone was getting what they wanted. Inej would get to do what she enjoyed, the citizens would have access to delicious pastries, and he would have someone watching her during the day.

"Follow me, and I'll introduce you," Manu said as he pushed back his chair and stood.

Inej trailed him around the counter past Shruti, Daas's wife, as she bagged candy for a customer, and through a curtain of hanging beads in a doorway to the kitchen, a place Manu hadn't been in years. He had spent countless hours there as a youngling, helping Daas as he and Manu's father talked. It brought back many memories.

The older elf smiled as he set a bowl aside and wiped his hands on a towel. His once midnight hair was now dusted with gray and kept short. Lines fanned out from the corners of his black eyes, while deep grooves cut into the brackets around his mouth. Daas had once seemed like a giant to Manu when he was a lad, but now, he only came to the top of Manu's chin. Still, he was strong and fit.

"Hello," Daas said with a warm look as he approached Inej. "I hear you're a baker. Manu can't stop talking about your pastry."

Inej's breathing was rapid, showing her nervousness as she issued a small smile. "I dabble."

Daas cut his black eyes to Manu before returning his gaze to Inej. "I'm eager to try your tarts. There isn't a lot of workspace here, but I believe we can share it."

"It's more than enough," she replied.

"Good. Good." Daas studied her for a moment. "Here is what I propose. Bake your pastry. If it's as good as Manu claims, then I will issue a two-week trial. During that time, if you have more goods you would like to bake, bring the ideas to me so I can see if I have the ingredients or can get them. As part of the deal, you would receive forty percent of the profits."

Her face went slack in surprise. "Forty?"

"Aye. Once the trial period is over, we will reevaluate to see if working together is favorable for both of us. Does that sound agreeable?"

Manu watched the disbelief, excitement, and caution play across Inej's face. She was usually good at keeping her emotions in check, but he knew her guard had slipped enough for him to see her true feelings.

"It's more than agreeable," she replied.

Daas shot her a wide smile and motioned to a cleared section of the counter. "That area is yours. Let me know if there's anything you need."

Inej took two steps forward, then halted and looked back, her brown eyes locking on Manu. The joy shining through was so bright it knocked the breath from him.

"Thank you," she said.

Manu dipped his chin, unable to speak. Once she walked to examine her workspace and the ingredients laid out for her, she forgot all about him and Daas. She pushed up her sleeves, wound her hair into a bun at the base of her neck, and reached for a bowl.

Manu walked to the front with Daas at his side. "Forty percent?"

Daas chuckled as they headed out of the store. "If she's as good as you say, she deserves it."

"You always had a gift for reading people. Better than most. What do you think of her?"

"I think she's hiding something, but I don't know what. She's guarded. That's expected, though. It could be because she's the only human here, or it could be the very thing you fear."

Manu looked out over the city. "We've been shielded from the chaos happening in the lowlands. The assassin coming on the heels of finding Inej is too coincidental."

"Your father never believed anything was a coincidence either. You've not led us wrong before, Manu. You won't now."

But what if he had? What if Inej was that fatal mistake? That's what he couldn't shake. He swung his gaze back to Daas. "Thank you for doing this."

"No thanks needed, lad. Now, go on. She's on my watch now," Daas said and jokingly shooed him away.

Manu chuckled as he walked out, but that died after a few steps when his thoughts turned to Jalall. It was only the second day, but he was already worried about his friend. Too much was happening for him not to look at everyone and everything as a potential enemy.

17

Shecrish and Idrias Border

The sun hung like a colossal ball of yellow fire in the sky, its merciless rays fixed on Dain. He had been waiting for hours among the tall grass, without any shade, for Esha's sister, Savita, to arrive.

Savita wasn't just any Sun Elf. She was a renowned Reader who took direction from the rune stones. Readers held staggering power, both politically and magically. Since only Sun Elves had the ability, that put their race in many positions of authority in the Above. Savita had made a name for herself in Belanore early on and soon took charge of the Asavori Rangers.

Dain knew she did it to keep an eye on Esha. Others believed that, as well. But no one would dare call Savita out on it. Readers swore to speak only the truth, and to claim that one lied was tantamount to death. Of course, just because Readers weren't supposed to lie, didn't mean they didn't do just that.

His worry grew as another hour passed. Savita was never late. And the longer he remained in the sunlight, the more it hurt. Not only had he pushed his magic to the brink traveling to Manu, but he hadn't rested before coming to the border. His retinas burned from the bright light, ensuring he was all but blinded.

He looked toward Idrias, the land of the dragons. It was a place meant only for the creatures and the Dragon Kings—dragons who could change shape at will into human form. They'd come from another world for the dragons, and while Dain had met a few of the Kings, he didn't know if he would be welcome on their land. The dragons themselves wouldn't tolerate anyone. They killed any who dared to cross their border.

But Dain couldn't wait any longer for Savita to get in contact with Esha. This gathering was outside the sisters' normal meetings, and he had no way of knowing if Savita had gotten his message in time. The border was the closest Dain had come to Idrias. He had no idea how big their land was, but if he didn't get to the Dragon Kings soon, Yasmin's children might die. Dain had already lost one child in his care. He wasn't about to lose more.

He gathered his shadows and headed west. He didn't stop until he reached a mountain range. Dain hid beneath an overhang to let his magic recharge, but he didn't lower his shadows. A roar echoed around him, seeming to come from right above him. Small rocks plunked against boulders right next to him before rolling downhill.

Dain broke out into a cold sweat at the knowledge that a dragon was above him. He had witnessed the kind of magic the Dragon Kings had, and he had no interest in taking on a dragon. The shadows gave him cover. It was the only reason he didn't bolt from his hiding place. He tried to relax, but it soon became apparent that several dragons were around him.

He stayed for as long as he dared before he continued westward. Kendrick had told him about the capital, Cairnkeep, that sat atop a mountain. Dain began searching every peak until he saw two identical structures. That had to be what Kendrick referred to. Dain headed for them, slipping inside a house and into a corner to nestle among the shadows.

There, Dain sat, his magic almost depleted as he listened and rested. The shadows hindered his view, but they didn't obstruct his hearing. There was no movement within the home. Outside, however, he heard the distant roars of dragons, seemingly from all directions.

Many elves believed the dragons had vanished from their lands because no one had seen any of the creatures in centuries. Kendrick's arrival on Shecrish had nearly started a war between their two races. The elves would've been slaughtered, and it was only with Kendrick's and the other Kings' quick thinking that it hadn't happened.

"I doona know who you are, but I'd advise you to show yourself immediately," stated a deep, commanding voice.

The accent was the same as Kendrick's, but it wasn't his friend. Dain parted the shadows enough to find a tall man with wavy, blond hair and eyes as black as the night sky. "I mean no harm," Dain said. "I'm looking for Kendrick."

"Show yourself," the voice demanded again.

Dain might not stand a chance against a Dragon King's power, but he was quick enough to get away with his shadows if necessary. He parted the shadows and let them fall away to reveal himself. Without a doubt, he stood before a Dragon King.

"Dain, I presume?"

Dain dipped his chin. "That's me. I know I came uninvited, bu—"

"I've alerted Kendrick. He'll be here shortly. For now, take a rest." The King turned and walked to a table before lowering himself into a chair.

Dain glanced around the house as he followed. If the King was upset about his arrival, Dain couldn't tell. He took the chair opposite the dragon. "I wouldn't have come if it weren't important."

"You helped Kendrick and Esha when they needed it. That's all that matters to me. I'm Con, by the way."

Con. As in Constantine, the King of Dragon Kings. The one dragon more powerful than all others. Some of the tension in Dain's muscles eased. If their King welcomed him, then maybe his journey hadn't been for naught. "Thank you."

"Is this about the slave bracelet we got from Jai?"

Dain shook his head. "I almost wish it was."

The door opened, drawing Dain's gaze. Kendrick's form filled the doorway, his black hair windblown, and his green eyes widening at the sight of him.

"Bloody hell," Kendrick said with a smile as he walked over. "It *is* you."

Dain rose and extended his arm. Kendrick shoved it away and embraced him, pounding Dain on the back. No one dared to touch him in such a way. No one except a Dragon King, that was.

Kendrick leaned back and searched Dain's face. His smile fell as he dropped his arms. "What happened?"

Dain looked between the two men. "It's Yasmin and Ravi's children."

"They were taken?" Kendrick asked, a deep frown forming.

Dain shook his head. "We were worried the Masters would try to go after them, so I hid them with Manu in the mountains."

"You thought that was a safe place because…?" Con asked.

Dain lowered himself back into the chair. "The Dangerous Peaks are a brutal place not easily navigated by anyone but the Mountain Elves. The Masters didn't know about Manu's involvement in helping us take down Shaldorn, nor had any Mountain Elves been kidnapped."

"Has that changed?" Kendrick asked as he crossed his arms over his chest.

"What changed was that someone entered Manu's mountain and tried to kill him."

Con's brows snapped together. "They live *in* the mountains?"

Dain nodded. "Entire cities within a mountain."

"Interesting," Con said. "I take it the Masters learned that Manu helped you."

"Maybe. We can't know for sure," Dain said. "They might have been after Manu, but we think they were trying to find the children. The Masters know if they get even one of them, it will draw out Ravi and Yasmin. The kids aren't safe with Manu anymore. There's nowhere on Shecrish they can hide. The Masters' grip is too tight. More and more are falling to their threats. I was hoping you might know of someplace. These children are innocent. They have no—"

"I know the perfect place," Con said over him.

Kendrick nodded. "Somewhere the Masters can no' reach."

Dain looked out the window and sighed in relief. Only when he had his emotions in check did he look at the two men. "When can I bring them?"

"Now," Con said.

It had taken both Dain and Arya to bring the children to Manu. This was much farther and would require several stops. "It will take me a few days."

"We have a way of getting them here almost immediately," Kendrick said with a smile.

18

Inej finished cleaning her side and moved to Daas's as he and Shruti closed up the shop. She had gone nonstop since first entering the kitchen. Inej was exhausted but also happy. There was a bubbly feeling in her chest that she had never experienced before, and she never wanted it to stop.

Even Shruti had warmed to her. A little. The elf wasn't nearly as personable as her husband, but that didn't bother Inej. Especially after both had tasted her tarts and loved them. They had sold every single pastry she had made.

Daas parted the beads and walked over, carrying a bag, his dark eyes shining brightly. "We had to send people away. They were lined up, waiting for your pastries. Word has spread about your baking. And this," he said, handing over a pouch, "is your cut."

Inej stared at the bag, fighting the urge to dump the contents out and count each one. She had never held so much coin at once in all her life.

Daas laughed softly. "I suspect there will be much more of that tomorrow. Be here at dawn."

"Of course," Inej murmured, still thinking about her earnings and all that she could do with it. Clothes. A new place to live. Food—all the food she could ever want.

"Manu said you knew the way back to Jalall's, but I'm happy to walk you if you need."

And just like that, her dreams crumbled to dust. For a little while, she had forgotten about Manu and why she had faced the Peaks' violent weather. She tucked the bag of coins into her pocket and smiled, but it was forced. "I can find my way, thank you."

"See you tomorrow, then. Be sure Manu feeds you well tonight. You've earned it."

Inej walked to the front. Shruti was putting away some leftover candy and glanced her way. Inej waved, but she didn't know if the elf saw her, nor did she care. Her feet were heavy as she left the shop and headed toward Jalall's.

How could she have forgotten about Krata? About why she had a vial of poison stuffed between her breasts? She couldn't trust Manu being nice. That wasn't who he was. So what that she was finally doing what she loved? So what that she had more money than ever before? None of that mattered when others were being taken from their homes.

She found herself standing in front of Jalall's front door without memory of how she had gotten there. In just half a day, she had almost ruined her mission. If she was going to be any kind of agent, she couldn't forget again.

Inej started to open the door, then thought better of it and knocked. She was a guest, after all. She waited and tried not to think about the weight of the coins pulling on her dress. She glanced at others walking by to make sure no one rushed her and attempted to take what was rightfully hers.

The door opened, and she found herself looking into Manu's eyes. Her irritation soared at the sight of his handsome face. Had he wooed humans with a smile and a kind word? Or had he simply grabbed them? Had Krata willingly gone with her kidnappers without realizing who they were? She was too nice. She saw the good in everyone. She had probably done just that.

"Why are you standing out there?" Manu asked as he moved aside. "Come in."

Inej crossed the threshold and headed straight for her room. Nay. It wasn't her room. It was simply the place where she laid her head. The only things that were hers were the coins. She had earned them. No one would take them from her. The bed, the clothes…they were on loan. One she could now repay.

She waited for Manu to order her to stop, but he didn't. Nor did he come after her. She entered her room and closed the door, leaning back against it as she scanned the room for a place to hide her money.

Her fingers grabbed the bag and tugged it out of her pocket. She dumped the contents onto the bed. Her jaw went slack at the sight of the coins earned from a single day. Not even a whole day. A half day. If she could earn this in a few hours, what could she accumulate in a day? A week?

She pulled her hand back as if burned. She wouldn't be here in a week. Inej looked at the door. She was alone with Manu again. It was time she formed a plan to give him the poison. She also needed to make sure she could get out of Navara.

Inej put the coins back in the bag and hid it. She grabbed fresh clothes from the wardrobe and made her way to the bathing room to freshen up. In record time, she walked out, the poison safely tucked between her breasts once more. The dress had a low neckline, making it easy for her to grab the vial. No one would come looking for Manu until morning, and if she dosed him at dinner, then she had all night to find a way out of the mountain.

She heard voices from the kitchen and headed toward them. Chanda laughed at something Manu said. There was an easy camaraderie between them. Inej's feet slowed as she approached, and she peered around the corner. Manu leaned back against the counter, his arms casually crossed over his chest. He wore an easy grin, following Chanda with his eyes as she moved about the kitchen. Chanda's smile was bright, her body relaxed as they bantered back and forth. It transformed the elf from pretty to beautiful.

Suddenly, Manu's gaze lit on her. Inej dismissed the shiver that curled down her spine as he slowly straightened. His gaze was intense, probing.

"I needed to wash off the flour," she said into the awkward silence.

His dark eyes looked her over before returning to her face. "The food is nearly ready."

"Good. I'm hungry."

She could have sworn she heard "*me, too,*" before he turned away to grab something out of the cupboard. When she drew her gaze away, it was to find Chanda watching her. The elf's smile was gone, and though it wasn't hatred directed at her, Inej still felt her disapproval. As if she had disrupted something between Manu and Chanda. Which she had.

Inej almost felt sorry for the elf. If she weren't there on a mission, she wouldn't have any designs on Manu. Inej would've cheerfully retreated so the two could find their way to each other. But clearly, Manu didn't think of Chanda as a lover since he had barely looked her way since Inej entered the room.

"We can finish," Manu told Chanda. "You said the meal was done, and I'm sure you'd like to get home."

The elf jerked her head toward him. "It's no problem to bring the food out to you."

"Jalall doesn't ask it of you, and I don't either. We'll be fine. And I promise I'll clean everything up, so you don't have to do it in the morning."

Inej turned and headed to the dining area, so she wasn't watching the exchange. It was obvious Chanda didn't want to leave her alone with Manu. But alone time was exactly what Inej needed. Hopefully, she could get the poison into his drink at dinner. If she didn't, she was prepared to find a way into his bed—maybe even that night if she was lucky.

At least he was handsome. That would make it easier to get through. Or she could just close her eyes and pretend he was someone—*any*one—else. That way, the only person to ever know she had given her body to someone so evil would be her.

The sound of the side door opening and closing told her that Chanda had departed. Inej turned as Manu walked into the room. Thoughts of sex made her imagine what he would look like without his clothes. Her gaze lowered to his large hands and long, thick fingers. Desire unfurled like liquid heat between her legs, startling her.

"Shall we eat?" he asked.

She swallowed hard, nodding. What had just happened? There was no time to think about it as they walked to the kitchen. She was hyperaware of his every movement. From the way his arm brushed her shoulder to his hand bumping into hers. His very nearness.

How would she get through a meal like this? She briefly thought about going into her room and easing the ache herself, but she couldn't miss another opportunity to slip him the poison. Others were counting on her. Before she knew it, they were seated at the table across from each other once more.

"I hear your pastries sold well," Manu said.

Inej looked at her plate, but she couldn't think about food when her body craved another kind of meal. She needed to get control. And quickly. "They did."

"Did you enjoy yourself?"

"Very much."

She lifted her eyes, her gaze tangling with his once more. Dark. Mesmerizing. Challenging. He was too much. His regard too fervent. She wanted to look away, to have a moment to catch her breath so she could participate in the conversation—or at least pretend to.

Somehow, she tore her eyes from his and found herself staring at his lips. It was a mistake, but she couldn't tear her gaze away. Images of his mouth kept running through her mind—on hers, wrapped around her nipple, kissing between her legs.

"You seem...different," he said.

Inej drew in a deep breath, thankful that his words had ended the fantasies rolling through her head. She had never been attracted to elves. Then again, she had never spent so much time alone in the company of a male elf before.

"I'm just tired, I suppose," she answered.

His eyes didn't leave hers. "You were just healed from a stab wound."

She looked away, unable to bear his piercing gaze for fear he might see the truth. He was despicable, evil. And an elf.

But she wanted him. Craved him.

Inej jerked to her feet so fast the chair fell backward, banging against the rug. She rushed around the table as Manu slowly rose. He watched her, but he didn't attempt to stop her. She hurried past him and then hastened to her room. Once behind the locked door, she walked to the bed. If she was going to give herself to him, she needed to be thinking clearly so she could control the situation. If she went to him as she was now, all she would care about was gratification.

She yanked off the dress and saw the vial fall from her breasts. Inej reached for it, but her fingers missed, and it tumbled against the rug. She gasped, frozen as it bounced twice and came to a standstill, thankfully without shattering. Her heart thudded wildly against her ribs as she carefully lifted it and tucked it under the mattress.

Her legs crumpled as she fell back onto the bed to stare at the canopy. The day had been unlike any other. It wasn't her dream job or even earning money that was on her mind. It was Manu. She squeezed her thighs together as desire throbbed deep within her. Inej slid her fingers between her legs and closed her eyes. Manu kept popping into her thoughts. She tried to think of past lovers, but she kept returning to his chiseled features, his wide lips, and that hard body.

A moan tore from Inej's lips as she chased the climax, her fingers circling her clit. In her mind, it was his hands on her, his mouth, his voice murmuring her name. She imagined him over her, his dark eyes watching, strong hands caressing her body, and the heat of him pressed against her.

Pleasure slammed into her, sharp and all-consuming. She bit her lip to hold in the cry and lifted her hips while shudders rolled through her body. When the waves finally ebbed, she lay still, her heart pounding and her breath ragged as the ghost of his touch lingered on her skin. She drifted to sleep with the fantasy of him beside her.

Inej woke suddenly. She sat up, disoriented, and looked around, half-expecting to find Manu in her bed. That was how real he had been in her head as she'd eased the ache in her body. But he wasn't there. Whatever had gotten into her head had caused her to lose another chance at finishing her mission. She was turning out to be an awful agent.

She stood and stepped onto her discarded gown. Since she couldn't go out naked, she put it on and headed to the door to get some water. Maybe some food after leaving dinner without eating even a single bite.

Manu was exiting the bathing room at the same time she walked out of her room. She halted at the sight of him, nothing but a drying cloth wrapped around his trim hips. He looked up before she could retreat to her room, and their eyes collided. She noticed the droplets of water beading his skin and dripping from his wet hair. Her gaze trailed one as it plopped onto his muscular shoulder and ran to his collarbone, skimming along it before rolling onto his chest and into the dusting of hair there.

Time slowed as she took in every inch of the fine specimen before her. Muscle rippled beneath his fair skin as if an artist had sculpted him from her fantasies. His broad shoulders flowed to strapping arms and a chest built for sin. Her gaze dropped to the ridged planes of his abdomen, where each muscle stood out in perfect relief.

An invitation her fingers itched to answer.

The moment her gaze reached the towel, she had the overwhelming urge to rip it off and feast her gaze on the rest of his magnificent body. Her mouth went dry as she imagined him pushing her against the wall and lifting her up before thrusting deep inside her.

The scene played out in her head, making her nipples harden and her breasts swell. He hadn't made a sound during any of this, hadn't even moved. But his eyes burned with the same fever that coursed through her veins.

They stood like that for several moments, each waiting for the other to make a move. Inej's breath caught in her chest when he took a step toward her. Her hand rose, ready to remove the towel, just as someone pounded on the front door, breaking the spell holding her. She stood stunned as he went to see who it was.

Leaving her with an ache, sharp and unfamiliar.

19

Manu hurried into his room and tugged on pants as he angrily stalked to the door to see who had interrupted what was about to be a very good evening. He yanked it open more roughly than usual, trying to curb his anger. It was no one's fault but his for standing there so long, drinking in the sight of Inej before he decided to act on it.

"What is it?" he asked the soldier. He was proud of himself for keeping the irritation out of his voice.

"A small group from the lowlands has been spotted heading toward Delnola Pass," she replied.

Manu pinched the bridge of his nose with his thumb and forefinger. More mercenaries. But this time, they might just be looking for him. "How many?"

"Seven. One is scouting ahead of the group."

Just what he needed. Manu dropped his arm to his side. "I want four guards posted in different areas around to watch them. I want to know where they're going."

"They wouldn't build another Shaldorn in the Peaks, would they?" the young female asked.

"I wouldn't put it past them. Make sure I get regular updates. I want to be prepared."

She nodded once. "Of course, my lord."

Manu closed the door as she walked away and rested a hand upon it. Factions of mercenaries wishing to cash in on the bounties moved about the lowlands constantly. If the group in the Dangerous Peaks were mercenaries, then they were looking for him or the children. Or both. He could withstand whatever was done to him and never break. Same with any of his allies—unless the children were used against them. Each and every one of them would hand over every secret they had to keep the children alive and unharmed.

He turned and headed back to the bedroom. When he reached Inej's door, he paused, but he didn't knock. He continued toward his room and stretched out on the bed with his hands locked beneath his head. He needed to get a little rest.

Manu eventually closed his eyes, but he couldn't shut off his brain. He sorted through various options for where he could put the children until Dain returned with—hopefully—good news. The city was built to withstand an assault, but not indefinitely. If mercenaries found them, they wouldn't relent. That would put the entire city in danger.

He and Jalall would lead their army to face whatever came at them, but soldiers and citizens alike would die. Not to mention those taken to fill the slave supply. There was a secret tunnel leading out to safety near his house. Only he and Jalall knew about it. It could be used to get as many out as possible. They wouldn't be able to go to the other tribes, though. Word would spread that the Masters were looking for him.

The majority of the tribes' leaders would remain hidden and keep silent, but not all of them. At least one would turn on him, whether out of fear or to align with the Masters. His people would be out in the Peaks on their own, huddling in any caves they came across. The young and the old would perish first. That was if they survived the assault and abductions.

While he hadn't announced his participation in taking down Shaldorn, his people knew he'd been involved when he brought two Dark Elves, a Sun Elf, and a human to Navara. But none knew about the other hits on the Masters, or how deeply aligned he was with his friends. Maybe it was time for his tribe to learn just how dire the situation was.

Manu tensed when he heard the front door open and shut. He swung his legs over the side of the bed and stood. The stone was cold beneath his bare feet as he made his way to the door. He peeked out the blinds and spotted Inej walking away, her long, dark braid hanging down her back.

He yawned and looked at the clock to see that it was almost dawn. He hadn't gotten any sleep. He strode to the kitchen and boiled some water for tea. As he waited for the water to heat, the side door opened, and Chanda walked in.

"Morning," she said cheerfully.

He smiled. "Morning. You know, with Jalall gone, you could take the day off."

"Who would feed you? Besides, someone needs to make sure she doesn't take anything."

"There is plenty of leftover food to feed us for today. As for the other, I wish you would give Inej a chance."

Chanda sighed as she crossed her arms and faced him. "You don't see it, do you?"

"See what?"

"She's after you or Jalall."

The kettle whistled as it came to a boil. Manu poured the liquid into a cup over his tea and set the kettle aside. "Is it because she's human?"

"It's because she's after something."

"Aye. A new life."

Chanda rolled her eyes. "All you see is a pretty face."

"You don't have to worry about her during the day. She'll be at Daas's. And I'll be with her at night."

"Alone."

Manu gently cupped her shoulder. "Take the day off. Rest. Read one of Jalall's many books. Do whatever you want."

"She's staying, isn't she? Permanently."

"I believe so."

Chanda left without another word, her disappointment in his decision palpable. Manu didn't know why she disliked Inej so, but he couldn't waste energy thinking about that when there were other pressing matters. Tea in hand, he returned to his room and dressed. It was early enough that he could get home to share the morning meal with the children.

He quickly drank his tea and put the empty cup on the counter before locking up after himself. Manu crossed the bridge and passed the candy shop. He looked inside but didn't see Inej. She was most likely in the back. To his surprise, there was already a line forming outside.

When he entered his home, he found his staff up and moving about. He'd risked that none of them would say anything about the children, and once he had explained the situation, they under-stood the importance of staying silent. And so far, they had. He trusted his people.

But should he?

Manu stood at the bottom of the stairs and listened to see if the children were awake. When all was quiet, he went to his office, figuring he would work until they rose for the day. He pulled out his chair and sat, then rubbed the heels of his hands into his tired eyes and yawned. That was all the time he gave himself before he dove into the pile of papers that had been waiting for him.

In moments, he was absorbed in the day-to-day running of the city. He had an ever-growing list of things that needed to be done and had just flipped over a page to reach for another when he heard a squeal from the doorway. He turned his chair in time to grab Jaya as she launched herself at him.

She was still in her nightclothes, her blond hair coming out of its braid. The moment she wrapped her little arms around his neck, his worries eased a fraction. He settled her on his lap as the other two younglings, Surya and Hadi, greeted him with hugs and climbed on his lap, too. Sameer, Malini, and Din filed into the room, though they didn't welcome him with as much enthusiasm.

"Anything from Jalall?" Sameer asked with all the seriousness of an aged warrior.

Manu tilted his head to the side, giving Surya access to his hair as she began braiding it. All six had been upset by the attempt on his life. The only silver lining was that they hadn't worried about their safety. That meant he was doing something right. "Nothing yet. He won't return for another four days."

"You're lying," the lad stated.

Malini put her hand on his arm as the two exchanged a look.

Then she turned hazel eyes to him. "We may be young, but we understand what's going on."

"I know," Manu said. "I hate it, and I wish I could change it, but I know. There's nothing to tell." There was, but he didn't want to give them more to worry about. They had enough. "When there's something definitive, I'll let you know."

"What if I have news?"

They all turned at the sound of Dain's voice as he stepped out of the shadows.

"Dain!" Jaya shouted enthusiastically, jumping from Manu's lap and rushing to the Dark.

It didn't matter how many times Manu saw the intimidating Dark Elf grin and drop to a knee for the child, he would always stare in wonder.

"Did you bring us something?" Din asked, alternating between wanting to be with the younger siblings and wanting to stay with the eldest two.

Dain shrugged. "Why would I do that?"

"You always do," Jaya said as she and the other two younglings began to root around in his pockets.

Hadi was the first to produce something. "I got candy!"

Jaya and Surya quickly found something. Then Dain stood and raised a brow at Din. He bit his lip, and after Malini gave him a nudge, he hurried to Dain to dig in one of his jacket's many pockets until he produced a wooden dagger.

"Thank you," he said softly and hurried back to his older siblings.

Dain then looked at Sameer and Malini. Neither moved, but that didn't deter Dain. He slipped his hands into his pockets and then held them out to them. Sameer's eyes lit up at the small, foldable knife, and Malini stared in wonder at the silver necklace.

"What? Nothing for me?" Manu teased the Dark.

Dain gave him a flat look. "Next time."

"You said you had news," Manu reminded him.

The kids all went still, their attention locked on Dain. The Dark Elf turned to Manu. "I've secured a place for the children."

All six began to talk at once, their fear at leaving another place they knew evident in their voices and how they clumped together.

Manu pushed to his feet and walked to them. He raised a hand, waiting until they quieted before he spoke. "I know this is scary. We all thought Navara would be someplace you could hide indefinitely, but that has changed. Everyone is doing what they can to keep you safe. That is our priority."

"Where are we going now?" Malini asked, her voice resigned.

"To the Dragon Kings," Dain announced.

Sameer looked between Manu and Dain. "We don't know them."

"I do," Dain said. "They're good people. The Masters' reach doesn't extend that far, and that means they can't hurt you."

Jaya looked up at him with her big, dark blue eyes. "Is Yaz and Ravi coming, too?"

"Not yet, little one," Dain said softly.

Manu looked around. "Is Arya coming to help you take the children?"

"Actually, someone else is doing that," Dain said.

Manu glared at his friend. "You brought someone in without telling me?"

"That was my doing," said a feminine voice as a woman with

black hair and silver eyes suddenly appeared. She waved long fingers, her nails painted gold. She was dressed in black like Dain, but their clothes were very different. Her pants were tight, and her long-sleeved shirt was see-through to a sleeveless shirt beneath. Her boots, however, had heels so high, that he wondered how she could walk.

"Hi. I'm Rhi," she told the kids.

Jaya tilted her head to the side. "You sound funny."

Rhi smiled as she bent over, her hands on her knees. "That's because I'm from a place called Ireland, far, far away from here." She ruffled Jaya's hair before straightening and looking at Manu. "I understand your annoyance, but I wanted to give Dain time with the children before I showed myself."

Dain caught his gaze. "You can trust her."

Manu sighed as he glanced at the floor. Dain was the one who'd had the interactions with the Kings, which meant he had to trust the Dark. Dain was good at reading people. If he said Rhi could be trusted, then Manu would trust her. "How are you able to use magic as a human?"

"I may look human, but I'm not. I'm Fae." Rhi flashed a bright smile.

"She's also mated to the King of Dragon Kings," Dain added.

"Shall I get him?" Rhi asked. "He'd love to meet you."

Manu hesitated. "Get him?"

A slow smile pulled at her lips. "Fae can teleport. At least to places we've been. Dain had to get me here, but now that I've been, I can travel back and forth easily."

"Teleport?" Manu repeated.

"She jumps from where she is to wherever she wants," Dain said.

Rhi shrugged. "I can go as far as I need to. It could be halfway around the world."

"All Fae can do that?" Malini asked, her eyes wide with wonder.

"Yep," Rhi replied with a grin. "And I can take all the children at once."

Manu was suddenly second-guessing this plan. "Where are you taking them?"

Her face grew serious, letting him know she realized how dangerous things were. "We've been taking in children for some time now. The place is secret and protected by dragon, Fae, and Star magic."

"Star magic?" Dain asked.

Rhi wrinkled her nose. "I don't know if now is the time to alert you that there are beings with unparalleled powers who can travel the stars, moving from planet to planet."

"Are they friendly?" Manu asked.

Rhi shrugged one shoulder. "A few."

Which meant others weren't. Just what he needed to learn. But that wasn't his worry for now.

"My point is that the children will be guarded by a slew of Dragon Kings, a Star Person, me, and many other magical beings," Rhi added.

"Many?" Sameer asked, his excitement evident in the way he was leaning forward.

Rhi nodded. "We have an Amazon, a Banshee, and a Seer, to name a few."

Manu always suspected that there were other beings out there, but to have them named was shocking. He wanted to know what they looked like, what kind of magic they had, and if he could meet them.

Something touched his hand, and he looked down to find Jaya beside him. He would miss her jumping into his arms, and especially her hugs. He looked at each of the children. It wasn't just Jaya he would miss.

"Is this what we should do?" Sameer asked him.

Manu lifted Jaya into his arms and faced Sameer. "Do you trust me?"

"Aye," all six answered.

"Do you trust Dain?" he asked.

"Aye," the children replied.

He looked at Rhi, who gave him a nod. "Dain trusts Rhi and the Dragon Kings, and I trust Dain."

"Then we'll trust Rhi," Malini stated.

Jaya wound her arms around Manu's neck. "Will you visit?"

He closed his eyes and held her against him. "As soon as I can."

"Watch over Yaz and Ravi," Sameer bade him.

Manu nodded to the boy. "I will."

He reluctantly gave Jaya a final squeeze before setting her on her feet. "Be good."

Jaya walked to Dain while Manu said his farewells to each of the children. Once they had all spoken to Dain, the group gathered around Rhi.

The Fae looked from Dain to him. "If you need me, all you need to do is say my name, and I'll come."

Manu raised his hand to the children. One moment, they were there. The next, they were gone. As was a piece of his heart.

20

Inej was no stranger to fatigue. She was used to working hard, but no amount of hard work could have prepared her for the stiff fingers, aching shoulders, or sore feet she experienced as she walked home from her first full day of baking.

Something light and effervescent had blossomed in her chest the moment her fingers sank into the dough, and it had only grown with every passing hour. She lost all track of time and people, as she worked. Only once did she glance through the beaded curtain separating the kitchen from the front and witness customers devouring her creations. Her treats were making others smile, and in turn, bringing her unimaginable joy. Daas had to turn people away yet again.

The bag of coins in her pocket was significantly heavier than it had been the previous day. Already, Inej was coming up with different ideas for pastries that she was excited to share with Daas and Shruti. And for a little while, she could imagine that this was her new life.

There was no sign of Manu as she entered Jalall's home and walked to her room. Inej couldn't stop smiling. A quick look showed she had the entire place to herself. She grabbed some fresh clothes and headed for a bath. Her tired muscles melted in the hot water. She stretched out, lulled by the candle flames dancing on the wall and the heat. Before long, she was so relaxed her eyes drifted shut.

Inej jerked awake and quickly washed before reluctantly rising from the tub. She briefly considered eating, but her eyes were so heavy that she went straight to her bed, intending to only rest for a moment. She woke in the same position she'd fallen asleep in and was stunned to discover that it was dawn. Inej rose and dressed, then hastily plaited her hair. When her belly growled, she slipped into the kitchen and found a quick bite before heading out the door—all without spotting Manu.

When she reached the candy shop, elves were already lining up, waiting for the doors to open. She had to slip past the crush of customers just to get to the door Daas held open for her. They said a quick hello, and then she was up to her elbows in flour.

Shruti forced her to take a break at noon to eat, watching over the pastries so they didn't burn. It was the only way Inej would leave the kitchen. Before she knew it, the day was finished. She might not have worn a smile on her face on the walk home, but it was there in her heart. Her work was longer now, but she was doing something she loved, and for some reason, that didn't feel like work.

Her eyes sought out Jalall's house. The walk seemed particularly long that day. It was too bad she didn't live closer to the shop. A place of her own without anyone watching over her. Her feet grew heavy as she came to a halt. What was she thinking? She would never have a place of her own in Navara. Her job was temporary. She was here to carry out a mission.

Inej drew in a deep breath and then slowly released it. A large portion of her joy disintegrated, scattered with that one thought.

She silently entered Jalall's. There were none of the sounds she attributed to Chanda from anywhere in the house. Inej longed for another long soak and to crawl into bed, but she had already lost several days in not carrying out her assignment. How many more times would she be alone with Manu? She needed to take advantage of the time she had before it, too, was gone. That meant staying up to have dinner with him. She glanced down at her flour-stained clothes and realized she needed to change. As she passed the closed door to Jalall's office, she heard voices on the other side and immediately halted.

"The children have settled into their new location nicely," said a deep voice she didn't recognize.

Manu asked, "You saw them?"

"I was taken to them."

She frowned and pressed her ear to the door when the voice lowered so she couldn't pick up the next words. They were abducting children now? It was the natural progression, but that didn't stop the anger that rose for her spending time baking while others were hurting. How could she have let herself forget about Krata and all the other missing? The loathing she felt for herself threatened to swallow her whole.

But she realized the conversation had revealed that Manu wasn't the one in charge. There were others, including the unknown male behind the door. If she killed Manu, someone else would step into his role and continue the horrors without missing a beat. She needed to get details on who all was involved and find a way to somehow get that information to Gita so other agents could take out the other individuals.

The creak of a chair had her bolting to her room before she was discovered eavesdropping. She softly closed the door behind her before putting her day's pay with the other coins. All thoughts of ridding the world of Manu that night fled. She needed information, which meant striking up a conversation. And that meant not only looking her best, but also being engaging—charming, even.

Inej dressed, then took her time brushing out her hair and making sure there wasn't a speck of flour anywhere. She hid the poison beneath the mattress and then paused before her door. It was only a conversation that night. While it sounded easy, she needed to be careful that she didn't ask pointed questions and let him guess what she was trying to find out.

She squared her shoulders and opened her door. The office was still closed. She didn't get close to see if she heard voices, even though she wanted to. Instead, she headed to the kitchen. There, she pulled out food she found and set about making plates for both her and Manu. She hadn't paid attention to how much he ate, so she was guessing on what to give him. She turned, her finger in her mouth to lick off some sauce, when she found Manu in the doorway.

"Oh!" She tamped down a flare of anger for being startled. "You have to stop doing that."

His lips curved into a crooked grin. "I didn't sneak up on you. You were absorbed in your thoughts."

"Try walking louder." She softened her words with a quick grin, remembering too late what her goal was.

He chuckled as he leaned a shoulder against the doorjamb. "I'll do that. How was your day?"

"Long." And then she found herself smiling. "But good. Daas said sales have never been better."

"I hear the pastries sold out yet again."

"They did. It's unbelievable."

He shook his head slightly. "I'm not surprised at all."

His words, spoken with such sincerity, left her dumbfounded. It was almost as if he were...proud of her. No one, since her mum, had ever been happy for her about anything. Silence stretched between them as they stared at each other. His dark eyes pulled her in, drawing her close before wrapping around her like the night.

Several feet stood between them, but it felt as if he were right before her. She should be scared. She should back up or at least look away to break the connection that linked them. Instead, she stayed where she was and let his midnight gaze swallow her.

Thoughts of Manu in the towel from the other morning filled her head. A raw, visceral hunger burned through her veins and settled between her legs. He was a monster, but that didn't curb her desire to know what his body felt like against hers. She didn't want to crave his mouth or long to run her hands over him. She desperately wished to forget the yearning to have him inside her.

"Shall we?"

She blinked, and he was beside her, carrying the plate to the table. Her legs were wobbly as she followed him. The meal was uncomfortable. Each time she looked at him, she saw him as he had been in the hallway, his naked chest gleaming with water. It made it nearly impossible to keep her thoughts on a conversation when all she wanted to do was crawl across the table and kiss him.

At least he wasn't having a one-sided conversation. He had barely said two words since they'd left the kitchen.

Manu rose to get more wine, which gave her an opportunity to get control of herself. She was supposed to be charming him to get information. He needed to trust her, and he wouldn't do that unless she gave him a reason to.

Sleeping with him would break down his walls. The thought sent a wave of pleasure straight to her sex. It would also give her body what it craved. Maybe then she could think clearly.

When he returned to the table and set down the bottle, she pushed her chair back and got to her feet. Whatever she had been about to say vanished the moment their eyes met. She went to move back, but her foot got tangled with the chair leg, and to her horror, she began to fall. His arms were suddenly there to pull her firmly against him. Her hands flattened on his chest on instinct, and she stared at his beige shirt as she felt the firm sinew beneath her palms. This was where she wanted to be, where her fantasies had taken her. She was bombarded with emotions. One half of her was impatient to see what happened next. While the other half was aghast that she wasn't recoiling from such a brute.

He said nothing, but the heat in his eyes seared her. Her skin warmed everywhere his onyx eyes touched. She became aware of his large hands—one splayed on her back, the other resting on her hip. Steady. Strong. Soothing.

A shiver of anticipation slid through her. She couldn't draw enough breath into her lungs. His scent—dark, rich, and mossy—filled her senses, swirling around them seductively like an enchantment. The longer she was in his arms, the more her pathetic defenses crumbled.

The hand on her back flexed slightly. It was a subtle movement, as if he needed to know she was still there. The attraction between them had its own gravitational force. Did he feel it? Was he as caught up in it as she?

Inej didn't know what finally prompted her to lift her gaze to his. Her heart missed a beat when she saw the desire blazing in his dark depths. His hand deliberately moved to the curve of her lower back and pressed. She sucked in a breath at the feel of his rigid cock pressing into her front.

His eyes dropped to her mouth, and her lips parted of their own accord. His nostrils flared, and a muscle tensed in his jaw. Desire glided, hot and wicked, over and around her, touching every inch of her before gathering between her legs.

"Inej."

He whispered her name, the sound both a caress and a plea.

His arms tightened as his head lowered. Her eyes closed a heartbeat before their lips brushed. It was over all too soon. She opened her eyes when she felt him lean back. He searched her gaze. She didn't know what he was looking for, and she didn't want to ask. Not now. Not when she needed him to quell the ache she felt inside.

She held his eyes as she rose onto her toes and caressed her hands up his chest to wind around his neck. Time stood still as their lips hovered, breaths away. She slid her fingers into the cool, thick strands of his hair and pressed her mouth to his in a lingering kiss.

A low moan rumbled from his chest before he deepened the kiss. He moved one hand upward to tangle his fingers in her hair. He bent her back over his other hand as the kiss heated, turning fiery and possessive.

And hungry.

She tasted his need, his yearning, and it drove her desires

higher, sharpening them. Every fiber of her body became attuned to him. She felt the rise of his passion, the urgency he fought to hold in check, the storm that demanded to be freed. She smelled it, tasted it, touched it, and she met it with her own.

Suddenly, he drew back. One moment, his lips were there, and the next, they were gone.

She grappled with the unexpected loss and looked up at him. Her lips were swollen, and she tasted him when she licked them. The fire still burned in his eyes. So why had he ended the kiss? "What is it?"

"I need to know you want this. That you aren't doing this because you think you must."

Her fingers cupped his face as she brought his mouth back to hers. "I want this," she whispered before kissing him.

Those three words snapped the control that held back his storm. He lifted her with ease, allowing her to wrap her legs around his waist. Then he walked to her room, their lips never breaking apart. She had sensed the power in him before. Now, it poured off him, intoxicating and compelling. And it heightened her desire.

He pinned her between the wall and his deliciously hard body. She felt his every move: the way his muscles bunched and flexed, his fingers digging into her. She was on fire, her blood scorching through her veins, when his lips trailed across her cheek to her jaw and then down her neck. She rolled her head to the side to grant him better access as he ground against her. She needed him inside her that instant.

Before she could gather the words in her head, he lowered her legs one at a time until she stood. Then, he spun her around so she faced the wall. Her hands were braced on the stone, one cheek pressed against it, as he gently moved aside her hair and left a trail of hot kisses down her neck.

She shivered, desire coiling tightly as he found one of her secret spots. She arched her back to shove her hips against him. The sound of his answering moan made her knees weak. She couldn't handle any more. She ripped off her pants and turned in his arms, only for him to seize her mouth in a kiss that stole her breath and sent the flames of passion burning higher, hotter.

He found the hem of her tunic and slipped his hands beneath the fabric. His fingers brushed against her hip before slowly moving upward. She shivered at the feel of his hand on her bare skin. It was a hint of what was to come. He broke the kiss to remove her tunic and toss it away.

21

Need, feverish and all-consuming, coursed molten and wild through Manu's veins, demanding that he take her. *Claim her.*

The sight of her lips, swollen from his kiss, brought a possessive reaction he'd never felt before. He looked lower to her well-endowed breasts, barely held by their bindings. His fingers itched to release them and cup the voluptuous orbs in his palms that instant. Somehow, he kept the urge in check to continue his perusal along the indent of her waist and over her hips, showcasing her hourglass figure and making his mouth water.

The soft cream material resting on her hips and covering her sex begged to be removed. Before he knew it, he was on his knees. His fingers brushed her ankles and stroked up her toned legs to her thighs. He hooked his thumb in the band of her underwear and traced upward.

Her breath hitched, making his blood run hotter. With his hands holding her hips, he looked up, their gazes colliding. He refused to let her look away as he leaned forward and pressed a kiss to the silky material just above her sex.

Her lips parted as her chest heaved. But it was her eyes, smoldering with need, that undid him. He tugged her underwear over her hips and down her legs until they dropped around her ankles. Then, never breaking eye contact, he ran his hand around the back of her calf to her knee to lift one leg before settling it on his shoulder.

She bit her bottom lip and flattened her hands on the wall as he brought his mouth to her core and licked her. A half-sigh, half-moan fell from her lips as her eyes closed. He then turned his attention to her sex. He parted the dark curls and found her clit, circling it with his tongue.

He licked and laved, teased and savored, until she trembled, her hips rocking against his mouth. Only then did he slide a finger inside her wet heat. Her fingers curled in his hair, holding his head against her as her moans became louder. He could feel how close she was and added a second finger to the first.

Inej was mindless with wanton pleasure. Nothing existed beyond Manu and what he was doing to her. She both yearned for release and pulled back from it, not ready for any of it to end.

She gasped as his fingers found that perfect spot, robbing her of breath and thought. Desire wound tighter and tighter, pushing her ever closer to orgasm. His fingers and tongue skillfully worked her body until all that mattered was easing the ache, reaching for the ecstasy that awaited.

The first wave of carnality slammed into her with unnatural

force. She clutched his head and ground against him, riding the hedonistic storm as if it were her last. It tossed her about, showering her with stars and dropping her into a void of never-ending bliss.

It could have been hours or days before she finally came back into her body. He placed light kisses against the inside of her thigh that rested over his shoulder. She loosened her fingers and released his hair. He was beyond tender as he lowered her leg. She only opened her eyes when he stood, his fingers trailing lightly up her body as he did.

She was snagged by the hunger, longing, and clawing need in his ebony orbs. She had never met someone with the same raging fire inside them as she had. Until now. Manu was nothing like she had expected. He ran hotter, burned brighter than anyone she had ever encountered. Now that she stood within his fiery blaze, there was no escaping, even if she wanted to.

His hands came to rest on either side of her head as he lowered his mouth to hers, kissing her deeply so she tasted the pleasure he had brought her on his tongue. As quickly as the kiss began, he pulled away to look down at her once more. She thought she knew what kind of elf Manu was, but she had been so very wrong. The thought that she could hold back in his arms had been laughable. He demanded complete surrender, and she had given it to him without a second thought. If she proceeded with this game, would she be the same afterward? At the moment, she didn't care.

She unlaced the bindings around her chest. His dark eyes lowered to her breasts as the material fell away. His nostrils flared, causing her stomach to flutter. Her breasts swelled beneath his gaze. Then, finally, he cupped a globe in his large hand, gently massaging it. His onyx eyes met hers just as he ran a thumb over her nipple.

The sight of Inej's magnificent breasts made his balls tighten, and his cock jump. They were glorious, and more than a handful. The weight of them felt right in his palm, but it was the sight of the pebbled, dark brown nipples begging for his mouth that he focused on.

He bent and wrapped his lips around the taut peak, swirling his tongue around it. She arched against him. Her hands gripped his shoulders as she moaned. He drew her nipple deep into his mouth and felt her shudder against him.

Her skin was softer than any fur. Her moans were the sweetest sound he had ever heard. Her supple body was as willing and eager for pleasure as he was to give it. Inej was quickly becoming his obsession—to learn *and* to claim.

He moved to her other breast and lightly nipped the peak. She cried out, the sound filled with surprise and enjoyment. He had wanted a taste of her, and now that he had it, he was addicted. Her scent, her touch...her moans. She was uninhibited, utterly abandoned. The fire within her matched his, something that he had never encountered before.

Manu lifted his head to look at her. She was gasping for air, her chest heaving as she looked at him through heavy-lidded eyes. He needed to be inside her, to have her clenching around his cock. But first, he wanted them skin-to-skin.

He reached behind his head and grabbed his shirt, yanking it over his head and tossing it away. He stilled at the sight of her hands poised above his chest, as if she were suddenly afraid of touching him. He forgot about removing the rest of his clothes as he watched her.

Inej had seen his bare chest, but that was before he had brought her such unbelievable pleasure. She hadn't dared to touch him then. Yet, even now, as she sought to feel his warm skin beneath her palm, she hesitated. Something inside made her pause, issuing a silent warning. Almost as if cautioning her about continuing down this path.

She had imagined that Manu would be like others, those she could share a respite with and then forget. There was nowhere for her to escape to this time. She was supposed to leave, wasn't she? She couldn't think with her body awash with desire that demanded she give in to it. There was something she was supposed to do, something important.

His fingers slowly, gently wrapped around her wrist. Her gaze jerked to his face. It was a mistake to look into his eyes again. She was already overwhelmed by her needs, but his were palpable—a living, breathing entity that wanted her, beseeched her, drew her closer. And she freely went.

He placed her hand on his chest and waited. She forgot about his striking eyes and found herself eyeing his chest. Heat radiated from him, seeping into her palm and running along her arm. She spread both hands over his impressive torso, feeling the strength beneath her palms. She glided lower, over the ridges and valleys of his abdomen, as it tapered to a trim waist and narrow hips. Her hands halted at the waist of his pants. Then all she could think about was the bulge she saw there.

A sound that was part growl, part groan filled the room, right before his arms locked around her, and his mouth seized hers for another breath-stealing kiss. She melted against him, wanting more. He kissed her as if she were the essence of life itself and he would die without her. She tasted his need, his longing.

And matched it with her own.

Something bumped into the back of her legs. Then suddenly, his mouth was gone. She tightened her grip on his shoulders, not knowing when she had latched onto him, and opened her eyes. Somehow, they had crossed the room to the bed. She became acutely aware of his arousal against her stomach. She wasn't sure when he had rid himself of the rest of his clothes, but it was one less thing she needed to take care of.

Inej turned him so that he backed up to the bed. Then, she gave him a gentle shove so he fell back. As he rose up on one elbow, she looked down at him. His clothes had hidden a glorious body rippling with muscle and power.

She glanced at his hands that could call his magic in an instant and strike her down. It was one of the reasons she had never bedded an elf, but that concern seemed as far away as the sun at the moment. Her gaze moved over his stomach to his cock, hard and straining upward. A bead of moisture formed on the head as if calling to her.

He froze, waiting, watching when she dropped to her knees and ran her hands along his powerful thighs. She caressed his skin, moving toward his arousal. He stopped breathing when she neared. The moment she wrapped first one hand and then the other around him, he finally dragged in a ragged breath.

"Inej," he growled seductively.

The sound of her name on his lips sent a shiver of excitement through her. She stroked up and down on his thick rod, marveling at his size. She leaned forward, her lips parted and ready to slide over him, when he stopped her. She looked up to find his face pinched.

"One touch. That's all it will take," he rasped.

Could she really do that to him? Her, a human? That kind of power was heady. She could finish him now. Her sex throbbed, making her squeeze her legs together. But that wasn't what she wanted.

She wanted a taste of him, and she would get it. But first, she wanted to feel him moving inside her. She crawled over him to straddle his hips, and if it were possible, the dark pools of his eyes blazed even brighter with longing.

He lay back as she halted with her hands on either side of his face. Slowly, she sat back. She sucked in a breath when her sex brushed his arousal. He moved his hands to rest on her thighs, his chest rising and falling rapidly. She rose up onto her knees and grasped his cock, holding him as she lowered herself onto him.

She was so wet. Manu fought against lifting his hips and let her take control. She was tight, causing her to move slower than he would've liked, but her body soon adjusted, and she took every inch. She flattened her hands on his chest and dropped her head back as she began to rock her hips.

Somehow, he held himself in check and allowed her that for several moments before he sat up and flipped her onto her back.

Her eyes widened with excitement as he began to move his hips with long, slow thrusts. It wasn't long before her nails raked across his back. He quickened his tempo, driving into her hard, fast, and deep.

He watched the pleasure play over her face and knew the moment she was about to climax by the way her breath hitched. Her lips parted on a silent scream as the walls of her sex clamped around him. He followed her as they orgasmed together, his seed spilling inside her.

22

Rannora

Rain pelted Dain, drenching the city and everyone in it. The droplets soaked his hair and ran down his face and neck, sliding beneath the collar of his leather coat. He didn't bother with his shadows. There was no need. The night hid him well enough.

The rumble of the storm stifled the city's usual sounds. He blinked away droplets from his lashes and shifted to better see past the large, arched opening chiseled out of the dark rock and into the pub. He had conducted business at The Crossing for years. Sidiq, the owner, was a Dark Elf who had once been a CCD agent. He'd built the bar so that it sat between the Below and the Above, which made it a beacon for the Dark as they ventured up from the depths of the world. Since other elves frequented it, as well, The Crossing made for a seamless meeting point.

Dain spotted Sidiq as he poured alcohol into a glass. The Dark was big and broad, a warrior in his own right, who had survived years of spying. Dain didn't know what the blue tattoos on the side of Sidiq's head meant, and he wouldn't ask. There were things others weren't supposed to know.

Sidiq had offered the pub as a safe place for Dain in case he needed to hide from the Masters. He wanted to trust Sidiq, but in his line of work, trusting could mean death. Just as not trusting could. Dain had been lucky so far, but how much longer would that luck hold out? He didn't mind taking chances. He kept to himself—as any spy should. That way, an enemy could never get to someone he cared about.

He wasn't alone anymore, though. He had those he fought beside, those he would die for. Friends. It was a different experience. He couldn't let himself get used to it, though, not with the Masters looking for a way to strike. So, Dain tried to keep a wall erected around him. And yet, he kept returning to The Crossing.

His attention caught on the newest hire at the pub, a human male with blond hair and a too-easy smile. He watched the man move about the tables, taking orders and making others laugh with his false charm. There was something about the man that rubbed Dain the wrong way. But the man wasn't the reason Dain was here.

He searched the pub, hoping for just one glimpse of her. He stayed rooted to the spot until he finally spotted the familiar, braided brunette locks as Reva walked from the back storeroom. She rubbed the side of her face against her shoulder and reached for a tray laden with drinks.

Dain clenched his hands into fists as he watched her dodge roaming hands as she passed out orders. Movement out of the corner of his eye drew his gaze, and he saw Sidiq heading toward the table. He must have seen the men attempting to grope Reva. Dain had only recently discovered that Sidiq was romantically interested in Reva. If nothing else, he knew Sidiq would keep Reva safe.

But the human man beat Sidiq to the table, smoothly getting between Reva and the elves intent on groping her. The man didn't raise his voice or threaten the patrons, just kept a smile on his face while shifting their attention. Dain hated him immediately.

Yet, he, too, seemed intent on keeping Reva safe.

Sidiq watched the man for a moment before the Dark slowly made his way back behind the bar, and Reva moved off to other tables, unaware of what had taken place. It was a busy night in the pub. Every table and seat was taken. Dain could slip in unnoticed. It would be good to catch up with Sidiq, and if Reva came into the storeroom, then he would have no choice but to speak with her.

Dain tensed when he felt someone moving up behind him. He whirled around, drawing out the blade he kept in his coat and pressing it against a throat in the next second.

"Is that any way to greet a friend?"

Dain bared his teeth when he recognized Salil. He spun the weapon in his hand and slipped it back into its scabbard as he glared at the DIA agent. "You should know better than to sneak up on someone, Wood Elf."

"You were late to our meeting." Salil's hazel eyes bore into Dain's before his gaze slid to the side to look toward The Crossing.

"I had other business," Dain said.

The Wood Elf ran a hand through the wet strands of his short brown waves as he flattened his back against the building. "This day has been utter shite. Tell me you have news."

"Nothing." And that was the problem. Things were too quiet. They had been for days, and that could only mean trouble.

Salil shook his head, sending water flying. "Fuck. You, too? None of my contacts had anything useful. I don't have a good feeling about this."

"Nor do I." Dain glanced over his shoulder at the pub. He wasn't ready to leave, but that was how it always was when he came.

"Durga wants to talk to you."

Dain briefly closed his eyes. He should've visited Durga days ago, but too much had happened, and it had kept him from it. She had climbed high in the DIA, and though it was rare for DIA and CCD agents to work together, they had found common ground after he'd brought her intel on Shaldorn. She had then brought in Ravi and Yasmin. There was no way Dain and Arya would've been able to bring down Gita and Shaldorn without Durga's help.

"I suppose I'd better go now," Dain said. "You tagging along?"

Salil shrugged. "I was headed there after our meeting anyway."

"Let's go, then."

Dain waited until the Wood Elf moved closer before he gathered his shadows and traveled them across town to Durga's home. He had given her special wards that kept out most elves, even the Dark. It was the same ones he had put around Reva's place. Unlike at Reva's, though, Dain had left a narrow entrance for him to get into Durga's office so others wouldn't see him.

Once inside the room, he listened to make sure no one was around before dropping the shadows. He spotted a half-empty glass of liquor and an open file on the desk. Neither he nor Salil moved from their location. Durga was Salil's superior, and while

Dain didn't answer to her, she *had* earned his respect. They wouldn't snoop.

It wasn't long before he heard the click of her heels as she walked down the hall, moving from rug to plank floor and back to rug. She opened the door, only to come to a halt at the sight of them. Durga had the same coppery skin that Salil did, which proclaimed them as Wood Elves.

Durga kept her brown hair in a bun, no strand out of place. Her hazel eyes had more gold in them than Salil's as she looked between the two of them. An olive green gown graced her tall, slender form, while gold earrings dangled to her shoulders, and gold tips adorned the top points of her ears.

She walked into the room and closed the door before making her way to the desk. She braced her fingertips on the surface. "I take it by your expressions that things didn't go well?"

"There's no news on my end," Salil said. "I spent the entire day pushing my contacts, but they know nothing."

Durga's gaze slid to Dain. "You always manage to get some kernel of information."

"Not this time. I didn't visit all of my contacts, however." Dain wouldn't say more about the children and the Dragon Kings in front of Salil. The fewer people who knew about it, the less likely the information would be leaked. And if it did leak, Dain would know who betrayed him.

Durga blew out a breath as she looked down at her desk. "The Masters have been one step ahead of us this entire time. Why suddenly go quiet?"

"My guess is that something big is coming," Salil said.

Dain nodded in agreement when Durga looked his way.

She straightened. "I, too, think that. Get some rest, Salil. You've been at it for days."

He dipped his head to Durga before nodding at Dain. Dain returned the gesture and waited until the Wood Elf was gone before swinging his head to Durga.

"I hope you aren't going to tell me I can't trust him. He's a damn fine agent," she said.

Dain shook his head. "This has nothing to do with him."

"Good," she said as she sat. She motioned to one of the chairs across the desk. "The deeper into this we go, the less inclined I am to bring on anyone new. I know the Masters have infiltrated our ranks, just as we have theirs. But I'd rather not have anyone privy to all our secrets."

Dain walked to the chair and lowered himself into it. "That is the way of war, no matter what side you're on. There's no getting away from it. One of us will eventually get caught. Arya already has."

"She freed herself, and if any of you *do* get caught, you know we'll come for you."

"You can't," he warned. "And you know it."

Durga rolled her eyes. "This isn't some mission about uncovering fraud. This is our very way of life. I want those on my team to know I will do anything for them."

"We know. But you can't come for us. You'd be delivering several team members to them at once. Then what?"

Instead of answering, she looked away. He noted the dark circles under her eyes. Some might think she had the easiest job since she wasn't in the thick of it, but in fact, Durga's was the hardest. She had to assemble the teams, sift through intelligence, and make decisions. She sent teams out. Then she had to sit back and wait to hear what happened to her people. It made for long, sleepless nights and more stress than one person should have to handle.

And there was no end in sight.

"When was the last time you slept?" he asked.

She laughed, the sound humorless as she met his gaze. "I could ask the same of you. We'll sleep when this is over. What information did you not want to share in front of Salil?"

"An attempt was made on Manu's life. The children had to be moved."

Durga sat up, her face creasing with lines of worry. "How did the Masters learn about him?"

"I don't know. Yet." But Dain would find out.

"Were they after him or the kids?"

"He isn't sure. And neither of us wanted to take any chances."

"I know we set up the coastal place for the team—"

"They decided to name it Serenia," he interjected.

"While it's secluded and relatively safe, it isn't a place for the kids, no matter how much Yasmin and Ravi want them there. There is no other place in Shecrish."

Dain nodded. "I couldn't agree more."

She stared at him for a long minute before she narrowed her gaze. "I see."

He had known she would figure out what he was saying without him actually having to say the words. Because they couldn't be too careful. Durga knew about his contact within the Dragon Kings. She would put two and two together.

"They're safe?" she asked, her voice pitched just above a whisper.

"Aye."

Her shoulders sagged as she released a breath. "I needed some good news. Thank you for that."

Dain stayed for another thirty minutes, going over plans, before he left. And found himself right back at The Crossing. But he didn't go in. Too many were looking for him. If someone saw him and reported it to the Masters, they might turn their attention to Sidiq or Reva. And Dain wouldn't let that happen. He had kept Reva out of their hands twice now, and he would continue to do just that. Because if they learned about her, and that magic didn't work on her, she would be dead within moments.

He waited in the rain until closing. Reva was observant and capable, but he still intended to follow her home to ensure that she arrived without incident.

"Reva, wait up!" the blond man said as he jogged from the back of the pub.

Sidiq's gaze was hard as he watched the human rush to Reva. Sidiq's gaze then shifted to look out into the night. Dain could show himself, but he decided to trail the couple instead. He told himself it was just to make sure Reva was safe, but he knew that for the lie it was.

"Thanks for intervening with those handsy elves earlier," Reva said.

The man shrugged. "Happy to do it. I was wondering if you'd like to get dinner sometime."

Dain strained his ears to hear over the rain, but he couldn't make out what she said.

"Perfect," the man said. "How about tomorrow?"

Dain hid between two buildings as they stopped beneath an overhang and talked about times. Reva waved and went to the right as the blond disappeared to the left. Dain thought about following the man, but he stayed with Reva instead. And just as he had done countless times before, he stood on the ground floor and watched her climb the stairs and go to the flat labeled 13.

He backed deeper into the shadows when she paused with the key in the lock and looked over her shoulder. Her eyes moved over him without seeing him. He still remembered the look of confusion and hurt the last time they'd spoken. He had been a fool to allow her to become one of his contacts. It had put her in jeopardy. Worse, he hated that Sidiq had been the one to point it out.

It wasn't just that Reva was human, magic didn't work on her. If she got hurt, there was nothing he could do. A Healer's magic wouldn't work on her, and neither would elvish herbs. Now, he would never know the pain of watching her be injured and being unable to help her. And that was the best for everyone.

He waited until Reva was safely inside her home before he disappeared into the night.

23

Inej's eyes flew open. She lay frozen on her side as she stared at the wall, afraid to move. She had fallen asleep next to Manu. That was a first for her, since one of her rules was that she always slept alone. She slowly rolled onto her back and looked at the spot next to her, only to discover it empty.

Her smile of relief vanished as she wondered why he had left. Had he slept beside her, or had he slipped from the bed as she usually did? She didn't know why she was irritated that he had left. Which only made her angry at herself.

She stretched beneath the covers and felt the slight pull of a body used well. Flashes of their night played in her head. His lust-filled eyes. His gentle touch. The way he so easily wrung climaxes from her. Her nipples hardened as she recalled how his tongue had rasped against the tight buds.

Inej looked at the empty pillow again. Perhaps it was good that he wasn't here. Otherwise, she likely would've had her way with him again. Except this wasn't her usual bed partner. She needed him to return to her so she could get close.

Remembering why she was in Navara doused the embers of desire that had flared to life once more. She had forgotten who he was in the moment, but she couldn't do that again. He had a fine face and fooled many people, including his own, but she knew. It didn't matter how much her body craved his touch, she was there to stop him—and everyone involved—if it was the last thing she did.

Inej threw off the covers and rose. She found a wrap to hide her nakedness and slowly opened the door so it wouldn't make any noise. When she didn't hear anything, she walked from her room and checked the house. She was alone, and it made her wonder if he had left to kidnap more unsuspecting individuals.

She wanted to get those he answered to, but if she couldn't, she would at least put a wrinkle in their plans by taking him out. That meant she had to maintain some sort of control over her body, so she wouldn't get carried away again. A look at the clock confirmed that it was past time for her to rise. She quickly readied for the day and left before Chanda arrived.

Despite being busy baking, her mind randomly recalled parts of her night with Manu. Most times, she was able to shove them out of her head, but a few lingered, causing her thoughts to drift to relive their first kiss, the way he'd pressed her against the wall, or how well their bodies joined.

"Inej?"

She jerked out of her ruminating, hitting her elbow on a rack and dropping the spoon she held. She hastily picked it up and moved it to the sink, flustered and embarrassed to be caught thinking about Manu. "Aye?"

Daas was astute, his dark eyes seeing everything, but he didn't ask what was wrong. Affable expression in place, he said, "You have a visitor."

"Visitor?" she asked with a frown. Who would come to see her?

The beaded curtains moved, and Manu's form filled the doorway. The room shrank when he entered. Had her thoughts conjured him? Unable to help herself, she looked at his mouth. Just then, she remembered that he had whispered something to her as she'd fallen asleep, but she couldn't remember what it was.

Inej became aware of Daas looking between them curiously. She cleared her throat, set the empty bowl she was supposed to have been cleaning aside, and wiped her hands on the apron. "Hello," she said nervously.

Daas chuckled as he turned to go. "Call it a day, Inej. I'll finish the rest of the cleanup."

Manu stepped aside to allow Daas to exit, his gaze following the older elf out. Then Manu's eyes were on her, the dark pools searching, probing. Her belly fluttered as she remembered the sounds of his raw, untamed groans as he kissed and touched her, how he had held his hard body over her as he thrust his hips.

Inej tried to swallow, but her mouth had gone dry. She turned, unable to hold his gaze for even a second longer. She saw the flour on her hands and wiped them, trying not to imagine where else the flour might be.

"You'll have to look at me sometime."

His voice was behind her, closer now. She closed her eyes, hating that she pictured him sliding his hands around her waist and drawing them closer, his lips on her neck as it had been last night—in that spot that drove her wild.

"I should finish." She said the first thing she thought of, belatedly remembering what Daas had told her.

"Regretting last night, then?"

She jerked her head to the side, glancing at him over her shoulder. "I didn't say that."

"Then look at me, Inej."

No one said her name like he did. It didn't matter that he'd pleasured her or how much she enjoyed baking. This wasn't a new start for her. She had a mission, and that meant she had to act the part.

She gripped her hands and turned to face Manu. She needed a reason for acting so strangely. "You left."

Heat flared in his eyes as he took a step closer. "Not by choice."

Had she been so relaxed and content that she hadn't heard someone enter the house? Now, she sounded petulant, and she was never that. "I thought you might have had regrets." That was better. She put it on him, which put her in a little better light.

"There are things I regret, but that will never be one of them."

As odd as it sounded, she believed him. It was on the tip of her tongue to tell him he would, but she swallowed her words.

"I thought we might take a walk," he suggested.

"Let me get cleaned up," she urged as she removed the apron.

He stepped aside, giving her room to maneuver to the tiny bathroom. She splashed water on her face, washed her hands, and got the flour out of her hair and the spots on her clothes. After one last look at her reflection, Inej walked out. She found Manu talking with Daas at the front of the shop.

Daas discreetly handed her another bag of coins when she reached them. "Good work today. I'll see you tomorrow."

Inej tucked the bag into her pocket as she and Manu walked

away. He turned them to the left, which was opposite of how she normally went home. She winced at calling Jalall's house her home again. It was a temporary place for her to lay her head, and the sooner she remembered that, the better.

"Is everything all right?" she asked. Then added, "With whatever caused you to leave this morning?"

His lips flattened. "For the moment."

They fell into an awkward silence—at least on her part. This is why she only slept with her bed partners once and never saw them again. She didn't know how to act, and now she wished she had at least some idea of what to do. Not only did she not know what to say, but they were surrounded by others walking past. Someone might overhear.

She looked ahead to the waterfall. "Are we going back to your spot?"

"I thought I'd show you my home."

Her brows rose in surprise. She knew which one was his, even if he hadn't pointed it out. How could she not? It was the grandest place in all of Navara. She looked at the stately home ahead with its grand turrets and columned entrance. Why did he want to take her there now? Did he really want to show her where he lived, or was he taking her there to be kidnapped?

Her feet became heavy as she imagined walking to her own doom. How did other agents handle this kind of situation? She looked around. There was nowhere for her to hide, nowhere to escape. If this were to be her end, she would face it with her head up, doing everything she could.

Manu made small talk, but she barely paid attention the closer they got to his home. It was so large that it was actually a manor. Strangely, he hadn't called it that, though. He brought her through the front door, letting everyone see them together. It was another surprise she hadn't expected.

While the outside was imposing and daunting, the inside was warm and inviting. He'd chosen a warmer palette than Jalall, with color everywhere. Coral, burgundy, and yellow combined in the spacious rooms with their amber lighting gave it a warm feel. She eyed the huge entrance and the high ceiling above her. It was painted with a picture that she couldn't quite make out.

A tall plant stood in a corner, its large leaves both elegant and soft. She caught a glimpse of a wall hanging to her left, but she didn't have time to study it as she followed Manu.

He pointed out rooms as they walked—sitting room, parlor, office, library. Some doors were closed, others open, but there was greenery everywhere her eyes touched. Massive pots on the floor, smaller ones grouped together, more hanging, and little ones dotting shelves or tables. It made her forget that they were essentially underground in a frozen, unforgiving wasteland.

She eyed the scattered sculptures, paintings, and wall hangings. There wasn't a show of great wealth like she had expected, especially coming from Gita's place. Instead, she saw a home, albeit a very large one. It was just one more thing that went against what she knew of him. Perhaps he hid his wealth. That made more sense. Though it wasn't as if his people lived in poverty. Everything she had seen so far said they were better off than many in Belanore.

They passed a few servants, all of which had warm smiles, even for her. He took her up a flight of stairs and then down a long corridor with doors on either side. Manu didn't tell her what they led to, and she didn't ask. Once they reached the end of the hallway, he paused. She stopped and looked at him.

He glanced at her, his expression unreadable, before he continued onward to yet another set of steps. She swallowed past her growing fear and trailed him. When she reached the top, she found they were in an outdoor alcove with a magnificent view of the waterfall. It was also hidden from view. Inej pulled her gaze from the falls and looked at Manu, who was off to her right.

His neck moved as he swallowed. "Stay here tonight."

She blinked, unsure if she'd heard him right. "You want me here?"

"Aye. In my bed. But only if you want to be."

"And if I said I didn't wish to be?"

He shrugged one shoulder. "I'd take you back to Jalall's."

"And if I say I do?"

"All I've thought about all day is you. It's everything I can do to keep my hands off you now." He drew in a ragged breath. "The choice is yours."

She walked to him and laid her palms on his chest. "I want your hands on me."

24

Six words, and the last of his control snapped. Manu slid his hands to her firm arse and yanked her against his hard cock. His fingers curled into her flesh when she made a soft sound of approval. Everywhere he turned, every thought, every sound, made him think of her.

The attraction was much more than just the need to ease his body. He was obsessed with Inej. Infatuated. Completely consumed.

Their lips met in a heated, sizzling kiss, each lost to the passion raging within them. Her fingers slid into his hair as she lifted a leg to wrap around his waist. He rocked against her, impatient to join their bodies once more. He needed days—no, weeks—of doing nothing other than wringing cries of pleasure from her.

Voices drifted up the stairs, penetrating the haze of lust. Manu ended the kiss to listen, but all he heard was their ragged breathing. He looked into her eyes, noting the flecks of gold in the luminous brown.

"Stay with me tonight. Here," he said again. "I want you in my bed."

She touched his face, her palm scraping against his whiskers, making him wish he had taken the time to shave. Her gaze lowered to his mouth, and her finger slowly traced along his top lip, then his bottom.

Finally, she looked him in the eyes. "Aye."

There had been a moment when he'd thought she might decline. He would've let her go. He had never forced a woman. He'd never had to, and he wasn't about to start now—no matter how much he hungered for another taste of her.

He released her and took her hand, leading her down the stairs to his chambers. The moment she was inside, he shut and barred the door before facing her. She stood in the middle of the room, watching him. There was so much about her that he didn't know, so much he *yearned* to know. He should be circumspect, but his body overruled rational thought when it came to her.

Manu removed his boots, then his shirt, and her gaze lowered to his chest. He bit back a smile and unfastened his pants before shoving them down, stepping free, and closing the distance between them.

Her pulse beat rapidly in her throat, her chest rising and falling quickly. There was no shyness, no coyness. Inej was a woman who knew what she liked and wanted and went after it. That was part of what drew him to her. She was an outsider, and a human at that, but he was utterly beguiled.

He brushed the backs of his knuckles against her cheek before sliding his fingers around to the nape of her neck and moving closer. He got lost in her eyes, finding the gold from before as well as some deep brown striations shooting from her pupil, and a band of bronze encircling her iris.

"I've never seen such beautiful eyes," he told her. "From the first time you looked at me, I was mesmerized."

A small smile pulled at the corners of her lips. "My eyes?"

"First, it was your eyes. Then your face, your hair, and then your glorious body."

Her grin melted as desire flared in her gaze. Together, they quickly divested her of clothes before Manu brought her against him once more. Her sigh as they kissed made his heart skip a beat. Did she know how that affected him? Was she doing it on purpose? He hoped she was as enthralled as he was.

His thoughts scattered when she began to kiss down his chest. He stood with his hands at his sides as her fingers slid sensuously down his body and her mouth followed. She left a trail of heat in her wake as she moved to his stomach and then lower. He held his breath when she dropped to her knees and pressed a kiss against one hip and then the other, all while her hands leisurely caressed down his thighs and up again.

The feel of her breath against his cock made it jump. He watched her kiss closer and closer to his arousal, driving him crazy each time he thought she would finally touch him, only for her to change directions. His cock strained toward her as he clenched and unclenched his hands.

Finally, she wrapped her long, slim fingers around him. Manu moaned, his eyes rolling back in his head as she used just the right amount of pressure while moving her hand up and down his length. He sucked in a breath when she circled the tip of his cock with her thumb, sending ripples of pleasure running through his body.

He felt her breath against him once more. Manu looked down and met her gaze as she parted her lips and took him into her mouth. The rasp of her tongue, the heat of her mouth, her hands. It was all too much. He tangled his fingers into her hair as her head bobbed, each stroke sending him closer and closer to orgasm.

It felt so good he never wanted her to stop. He tightened his hold on her head and reluctantly pulled his cock out of her mouth. Her lips were wet, her eyes half-closed. He pulled her to her feet, but before he could do more, she backed to the bed and sprawled on the mattress, her legs parted.

He was over her in a heartbeat, one hand braced by her head, his other gliding up her thigh. When he skimmed a finger along the folds of her sex, he groaned. "Fuck. You're so wet."

"You do this to me," she murmured.

Inej arched her back as he pushed a thick finger inside her. It felt good, but it wasn't enough. She wanted him rocking inside her once more.

As if reading her thoughts, he withdrew his finger, and the head of his cock rubbed against her folds. She bent her knees up to her chest, spreading her legs wider. He pushed inside her, stretching her the deeper he went. She grasped his sides to pull him down atop her so she could feel his weight.

He loomed over her, big and powerful, his neck straining as he pulled out some and thrust hard. She gasped as he went deep enough to touch her womb. Then, he was moving inside her, the friction just what she needed.

She lifted her head to watch their bodies coming together again and again. The sight of him sliding inside her, combined with the wild look in his eyes, stole her breath. His stamina was unlike anything she had experienced before. Long and hard. Fast and shallow. He knew just what she needed.

The climax began before she was ready. She put her hands on his chest to tell him to stop, to make it last longer, but he only thrust deeper, harder.

"Come for me," he demanded.

She was already in the throes of the orgasm, but his words sent a fresh wave of pleasure swimming through her, sending her higher. She felt his body pumping inside her, prolonging the climax as she floated from one surge to another.

Inej's face as she came was a sight to behold—the pleasure radiating from her as her cheeks flushed and her eyes fluttered closed. Then there was her body shuddering around him. Manu reached for the orgasm and let the tight walls of her sex milk him until he could barely hold himself up. The mind-altering pleasure was even more intense than it had been the night before.

He came back into his body and found his head buried in her neck as her hands moved over his back. He was still semi-hard deep inside her. Every now and again, a small tremor ran through her body, causing her to tighten around his cock and sending ribbons of pleasure through him.

Manu rose up onto his forearms to look at her. Her brown waves were spread out around her like a dark crown. He didn't know what he liked more, her hair draped around him like a curtain or spread as it was now.

"You are exquisite," he said.

Her smile was soft as she gazed up at him. "So are you."

He wanted to remain just as they were, but he'd promised her they'd eat. Manu pulled out of her and got to his feet. "Our meal should be here shortly."

"Assumed we'd be here, did you?"

He chuckled. "I hoped. Since we aren't downstairs, they know to bring the food up here."

"Oh." Some of the light went out of her eyes as she sat up and turned her back to him.

Manu inwardly winced at his thoughtlessness. "Mountain Elves have always been unrestrained when it comes to sex and partners. No one will say anything about you being here, if that's what you're worried about."

"They may not say it, but they'll think it."

"Perhaps we should've remained at Jalall's."

She glanced at him over her shoulder and shrugged. "Chanda already thinks I'm after you. I don't think it matters."

"Would you like to return to Jalall's?" He held his breath, waiting for her answer.

Inej pushed to her feet and faced him. "I've never apologized for heeding what my body needs, and I won't start now. What I would like is a soak in that," she said, pointing behind him.

Manu looked to the rectangular tub cut out of the mountain, large enough for three. The inside had been ground down until it was smooth. Two steps led into the tub. He went to the faucets and knelt to turn them until water flowed through the spigot. He straightened and found Inej looking around his room. She glanced over and saw him observing her.

"Is the room not what you were expecting?" he asked.

She shook her head, the ends of her hair swaying with the movement. "Nay."

He looked about the room, taking in the shelves of books he'd built from a fallen kocracia evergreen, showing the dark umber color, to the burnt amber and gray rug, to the chairs covered in a bluish-gray, and then finally to the bed, where pelts of white and gray fur had been sewn together and pulled back to reveal the comforter that was a muted, ashy dark blue.

"The colors suit you," she said as she faced him.

He quirked a brow. "Oh?"

She walked to him. "This room feels calm, peaceful. Like you."

"I'm far from calm."

"You hide it very well." She stopped before him.

He reached for a lock of her hair and let it run through his fingers. "It keeps my people relaxed."

"What about you? What keeps you composed?"

"I don't think any leader can be."

She moved down the steps and into the tub, standing as the water rose, winding her hair atop her head. After a moment, she lowered herself and reclined with her legs out. Then, she looked at him and raised a brow. "Are you coming?"

Manu stepped into the tub and sat facing her, their legs tangling as he stretched out. Tendrils of her hair had come loose and stuck to her skin as the heat from the bath dampened it. Her gaze was questioning, which prompted him to ask, "What is it?"

"I'm trying to figure out why an elf like you doesn't have a wife."

He grunted and glided his hands over her calves. "It isn't required."

"I've seen the way the females look at you. You're not only

handsome, but also in a position of power. You could have your pick of women."

"Maybe I've not found the right one."

Her brows shot up. "Don't tell me you're waiting on love."

"You say that as if you don't believe in it."

"You do?" she asked in surprise.

He tugged on her leg, bringing her closer. "Why don't you?"

25

It was a good question, and one Inej wasn't ready to answer. Warm water swirled gently around her as Manu brought her ever closer until she straddled his hips and rested her hands on his chest.

"I find it hard to believe that a woman like you doesn't have someone special in her life," he said.

She felt him growing hard once more while his hands caressed along the curves of her arse and up to her back. His appetite, it seemed, was as ferocious as hers. "Who said I don't?"

Some emotion she couldn't name moved behind his eyes as he stilled. "Do you?" he demanded softly.

Had her teasing words really caused such a reaction? Could this elf who kidnapped others for who-knew-what-purpose really have standards? It appeared so. The realization made her uneasy, as she couldn't reconcile that with what she had heard about him.

"Nay," Inej replied. "I don't."

Manu relaxed. She didn't let the tension ease from her muscles until his hands continued their exploration of her back. He never looked away, as if he were trying to see into her thoughts.

"Because you don't believe in love?" he asked.

"That's part of it."

"And the other?"

She could lie. She had one ready, but that wasn't what came out. Instead, she found herself speaking the truth. "You think having someone to share my life with would make it easier? I've seen the reality too many times to know it won't. The struggle doesn't get easier. It gets harder. Plus, there's always one who wants a child, and with infants continually needing homes, the Domestic Ministry is all too ready to give one to a couple looking, no matter their situation. Then, there'd be an additional mouth to feed with what is already too little. There are the couples who actually elevate themselves somewhat with both of them working —until one of them stops for whatever reason. Then it's up to one person to feed both, along with any children. No, thank you. I know what I need to do to support myself."

He didn't argue or try to press any point he may have had. He listened, his dark eyes noting everything. Somehow, that made it worse.

"I don't want your pity," Inej said. "If that's what you're thinking, stop."

He sat up so their bodies were pressed together. His mouth hovered next to hers. "That isn't what I was thinking."

"What were you thinking?" The words came out as a ragged whisper as she slid her arms around his neck.

"Let me show you," he murmured, right before he kissed her.

It wasn't the wild, ravenous kisses from before. It was slow, sensual, and utterly erotic. His lips were soft and firm as they pressed against hers deliberately before he languidly slid his tongue against hers. She was so absorbed in the kiss that she barely felt his large hand splayed upon her back, or his other hand stroking up her side to graze her breast.

She tightened her arms as the kiss deepened, moving her past lust and into something else entirely. Everything in her rebelled. It was too...intimate. Too romantic. She readied to shove him away, only she couldn't. She had come to take down evil, which meant she had to go with things, even if they were hard.

Even if she knew she might never be the same.

Because she was already different. She could feel the changes.

His thumb glided against the underside of her breast, causing her nipple to harden. She forgot about missions, the past, and the future. She forgot about everything but him and the pleasure that awaited. She sank into the kiss, into him.

Into the bubble of pleasure and decadence.

A moment later, a knock shattered it. A frown puckered Manu's brow as he turned his head toward the sound.

"Is it the food?" she asked.

He shook his head slightly as he gently moved her off his lap. "It's too early."

She returned to her side of the tub, watching him rise, water sliding from his body as he stepped out and walked naked to the door. She locked her gaze onto his back, watching the play of muscles. He cracked open the door wide enough to look through as she eyed his tight arse and thick legs. Someone spoke softly, preventing her from hearing anything. Almost immediately, Manu shut the door and began to dress.

"What is it?" she asked.

"Stay for as long as you'd like. You may remain here to wait for me if you wish, though I'm not sure when I'll return."

Was he going on another kidnapping spree? Panic seized her as she stood and exited the tub. He walked to her and cupped her face in his hands before pressing his mouth to hers for a lingering kiss. He offered her a smile and then walked out of the room.

Inej stared at the door for a long time before racing to the window, grabbing her clothes as she did. She dressed and peered outside, trying to catch a glimpse of him, but it was the wrong angle. She spun around, her gaze sweeping the room. The need to snoop was strong, but she doubted she would find anything of value here. It was more important for her to follow him and see why he was rushing away.

She looked longingly at the huge bed before hurrying out of his room. She took a wrong turn and got lost, which made her have to backtrack. His home was massive, and she knew there were more levels and rooms she hadn't seen. His people were loyal. They wouldn't tell her anything, so it was pointless to remain. This time, at least.

Inej only saw one servant as she made her way out. She tried to keep her pace normal, but urgency quickened her steps. She had just crossed the bridge when she noticed a commotion near the entrance that had made a crowd gather. Something big was going on, and no one was trying to hide it. Unfortunately, by the time she reached Jalall's, Manu and his squad were gone.

With nothing else to do, Inej used the side entrance. The house was empty, and she was relieved not to have to deal with Chanda. She scrounged up some food and cleaned up before she bathed and went to bed. Sleep was slow to come, however. She tossed and turned for most of the night, only dozing in short spells.

When she finally gave up and rose, she was tired and anxious, and ended up getting to the candy shop thirty minutes early. She sat outside, waiting for Daas and his wife to open. Inej tried to bury herself in baking, but she couldn't shut out the world as she usually did.

"Shite," she murmured when she realized her pastries were burning.

She set them aside to cool and looked them over, trying to see if she could salvage any. Two had the barest hint of burn. She would put those aside.

"We're all worried."

Daas's voice made her head jerk to the side, looking to where he stood watching her. "Do you know why he left?"

"I suspect it's because the Masters are getting close."

His response shocked her. "Who are the Masters?"

"The group responsible for the abductions in the lowlands."

So, Manu's people didn't know he was leading the Masters. "How do you know what they're called?"

"Manu alerted us to their practices. Don't you worry, dear," the elder elf stated with a nod. "Manu will be back."

He'd better return. She still needed to get information from him. She had spent time and energy getting close to him. If he died, she'd have to start all over. Someone might get suspicious then.

Daas walked out of the kitchen, leaving her to her thoughts. Twice, she messed up a recipe and had to redo it, but neither Shruti nor Daas said anything. Customers were steady, but things had slowed from the previous days. She suspected it was because Manu had left in such a rush.

The day dragged at a crawl, and tensions continued to rise

through the city. She wasn't looking forward to another sleepless night, but she was ready to treat the burns she had gotten from her carelessness and lack of concentration. Daas handed her another bag of coins before they walked out together. She was waving goodbye when she noticed a commotion near the entrance.

Inej forgot about Daas as she rushed forward with dozens of others to see what was happening. Wails started the moment some soldiers carried in a stretcher. She rose on tiptoe to see if it was Manu, but she couldn't see a face. She leaned around those in front of her and scanned faces, looking for him.

Finally, she spotted him directing some soldiers before speaking to a small group. He turned then, and she saw the blood on the side of his face. It had dried into ice crystals in his hair and on his skin. More blood was matted in the fur of his coat. He looked toward Jalall's home for a moment and then turned his head in her direction as if searching for her. She was rooted to the spot as others continued to rush forward.

His gaze collided with hers. They stared at each other for a long time, neither of them moving. She was unnerved at the relief that filled her. Someone shouted his name. He tipped his head to her, then turned away.

"I told you he would return," Daas said, moving up beside her.

Inej glanced at his kindly face. "So you did."

"I've known him for his whole life, and I've never seen him look at anyone the way he looks at you."

"I'm sure it's because he feels responsible for me."

Daas laughed softly. "And he takes all of us to his home for dinner? Look harder. You'll see what I see."

She swallowed, unsure how to reply. Daas walked away, chuckling. She watched others moving around her, and it was long minutes before she finally made her way to Jalall's. The moment she entered, she heard Chanda in the kitchen and grimaced.

Inej wasn't up for dealing with the elf, so she went straight to her room. She checked to make sure the poison was still under the mattress before falling back onto the bed and looking up at the canopy. She hadn't been able to sleep last night, but now, she couldn't keep her eyes open. Chanda's presence kept her out of the kitchen. She would wait until the elf was gone before going to eat.

Inej must have dozed off, because when she opened her eyes, she no longer heard Chanda. She crept out of the room and checked the house. She smiled when she realized she was alone and headed to find food. She was at the counter when the hairs on the back of her neck rose. There was only one individual who could cause such a reaction: Manu.

A large hand wrapped around her waist as he came up behind her. He moved aside her hair and pressed his mouth to her neck. Her eyes rolled back in her head as pleasure spread through her. She turned her head toward him, and their lips met in a hungry kiss.

He gathered her dress in his hands, pulling it higher. She moaned when he yanked down her underwear. She leaned forward, and he entered her with one hard thrust.

26

Manu gripped Inej's hips as he drove into her again and again. He had only intended to kiss her, but he lost all reason when he was near her. Every moment with her deepened the ache, stoked his desire. She wasn't just under his skin—she was becoming a part of him.

She issued a breathless groan. The sultry, seductive sound drove him wild. Her sheath was snug around his cock. All he had been able to think about for the entire day was getting back to Navara.

Back to Inej.

Pleasure built quickly. His orgasm was almost upon him, but he wasn't going without her. He flattened his hand on her abdomen and slid his fingers down until he breached her dark curls and found her swollen clit. Her breath hitched as he circled it once, twice.

"Aye," she urged.

Her moans grew louder as she rocked back against him,

meeting his thrusts. The feel of her was simultaneously too much and not enough. His hunger grew with every breath—quiet, relentless.

Consuming.

A scream was wrenched from her lips as her body tightened around him. Thoughts ceased. He drove into her and bellowed as the orgasm slammed into him, robbing him of breath. His body shook as he came undone, drowning in brutal, blinding pleasure he never wanted to end.

He was slow to come down from the glorious high. The sound of their ragged breaths filled his ears. He felt her soft curves as the room came back into focus. Manu drew in the scent of their love-making. A violent, possessive sensation overtook him. Something urged him to mark her as his, to claim her so no one would ever harm her. The reaction was so immediate and intense that it shook him.

Manu kissed the exposed portion of her neck and slowly pulled out of her. She turned to face him, her skin flushed from her climax. Her brown eyes searched his face before she gently touched his cheek. He covered her hand with his and felt stubble on his fingertips. He had only hastily scrubbed the blood and ice from his body, changed, and come to find her.

"I saw blood earlier," she said.

He leaned his cheek into her palm and closed his eyes for a heartbeat. "It was minor."

"You were hurt."

"Nothing herbs couldn't heal."

She studied him for a moment longer and then almost reluctantly said, "I was worried."

He took her hand and brought it to his lips, kissing her knuckles. "All I could think about from the moment I left you in my chamber was getting back. To you."

Manu knew he had said too much when he felt her retreat. She didn't pull away physically, but there was no doubt that a wall had come down between them—one that hadn't been there before. His feelings for her were growing into something serious and lasting. And yet, he couldn't forget that she didn't believe in love.

He glanced behind her and saw the plated food. "I interrupted your meal."

"I promise, I didn't mind," she replied with a grin.

"Let me fix a plate, and we can eat together."

She withdrew her hand, and he wanted to call it back. He couldn't rush her. There was a good chance that what he felt was real, and he knew she felt something for him. It might not be love —yet—but he was willing to take it as slowly as she needed. Because he wasn't giving up on her.

They walked to the table together, taking their usual seats across from each other. He focused on his food instead of shoving it off the table and laying her across the surface so he could take her again. She was addictive. Every second in her presence left him needing more.

"Can you tell me what called you away?" she asked.

He swallowed the bite and set down his fork. "Some tribes have no desire to know who might be in the Peaks or why. That isn't how we do things in Navara. I've always kept an eye on the mountains and who might be trekking across them—especially if they come from the lowlands."

"That's how you knew I was out there."

"Indeed. We keep an eye on anyone coming from the lowlands in case they get into trouble. More often than not, they do. Others, coming from the other directions, do so for several reasons. Trade, visiting, or aggression."

She paused with the food halfway to her mouth. "Which was it this time?"

"We noticed a group from the lowlands a few days ago. They weren't..." He trailed off, wondering how much to tell her.

"Weren't what?" she pressed.

He flattened his lips. "Friendly."

"They attacked you?" she asked, her eyes widening in alarm.

"They did after we stopped them from continuing deeper into the Peaks, aye."

Her brow creased in a frown. "Do you often stop people from traveling?"

If he weren't so tired—yet wired—he wouldn't have let the conversation get this far, but it was too late now. "They weren't a group of travelers. They were mercenaries who got too close to Navara. They attempted to take me, but things didn't work out too well for them."

"Take you?" she repeated, her face frozen in disbelief.

Manu rubbed his forehead. He hadn't wanted her to know that the Masters were so close. "They won't get into Navara. I won't allow it. None of my people will be taken. That includes you."

"You're talking about the Masters. Daas mentioned them."

He pushed his plate away, no longer hungry. "What do you call the group abducting people in the lowlands?"

"I've not heard them called anything."

The Masters had kept themselves hidden for a long time, but now that Manu and his friends were causing havoc, their name was spreading—as was word about their organization. Maybe it hadn't reached Belanore.

He rose, grabbed a bottle of wine and two goblets from the sideboard, and brought them to the table. He filled both glasses and handed one to Inej, then sat once more. "Their organization is large, and their reach is far and wide."

"Even in the Peaks?"

"In a manner of speaking. They had a place in the mountains once."

"Shaldorn?"

His heart thudded in his chest as she casually dropped the name few were aware of. He and other Mountain Elves had known of its existence for decades, but he'd been unable to get inside to do anything about it. It was only after Yasmin escaped and he found her that he had learned the true horrors of the place.

Yasmin was the first and only human to escape Shaldorn and live to talk about it. Even those who managed to get free when he and his friends shut it down had disappeared into the lowlands, hoping the Masters never found them. They wouldn't speak of it to anyone. So, how did Inej know about Shaldorn?

"How did you hear about that?" he asked, keeping his voice casual despite his tense muscles.

Had he been wrong to trust Inej? Was she a spy sent to...to what? Kill him? She had saved his life. If she wanted him dead, she would've let the assassin's blade find him. Still, he waited for her answer.

"I clean for the wealthy, remember? I overhear things," she answered.

She didn't display any hesitation or nervousness that he could see. Maybe he was overreacting. "Just one family?"

"Many. I work for an agency that places us. I've not been lucky enough to find one place to remain."

"Do you remember which family you heard talking about Shaldorn?"

She shifted nervously in her chair. "You're making me anxious. Am I not supposed to know about it?"

Instead of answering, he asked, "Did the family speak about what Shaldorn was?"

Inej gave a quick shake of her head.

He downed the wine and refilled his glass, wary now. "The ruins are quite a ways from Navara. It's why I wasn't aware of its construction. It sits atop one of the lower peaks, shielding it from view. By the time the tribes learned of it, the project was already complete. There was only one way in and one way out, and only those with invites gained access."

"Invites?" she asked in confusion.

He was edgy, tense. He couldn't help but wonder if his desires had overshadowed caution. If Inej were an elf, he wouldn't have been so lax. He was more grateful than ever that the children were with the Dragon Kings and far from the Masters' reach.

Manu couldn't sit any longer. He rose and walked to the wall, leaning a shoulder against it as he swirled the wine in the goblet in an effort to conceal his unease. "They built a road. Every so often, dozens of carriages would make their way to the stronghold. The walls were high and thick with few windows. Everything was kept contained within, so we had no way of knowing what went on inside. It was only after I found a half-frozen human female named Yasmin that I learned the truth."

"Which was?" Inej urged when he paused.

He took a long pull of wine. "Evil. Pure evil. A Moon Elf had lured Yasmin there with the promise of a better life. What she got was enslavement. Hundreds of humans were brought there. Put to work cleaning, cooking, and serving."

"Why do I get the feeling the *serving* you're referring to isn't meals?"

"Because it wasn't. Those who received invitations, all had particular proclivities they couldn't slake anywhere else. The stronghold gave it to them. Anything they wanted, anytime. And I do mean anything. Shaldorn was the secret playground of the wealthy elite. They did a good job of hiding it, but word eventually leaked, and others began asking questions and digging for information."

She nodded to him. "You mean you asked questions."

"I remained in the mountains, keeping an eye on the comings and goings at Shaldorn while also making sure no one ever got close to Navara. Others more adept at uncovering secrets got to work. Those individuals came up with a plan, and with Yasmin's help, they got into the stronghold. I was on the outside, waiting to help if they needed it, which they did. We were victorious in shutting down Shaldorn, but that wasn't the end of things. We soon discovered that the Masters had been the ones abducting people, and they ran Shaldorn. They didn't take our meddling well. They learned who had been involved in closing down the stronghold and put a price on our heads. All except for me. They didn't know about me until recently."

Inej raised her brows. "What are you going to do?"

"Fight to my dying breath."

She looked down at the table and folded her hands in her lap. "Now I understand your suspicion when I brought up Shaldorn. You think I'm with them."

"Are you?"

"You think they would turn to a human for help?" she asked with a grin.

He didn't return her smile. He couldn't. Because he feared she was a spy, even as he reminded himself that she had saved his life. He couldn't discount the things he had overlooked before.

She pushed back her chair and stood before walking around the table to stand before him. He straightened from the wall and stared down into her beautiful face. Not even the worry that she might be with the enemy dampened his desire. Not one iota.

Inej held his gaze. "I'm a nobody who often went without meals to keep a roof over my head. I walked amid the wealthy, cleaning their messes and straightening their homes. Plenty of times, I had opportunities to steal something that would have fed me for a month, but I didn't. I kept my head down and worked, doing my best to get through each day. If you think I'm with the enemy, then you should've left me to the wolvites."

"If I had done that, I never would've learned the taste of your kiss or discovered how good it feels to be inside you."

Her gaze dropped to his mouth, and he saw her pulse quicken in her neck. "Don't do that."

"Do what? Be honest?"

"Change the subject."

He set his goblet on the table and moved closer to her. Her eyes lifted to his again, exposing the passion in her that ran as hot as his. He should keep the conversation on her past, but his body had other ideas. "Tell me you aren't thinking of my cock inside you. Tell me you don't want my mouth on your breast or my finger teasing your clit."

Her throat bobbed as she swallowed. "I...can't."

The air crackled with sexual tension as they stared at each other.

She grabbed his head and pulled it down to her. Right before her lips touched his, she said, "I'm not your enemy."

He wrapped his arms around her as he molded her to his body, kissing her deeply. He hoped to hell she wasn't. Because even if she *were* an enemy, he couldn't stay away from her. He was in too deep, and there was no way out for him.

27

Belanore

The balcony doors were open, allowing the sounds of the city below to drift up to the tower's top floor. Gita stood in front of the floor-length mirror and studied her reflection, turning one way and then the other to look at her new royal blue gown. It was adorned with white and silver beads that made her icy blue eyes almost glow.

She looked down and adjusted the skirt, running her hands along her trim waist and the exposed section of skin at her stomach, then to the top that began right under her breasts. She flicked her long, blue hair back and froze when her gaze locked on One's reflection in the mirror.

Gita lifted a brow. "An audacious move, entering my room."

He remained silent as he stared, his expression giving nothing away. She had chosen him to work at Shaldorn because he never let his emotions rule him. One was...well, he was exceptional. And unique. His violent streak rivaled hers. Moreover, he had been loyal and dependable in keeping the workers in line. Even Two and Three had given him a wide berth—which was saying something.

She thought she knew him. He had never attempted to get into her bed or wrest away control of Shaldorn. He had known his place and remained in it. Yet the dynamic between them had shifted since they'd left the stronghold. She couldn't name the exact place or time for *when* the change had happened, but it had. Her greatest concern was that, somewhere over the weeks, she had gone from being the one in charge to *him* commanding *her*.

And she didn't like it.

Gita turned to face him. One always dressed impeccably. She had seen him garbed in clothes that bordered on feminine at times, the attire of a warrior at others. No matter how he dressed, it was done to impress. She had never been able to figure out his clothing choices. Today, a tunic in soft gray draped pleasingly over his torso, and charcoal gray trousers encased his trim hips and long legs. The pieces were simple and unembellished, but the cloth was luxurious.

He had a talent of altering his looks in a blink—with or without clothes. But One's greatest achievement was the stony face he displayed now. There was no way to tell what he was thinking or why he had come. And that instantly put her on edge.

Their staring challenge continued. Gita might be alone, but she could more than handle herself. She hadn't climbed to her lofty position within the Masters' ranks by being a pretty face. She had gotten her hands dirty, and she wasn't above doing it again. Besides, she hadn't wasted those years with One. She had watched him, learned his techniques so she could anticipate his reactions should he ever challenge her.

Minutes ticked by as neither uttered a word nor moved an inch. Had he come to kill her? Gita didn't think so. If the Masters wanted her dead, they would've extinguished her life after Shaldorn, instead of putting her in the tower. They knew how valuable she was. So, what was One's problem?

She caved first. He would stand there for days if she let this continue. "What do you want?"

"Did you think the Masters wouldn't find out about Inej?"

Gita rolled her eyes as she laughed. "I took initiative. She's a human. So what if I sent her to find a Mountain Elf? If she makes it, Manu will never expect her to betray him. He's a do-gooder who helps others."

"And Inej was the perfect bait."

Gita grinned as she drew in a breath and slowly released it. "Admit it. You're upset I came up with a perfect plan before you."

"Who is Manu?"

She had been waiting to see if One would ask that. If he hadn't, it meant he had already known about Manu, and, therefore, had been working against her. She studied him for a long moment before answering. "He helped Ravi and the others at Shaldorn."

"I didn't see him. And you never mentioned him."

"New information came to me."

One hadn't so much as blinked yet. "And you believed sending Inej to the Peaks would get you out of the tower?"

"I don't belong here!" she bellowed, her control snapping at his arrogance. She wasn't meant to be confined or restrained. If she didn't get out soon, she would lose her place with the Masters.

One's purple eyes narrowed slightly.

Gita looked away as she rested her hands on her hips. How she hated it when her anger got the better of her. If a male did it, he was strong. *She* was always labeled as unstable. Gita had learned to control that part of her years ago. However, being locked away and forgotten in the damn tower had cracked the façade she had built around herself. She had to get out. Needed to remind the Masters why she was still relevant.

"My servants were friends. When one of them was taken, I saw a prime opportunity." She swung her head to One. "You would've done the same."

He crossed his arms over his chest and widened his stance. "Perhaps. You disobeyed a direct order, however."

"If I can get Manu, it won't matter, and you know it. He was instrumental in helping Yasmin and Ravi bring down Shaldorn. They all deserve to feel the full weight of the Masters' retribution. *My* retribution."

"You sound certain about Manu."

She preened. Let him wonder where she got the information.

"And if you fail?" he asked.

She lifted one shoulder in a shrug. "No one else has gotten close to any of those on the list."

"The Masters haven't changed their minds about letting you out."

"They will. Wait and see."

He chuckled. The sound grated on her already frayed nerves. One was handsome and magnetic, but his smile never quite reached his eyes. Few realized that, however, as they were taken in by other parts of him. *She* had noticed.

She always noticed.

"They will," Gita insisted. "I'll take my place and run the new Shaldorn."

"Indeed."

It was her turn to narrow her eyes. "You want the position, don't you?"

"Do I?" he replied in a soft voice.

It immediately made her hackles rise. "Odd how you were at Shaldorn with me, but I'm the only one locked in this fucking tower."

"Shaldorn was yours. You made that known far and wide. When things went as planned, you got all the credit. It's only right that when it all went to shite, you took all the blame."

"Tell me, One, how is it you survived when Two and Three didn't?"

"Tell me, Gita, how is it you came out alive?" he retorted icily.

Anger erupted in her chest, spewing violence and aggression. Magic was in her palms before she had time to think about it. If she thought she could kill One, she'd end his life right then. It wasn't time for that, though. Yet. "Get out."

"This isn't your home, where you can order me about. This is a safehouse. A place the Masters have placed you. I am your contact to the outside world. Your *only* contact."

She sneered at him. "Hardly."

"Oh, you mean the servants? One was abducted, and you sent the second away. I've had to find replacements. I wouldn't bother talking to them, though. They won't be able to respond to you. In *any* way."

Gita wanted to scream in outrage, but the ice in her veins froze her to the spot.

"You went against the Masters," One repeated calmly. "How did you think that would go for you?"

"I'm trying to *help* them," she declared.

One dropped his arms to his sides. "They were about to release you."

She jerked back, his words like a slap. "You're lying."

"Am I?"

"Why didn't you tell me?" she demanded.

He turned on his heel without a word. She stumbled forward a step to follow, her mind refusing to accept what she had heard.

"One? Why didn't you tell me?" she repeated.

He said nothing as he walked.

"One!"

He opened the door.

"ONE!"

He shut the door, cutting off Gita's scream, and stood in the hallway, taking a deep, satisfying breath before walking to the lift. She wouldn't come after him. Even if that's what she wanted to do. Her fear of the Masters and what they might do kept her inside.

He leaned against the back wall of the lift and closed his eyes as it made its way to the main floor. His body needed rest, but he had another appointment to keep first. Maybe he would be able to find a moment or two to sleep afterward.

The bell dinged, announcing his arrival. He opened his eyes and straightened before striding into the building's lobby. As usual, there was no one in sight, but he always prepared himself, just in case. He never let his guard down when he wasn't in his space. He hadn't survived this long by being reckless.

He walked for three blocks and crossed two streets before hailing a hack. "Reader Temple," he bade the driver.

The carriage lurched forward as the horses began walking. He kept the curtains open to allow for airflow. Being inside the carriage was too confining, but it was the quickest way to get through the crowded city. He sat with his hands on his thighs and concentrated on his breathing.

A bead of sweat ran from his temple down his cheek and into the collar of his tunic. He wanted to shove the door open and jump out, but he didn't give in to such rash displays of emotion. Ever. They never served a purpose other than to announce someone's fears and inadequacies. And it would also draw attention to him. Today, he wanted to blend in and not be seen. That meant he had to endure the horror of the carriage.

It suddenly slowed and then came to a stop. He drew in a breath and peered out the window. They were still quite a ways from the temple. The chilly breeze couldn't alleviate the stuffiness inside the carriage, making it difficult to breathe. He yanked at the already open curtains, hoping to cool his heated skin. He could get out. No one had to know why. No one would even think twice. But he stayed. Not because he didn't want to walk, but because he needed to push at his fear. He wouldn't let it be used against him again.

Instead of thinking about the heat or the enclosed space, he went through the Masters' voices, laying them out in a circle just as they had been in the chamber. Except this time, he was looking down at them. He had his suspicions about one of the Wood Elves. If he were lucky, he would soon learn the male's identity.

The carriage suddenly lurched forward again. One flexed his fingers on his thighs, the only show of relief he would allow himself. The rest of the ride to the temple went without incident. A steady breeze found its way into the carriage and caressed his heated skin.

By the time he reached his destination, he was as composed as he'd been when he entered the carriage. He flipped a coin to the driver and looked up the stairs of the building that was sacred to all elves. It might be the home of the Readers, but it was a place where everyone could connect with the sacred and divine. The temple's design symbolized the universe, encompassing both good and evil, as well as the elven experience.

The first time One had visited, he had pondered where he fit in the universe. The answer had come shortly afterward. Knowing didn't make things easier, however. In many instances, it made it more challenging.

The temple was powerful, not just because of its placement within the city center, but also because of its architecture. The central tower was a step pyramid supposed to resemble the mystical mountain home of the gods. Smaller towers were scattered around the grounds. He headed toward one of the gateways adorned with statues and carvings of the gods. As a boy, he had been mesmerized by the gateways so much that he had thought to become a sculptor himself.

He made his way to one of the sacred bodies of water used for purification before entering the temple. He did his prayers of absolution and got to his feet to proceed to the main sanctuary.

While various races of elves—and even some humans—were at the temple, the majority of those walking the grounds were

Readers in their white clothing. Each Sun Elf Reader had a bag tied to their belts, holding the special rune stones they used to divine answers and see the future.

He slipped between two enormous columns, his gaze scanning the many Readers until he found the one he sought: Savita.

28

Inej tried to turn over, but something weighed her down. She opened her eyes and found Manu on his stomach, using her chest as a pillow. He had one leg thrown over hers, and both arms wrapped around her middle.

She dropped her head back onto the mound of pillows behind her with a vague recollection of Manu throwing them onto the bed. She'd lost count of the number of times they'd had sex. There was the kitchen, twice in the tub, the hallway getting to the bedroom…but once they were on the bed, she'd lost count.

How had they gotten into this position? She didn't remember much after the last orgasm he'd wrung from her. This was why she didn't linger with her partners. She wasn't sure what to do now. She had to admit she was comfortable. In fact, she rather liked him against her.

She tentatively slid her fingers into his hair. Her other hand softly glided up to his shoulder from where it had rested on his arm. No one had to know she was touching him—or enjoying this quiet moment. She shouldn't want it—not with the kind of elf he was. But her traitorous body couldn't refuse him.

Lying in bed with Manu was what a lover would do. It's what she should do as an undercover agent. Why then did she feel so guilty?

She thought back to dinner and how she had nearly blown her cover by asking about Shaldorn. His entire demeanor had changed the moment she spoke the word. He'd become guarded, cautious. The way his eyes had hardened had sent a foreboding chill down her spine. She had recovered quickly, but she couldn't afford to make that kind of mistake again.

Yet that wasn't what bothered her. She couldn't stop thinking about his story about Shaldorn. He'd sounded so believable. The way his voice had trembled with anger when he spoke about Shaldorn's purpose had been genuine.

Who did she believe? Gita, whom she barely knew? Or Manu, who she also barely knew? How could she untangle the truth?

The one thing she knew for certain was that everyone lied. Uncovering who was being dishonest this time wouldn't be simple or easy. Manu had sounded heartfelt while telling his story. But it was more than that. It was the way he'd described what went on at the stronghold that troubled her the most.

Had she been too hasty in trusting Gita? Possibly. She had been drowning in the guilt and shame of how she'd treated Krata, and Gita had given her the answers she needed and a way to get revenge. Even if Inej knew it had been a fool's errand from the very beginning.

As if a human could stand against an elf. Especially one like Manu.

Where did that leave her, then? She couldn't come clean to

Manu, in case he was the one responsible for the abductions. Did she remain and keep up the pretense? This was the first time she'd had money, and she was doing something she loved. Not to mention, if Manu *was* the one controlling the abductions, she was safe in his city.

On the other hand, she could leave. Manu had offered to take her back to the lowlands. What then? It wasn't as if she wanted to return to her cleaning job. Nor could she go to Gita, in case she *had* lied. There was Rannora, or one of the other smaller settlements in the rainwood, but she would have to live hand to mouth again.

She had gotten herself into a problematic situation with no clear path to truth or freedom. Her gaze lowered to Manu. At the moment, she had nothing to gripe about, however. If only she knew the facts. When she was with him, it was easy to believe him, to accept everything around her. She could even forget things for a little while. Inevitably, something would make her think of Krata or the poison, though, and she would remember all over again why she was in Navara—and why Manu was in her bed.

She nestled into the pillows and closed her eyes. The next time she woke, she was alone. The place beside her was cold to the touch, which told her that Manu had been gone for some time. A sound from the kitchen drew her attention. She swung her legs over the side of the bed and stood. She spotted Manu's tunic on the way to the door and slipped it over her head. It hung to the tops of her thighs, and the sleeves were so long they fell past her hands, making her need to shove them up to her elbows.

She cautiously made her way to the kitchen and peeked around the corner to find him at the stove in nothing but his trousers. Inej silently admired him and the play of muscles as he moved.

He looked up then, a smile pulling at his lips. His dark eyes held a warmth that made her breath catch. "Morning," he said.

Her lips moved of their own accord, effortlessly returning the grin. Warning bells went off in her head, telling her that she was letting her guard down. "Good morning."

"You weren't supposed to wake up."

"Were you trying to slip out?" she teased. She turned her face away to hide her grimace. She didn't tease. What was wrong with her?

He chuckled as he walked to her. "On the contrary. I intended to bring you breakfast before you went into the shop."

"You were...?" Her brain seized, making words impossible. No one had ever done that for her.

He looked down at her and slid his hand around the back of her neck, his thumb moving softly back and forth along her jaw. "Aye. But seeing you in my tunic has my mind turning to other things."

The monster she'd come to the mountains believing him to be wasn't meshing with who she was getting to know. People had secrets and often showed the world what they thought others wanted to see. Is that what he was doing?

"I shouldn't have kept you up so late," Manu said.

"I played a significant part in that, too."

His crooked smile made her heart skip a beat. "So you did."

She curled her hands into fists when he turned away so the food wouldn't burn. Inej couldn't take her eyes off him as he finished cooking and plated their meal. Images of their night kept replaying in her head, making it even more difficult to extract the truth.

He moved behind her, his fingers trailing over her arse. They exchanged a smile and, plates in hand, turned toward the dining room. They didn't get two steps before the side door opened, and Chanda walked in with a beautiful elf. Both Chanda and her friend looked from Manu to Inej, and then down at the tunic she wore. She fought the urge to move behind him so they would stop staring.

"Oh," Chanda said, casting a distressed look at the other elf.

Manu didn't seem fazed by their arrival. "Chanda. Tahmine." Manu then put his hand on Inej's back and gave her a slight push as he said, "Your food is getting cold."

There was no mistaking the hurt look on Tahmine's face. Inej turned the corner to the dining area and took her seat.

"I'm sorry about that," Manu said.

"Is she yo—?"

"Nay," he said before she could finish. "Never. It was casual."

Inej glanced at the doorway, thinking of the elf.

"I made it very clear on my part that there was nothing serious between us. She agreed to it," he added.

Tahmine had likely acquiesced, hoping he might change his mind. Inej didn't tell Manu that. She could tell by his darkening expression that he had already figured it out.

"Tahmine wasn't supposed to be here. Chanda shouldn't have brought her."

Inej reached across the table and put her hand on his. She waited until his gaze met hers. "You need to talk to Tahmine."

"I know," he said with a sigh. "This isn't how I wanted your day to start."

"Don't worry about me."

He tilted his head to the side, considering her with his dark eyes. "You aren't angry?"

"At what? Someone walking into a house that isn't mine? We aren't a couple."

"I suppose not," he said carefully.

She was talking like Inej and not an agent. If she wanted the truth, that meant she had to get it any way she could. She wanted the kidnappings to stop, but she didn't want to take an innocent man's life. She swallowed and tried again. "I'm a human, and you're an elf."

"That matters because...?" He arched a thick brow.

"As your tribe's leader, your people expect you to take an elf as your wife."

He set down his fork. "What if I've found someone else I want?"

Inej panicked at his words. Her heart began to race as she fought for a response. "You don't know me."

"I have a pretty good idea of who you are after last night."

Inej swallowed and sat back, letting her hand slide from his. "You don't know me," she repeated.

"I know your body. I know the place on the back of your neck that makes you shiver. I know that your nipples are incredibly sensitive. I know just how much pressure to use on your clit to make you cum." He rose and walked around the table to kneel beside her. He turned her chair so she faced him. "Tell me you don't feel the same draw to me."

Her lips parted, but the words wouldn't come.

"Inej, I wa—"

Some loud banging on the door drowned out his words.

Manu's brows snapped together as he jumped up and strode out of the room. She didn't follow. She wasn't sure her legs would hold her. Not after his declaration. She heard voices, and a moment later, Manu was in the doorway, pulling on his boots.

"I have to go," he told her.

She got to her feet and held onto the table to stay upright. "What is it?"

"I'll be back as soon as I can." He was breathless as he rushed to her and pressed a kiss to her lips.

"Wait," she called as he turned to leave. "You need your shirt."

He flashed her a smile. "I'll get another."

Then he was gone. Leaving her alone in the house with Chanda and Tahmine. Inej looked at the food, but she couldn't eat it after their conversation and his quick departure. She should take the plates to the kitchen, but she wasn't in the mood for an exchange with the two elves. Inej made her way to the bathing room and cleaned Manu's smell from her body before dressing. Back in her room, she folded his tunic and left it on a chair. Then, she slipped out of the house, braiding her hair as she made her way to work.

She was early again, but she would rather wait there than at Jalall's. As soon as Daas arrived and let her in, she went to the back and gave herself up to the baking, whipping up one kind of pastry after another.

Work kept her hands and mind busy. The only time she thought about Manu was when she was idle. She knew she should probably consider how to respond to him when they next saw each other and picked up their conversation. He didn't seem the type to let things go without clearing the air. It felt as if she had been dropped into a game she had only been given partial rules to, and she was expected to figure it out as she went. The problem with that was that she was doing a bad job of it.

Inej reached for her bowl, only to find it gone. She turned in a circle, looking for it, only to see Shruti had washed it, and it was drying with the others. Which meant there was no more baking to be done. How had the day passed so quickly?

Inej glanced through the beaded curtain to the front, hoping to spot Manu, but there was no sign of him. She remembered the sight of the blood on him the last time he had returned. He'd said a group had tried to take him, but she realized now that they had attempted to *kill* him. Just as the Mountain Elf with the dagger had.

Just as she was meant to do with the poison.

She placed her hands on her stomach and doubled over. Gita wanted him dead. The Masters wanted him dead. How many more attempts could be made on his life before someone succeeded in killing Manu?

Inej was numb, her mind overloaded with bits of information she was trying to decipher and form into some semblance of truth as she helped close up the shop. Daas and Shruti kept asking if she was okay. It wasn't as if she could tell them the truth. She thought about it for a moment. Someone had to know something that might help her figure out if Gita was right about Manu. But in the end, Inej didn't chance it.

When she reached Jalall's, she hesitated for only a moment before entering. She quickened her steps when she heard sounds coming from deeper in the home, thinking it was Manu. She swallowed her disappointment when she found Chanda putting away some clothes.

They looked at each other before Inej pivoted and went to her chamber. She stood in the middle of the room, looking at the bed where she and Manu had shared endless hours of pleasure the night before. She sank onto the corner of the mattress and listened to Chanda moving about the house. Inej remained in the room until she heard the side door open and close, signaling that Chanda was gone. She left her room and walked through the house, looking into every room for a person who wasn't there.

29

menacing sky filled with dark, angry clouds hovered over Manu and his soldiers. Another storm was about to unleash upon them. Each of them was equipped to handle the volatile weather, but it wasn't the impending blizzard that vexed him. It was the letter from Jalall delivered that morning.

Or rather the note that *claimed* to be from his friend.

Manu pushed northeast. They'd had to put their snowblades on to trek through the thigh-deep snow. It was slow-going, but that was nothing new for any of them. Yet Manu chafed at their sluggish pace. Jalall was in trouble, and he needed to get to him quickly.

Navara and all those within the mountain were secure from any threats. Manu and his team were a different story. They kept off the peaks to remain out of sight, but that couldn't last forever. Eventually, they would have to cross a mountain, but he had chosen one with boulders to shield them the majority of the way. They just needed to reach it before the storm unleashed its fury.

He ducked his head against the ever-increasing wind and plowed forward, one foot in front of the other as bits of ice pelted any exposed skin. He raised the fur around his lower face as his thoughts turned to Inej. His body hungered for her as if he were starving. She was never far from his thoughts, and, worse, he couldn't stop seeking her out.

It didn't matter that she was human. Nay, what unsettled him was the nagging feeling that she knew more about Shaldorn and the Masters than she let on. At first, he'd thought he was being overly cautious and seeing enemies everywhere. Now, he wondered if he was falling for the enemy. Because he *was* falling for her. There was no getting around that fact.

Unease trickled over Manu. He halted and looked to his right up the slope, catching sight of someone just as they ducked behind a boulder. There was a shout from behind him. He looked over his shoulder and saw his team fending off an attack that came from their flank. He spun, dropping to one knee as he raised his hands and released a blast of magic from both palms to help his warriors.

He jerked around at the sound of a loud crack, expecting an attack from the front, but there was none. A sense of dread filled him when a second booming crack sounded. Manu looked up at the towering peak above them and saw the shelf of snow splitting in half. There was a moment of silence before the ridge broke off and thundered aggressively down the slope.

"Avalanche!" he shouted.

Everyone scattered as fast as their snowblades would let them. The safest place was just ahead, where a large overhang of rock could protect him, but there was no way he would get to it in time.

His next option was about fifty feet below. He wouldn't make that either.

Manu darted to his left, hoping to get clear. He heard his team yelling, but their voices were soon drowned out by the hissing of the snow, rock, ice, and soil as it rumbled swiftly and violently toward them.

He glanced toward the wave of white descending far too quickly and tried to brace himself by dropping to his knees and hugging his arms against his body. The impact was unforgiving, mercilessly sweeping him up in the snow and tossing him about. The world was white as it spun haphazardly. Snow was shoved into his mouth, nose, and ears as he tumbled inside the landslide.

His arms and legs were yanked in different directions, as if the snow were attempting to rip him apart. That pain was soon forgotten as he crashed into a rock, bending him backward until his head slammed against it. Agony radiated from the base of his skull and throughout his body as he was swept away once more and lost consciousness.

Manu gradually came to buried beneath the snow. His left arm was twisted awkwardly behind him. For several minutes, he didn't move as he tried to take stock of his body. The snow was pressed too close to his face. He needed room to breathe, but more than that, he needed to dig himself out. The problem was, he wasn't sure which way was up.

He shifted his right shoulder to dislodge some of the snow so he could wiggle the arm beneath him. Eventually, he was able to move his hand up near his chest. He then turned his palm outward and called to his magic, using only a fragment of it at a time to break through the ice to create space around him.

Once that was done, he drew in a deep breath. Time was

running out, though. He had no idea how long he had been buried. The longer he remained covered, the less likely his chances of survival. The space he created allowed him to turn over so he could attempt to lay on his back. That small movement sent spasms of pain through his twisted arm.

Manu clenched his teeth and gripped his injured arm with his other hand. Then he gradually righted the limb until it was against his abdomen. He realized he was breathing much too fast and attempted to slow his inhales and exhales until the worst of the discomfort had passed.

What he needed was herbs. He used his right hand to feel around him for the belt beneath his coat where he kept the herbs and a water flask. But it wasn't there. He lifted his head to look down and saw that his coat had been ripped apart, and the belt was gone. Not only didn't he have the herbs, but he also didn't have water.

This wasn't his first avalanche, nor was it the first time he had been buried. It also wasn't the first time he'd had items ripped from him. He blinked up at the snow above him, wondering if that was the way out, or if it was in another direction. It was impossible to tell.

He touched the back of his head and winced at the contact. When he pulled his fingers away, they were covered in blood. That explained his aching head. He had one good arm, his legs, and magic. That was all he needed to get free.

Manu pulled his knees up to him, only to bellow at the throbbing in his right ankle. He gripped his thigh and rode the worst of the pain until he could think clearly again. That pain was worse than his arm, which wasn't a good sign. His right hand shook as he lifted it and watched thick, bronze beams shoot from his palm in pulses as he carefully chipped away at the snow to create an arc over his legs.

When he got as far as he could, he returned his attention to the ice above him and made that area bigger so he could sit up. The act of rising was another excruciating moment that made his stomach roil dangerously. But once he was up, he saw the state of his ankle and the blood coloring the snow.

He stared at the bits of muscle and cartilage that kept his foot connected to his leg. His snowblades had been ripped off, which was likely the cause of his ankle injury. Getting free had just become that much harder. If he moved, he could lose his foot, but if he stayed, he would surely die. He suspected the avalanche hadn't been an accident. It didn't matter if it was the Masters' goons or mercenaries, someone wanted him dead. But they would have to do better. As long as he was breathing, he was fighting.

Manu tugged off what remained of his coat, then used his hands to scoot himself closer to his injured ankle. He had to bind it somehow, and the only thing he had was his jacket. He took a deep breath and leaned forward. Sweat beaded his brow from the agony the simple movement caused.

Since he only had the use of one arm, he had to shift his leg a few inches to the left to use the snow to help hold up his foot so he could work with his right hand. It seemed simple enough until his muscles tightened, and he tried to lift his leg.

Manu fought against the rising bile and the black dots edging his vision. He couldn't lose consciousness again. Every second was one closer to death. If he stopped, if he gave up, it was over.

Little by little, he moved his leg to where he needed it. Next came lifting his foot. By hand.

He did it in one motion. Manu swallowed his shout of pain,

focusing on his breathing instead to stay conscious. He had two of the three steps completed. Now, all he had to do was wrap his coat around his foot to keep it in place. All of which was harder than he'd anticipated. It took four attempts before he found a way to not only hold his foot but also keep the coat in place. It was fine now, but it wouldn't hold up while walking.

It was getting harder to breathe. He could wait no longer. He had to start digging himself out. Manu looked up at the snow packed above him. It seemed the logical place to start. If that way was up. He didn't feel as if he were upside down, but he was disoriented, in pain, and quickly running out of air.

He adjusted his position as magic filled his palm. He directed it at an angle above him in case the snow and ice fell in—at least it wouldn't fall directly on his head. As he worked, he pictured Inej baking with flour on her face, her brown eyes alight with contentment. She was a different woman when she was in her element. She glowed from within. Baking was her passion, her calling. That was when she let her guard down. It was also the first time he had seen her smile. It hadn't been a bright one, but one of inner joy. A true smile that lit her from within.

What would become of her if he didn't make it back? Would she remain in Navara? Would she miss him?

An hour into digging, and Manu had made little progress. He increased the amount of magic he used, but that in and of itself brought dangers of a cave-in. He didn't know if the rest of his team was even alive. They might be waiting on him. Then there was Jalall and his men waiting for his help.

Manu dropped his arm to his side. The air was too thin. He wasn't going to make it. There was no way around that. He had so many things he wanted to say to Inej that would never get said now. He fell back into the snow, his gaze locking on the small hole he had made in the ice. He could be three inches from freedom or three feet. It was impossible to tell.

Any others from Navara who came looking for them would see the evidence of the avalanche and put the pieces together, but without a leader, it was likely no one would go after Jalall. His eyes were getting heavy. Too bad there wasn't a way for Dain to find him.

A thought attempted to intrude. Manu focused on it, but everything was hazy. Then he remembered. Gathering the last of his strength, he called out, "Rhi."

Iron Hall

Rhi found a stash of freshly baked bread and stole a loaf. She brought it to her nose and inhaled the wonderful, yeasty aroma. Her stomach rumbled with hunger. She was eating for two now and couldn't seem to stop stuffing her face. Con kept saying how adorable it was. Though he hadn't found it so cute when she refused to share her food with him the night before.

"We'll see if he finds me adorable when I'm the size of a house," she whispered before pulling off a section of bread and stuffing it into her mouth.

She was chewing when she heard her name being called and recognized Manu's voice. She forgot about the bread and teleported to Con in the great hall of the underground city. He was in the middle of a conversation with several other Dragon Kings when he caught sight of her and stopped mid-sentence.

"It's Manu. He called to me. Something's wrong. I hear it in his voice," she alerted him before teleporting to the Mountain Elf's location on the side of a frozen mountain. She wouldn't usually take that small amount of time, but with her carrying their child, she owed it to both of them to let him know where she was going.

The moment the frigid wind whipped into her, she used her magic to create some attire to keep herself warm. She stared in shock at the destruction from the avalanche in all directions. Her gaze snagged on fur poking through the snow thirty feet away.

Rhi dropped to her knees and began digging, her magic having taken her directly to Manu. When her fingers became too numb, she used magic, but she never stopped. She should've brought Con with her, because she was afraid Manu might need Con's ability to heal.

Her muscles strained as she shoved aside ice, going deeper and deeper as she revealed more of the fur that she soon recognized as a coat. Then, she spotted the dark splotches of blood and quickened her pace. A few moments later, and she uncovered his leg. Her breath puffed around her as she worked until she finally uncovered his face.

30

The house was too quiet. Everywhere Inej looked, she saw Manu. There wasn't a room she could be in that didn't have a memory of him. She didn't want to think about him—or their conversation from that morning—but that was all that was on her mind.

She stared at her bed for a long time, recalling how he had fallen asleep on her. She had liked it. Too much, actually. There was even a memory of him tugging her onto his chest. At least she thought he had. It might have been a dream. How was she going to climb into that bed now when his memory was all around her?

Worse, what would she say when he returned? He would want to finish their conversation, and she wanted to know what he had been about to say. What did he want? Was it her? The thought filled her with both excitement and dread.

She needed to start with what *she* wanted. That was easy. She wanted the abductions to cease and for those responsible to be caught and punished. Therein lay the problem. Because Manu might be one of those people.

"What if he is?" she asked herself. Inej shrugged. "Then justice should be served. But if he isn't...?"

Gita had every reason to lie. Everyone *always* had some reason to lie.

Inej leaned against the doorjamb to her room, her gaze still on the bed. What if Gita had lied? She had said elves couldn't get to the Peaks, but based on what Manu had said, they came all the time. If Gita was dishonest about that, the only conclusion Inej could come to was that Gita had needed her to find Manu. Because he helped humans who were stranded.

It sounded reasonable, but that was assuming Manu was honest.

If he was everything Gita said, why be so nice to her? She was no one. Why not put her with all the others he kidnapped? Why take her to his city, give her food, shelter, and clothing? And a job she loved. Why take her to his bed and tell her the story of Shaldorn?

Maybe to see if she was working for the other side?

That, too, sounded plausible.

How would she ever figure out the truth? She couldn't exactly lay it out to Manu to see what he might say. Nor could she ask around. Manu's people were loyal. It would get back to him, which would be like her asking him herself. She also couldn't check the things Gita had told her. Even if she had thought about questioning Gita before heading out to the Peaks, she likely wouldn't have gotten answers. Inej wouldn't have known who to ask or how to prove if any of it were true.

She had gotten tangled in a snare so thick and unclear that she wasn't sure she could untangle herself. She could leave, but that would only save her for a short time. If the wolvites or weather didn't get her, she was sure the Masters would. Her one and only choice was to remain in Navara. Yet, it felt wrong.

The click of the front door opening yanked her from her musings. Manu was back, and she was no closer to knowing how to finish their conversation than before. She looked down the hall to the door, expecting to see someone, but the corridor was empty. A shiver of apprehension slid down her back.

A cacophony of voices rose from outside the house. She hurried to the door and yanked it open to see a crowd gathering. Shock reverberated through the mass. She stepped out onto the landing to see what was happening when the wailing began as it had the previous night. Inej steeled herself as she gathered with others along the street to watch the procession of elves carrying stretchers with unmoving bodies.

One passed right in front of her. She couldn't take her eyes off the clusters of ice or the bluish tint to the skin. The elf was dead. Were they the ones who had left with Manu? She swung her head back to the entrance, fully expecting to see him coming in covered in blood again. She studied every face on the stretchers, silently rejoicing when none was his.

There was one more stretcher being carried in. She thought to see Manu walking beside it. Instead, she found him on it. The men carrying him hurried past her, giving her only a glimpse of his face with his eyes closed. His skin was pale, but it didn't have the bluish tint. And they were racing him to his house. But there had been so much blood in his hair and on his face.

"What happened?" she asked, hoping someone would tell her.

But everyone seemed to be as shocked as she. With the last of the dead and wounded brought in, people began preparing for funerals. She stood helplessly, watching it all. She wanted to do something, but she didn't know any of the families to help with the burials. Her head turned to Manu's home. Would they let her in if she went to him?

She didn't want to try to find out. Inej returned to Jalall's house and softly shut the door. She leaned her forehead against it as Manu's image flashed in her head: him lying so still and bloodied. He had always been larger than life and strong. He might get hurt, but nothing serious. She turned and put her back to the door. He wasn't dead. Nor would he die. He was the leader of Navara, and his people needed him.

You came to kill him.

The thought came unbidden. Inej put a hand to her belly and another over her mouth as she closed her eyes. She *had* come to end his life. The poison was still tucked under her mattress, waiting.

The hate and anger that had driven her into the mountains had simmered to banked coals. She was confused. The facts were muddied. How could she take someone's life—anyone's—without knowing if they were responsible for the abductions? The doubt would eat her alive. Some undercover agent she'd turned out to be.

She dropped her arms and pushed away from the door, needing to do something to occupy her time until she could get word about Manu. A long bath might help. Then, she'd get into bed early. She likely wouldn't sleep while worrying about him, but the attempt had to count for something.

Inej was halfway to her room when she heard someone behind her. She started to turn when she saw a flash of bronze magic right before it slammed into her. The force had her careening into the wall, where she bounced off and into the other side of the hall as another strike brought her to the floor.

Her mind screamed for her to get up and run. Something was burning. Debris was falling around her as if in slow motion. She looked toward the kitchen and used her arms to pull herself toward it. Footfalls thumped ominously behind her. Her attacker was still there and coming to finish the job.

She didn't try to see who it was. It didn't matter. There was no way she was getting out of this alive. Her fingers curled against the smooth stone floor, and she dug in as much as possible, pulling her body forward. She had been hit, but oddly, she didn't feel any pain. Maybe she was already dead and just didn't know it.

A boot pressed into her back, pushing her down and ending her pathetic attempt at escape. She was the only human in the city. How else had she expected this to turn out? She had believed she was safe because Manu had said she was. She knew better than to get comfortable, and she was paying for that now.

Her cheek was pressed to the cool stone, and she found her gaze falling into her room and onto the bed, where the previous night had been the closest thing to paradise she had experienced.

Suddenly, the boot was gone. She heard the reverberations of someone running, but it didn't matter. Nothing mattered anymore. At least now, she no longer had the weight of whether to take Manu's life. Death tended to erase such complications.

She heard a voice as if from a great distance. She couldn't tell much about it, and there was no point in answering. Her eyes closed of their own accord, and she felt herself drifting.

Something nudged her side before shoving her onto her back. She was yanked back to the living by the pain that ratcheted through her body. There had been no pain in the place where she'd drifted. There was just darkness and quiet. That's where she wanted to be. She clung to it, pushing the agony away.

A voice came, joined by a second. Was there a third? She couldn't bring herself to care. They weren't attempting to help her, and that was okay. They were her killers. Her soul still lingered, though she wasn't sure why. She was ready to go and get away from the horrors.

Not everything had been bad. There had been Manu.

The pain was there, but it was fading, becoming a distant memory.

31

The chaos was overwhelming as elves ran about getting Manu to his chamber and onto his bed. Rhi kept herself veiled since the only one she knew was Manu, and she didn't want to find out how the elves might greet an outsider who just popped into their home without them being any the wiser.

She wasn't completely ignorant of their race. Esha had been very forthcoming about elves and Shecrish, in general, but that didn't mean Rhi knew everything. The harried, distraught faces of those in the room told her she needed to be worried about Manu. She could get Con and be back in a flash. Well, not exactly that quickly. He would want to know what was going on, and rightly so. Those were minutes she wasn't sure Manu had.

But Con could heal him with a touch. At least, she hoped Con could. Rhi stayed out of the way in a corner as she looked from face to face.

"We need a Healer," someone said.

It didn't seem to be a command, but rather a statement. The

kind that meant they didn't have someone there who could heal Manu. Dain might know what to do, but she had no idea where to find him.

"Found them!" another elf said after opening a drawer and holding up a jar of herbs.

Those looked like the magical herbs Esha had shown her. They were just as effective as the...she winced, unable to remember which of the races could heal. It didn't matter. The herbs could work. They just had to get them into Manu.

Rhi watched the men and women crowded around Manu's bed work to get the herbs, now in water, down his throat. He hadn't woken or even stirred. He was breathing, at least. Which he hadn't been when she first found him. She had done the only thing she could think of by jumping to Navara and whispering in a few guards' ears that Manu was in danger. It had taken them longer than she would've liked to heed her suggestion and head out to look for him, but they had eventually found him and dug up the rest of his party. Sadly, he was the only survivor.

Her attention moved to the doorway as another elf ran in, breathing hard. He slid to a stop at the sight of Manu.

"I need an update," the elf demanded as he took a tentative step forward.

"Jalall," a female said, surprise causing her voice to rise.

He looked at her. "What happened?"

"There was an avalanche," one of the males replied. "He's alive, but barely."

"He went in search of you," another stated.

Jalall's forehead crinkled as he raked a hand through his short, dark hair. "We were attacked on our way back, which delayed us."

The room grew quiet as Jalall moved closer to the bed, his gaze locked on Manu. Worry bracketed his mouth and furrowed his brow. The two must be close. Given the way the others deferred to Jalall, that made sense.

Suddenly, Jalall looked up and scanned the room. "Where's Inej?"

No one answered, but he also didn't wait to hear any responses. He ran from the room. Rhi had so many questions, and she wouldn't get any answers from Manu anytime soon. Jalall, however, might just give her what she needed. She slipped past some elves and raced after him.

He strode with purpose out of Manu's home. Others took one look at him and hastened to get out of his way. Rhi followed two steps behind him. Whoever he was, he seemed to be someone who was at least partly in charge. She glanced around her, taking note of the light coming in from above and reflected in mirrors, giving the otherwise dark places luminosity. There were plants, as well, but it was the homes cut into the mountain that impressed her. The road system, along with the bridges over the river, and the stairs leading to the various levels above them, was well thought out. The Mountain Elves were self-sufficient and well hidden.

"Jalall!"

The elf drew up at his name. Rhi saw an older male running up, apprehension cut into the deep grooves of his face. Rhi knew each elven race had different coloring, but the Mountain Elves were the ones closest to looking human. Their skin ranged in color from as pale as hers to a light tan.

"Daas," Jalall said in greeting. "Can this wait?"

"I can't find Inej," the other elf stated.

A muscle in Jalall's jaw bunched. "I was going to check on her now."

"Mind if I tag along?"

Jalall motioned the elf along, and they continued. Rhi moved closer to the duo when she noted that their voices had lowered.

"How have things been here?" Jalall asked.

"Good. Quiet. Inej began working with me right after you left. She's been nothing but amazing."

Jalall grunted. "Has there been anything between her and Manu?"

"Aye. It was clear to anyone who looked. He took her to his home for dinner once that I know of."

Jalall's head snapped toward the elf, shock reflected on his face before he carefully hid it. "Did he?"

Rhi suspected Jalall had known about the children, but since he hadn't been there when Manu sent them away, he wouldn't know about her and Dain's arrival.

"Manu's interest in Inej was clear," Daas said. "Just as hers was in him."

"I saw that before I left." Jalall glanced over his shoulder.

Could he detect that someone was there? Rhi should put more distance between them, but she wanted to hear what they were saying.

"How is Manu?"

Jalall gave a quick shake of his head as they headed across one of the bridges. "He's alive but in bad shape. It's going to take time for him to heal."

"Do we have that kind of time?"

"I don't know."

Rhi hated not knowing what was going on. She was getting bits of the puzzle and trying to put them together, but she didn't have nearly enough. Her instinct was to get Con, but this was elven territory, and she wasn't sure how the Mountain Elves would take to the arrival of a Dragon King—even if he did come to help. So, she stayed and listened.

They headed to a large, dark house. Jalall went to the door first and stared at the handle for a moment. That's when Rhi saw that the door hadn't been closed all the way. Both Jalall and the other elf held out their hands, their magic at the ready. Rhi did the same. She might be invisible, but she would protect herself.

Jalall nudged the door open with his foot. The inside wasn't completely dark. A small light illuminated the first room, but there were still way too many shadows about for her liking.

"Inej!" Jalall shouted and raced down the hallway.

The elder elf ran with him. Rhi lingered as she turned in a circle. When no one jumped out at her, she teleported to the other end of the hall to shield them in case someone came out from that way. She glanced over her shoulder and saw Inej on her back, her clothes charred, and her skin bloody from an attack.

"Inej. Fuck." Jalall dropped down beside her. "Oh, fuck."

Rhi quickly moved about the house to make sure it was clear. She returned to the hallway to see both elves leaning over the human.

"She's barely breathing. Daas, get the herbs in my room, there," Jalall said and pointed to the right. "Third drawer."

The older elf ran into the room and searched for the herbs as Jalall gathered Inej into his arms and headed into a bedroom. Rhi followed, once more debating whether to get Con. If it were only Jalall, she might, but she didn't know Daas.

Con could heal Inej instantly. Well, if she wasn't dead. If she were no longer alive, there was nothing her mate could do. But if she brought Con, it could start a war. The Dragon Kings had their own issues to deal with. There was no need to add yet another thing to that ever-growing pile. Still, Rhi hesitated. Someone had attacked Inej. Those marks had been made by magic. Someone had gone after a human with no defenses, and that made Rhi want to hunt them down.

Daas raced back into the room with a small, cinched bag and a filled glass. He dumped a large amount of the herbs into the water and swished it around before kneeling on the opposite side of the bed from Jalall. The two elves worked silently to get the mixture down Inej's throat, much like the others had been doing with Manu. Was it a coincidence that they had both been attacked?

Dain and the rest of their crew needed to know, in case this was the Masters. Even if it wasn't the organization, they needed to be made aware of how close to death Manu had come.

Finally, Daas got to his feet and set the herbs and glass aside on a table. "Who would do this to her?"

"I've been asking myself that question. Has she clashed with anyone?"

"No one," Daas said with a shake of his head. "She spends her days at the shop baking and comes here when she's done."

Jalall dropped into one of the chairs. "Where Manu stayed with her. Fuck." He sighed and slumped backward. "He hadn't wanted to leave her alone in my house, and we didn't want to assign someone to her."

"If there was something budding between them, they had time alone. So what?" Daas said.

"Tahmine."

Rhi perked up at the name. It was good that Jalall already had a suspect.

"Surely not," Daas stated.

Jalall looked at Inej's still form. "Tahmine has made no secret of the fact that she's been in love with Manu. I warned him not to continue their affair. He told me he made sure she knew it was casual."

"You think she tried to kill Inej out of jealousy?"

Jalall slid his gaze to the elder elf. "Do you have another suggestion?"

"Well, then, we'd better find out the truth before Manu wakes and discovers Inej like this."

"Agreed. Can you stay with her?"

Rhi's lips parted, ready to jump in with a warning. How did Jalall know Daas hadn't been a part of Inej's attack? She bit back her words and chose to follow Jalall out the side door. No one was about to see them, making it a perfect place for her to speak to him.

She touched his shoulder, and he immediately whirled around. Rhi ducked the fist that came flying at her, as well as the flash of bronze.

"Stop," she said as she dropped her veil and kicked his legs out from under him. She held her hands over his face with her foot on his chest and looked down at him. "I came with Dain earlier to bring the children to safety. I'm a friend."

"Friend, huh? Are you the one who attacked Inej?"

Rhi rolled her eyes. "I may look human, but I'm not. I'm a Fae."

To prove it, she veiled herself once more and then dropped it. Then, she teleported into the house and back again.

"If I wanted to hurt you, I would've done it in Manu's room when you came running in," Rhi stated. "I've been veiled the entire time. He called for me when he couldn't get out of the avalanche. I dug him out and then whispered to the guards to go find him."

Jalall slowly sat up and stared at her with black eyes very similar to Con's. But that's where the likeness ended. Con was several inches taller with blond hair compared to Jalall's dark brown.

"How do I know you're telling the truth?" Jalall asked.

She shrugged. "You won't until you're able to talk to Manu. Like I said, if I wanted any of you dead, you would never see me coming."

"Your accent is different," he said as he looked her up and down.

"Because I'm not from this world. Listen, we can talk about that later. I'm not sure you should leave Daas alone with Inej."

Jalall accepted the hand she offered to pull him up. "I trust him."

"I bet you said the same thing about Tahmine."

He grimaced at the name. "I get your point, but there's only me."

"There's also me. I'll stay behind and watch over her."

"Manu will be awake soon."

She grinned at the threat. "If Dain were here, he could vouch for me."

"But he isn't. I also think it would be better if no one else knew you were here."

"Way ahead of you," she said and veiled herself. "Be careful," she called before teleporting back to Inej.

Seven hours, twenty-seven minutes, and forty-four seconds. That was how long Rhi had been silently guarding Inej. Daas had been relieved by his wife, Shruti, who managed to get more herbal water into Inej, but she still hadn't stirred.

The elves didn't seem worried by that, but Rhi certainly was. She had gotten used to Con being there to heal whoever needed it. The Fae healed quickly, but they could be killed. Elves seemed to have the same rate of healing as humans. The difference between them was that elves had Healers and the herbs that were more readily available to them.

With all Rhi knew about the human race, she was surprised they managed to live—and most times thrive—when surrounded by magical beings who could wipe them out with a snap of their fingers. What made humans so special?

And so damn resilient.

Rhi drummed her fingers on her thigh. She was getting antsy. Not only did she need to check in with her mate before he unleashed hell on the elves, but she also hadn't seen Jalall since they'd parted ways hours ago. She had no idea how Manu was, or if Jalall had tracked down Inej's attacker.

Unlike most Fae, Rhi could stay veiled indefinitely, but that didn't mean it was easy. She couldn't make a sound, lest someone hear her. Things would be so much easier if she could get in touch with Dain so he could stand guard over Inej.

"How is she?" Jalall asked as he walked into the room.

Rhi pushed away from the wall. Her elation dimmed when she noted his harsh breathing, his fisted hands at his sides, and his tightened face. She was about to speak when she remembered that she was veiled and had to hold her tongue. This was the part she hated the most. She had questions, and she wanted answers.

Shruti rose and shook her head. "There's been no change in Inej. Her wounds are healing, but slowly. I don't know enough about humans to say if this is normal or if her body is rejecting the magic."

"The herbs healed her before," Jalall said as he walked to the bed. "Thank you for watching her. Go home and get some rest."

Rhi waited until she was alone with Jalall before dropping her veil. "You've been gone a long time."

"I know," he replied wearily. He didn't even look at her as he ran a hand down his face.

"You didn't find Tahmine, did you?"

He shook his head and finally swung his dark eyes to her. "She and Chanda left to do some foraging."

"Who's Chanda?"

"Besides being Tahmine's closest friend, she, Manu, and I grew up together. She also manages my house."

Rhi blew out a frustrated breath. "Tahmine has to return eventually. We'll get her then. How is Manu faring?"

"I was on my way there, but I wanted to stop here first. If he's awake, he'll want news about Inej."

"My mate can heal her with a touch."

Jalall's brow creased in a frown. He stared at her for a long moment before saying, "Your mate is…?" He paused and swallowed before dipping his voice to a whisper. "He lives outside our borders, doesn't he?"

Rhi wasn't sure if the elves feared or hated the dragons, but in the end, it didn't matter. If elves couldn't venture onto dragon land, then dragons couldn't cross onto Shecrish. "He is. I can get him in and out quickly. No one ever needs to know either of us was here."

"I—"

Jalall never got to finish as a form filled the doorway. Both of them were taken aback by the sight of Manu still wearing his soiled clothing, though someone had cleaned most of the blood from his face and hair. His left leg bore all of his weight, and he leaned heavily against the doorway to keep himself upright as his gaze locked on Inej.

"What happened?" Manu demanded, his voice breaking.

Worry creased Jalall's face as he took a slow step toward Manu. "I was coming to you."

"What happened?" Manu asked again, his voice hardening as he pinned Jalall with a dark look.

Rhi took pity on the men and said, "Someone tried to kill Inej."

"Tried." His black eyes slid to her, filled with regret and blame. "You said tried. That means she's still alive."

"We found her in time," Jalall told him.

Manu limped forward, but his leg buckled. He hit the floor hard. Rhi and Jalall rushed to his side, but he held out a splayed hand at them. "Don't!"

Rhi froze and looked down at his foot. It was heavily bandaged, and blood stained the dressing. "You shouldn't be out of bed. Your foot isn't healed."

Manu breathed heavily, his guilt palpable. "I heard others whispering about her. I had to know."

Jalall looked at Rhi. She shrugged, unsure what to do. Manu got his good foot beneath him to stand, but his balance was off. This time, when Jalall gripped his arm, Manu let his friend pull him upright and help him to a chair.

"Sit before you lose your foot," Jalall ordered.

Manu sank into the chair and sighed. "Tell me what happened. All of it." His voice was soft, as if saying the words cost him a great deal.

"Where do we start?" Jalall asked.

Manu leaned in and stared at Rhi. "I take it you heard me, then?"

"I did. It was close, though. You should've called for me sooner," she chided softly.

His gaze briefly dropped to the floor. "Thank you for coming to my aid. Did any of the ot—"

"They did not," she said over him. "As for Inej, she has at least four wounds. One on her side, two on her back, and one on her front."

Manu winced as he shifted his injured leg. "They attacked from the front, and she turned to run."

"Actually, I think her attacker or attackers came at her from behind." Rhi glanced out of the room to where it'd happened. "I've had plenty of time to study the scene and her injuries. It seems she was walking down the hall from the front room. She must have heard something and started to turn. That's where the side wound came from. The hit propelled her to the side and back against the wall, where I discovered marks where more magic struck. There are more strikes on the wall, moving in a gradual downward angle, suggesting they continued to fire as she fell. Based on the position of one of her back wounds, I think she got hit *as* she fell."

Manu swallowed heavily, a mix of outrage and distress clouding his face. "And the injury to her front?"

Rhi shot a quick look at Inej. "I think they flipped her over to see if she was still alive."

"We found her on her back," Jalall added. "That does seem to add up."

Manu braced his hands on his thighs as he shook his head. "I told her she was safe here. I swore no one would harm her. Who would do this?"

Jalall shifted his weight from one leg to the other as he leaned back against the wall. "I, uh, I've been looking for Tahmine and Chanda to question them."

Manu didn't react. Seconds passed in heavy silence before he sat up, every line of his body taut with barely contained fury. His gaze, hard as forged steel, locked on Jalall. "What do you mean you've been looking for them?"

"They left the city to forage."

"You think they did this?"

Jalall threw up his arms, his face twisted with exhaustion and frustration. "Maybe. I don't know. Neither of us will know until we speak to them. But that isn't our only problem."

"What could be more important than finding Inej's attacker?" Manu demanded, anger dripping from every word.

Jalall's lips flattened. "How about the fact that eight of our people were killed, and you nearly died? I sent some men out to check the area to see if it was an accident."

"It wasn't," Manu stated calmly. "We were ambushed."

Rhi asked, "Did you see who it was?"

"They were too far away. I was on my way to find you," he said to Jalall.

Jalall frowned. "How did you know to come looking? We'd been fending off an attack for over a day before we finally got them all. I got here right after you were brought in."

"Seems someone went to a lot of trouble to get both of you outside the city," Rhi said.

Manu rubbed his eyes with his thumb and forefinger. "I and a small contingent confronted a group of mercenaries who were looking for me a few days ago. They never got close to Navara, though."

"Then who could?" Rhi asked.

The two elves looked at each other.

"Someone inside," Manu said. He asked Jalall, "Did you see who attacked you?"

Jalall sank into the other chair as he shook his head. "Their faces were hidden, but I don't think it was Sachin's tribe. The assassin was one of his people, but Sachin was shook up about it and wanted me to assure you that he had no part in it."

"Do you believe him?" Rhi asked.

Jalall nodded slowly. "I do."

"I get coming after me, but they wouldn't go after Inej," Manu said after a beat of silence.

Rhi twisted her lips. "They might."

Both men turned their gazes to her. "Explain," Manu urged.

Rhi glanced at the floor. "What do you know about Inej?" When Manu parted his lips to speak, she held up a finger. "I am speculating, but hear me out, please. She's new, as well as human. You would be wary of an elf you didn't know, but would you be as guarded against a human?"

"I went through this same argument. We took precautions," Jalall said.

Rhi crossed her arms over her chest. "Did you?"

Anger flashed in Manu's dark gaze. "You don't think I can protect my people?"

"I think you do an admirable job with your people. Just not yourself." His nostrils flared in response. She dropped her arms to her sides. "What if you were the target?"

"Again, we went through this," Jalall stated.

Manu nodded. "Inej saved my life. Why would she do that if she wanted to harm me?"

"It could've all been a ruse to get you to trust her," Rhi said.

Manu scrunched his face in denial. "She almost died."

"And it convinced you that she meant you no harm. And," she hurried to say when Manu's lips parted, "she got close to you by becoming your lover."

Jalall snorted. "I'll admit, you have a point. But she's human."

"Elves can still be killed," Rhi stated. "A knife in the heart while Manu sleeps. Poison slipped into his food. Sending him into a trap."

"She didn't send me," Manu countered. "Inej had no idea where I was going."

Jalall scrubbed a hand down his face. "I still don't see how your theory connects to Inej's attack."

"They were tying up loose ends," Rhi said with a shrug.

Manu shook his head. "I don't believe it. Any of it."

"What if Rhi's right?" Jalall asked. "What if Inej was sent by the Masters? Even you have to admit she is a perfect decoy."

"And what if she wasn't?" Manu asked as he looked between Rhi and Jalall. "What if she's a victim in all of this, and it's just a coincidence that we were both hurt?"

"If she's innocent, then she'll understand why you're being cautious," Rhi said.

Manu bent forward and dropped his head into his hands. Rhi had seen enough of the Kings falling in love to know that Manu was head over heels for Inej. Which meant it was possible he'd be too blinded by his feelings to see the truth.

If Inej were in Navara to harm him. Rhi had given one theory. It was time she talked about all the ways Inej could be innocent. But even as she considered them, the pieces were harder to put together.

"If the Masters sent Inej to kill me, they wouldn't remove her before the job was done." Manu lifted his head and pinned Rhi with a hard look. "As you said, she got close to me. So, why go after her? There isn't an answer because the two events aren't related."

"Are you saying you think her attack was motivated by jealousy?" Jalall asked.

Rhi cringed at the pain that flashed over Manu's face. If he claimed it was jealousy, then the focus shifted to two of his friends, one of whom he'd had an affair with. Either way, he was on the losing end.

"You need to rest and heal," Rhi told him. "I can bring Con for you and Inej. His touch heals in an instant. That way, you can start getting to the bottom of things. Or I can bring both of you to him, if you'd rather."

Jalall nudged Manu when he didn't answer. "We need you. And that means you need to be at your best. Take Rhi's offer."

"Fine," Manu said. "But I'm not leaving Navara."

Jalall got to his feet. "I'll make sure no one enters the house, so we aren't disturbed."

"I'll be back," Rhi told them.

33

Manu's ankle throbbed with every beat of his heart. It had taken everything he had to get to Jalall's, and he had done considerable damage to the recovery of his foot in the process. But he hadn't been thinking about any of that once he learned that Inej was hurt. All that mattered was getting to her.

Seeing her had only made his pain worse, because he hadn't been there to protect her. She had faced the attack on her own. Navara should have been a safe place for her, but she had found the opposite. Was he so blinded by his people that he couldn't see the possible enemies in his midst?

He should've done more to keep her safe. He choked on remorse, wondering if she had cursed him as she lay helpless and in pain. If he couldn't protect even one person, how was he supposed to keep an entire city secure? Especially if someone he knew was plotting against him.

Manu couldn't imagine anyone who would purposefully send

him and others to be killed by an avalanche while trying to take out Jalall and his team at the same time. As for Inej, he hadn't seen or heard anything that had made him believe she wasn't welcome in Navara. He couldn't deny that he didn't know his people as well as he thought he did, though.

"Do you want to talk about it?" Jalall asked softly.

Manu would rather stay in his thoughts, but he needed another perspective. "Not really," he admitted. "But I need to. What do you think about what Rhi said?"

"I think she made a lot of sense."

Manu squeezed the bridge of his nose with his thumb and forefinger. That was the rub. Rhi *had* made sense. He dropped his hand and sighed. "You think Inej is working with the Masters, that Tahmine attacked someone I gave shelter to out of jealousy, and that both your team and mine were targeted to be killed?"

"I said her connections made sense. None of it may be true."

"Or all of it may be true." He met Jalall's gaze. "I owe it to everyone to look at all possibilities."

Jalall scratched his whiskered cheek. "You won't be doing this alone."

"I fell for Inej. I saw a future with her. I..." He trailed off, unable to finish. Manu looked at the bed and felt the compulsion to go to her. She was too pale. And too still.

"We'll figure this out."

Manu snorted as he looked at the floor. "What is there to figure out if Inej is the enemy? Or if Tahmine tried to kill her? By law, both will have to be punished."

"I don't want Tahmine to be responsible any more than you do. As for Inej..." Jalall said and glanced at the bed. "We were cautious from the beginning."

And it was restraint Manu had thrown to the wind as the attraction between them developed. Was there something between them? Had it all been a lie so she could get close to him? Nay, he refused to believe that. She hadn't been faking the pleasure or the way she kissed him.

"Inej had plenty of time alone with me to make an attempt on my life. She didn't," Manu said.

Jalall braced one foot on the wall behind him. "Maybe she was securing her place by your side first."

"If even half of what Rhi speculated is the truth, then I've made a real muck of things. As leader, I should've seen throu—"

"As much as many believe you're perfect, you aren't," Jalall said with a grin. "You make mistakes, just like any of us. If you missed something, then we have time to fix it." He paused and cleared his throat, his gaze briefly dropping to the floor. "To that end, I spoke with Daas already. Inej was with him all day. He said she never left the back of the kitchen until she returned here."

"Then she couldn't have been involved in setting me up for the avalanche." Manu tried to keep the relief from his voice, but he wasn't sure he'd succeeded.

"Unless she's working with someone inside Navara."

The truth crushed Manu's respite to dust. "Inej only had contact with me, Daas, Shruti, and Chanda."

"She could've spoken to others as she walked to and from work."

Manu had no rebuttal for that. "She could've. Also, Chanda brought Tahmine here the other morning. She saw Inej in my tunic."

"That does look bad for Tahmine."

"She's someone to speak with. I'd like to talk to everyone who stood guard yesterday. I'm going to need a list of each individual who left the city over the last week, no matter the reason."

"You're not going anywhere until that foot is healed."

Before Manu could answer, Rhi appeared without warning or sound. Beside her stood a man with wavy blond hair cropped short on the sides. His shirt clung to his frame, the thin fabric doing little to hide the strength beneath. It was tucked into dark blue pants. Assessing, black eyes swept the room before landing on Manu. The stranger looked human—at first. But the air shifted around him, thick with power and authority.

Rhi looked up at him with eyes filled with love and devotion. "Lads, this is Con, the King of Dragon Kings. Con, this is Manu, leader of Navara, and Jalall."

Con dipped his head to Jalall before turning his gaze to Manu. Then he spoke with a unique vocal lilt. "Rhi told me of your injuries. I'm here to help."

"All he'll do is touch you," Rhi added.

Con slid his gaze to her for a heartbeat. "I've never attempted to heal an elf. My magic should work, though."

Manu was ready for the pain to be gone so he could sort through the jumble of thoughts ricocheting in his head. "The herbs will work, but it will take more time than I'm willing to give. Please, do what you can."

The Dragon King stood before him in three strides. Con dropped to his haunches as he studied the ankle Manu had extended to keep pressure off his foot. Manu tensed when Con reached out a hand and lightly set his fingers on his lower leg. A peculiar buzz rushed outward from Con's touch and flowed through Manu's body. One moment, the pain was there. The next, it had vanished.

Con straightened. "Take off the bandage."

Manu hesitated, still reeling a bit. Magic was part of elven life, but what he had just experienced was nothing like what he was used to. Jalall dropped to one knee and tentatively lifted Manu's foot to unwrap the bandage. Manu knew before the last of the bindings had been removed that he was healed. Yet he couldn't stop staring at his flesh that had, moments before, been throbbing as the ligaments, muscles, and skin stitched themselves back together. Even the Healers couldn't work as fast as Con.

"That's astounding," Jalall murmured as he touched Manu's healed flesh.

Manu twisted his ankle one way and then the other before flexing and curling his toes. He set his foot on the ground and stood, testing his weight upon it. He then rotated his left arm to find that his shoulder was also healed. He looked at Con. "Thank you."

"My pleasure," he answered.

Jalall was slower to get to his feet. His face was slack with shock when he turned to Con. "You did all that with just a touch?"

"Dragon magic is particularly powerful," Rhi stated proudly.

Con grinned at her before glancing at Inej on the bed. "Shall I tend to her now?"

"Wait," Jalall said hurriedly.

Manu cut his eyes to his friend, fighting a flare of anger. "Why?"

"Should we get information first?" Jalall asked. "That way, if she's innocent, she need never know what we did to prove it."

"Or if she's guilty, we can carry out her sentence," Manu replied.

Jalall shrugged. "That, too."

Manu's gaze was drawn to the bed and the woman who had somehow found her way into his heart. "Someone tried to kill her. I *will* find out who it was."

"*We'll* find out," Jalall corrected.

The fact was that Inej wasn't safe at Jalall's anymore. There was only one place in Navara that Manu knew he could protect her. He turned to Rhi. "Can you bring Inej to my chamber? I don't want anyone to know she's there."

"And if she's your enemy?" Con asked.

Manu sighed. "Then I'll handle it."

Rhi walked to the bed and stood beside it before Con joined her. Manu made his way to Inej and grabbed her hand when Rhi directed him. Jalall nodded, and the next instant, they were in his chambers with Inej on the bed. Manu released her, his heart heavy.

"Are you ready for me to heal her?" Con asked.

He met the Dragon King's eyes and nodded.

"She's alive," Rhi said to Manu. "The herbs are keeping her stable. You could leave her like this until you conduct your investigation."

"We could also bring her with us," Con offered.

Manu walked to his window and looked out over the city. "I'm not sure I'm qualified to make such decisions anymore."

"I might have gone a bit overboard when we spoke earlier," Rhi told him.

Manu shook his head. "You saw things I didn't or couldn't. If this is going to get sorted, I need to look at all the possibilities. Even if I don't want to."

Con walked up to stand beside him. "Your city is beautiful."

"It used to be safe. I always knew the Masters would find their way here, but I thought I'd have more time. I also never accounted for Inej."

"Maybe she was meant to be a blind spot for you. Maybe she wasn't. You care about her, and you want her safe." Con turned his head to look at Manu. "If it will ease you some to keep her sleeping here, then do it."

Manu dropped his chin to his chest. He wanted to talk to Inej, but he didn't know if he could believe anything she said. Not until he knew more. "I can ensure that no one will enter this room."

Rhi walked to Con's other side. "Then that's what you should do. Once you've seen to that, what do you want to do?"

"That's easy. I want to find who attacked my guards and me and uncover who tried to kill Inej," Manu said.

Con quirked a dark brow. "And?"

"I want to eradicate the Masters forever, so all of Shecrish is safe." When Con continued to stare, Manu blew out a breath. "I also want to be with Inej."

"Will your people accept her?" Con asked.

Manu shrugged one shoulder. "I don't know. We haven't had many interactions with humans."

"Would you give up your position for her?" Rhi questioned.

Manu had only ever known the life he had now and his role in it. The burden of so many souls resting upon him and his decisions to keep them protected was debilitating at times. It's why he went alone into the mountains.

With Inej, he'd found comfort and a calmness that had always escaped him. Being with her was like coming home. He sought her out instead of the Peaks—her smile, her kisses, her arms.

Manu nodded once. "I would. But can I keep both her and my people safe?"

"You need facts before you can answer that." Con swung his gaze back to the city.

Manu turned away from the window. "Then I'd better get started."

"Inej might have seen something that could help uncover the identity of her attacker," Rhi said.

Con's brow furrowed as he slowly turned around. "She might have, indeed. If I heal her, will she remain in this room willingly?"

Or would she need to be locked away? Con didn't say the last part, but Manu didn't need him to. He didn't want to shut her up anywhere. Keeping Con here indefinitely to heal her also wasn't an option.

"May I make a suggestion?" the Dragon King asked. "We have a little time before we must get back. Rhi and I can take a look on the mountains and see what we can find. We'll be veiled so no one will see us. And before you say we doona know the terrain, I should mention we'll be in the air."

Manu would love to see Con in his dragon form. Maybe he would get that privilege in the future.

"We'll be able to see a lot from the sky," Rhi added.

It was something that would take Manu days or weeks to sort through on foot. "I would appreciate that."

"We'll be back." Con looked at Rhi. As soon as she touched him, they were gone.

Manu stripped out of his dirty clothes and tossed them aside. He took a quick bath to scrub the dried blood away before putting on fresh clothes. His feet halted at the door, and he turned to Inej. She looked as if she were sleeping. He hoped he was doing the right thing by leaving her to let the herbs work.

"I'll return as quickly as I can," he promised her before walking out, then closing the door and locking it behind him.

No one would enter without his permission. If his staff was startled to see him leaving again, they didn't show it. He headed straight to the candy shop to talk to Daas and his wife. They confirmed that Inej had been with them the entire day. In fact, they said she had been waiting for Daas when he arrived, making Manu think she'd left shortly after he had.

Manu's next stop was the guardhouse. The rotation of guards at the door had been diminished with both him and Jalall taking soldiers out with them, which left only six he needed to speak with. All corroborated that Inej had never approached them to leave the city. When Manu left, he had a list of everyone who *had* left Navara.

Tahmine and Chanda were on that list. But they still hadn't returned, which meant he couldn't speak to them yet. Manu summoned guards and gave each of them a name of someone to bring back to him. He paced impatiently in Jalall's office at the barracks, waiting for the individuals to arrive for questioning.

The door opened, and Jalall walked in. "I figured you'd be here."

"I'm not leaving you out," he began.

Jalall held up a hand. "I understand. You need to do this. While you're talking to suspects, let me take some guards and go look for Chanda and Tahmine. If I'm not back by the time you finish here, come find me."

Manu blew out a breath. "All right."

He watched Jalall head out, his gut twisting with worry and dread. Enemies had infiltrated his city, and he had missed it. How many more would die before he uncovered the one responsible?

34

The Crossing Pub

The bar was louder than usual. Reva was used to the crowd of people, but there was something different about tonight. A customer scooted back his chair, bumping into her, which caused the tray to tip and ale to splash on her sandaled foot. She looked down at the mess as a wave of body odor hit her. She bit back a gag and backpedaled to find another way to deliver her current order.

She eagerly set the last mug in front of the patron and moved on to her next table. It wasn't until she made her way back to the bar for more drinks that she looked out through the doorway into the city streets. It was raining again, the sound beating a steady tempo, and the downpour doing its best to block out the light of the double moons. She wasn't looking for light. She was searching for shadows.

For Dain.

It had been days since she had seen him, and their last encounter had made it seem as if he had no intention of returning. As far as she knew, he hadn't been back. Sidiq never spoke about him, and the one time she had tried to bring him up, it hadn't gone well. It was no secret that Dain, Arya, and the others had a price on their heads, but they had saved her life. She would never turn on them. They had to know that.

Dain had once asked her to collect information for him that she overheard. She had loved the idea of helping him and the others in their quest to stop the abductions. Reva had thought she was doing a good job. Then, for some reason, he'd ended their agreement. That hadn't stopped her from continuing to gather information, however.

None of the elves at the pub paid her any attention, other than to attempt to slap her arse or ogle her breasts. Even the few humans who had enough nerve to enter didn't really see her. The more they drank, the more their voices rose, making it easier for her to pick up bits of conversations. She kept everything filed away for the day Dain returned.

She shook herself and called out the drink orders. Sidiq moved quickly and fluidly for his height. He caught her gaze and lifted a white brow. It was his silent way of asking if she was okay. She smiled and nodded once to let him know she was fine. He looked out for everyone who worked for him.

"Hey," Darshan said as he came up beside her and unloaded some empty tankards, his blue eyes crinkling at the corners. "Walk you home tonight?"

She shrugged. "Okay."

Reva wasn't sure how she felt about his attention. Darshan was attractive enough, with his piercing eyes, blond hair, and handsome face, but he was missing something. She needed to let him know soon that she only thought of him as a friend.

Darshan left, and she lingered a moment. She didn't need to look where he was since she could pick out his booming voice over the others. Whereas she was pleasant to customers, Darshan teased and joked with them. A few had propositioned him, but he didn't have to dodge grabby hands like she and the other females did.

"Want me to talk to him?" Sidiq asked as he set the drinks on her tray. "I can tell him to leave you alone."

Here was a Dark Elf who could quell customers with a look, wanting to help her when, not too long ago, elves had held her prisoner and tortured her repeatedly. She'd had to kill to escape, and had been looking over her shoulder ever since. There were only two individuals who made her feel safe—Dain and Sidiq.

Both Dark Elves, who looked anything but agreeable. Maybe that was why she felt secure in their presence. Oh, sure, Sidiq smiled and laughed, but his demeanor could switch with a snap of a finger. With Dain, everyone knew not to mess with him. It was there in his stance and the way his golden eyes cut right through someone.

"He's harmless," Reva told Sidiq.

Gray eyes slid briefly to the side before returning to her. "Don't let your guard down with anyone."

"I won't," she promised.

That seemed to mollify Sidiq as he moved down to tend to a customer. Reva lifted the tray, carrying it over her head, balanced on one hand as she wove her way through the crowd. She greeted her customers with a smile as she set down their drinks, but a conversation behind her snagged her attention.

"In the mountains?" the male asked skeptically. "You're full of shite."

"I'm not," answered another.

The first snorted. "There's no way anyone could get around the Peaks against the Mountain Elves."

"I heard they sent a human."

"Another one of her lies." Another snort, this one louder.

Reva turned slightly and spotted a Moon Elf slumped in his seat, his lips twisted in a sneer. "And what news do you have?"

"I have better than you."

This came from a Dark Elf with short, white hair. His face was turned away from her, so that she couldn't make out his features. Reva moved to the side to check on her next table while trying to get a look at his face.

"I know where they're building the replacement for Shaldorn," the Dark stated smugly.

The Moon Elf's blue eyes widened in surprise, but it quickly became anger. "You promised to get me in on that."

The Dark Elf laughed and took a long swig of ale. "Did I?"

Reva wasn't able to hear the rest of the conversation since she had to take another order. When she looked back at the table, both elves were gone. She hadn't gotten to see who the Dark was, but she could describe the Moon Elf.

No matter how closely she listened to the others around her, she didn't pick up anything else. But what she had heard was vital intelligence that Dain needed. She looked at Sidiq. He was her best way of finding Dain.

The rest of the night was a blur as Reva hurried from one table to the next until, finally, Sidiq yelled for last call. A surge of renewed energy filled her as she got in the last orders and started cleaning. She brushed strands of hair back from her face that had fallen out of her braid. She was hot and sweaty and couldn't wait to get off her feet. She looked a mess, and likely smelled it, too. Darshan, on the other hand, looked as if he had just gotten to work. He never broke a sweat or smelled of spilled ale. It was too bad she wasn't attracted to him. He could be a nice diversion.

Reva was mopping when Sidiq ran the last of the customers out of the pub. Darshan began to whistle as he wiped down tables and set the chairs on top, and Sidiq cleaned up behind the bar. It was their regular routine, one they did together several times a week, but tonight, she wanted to tell Darshan to go so she could talk to Sidiq.

She took her time mopping, and it was no surprise that Sidiq noticed. He eyed her but didn't say anything. She'd have to thank him for that later.

"I'll grab the other mop to help," Darshan said.

Reva waved him off. "I'm fine. I just have a little more to go."

"We can leave quicker if I help," he argued.

Sidiq braced his hands on the bar. "Actually, you'd better go now. I need to talk to Reva."

Darshan frowned as he looked from her to Sidiq, then back to her. "What did you do?" he whispered.

She shrugged and wrinkled her nose. "I don't know."

"Good luck," he said and made his way out into the city.

Sidiq followed and set his hand on the center of the giant mandala that covered one side of the rock entrance. Black magic shot across the space in a slender beam before fanning outward and meeting his palm once more. She had never seen him lock the pub before. He said nothing as she wrapped up her mopping and tossed out the dirty water.

Reva rubbed her hands on her thighs as she headed to the bar, where Sidiq waited. She parted her lips to speak when he put a finger to his mouth. Then, he walked past her to the door that led into the tunnels and down into the underground world of the Dark Elves. He used the same kind of magic to lock the door to the city. When that was finished, he motioned for her to follow him into the storeroom.

Once she was inside, he shut the door and locked them in with more magic. Before she could ask what was going on, he shoved her behind him and threw out his hands to the side as dozens of thin lines of black magic exploded from his palms around the room without a single one touching her. When he turned, she turned with him.

"All right," he finally said and took a step to the side before facing her. "I needed to make sure we didn't have any unwanted observers."

"You don't ward the bar?"

He crossed his arms over his chest. "To do that would alert others that I'm trying to hide something. You wanted to talk."

She didn't bother asking how he knew. He and Dain seemed to have a sense about those kinds of things. It had to be something in their training. She didn't know for sure if Sidiq had been a spy, but he moved and acted much like Dain did. And they knew each other. It seemed pretty obvious to her.

"I have a favor."

Sidiq's gray eyes studied her. "Ask it. If I can help, I will."

"I need to talk to Dain."

There was no outward show of emotion, but the atmosphere in the room shifted slightly. He looked away, and she could've sworn she saw disappointment on his face. She looked at the blue tattoos covering the left side of his head.

"I wouldn't ask if it weren't important," she added.

Sidiq dropped his arms to his sides and returned his gaze to her. "There's a price on his head. Anyone who gets close to him will get the same."

"I know."

"He's dangerous, Reva."

She swallowed. "So are most of the customers who come into the pub."

"He's in another class."

"He saved my life." She blew out a breath. "I wouldn't be here if not for him."

Sidiq's shoulders lifted as he inhaled. "I can move around in that world much easier than you. Tell me what you want to say to him, and I'll pass it on."

"I can't." The hurt that flashed across his eyes made her feel horrible, but she held firm.

"You don't trust me."

The statement made her wince. "Like you said, anyone connected to him will be hunted. I'd rather not involve you."

"You would risk your life for him?"

There was no heat in the words, but she detected another emotion she couldn't name. "This isn't about Dain. I'm willing to risk my life for everyone."

His eyes narrowed slightly. "You won't trust me with the message, but you'll trust me to get Dain?"

"You gave me a job when others wouldn't. You've looked out for me by keeping the customers from groping me. Maybe I'm overstepping, but I consider you a friend. That isn't something I say to many. I'm not telling you the information I have because I'm trying to protect *you*."

Sidiq sighed deeply. "Does it have to be Dain? I might be able to find Arya."

She wanted to insist on Dain, but that was only because she wanted to see him again. She didn't have an argument for why it had to be Dain, so she forced a smile. "That would work just as well."

35

Snow flurries drifted aimlessly in the air as Manu waded through knee-deep snow. Every name on the list of people who had left the city had been interviewed, their movements checked and verified, leaving him just as bewildered as before.

Rhi and Con hadn't returned yet, and Manu hadn't been able to stay inside a moment longer. He didn't go to where the avalanche had occurred. Instead, he headed toward Jalall and his team. Their tracks were easy to follow in the thick snow.

He looked up at the clouds and blinked the flurries from his lashes. Chanda and Tahmine had lived their entire lives in the Peaks. They knew when to take shelter if they were out overnight. Every Mountain Elf did. Manu wanted to find them, but he also dreaded what could come to light once he did. They could have been victims of an attack, or they could be Inej's would-be murderers. There was also a slight chance it was a mere coincidence that they had left the mountain when they did and weren't involved in anything. Manu wanted answers. Yet whatever he found had the potential to destroy Navara's tight community.

Breath puffed from his lips as he kept moving. He had grown up knowing his role and what was expected of him. Today, he hated it. Mostly because he didn't know what to do—about anything. A leader who couldn't make a decision wasn't a leader at all.

Did he stay in the city by Inej's bed?

Should he have allowed Con to heal her? He would've been able to talk to her, but he would've also had to keep her locked away.

Could he trust those around him?

Who in the city had been swayed by the Masters?

The only thing he knew for certain was what he would do to any individual who tried to kill Inej. And how he intended to avenge those who had died in the avalanche.

He paused and looked up when he heard what sounded like a shout. That's when he made out a form in the distance, waving their arms. Jalall's whistle sounded quickly after. At least he had found them. Manu raised his hand to let his friend know he had seen him and continued onward.

The group was somber when Manu reached them. He looked around at the soldiers, some of whom were standing guard while the others looked at the ground. Manu altered his direction and headed to where Jalall stood.

"I was about to send someone for you," his friend said.

Manu pulled down his fur to expose his face. "What did you find?"

Jalall stepped to the side. That's when Manu saw the body half-covered with snow. He recognized the dark fur coat with the white fur collar.

"Tahmine," he said.

Jalall's shoulder brushed his as they stood side by side. "It looks like she was struck in the back with magic."

Manu didn't want to look, but he had to. He moved closer and peered down to see the burnt fur that exposed the scorched flesh. She had been running away. But from whom? Ever since he'd learned of Inej's attack, he had suspected Tahmine. He'd even condemned her in his mind.

"Where is Chanda?" he asked.

"We've not found her yet."

Manu turned away from Tahmine. He had yet another slaying to solve. The weight of all he carried was crushing, but he refused to buckle beneath it. He lengthened his spine and looked at Jalall. "Mark this location so we can retrieve her body when we return."

Jalall motioned to one of the soldiers, who marked the area.

"Any movement?" Manu asked.

Jalall shook his head once. "Nothing. Chanda could have found cover."

"Or she could be dead." Manu scanned the mountain slope. "Tahmine fell facing south."

"I'll fan the guards out so we can search the mountainside," Jalall said.

Manu looked at the sky again, wondering where Rhi and Con were. They would be able to find Chanda, but they were already helping in other ways. It didn't seem right to ask for more.

Jalall slapped him on the shoulder after he'd finished giving the orders. The soldiers spread out. Manu headed toward the peak, following a hunch. He knew the mountains surrounding Navara well, especially where someone might go if they needed shelter.

The gravity of the situation hung in the air, as foreboding as the gray clouds above them. They were silent as they continued the search. The wind whistled softly through the evergreen branches laden with snow as their feet crunched on the ground. There were no tracks to find, no trail to follow.

He had no idea when Tahmine had died. She could've been murdered yesterday morning, giving her killer plenty of opportunity to get away and the wind and fresh snowfall time to cover their footprints.

Manu drew up when he reached the cave. He used one of the bird calls he had mastered to get Jalall's attention. When his friend looked up, Manu pointed to the cave. Jalall came around and up so they could enter it from either side.

Since he didn't want to alert anyone to their presence, Manu moved slowly toward the entrance. He reached his position before Jalall. It gave him time to stand and listen for any sounds coming from within. He couldn't hear anything, but the cave stretched back a bit. They could be farther inside.

Finally, Jalall reached him. Manu entered first, hands up and magic at the ready. Two steps in, and darkness consumed them. He kept to his side of the cave while Jalall took the other. They crept forward, one measured step at a time, moving farther and farther from the entrance and light. It was impossible to see anything. The only way they could pick their way forward was by using the walls.

Manu was about to turn them back when he heard something. A few steps later, he saw the soft glow of firelight dancing on the walls and the ceiling ahead of him. He glanced at Jalall, who gave him a grim look. The tunnel curved to the left. Manu leaned forward and tried to see around the bend where the light grew brighter.

"Manu," Jalall whispered.

He knew his friend's restrained, controlled tone meant danger was near. Manu tensed and slowly turned to look behind him. Standing in the middle of the tunnel was the alpha wolvite that had gone after Inej. If he was here, that meant the sounds Manu had heard ahead must be the rest of his pack.

But wolvites didn't light fires.

Manu and the animal were locked in a staring contest. The wolvite's head was lowered, his yellow eyes fastened on Manu. He hadn't growled, but that didn't mean anything. Manu and Jalall were trapped, and the beast knew it.

"Fuck me," Jalall murmured.

Manu kept eye contact with the wolvite. "What is it?"

"I just looked around the corner. The rest of the pack is in there. And they, uh…" Jalall cleared his throat. "They're eating."

"Is it Chanda?"

"I can't tell."

The alpha apparently didn't like them talking, as he finally issued a low, warning growl. The only way out was past the animal, and the beast didn't seem keen on letting them pass.

"We can take him," Jalall said. "If we attack together. We can probably get out before the others attack."

Manu looked at the wolvite, who was doing nothing but protecting his family, just as Manu had been trying to do since the day his father had died. He knew the animal's strength, just as the beast knew his. The wolvite could've attacked them from behind, but he hadn't. Maybe that was because he didn't want to. Or maybe he was waiting.

"Manu," Jalall urged.

He dropped his hands to his sides and inclined his head to the animal. "We're not here for you or yours," he told the wolvite. "We're looking for those like us."

The wolvite tilted his head slightly.

"You're fucking talking to it?" Jalall asked incredulously.

The animal swung its huge head to Jalall and bared its teeth.

"Ignore him," Manu said to get the wolvite's attention again.

Yellow eyes trained on Manu once more.

"We'll leave if you let us pass. And we won't come back. Your family will be safe," he promised.

There was no way he and Jalall could retrace their steps as they were. They needed to be on the same side of the tunnel so they could give the wolvite a wide berth. Since the animal didn't seem to like Jalall, Manu would have to cross to the other side.

He took a deep breath and slid his right foot out. The beast didn't pay it any attention. Manu then shifted his weight to that foot. The wolvite still didn't react. He pulled his left foot against his right. Jalall remained silent. Manu darted a glance at him to see that his attention was focused deeper in the cave and on the other animals.

His heart thudded against his ribs as he skated his right foot out again. Manu moved slowly and deliberately. Before he knew it, he stood in the middle of the tunnel with the wolvite just ten feet in front of him. When he continued toward Jalall, the animal side-stepped away from them. They repeated the dance until Manu was with his friend, and the beast was against the far wall.

"We'll leave now," Manu said and tugged on Jalall's jacket to get him to move first.

Jalall backed away a few steps. Manu lingered for a moment. He and the wolvite shared a look, and what he thought was mutual understanding. They were both trying to survive in the unforgiving, merciless Peaks.

Manu bowed his head, and to his surprise, the wolvite trotted off to his pack. Manu didn't wait around to see what would happen. He spun and ran out of the cave to where Jalall was waiting.

"Let's not do that again," his friend said, breathing heavily.

Manu moved them away from the cave. "Agreed. I wish we could've gotten to see who their dinner was."

"I didn't spot Chanda's fur. I saw several packs, though. It looked like whoever it was intended to set up in that cave for a long period."

"Which is too close to Navara for my liking."

Jalall twisted his lips. "Could be more mercenaries."

"Could be."

"They could be the ones who attacked me or caused the avalanche."

Manu adjusted his fur to cover his lower face. "Any of it is possible. We can't find out now. Everywhere we turn, we still come up empty for answers."

"Inej didn't say anything?"

He glanced at Jalall as they caught up with the others. "I didn't want to lock her in my room, and since the herbs were working, I left her unconscious."

"Where are our other...guests?"

Manu pointed at the sky. "They're taking a look at the avalanche sight."

"She can keep a...I mean *him*...veiled, too?"

"She said she could."

Jalall whistled softly. "A Fae. Who knew such a thing existed? I wonder what else is out there?"

"Right now, I'd settle for knowing where Chanda is."

36

Inej opened her eyes. The pain had dulled to a whisper, a shadow of what it had been. Worse, though, was the realization that she was alive. She had accepted her death, welcomed it, even. No one had asked if she wanted to be healed. They had done it without her permission.

Her anger was swift as she rolled to her side and pushed herself up to see if she was alone. The ire turned to fury when she realized that she was in Manu's bed. Hot tears rolled down her cheeks. She'd had a simple life in Belanore. It hadn't been great, but at least she hadn't worried about being killed.

Or having to take Manu's life.

She dashed at her tears, but more came—as if a floodgate had been opened. She tucked her legs against herself and dropped her head into her hands, giving herself a moment to let it all out before lifting her head and drying her eyes. She had gotten herself into this mess, and she would find a way out.

Inej cautiously slipped her legs over the side of the bed and stood. She was weak, but not so much that she couldn't stand on her own. She grimaced when she found she was still in the clothes she had been wearing when she was attacked. It looked like someone had cleaned off some of the dried blood, but she would feel better after a long soak.

Once she started the water in the tub, she walked to the mirror and looked at herself. The person staring back at her might have her same features, but she felt different now. Was it because she had come so close to death? It was like she had aged a hundred years since leaving Belanore and crossing the Dangerous Peaks. Where once she had been so certain, she was now doubtful and indecisive of everything and everyone. She could no longer tell what was the truth and what was a lie—if she ever could.

The urge to leave, to run away and act as if none of this had ever happened, was strong. That was the simplest way, but she would regret it later. As strange as it seemed, she liked Navara. She had found a place for herself. Well, aside from the fact that someone wanted her dead.

Inej slipped out of her clothes and into the water. The last time she had been here was with Manu. She didn't know where he was, but if she was in his room, then he must have brought her. He would return. That would bring discussions about who had attacked her, and the continuation of the conversation they'd begun before he was called away.

Her hand moved across the steamy water as she reclined. She wanted to believe that Manu was the elf he had shown her. She could easily imagine what their life could be like if he were. Her moving into his home and becoming his wife. They might even raise a child or two.

But always in the back of her mind, she would fear that he

might discover why she'd really come to his city. And when he did, everything they had built together would be ripped apart. She wouldn't survive that.

She could come clean and tell him everything. He might kill her, lock her away, or send her away—after he got all the information from her, of course. Whether he was the monster she'd first thought him to be, or the elf she hoped he was, his first and foremost concern was the safety of his people. He would sever all ties with her.

Or...she could do what she had come to do. She could feed him the poison without knowing if she had the correct villain. She'd never make it out of the mountains—if she even got free of the city. Jalall would hunt her down and kill her the moment he found Manu's body.

In every scenario, she ended up hurting, and either alone or dead.

She slipped beneath the surface to wet her hair and then came up for air. She took her time cleaning herself. The wounds were healed, but they were still very tender. Every movement taxed her. When she finished, she drained the water and rose to dry off.

There were no clothes for her, so she searched Manu's wardrobe and found one of his shirts, slipping it on. At least she would be clean and covered for whoever walked through the door. She sank onto the foot of the bed and used his comb to begin the arduous task of detangling her hair.

She had come close to death three times now, which was three times too many for her. She couldn't do a fourth. It was too much emotionally to accept and sort through in the aftermath. If they had let her die, she wouldn't be faced with the decisions before her now. There wasn't a good answer, no matter how she looked at it.

Gita must have been blind to think she was capable of carrying out this undercover work. Granted, she had been right about Inej getting into Navara, but not about the rest. Inej was tired of being deceitful and finding ways to talk around things so she didn't outright lie. But an omission was still a falsehood. She was just tired of it all.

She smoothed the comb through her hair one final time before she returned it to its place. As she turned away, Manu's shirt brushed the healing flesh of her abdomen. She faced the mirror and lifted the garment to reveal the jagged, pink flesh. All of her wounds were sensitive and tender, but the one on her abdomen was more so.

Her fingers loosened, and the shirt fell back into place, covering the injury. She tried to remember the attack, but her memories were fuzzy. Had she heard something? She must have, because she'd turned around. She couldn't recollect a face, clothing, or even a voice. They had struck her three times, which could only mean they had come for her.

Could it have been Chanda? Or Tahmine? Or was it someone else? Inej may never find out, which was disturbing. She could stand next to her assailant and never know.

She turned away from the mirror and peered around the room. Manu's space. His sanctuary. She saw him everywhere her eyes landed, and feared that she would always feel him, no matter where she went.

Her gaze stopped at the window. She slowly made her way over, ensuring that she couldn't be seen from below. Nothing seemed out of place in the city. Everyone was going about their days as usual. Was that because her attacker had been caught? Or because they didn't care that someone had tried to end her life?

Inej tried to see the candy shop from the window, but it would require her to get closer. An elf had tried to kill her, and she wasn't ready to show herself to a city full of them just yet. Her gaze then slid to Jalall's home. She observed the outside, thinking about the layout of the residence, when she saw a familiar figure striding toward the house. Her breath caught in her throat at the sight of Manu shrugging out of his coat, covered in snow and ice. He raked a hand through his dark hair, dislodging more snow. She waited for him to look in her direction, but he was in conversation with Jalall as they hurriedly walked through the front door.

She spun around and scanned the room. How long until he came home? She didn't want him to know that she had seen him. Did she get back into bed? Maybe sit in the chair and pretend to read? Would someone who had almost died do that? She looked down at her bare legs. He might be at Jalall's to get her some clothes.

Finally, she decided on the chair. Yet the moment she sat, she couldn't get comfortable. She tried tucking her legs against herself, then crossed one over the other, but nothing felt right. She was nervous, and that made everything worse. The chair wouldn't do. She rose and returned to the bed, sitting on the edge with her hands clutched. She had no idea what she would say when she saw Manu.

Her pulse kicked up the moment she heard someone outside. Hope bloomed, fierce and reckless, as she stared at the door, willing it to be him. But when it opened, it was Chanda who filled the doorway. Something inside her quietly shattered.

The elf tossed clothes onto the bed. "Get dressed. Manu wants to talk to you."

Inej had never been modest. Women all had the same parts,

just in different shapes. But something about Chanda's appearance —and tone—rubbed her the wrong way. Inej kept her irritable comments to herself as she stared at the elf.

Chanda crossed her arms over her chest and stared back, her black eyes flashing dangerously. Defiance flared within Inej as she lifted Manu's shirt over her head and laid it on the bed. If the elf wanted to see her body, Inej would give her a show. She didn't notice the coat until she reached for the clothes. Apprehension curdled her stomach. Had Manu learned who she was? Was he sending her away?

"Are we going somewhere?" Inej asked.

"I'm simply doing as Manu wants."

Inej dressed, surprised by the fur-lined boots. They were another confirmation that she was leaving the city. She grabbed the coat and waited. Chanda rolled her eyes and motioned for her to follow. They walked wordlessly from the room. Inej wanted to know where they were going, but Chanda wouldn't tell her. She cut the elf a side-eye, wondering if she was the one who had attacked her.

They didn't run into a single person as they left the manor through a side exit, but even then, Chanda didn't take her toward Jalall's. Instead, they headed in the direction of the waterfall. Every step felt definitive, as if her time were ending.

Chanda easily maneuvered the steep steps hidden by the manor while Inej fought to keep up. The climb was short but strenuous after her healing. Suddenly, Chanda pushed her into a narrow tunnel. The elf stayed right behind her, making sure Inej didn't attempt to run off. Not that she would know where to go.

"What is this place?" Inej asked after several minutes in the dark tunnel.

"An escape in case the city is ever invaded. Only the leader's family knows of it."

"But you aren't Manu's family."

Chanda chuckled, which was reply enough.

The floor dipped and rose beneath her feet as they wound their way through it. Inej kept her hands on the walls to either side of her to guide herself. Twice, she jabbed a finger into a protruding rock. She wanted out of the tight space and into the light, even if that meant going into the elements.

But why was Manu taking her from Navara? Had he discovered the poison? Did he know Gita had sent her? The thought that he had saved her, only to deliver a death blow, made her sick to her stomach.

"Go," Chanda bit out, shoving her from behind when Inej slowed.

She picked up her pace again. What was she to do against an elf? "Where are you taking me?"

"You'll find out soon enough."

The cold smashed into her like a wall, stealing her breath. She heard the wind howling faintly as fingers of light seeped into the darkness. Her teeth began to chatter, and she clenched her jaw tightly, refusing to let Chanda hear the fear rattling her bones. Because it was fear. Raw, bone-deep terror.

The elf shoved her forward again, driving her the last few feet into the swirling snow. Inej fumbled to fasten the long coat, her fingers stiff. She wrapped her arms around her middle and curled her hands into fists for more warmth. How had she forgotten how the wind cut through everything?

Chanda stayed at her back, silent but ever-present, forcing her onward. Inej sank into the thick snow, the cold biting through the fur of her boots. She dared a glance behind her. There was no time to think about what to do. It seemed the decision was out of her hands. Someone had made it for her. She focused on putting one foot in front of the other as the mountain—and everything within it—disappeared behind her.

37

"Here," Jalall said as he set some food down.

Manu pushed the bowl away and walked from the kitchen, his thoughts rotating between Inej, Chanda, Tahmine, and the Masters. The last thing he wanted was a meal.

"You need to eat to keep up your strength," Jalall said as he followed. "We've been out all day."

Manu shook his head and continued down the hallway. His patience was unraveling quickly. Every passing second spent waiting for Rhi and Con chipped away at his calm. He clenched his fist, his breath tight in his chest. An overwhelming sense of urgency slammed into him, demanding he get to Inej.

He had his hand on the knob and the door open. As he began to step out, Jalall shouting his name made him pause. Manu looked back to find Rhi and Con standing in the front room. Still, he hesitated. Manu looked toward his house. No one could get to

Inej there. It was only apprehension that made him think she was in danger. Inej would remain safe—and sleeping—for another few moments.

Manu set down his foot and slowly closed the door. His hand wouldn't loosen on the knob, however. He pried each finger away, and when he turned to face the Dragon King and Fae, the insistence to get to Inej doubled. He parted his lips to tell them he would be right back when Rhi's words silenced him.

"Sorry it took so long," she said. "But we wanted to be sure."

Manu frowned as he looked between the couple. "Of what?" Then he raised a hand to stop them as his chest tightened. "This will have to wait. I need to get to Inej."

"What is it?" Jalall asked.

Manu shook his head. "I don't know. I can't explain it."

"Rhi," Con said.

She was striding toward Manu and Jalall. "Already ahead of you, my love."

Even though Manu expected to be jumped, he was still dazed to suddenly find himself in his chambers. He spun to the bed to find it empty. Inej's bloodstained clothes were piled near the tub, and one of his tunics had been carefully laid out at the foot of the bed. He brought it to his face and inhaled, his eyes closing as Inej's scent mixed with his soap drifted through his senses.

Manu tightened his fingers on the shirt as he opened his eyes. "She woke up alone. I wasn't here. I should've been here. Someone should've been with her."

"How did she get out?" Con asked.

Manu forced himself to release the tunic and drop it onto the bed as he scanned the room. "There's no way she could've left. Nor could anyone have gotten in."

"That's not entirely true," Jalall stated.

Anger blazed unchecked as Manu swung his head to his friend. "What do you mean?"

"I can pick your magic. Same as you can pick mine." Jalall swallowed and glanced at the floor.

Manu's legs went weak as he realized that Jalall was right. He scanned the room, looking for something, anything, that would give him proof.

"Would someone please explain?" Rhi asked.

Jalall ran a hand down his face, weariness creeping into his voice. "Manu, Chanda, and I used to pick doors locked with magic. No one was better at it than Chanda."

"Which means she had access to this room, and thereby, Inej," Rhi said.

Manu couldn't imagine Chanda doing such a thing, but the facts were indisputable. "Why would she do this?"

"You can ask her once we find her," Con said. "Where would she go?"

"She knows the city as well as either of us does," Jalall answered. He suddenly swung panic-filled eyes to Manu. "Does she know about the tunnel?"

Manu shook his head and looked at the others. "I never told her, but it's the only way she could get out of Navara without being seen."

"Then let's assume she knows. Where would she take Inej?" Rhi asked.

Manu wrenched open the door. "I aim to find out."

"Wait," Con called, halting him.

Manu glanced back at Con to see the Dragon King watching him with an intense look. He stared down the hall, the need to hurry after Inej warring with the desire to learn what Con and Rhi had found.

"If Chanda wanted to kill Inej, she would've done it here," Jalall pointed out.

That didn't help Manu any. The fact that Chanda had taken Inej was enough to make him want to flatten every peak in the range. He shut the door and turned to the others. They had two minutes.

"You were right," Con told him. "The avalanche was intentional. There are black marks in the ice that suggest magic was used."

Rhi nodded, her silver eyes meeting Manu's. "We didn't uncover much there to track. But we did find where Jalall and his team were attacked. The group responsible for that was large enough that they left deep grooves in the snow that had yet to fill up."

"Which made it easy to trail them back to a meeting point," Con added.

Had Chanda gone to them? Had his friend taken Inej there? Manu had to know. "Where are they and how many?"

"There are fourteen in total. They seemed very confident they wouldn't be found," Rhi answered.

Con grunted. "That will be their downfall."

"Where are they?" Manu repeated through clenched teeth.

It was Con who caught his gaze. "Two peaks southwest of the avalanche site."

Jalall asked, "What do we do? Go after the group, or Chanda and Inej?"

There was only one place Manu needed to be. Others wouldn't understand, but he didn't care. He turned to Jalall. "Take thirty soldiers and go after the group. I want to double the sentries while the rest of the army waits here."

Jalall's frown deepened. "You can't go after Inej alone."

"He won't be," Con replied.

Manu looked from Jalall to Rhi and finally to Con. "All right. We'll carry out dual strikes. I want to make sure Chanda believes I'm alone."

"No one will see us," Rhi vowed as she tied her hair back from her face.

"We'll trail you and only take to the skies if needed," Con told him.

Jalall grinned eagerly. "I like this plan."

Manu clasped his friend's forearm. "Be safe, and good luck."

"Same to you," Jalall whispered.

Rhi and Con vanished from sight before Jalall opened the door. Manu grabbed his coat and exited his home. He ran, uncaring that his sprint caused others to notice. He just raced straight for the waterfall and the hidden stairs.

His father had made him climb this path blindfolded, weighed down with items, and in a full-out run. Manu knew exactly where to put his feet, when to grab a rock to hoist himself up, and when to duck low-hanging rock shelves. He sped up the incline, pushing himself harder and faster than he ever had. Horrors of all kinds of things being done to Inej filled his mind. He shut them out and focused on what he could do—track.

Manu finally reached the tunnel and turned to the side to squeeze his shoulders through. The fit was uncomfortably tight, but that didn't slow him. The only thing that would stop him now was death.

He barreled through the passage in a frenzied fury, not slowing until he saw the exit. Every instinct told him to keep running, but he had made too many mistakes. A couple of seconds here could save Inej's life.

Manu crept to the entrance, magic in his palms, and squinted against the piercing brightness that momentarily blinded him. He blinked rapidly to let his eyes adjust. The first thing he saw was two sets of footprints. Given the tracks' small size, they were women's. He looked ahead, hoping to spot Inej and Chanda, but there was nothing but white. The snow was coming down thicker now. Soon, it would wipe out the trail.

"Where are you heading, Chanda?" he whispered as he stepped into the snow.

Manu sank to his knees before using the path already forged. Within a few feet, the two sets of tracks became one. He started running along the packed snow to catch up to them. It didn't matter which of them was leading. It would be slow-going. Yet no matter how fast he ran, Manu caught no sight of them.

He had to know if Inej had left of her own volition. Because no matter how he looked at it, he couldn't imagine Chanda—who he thought of as a sister—forcing her to leave. Chanda had always been the voice of reason in their trio. Had something changed that he'd missed? Were there signs he had been too blind to notice?

Manu raced up an incline. He could jump, but he needed to be cautious. He had no idea what awaited him once he reached the top. But he wouldn't be alone either. He didn't look behind him for Con and Rhi. They were there.

Finally, he crested the mountain. His palms pulsed with magic waiting to be released. A cruel wind battered him and whipped snow from atop boulders. Icy shards pelted him as he hunkered next to a set of rocks and scanned the long, wide mountaintop and down the opposite slope.

There, halfway down, he spotted two figures. He didn't recognize either of the coats, but Chanda could've traded hers to throw him off. He scrutinized the trees and the nearby mountains, looking for anything that moved, anything that could be a threat. There was nothing but the two figures. But there were hundreds of places to lie in wait to ambush someone.

"Is that them?" Rhi's voice asked from beside him.

He glanced over and saw shoe impressions but nothing else. "I think so. I can cut them off, but I wanted to make sure no others were waiting."

"We'll take care of them if there are," came Con's deep brogue from behind him.

Manu slipped from behind the boulder and ran to the edge of the mountaintop before launching himself into the air. His strong legs helped him soar down the slope, his eyes locked on his targets. He landed behind the two figures and yanked them both backward to the ground.

But it wasn't Chanda and Inej looking up at him. Two unfamiliar Mountain Elves stared up at him. Confusion filled him as he stumbled back a step, his chest tightening with panic. This wasn't right. The tracks had led him there. So, where was Inej? His pulse roared in his ears as dread rose quickly.

"Who are you?" he demanded of the females.

The one on the left smiled as she raised her arm. He anticipated her magic and blocked it, but he wasn't quick enough against the other. Tight fingers of magic wrapped around his left arm and sank into his chest. Pain erupted through him like lightning, skimming along every nerve ending before latching onto his heart.

He dropped to his knees, unable to move as darkness closed in around him. All the while, laughter rang in his ears.

38

Inej had made a mistake. A big one. And now, she was neck-deep in something far more dangerous than she had expected. The structure was a graveyard of shattered stone, broken relics, and bodies locked in frost, like a grotesque echo of whatever horror had befallen the place. Chanda moved ahead, silent and steady, guiding her through level after level of a place that had once dripped in wealth but was now nothing more than a ruin steeped in death.

It was hard to know what was more treacherous: Chanda or the building.

The rooms were enormous. Windows above them let in small slivers of light that blinked off the jewels adorning the dead. Frost scaled the walls and curled around banisters to produce beautiful, haunting designs. Inej's heart lurched into her throat when she slipped, barely catching herself before she fell. She held out her arms, her heartbeat and breathing labored, as she stared down at the icy floor. She had been too intent on looking around to think about how treacherous the floor was.

Inej slowly straightened, realizing too late that she must be in Shaldorn. She looked behind her and saw a set of double doors with the glass blown away. She didn't understand why Chanda hadn't brought them through there, but it didn't matter. It was a way out, and Inej wanted out of the stronghold.

Manu had practically spat its name when he spoke of it. Why would he bring her here? Inej turned and found Chanda, who had halted midway up one of two curving staircases, and stood watching her. At least she thought Chanda watched her. The hood of her coat was pulled up so that Inej couldn't see her face.

"Where's Manu?" Inej demanded.

"Hopefully, running around Navara searching for you."

Icy fingers of terror coiled ominously around Inej. She had willingly followed Chanda out of Navara to Shaldorn. There was no way out. No one would be coming to her rescue. Because who would think to look for her here?

"Why are you doing this?" Inej asked.

"To finish what you began."

So, this disturbing, despicable place would be her tomb. But that wasn't what scared Inej. It was Chanda's words. If she knew that Inej had come to the Peaks to kill Manu, then that meant Chanda planned to bring Manu here.

Inej wished she had never left his room. Why hadn't she waited for him? She'd known in her gut that something wasn't right, but she'd gone with Chanda anyway. A human facing an elf. There wasn't much Inej could do now.

Chanda pushed back the hood of her coat to reveal her face. Black eyes as cold as a grave and just as unforgiving watched Inej.

There was no warmth or mercy anywhere to be found. The monster Inej had sought hadn't been Manu. It was Chanda.

The elf's smile was chilling. "I see you're putting it all together now. You dismissed me because you saw me as nothing more than a servant."

"Manu and Jalall are your friends. How can you do this to them?"

"Friends?" Chanda repeated with a bark of laughter. "They stopped being friends when they forgot about me. Jalall thought he was being kind by giving me the job of keeping his home. I wanted to spit at his pitiful offer, but it was a way in. They spoke freely around me, which allowed me to gather information."

Hatred coiled through Inej, dark and venomous. "You gave Gita the information on Manu."

"I've been working with her since she first built Shaldorn." Chanda lifted her hands and turned in a circle. "You should've seen this place when it was in its prime. It was spectacular." She stopped and looked at Inej. "Gita recognized my potential. We made a fortune together, and in the process, I've worked my way up the ranks of the Masters."

"Was your husband part of it?"

Chanda rolled her eyes and wrinkled her nose in distaste. "He was a means to an end. A few months after our marriage, I made sure he had an accident, so I no longer had to suffer his attempts at sex."

"What was your excuse for trying to kill me?"

The elf chuckled and walked to a nearby corpse before taking a bracelet from its arm and putting it on hers. "That was Tahmine. She was beside herself when she learned about you and Manu."

Tahmine would have been her second guess. "So, you saved me for this?"

"Oh, I didn't save you. I saved Tahmine. I got her out of the city before someone put things together."

"She's in this with you?"

Chanda's smile grew chilly as her amusement waned. "Tahmine is dead. She couldn't get over Manu, and then she rejected my advances. Now. Enough with the questions. You need to prepare yourself."

Inej swallowed hard as trepidation churned in her belly. "For?"

"You came to the Peaks to kill Manu, and that's exactly what you're going to do. I gave you plenty of time, but you let every opportunity pass."

"Why don't you do it?"

Chanda strode down the steps and grabbed Inej's arm, her fingers digging in deep as she dragged Inej up the steps. She was surprised at the elf's strength.

"You're the perfect scapegoat. Manu will die, Jalall will be killed while searching for you, and all of that will allow me to step in and take over the city, giving the Masters a foothold in the mountains," Chanda declared.

"It'll never work."

"Oh, it will. Manu is tracking what he thinks is our path. It won't be long before he's brought here, and we can wrap this up."

Inej waited until they were at the top of the steps before jerking her arm free. "And when do you take my life?"

Chanda grinned. "You can walk away if you do what I say."

"You expect me to believe that?" Inej asked dubiously.

The elf shrugged and started walking. "I don't care if you do or don't. You can either take the path I'm offering and potentially go free, or you can refuse, and I'll make you watch Manu die horribly before I kill you."

Inej looked over the banister to the ballroom below. She wouldn't get far if she tried to run. Humans learned to survive among the elves by bowing to their dominance and biding their time. It made for a degrading, miserable life. Humans had been able to outwit the elves a few times, however. Inej's chances were slim, but it was all she had. She didn't even have a plan, but she would meekly do as Chanda commanded while she tried to come up with one.

She looked at the doorway once more before following Chanda. The room they ended up in was filled with equipment Inej didn't have names for, and she never wanted to. There were sharp spikes on one, a glass box that looked like a coffin, and other ghastly items obviously used to inflict pain.

Inej should've listened to Manu's descriptions of Shaldorn more carefully. He'd told her everything she needed to know, had she but heard him. No one who sided with the Masters would feel such disgust and horror. Manu had shown her who he was, but she had been too blind to see it.

"Make yourself comfy," Chanda said with a chuckle.

Inej wished more than ever that she had a weapon or magic she could use. But she didn't have either. She was at a clear disadvantage in every way she looked at it. Unless she freed Manu. He could take on Chanda and anyone else. Whether she liked it or not, he was their only way to freedom.

She meandered through the many apparatuses, looking for anything she might be able to use as a weapon. There were plenty of sharp instruments, but nothing she could remove for her own use.

"Why side with the Masters?" Inej asked. "Why turn on your own people?"

"Why do you care?"

Inej glanced over her shoulder to find Chanda leaning a hip against a desk. The elf's dark eyes followed her. "I'm curious."

"Fine. You want to know. I'll tell you. Manu has a position of power he doesn't use. He could rule the Dangerous Peaks instead of just our mountain, but he doesn't. He believes the other tribes should be able to live as they always have."

"What's wrong with that?"

Chanda snorted loudly. "He could have a sizable army by ruling all. I knew when he proudly announced that he had helped shut down this place that he would never be the one we needed. Nor would he understand what aligning with the Masters could bring the mountains."

"I suppose you don't care that your people will begin to disappear."

"It'll be months yet. There are still plenty to be taken in the lowlands."

Inej was appalled by how indifferent Chanda was about it all. "Do you know what happens to those who are taken?"

"You expect me to believe you're concerned about elves?"

Inej turned to face the elf with more strength than she felt, then asked louder, "Do you know?"

"I do. Do you want to know?"

Chanda's voice was lilting and soft, but the excitement burning in her eyes terrified Inej. She should let it go. Forget it. But she couldn't. For better or worse, she had to know.

"Aye," Inej croaked, her voice a broken whisper.

The elf's delight was palpable. "They're turned into slaves. At least the ones who survive being broken."

Inej's throat clogged with emotion—outrage and disgust threatening to swallow her. She thought about Krata's bright smile and cheerful disposition being wiped away forever. "All of this for...slaves?"

"Life is hard. And if you're going to survive, then you need to learn who's in power and join them."

"Even if they're criminals?"

Chanda grunted. "Don't be so naïve. Nothing is as black and white as you think it is. You believe what we're doing is unethical, but you don't see the big picture."

"Explain it to me, then."

"I don't need to explain or justify anything to you, human. The gods put your kind with us to be dominated and subjugated. If you meant anything, you would be able to stand against us." Chanda motioned to her with disgust. "Without magic, you have no defenses. You are pests to be used as we see fit."

Inej turned away. Chanda had lived alongside Manu and Jalall, pretending to be their friend, all the while plotting their deaths to take control of Navara and enslave her own people. There had to be something Inej could use in this evil place, if not to free Manu, then to protect herself. She needed to alert everyone in the city so they could take a stand. It wasn't just getting out of Shaldorn. Inej would need to traverse the Peaks once more. She had looked back often as they walked to help her navigate a return, but all it took was one misstep before the mountains claimed her.

"Keep looking. You get to decide which of these we'll strap Manu to," Chanda said with a laugh.

Inej was appalled that Gita had been able to manipulate her so easily. Worse, Inej had willingly believed her without hesitation. Inej might not have carried out Manu's death sentence, but she had been dishonest and deceitful to everyone at Navara. That made her as guilty as Chanda and Gita.

Chanda had dangled freedom before her, but Inej wouldn't be allowed to live. All she needed was to get Manu free. She got to pick which of the torture devices he was put in, which could give her some kind of advantage. She swiftly perused the numerous devices and realized that each one got progressively worse. She didn't understand how half of them worked. It didn't take long for her to understand that none of the devices *wouldn't* inflict the utmost torture.

"I do believe Manu has arrived," Chanda said into the silence.

Inej whirled around and saw her walking away from the desk. Chanda waited near the doors as two female elves dragged in an unconscious Manu. They first appeared as Mountain Elves, but the longer Inej stared at them, the more they started to look like Dark Elves.

They had Manu's hands covered and bound so he couldn't use his magic. The women spoke to Chanda in low voices. Inej moved closer, hoping to pick up bits of their conversation, but the trio noticed her and ended their exchange.

"Which one shall it be?" Chanda asked her.

Inej nodded to the desk. "The chair."

"Nice try. Pick again."

"You didn't specify that it had to be one of the apparatuses," Inej argued.

Fury contorted Chanda's pretty features into something dreadful. "You had your chance to kill him with the poison. This is your last chance to choose. Or I will."

"Fine," Inej hurried to reply before the elf could say more. She pointed to her left. "That one."

Chanda followed her finger as a smile slowly pulled at her lips. "You heard the human. Get him hooked up."

39

The second Manu woke, he knew he was in trouble. Agony lanced up his arms, his muscles screaming, and joints pulled to the edge of tearing. He hung suspended by his wrists, and with the numbness in his fingers, it seemed he had been there awhile.

His head was bent forward, and he cracked open one eye to see where he was. He noticed that someone had removed his boots, and his feet dangled several inches above the ground. His stomach curdled in horror as he recognized the flooring as Gita's torture room at Shaldorn. He stopped himself from jerking away in disgust, just in time.

Each time he drew in a breath, it felt as if dozens of blades scored his lungs. He wouldn't be able to keep himself still for much longer. He might as well let his captors know he was awake and get things moving.

Manu took a deep breath, bracing himself for what he would find, and lifted his head. At first, he didn't see anything but the many torture devices. He looked up to see that he dangled by a metal bar, his arms outstretched. They had bound and covered his hands as an extra precaution against his magic. As torture devices went, it didn't seem that bad at first glance. But Gita wouldn't have something in the room that didn't deliver the utmost agony.

His coat had also been removed. The pain from hanging was so severe that he hadn't realized he was freezing until that moment. His body began to shake uncontrollably, making the chains rattle. He continued to scan the room until he spotted Chanda standing by Gita's desk, her arms crossed over her chest.

"It's about time you woke," she said. "I was growing weary of waiting."

"What are you doing?" he demanded.

"You've always believed yourself smarter, stronger, and faster than the rest of us. Surely, you know the answer."

"I've known you for my whole life. You're like a sister. This isn't you."

Her smile was cold and filled with malevolence. "You know nothing about me."

"Then tell me," he bade. "Tell me why you hate me so much that you would do this."

"I knew you were the wrong person to lead Navara when we were only ten. Your inability to grow into your full potential would allow someone else to rule the Peaks and all the tribes. I realized then that I had to find a way to remove you."

Manu's blood ran with ice as he stared at the woman he had considered a friend. He had been afraid that someone in Navara had betrayed him, but he never would've suspected Chanda. "When did you join the Masters?"

"I found Gita when Shaldorn was being constructed," she said, dropping her arms to her sides as she walked to him. "I saw the power Gita wielded, and she saw how I hungered for more."

Chanda had been working against him all these years. Now, he knew how the Masters had learned about Ravi, Yasmin, Dain, Arya, and his identity. He had been the one to share how he'd helped them with Jalall and Chanda.

"You might kill me, but you won't get to Jalall," Manu said.

Chanda grinned. "I wouldn't waste what little time you have left worrying about him. If he isn't already dead, he will be soon. As for your precious Navara, I will take over."

"And hand our people over to the Masters?"

"Of course. Right after I take control of all the tribes."

He shook his head. "It'll never happen."

Chanda snapped her fingers.

Manu saw movement on his periphery and turned his head. A jolt of surprise ran through him when he spotted Inej. He stared at her, waiting for her to meet his gaze, but she wouldn't look at him. Her eyes were focused on Chanda. Manu looked at his childhood friend and saw Chanda's obvious delight as she looked between them.

Chanda waited until Inej stood beside her before slowly walking around the human. "You came racing after us, but you haven't asked about Inej once since waking." Chanda tsked.

Manu stared at Inej, silently willing her to look at him. He hadn't forgotten her. She had to know that.

"Ever the champion, you brought your executioner into Navara and right into your bed." Chanda laughed as she stroked Inej's hair while looking at him with unbridled glee. "I bet that stings."

He waited for Inej to deny it, but her silence spoke volumes. An image of Inej straddling his hips, her head thrown back as he massaged her breasts, filled his mind. The pleasure had been real. But she had said she didn't believe in love. All the while, he had thought he could love enough for both of them. She had, indeed, been a blind spot that nothing could have prepared him for.

Chanda pulled a small vial from her pocket and held it up. "Gita gave her poison to use. We fully expected her to administer it within the first few days since she held such hatred for you. Of course, that's because her employer told her you were the one who led the kidnapping group. Gita played her part marvelously."

Manu had never thought to ask who Inej worked for. It hadn't seemed to matter at the time. Even if he had, he doubted that Inej would've told him the truth. She hadn't spoken much about her past, and he hadn't asked. She had been looking for a fresh start, and he had wanted to give it to her.

"You can also thank Inej for the device you're in now." Chanda winked at him as if this were some game.

Manu's arms were going numb. At least it helped alleviate some of the pain. "You killed Tahmine."

Chanda's smile slipped as she turned away. "She went against my order to leave Inej alone."

"She was working with you, then?"

"She only saw you and the future she wouldn't let go of as your wife," Chanda bit out as she spun back to him. "Then you flaunted your affair with a human in front of her. How did you think she would react?"

There was something more there. Something Chanda didn't want him to know. Manu had always known how to push her to get what he wanted, and he used that knowledge now. "I was clear with her about where I stood. It was casual and nothing more."

"You should've cut her off! Then, she might have seen me!"

He frowned at Chanda, taken aback by her shouted confession. "You should've made your intentions clear to her."

"There's nothing you can do for her anymore." Chanda turned Inej toward him and leaned close to her. Then, in a fake whisper, she said, "It's time."

Manu slid his gaze to Inej. He had held her, kissed her, and pleasured her untold times. Chanda had cautioned him about her, but he had ignored everyone's warnings. Nothing had mattered but what he felt for Inej. He was a fool for not seeing what had been right in front of him. He didn't care about his life. He was only concerned about his people and Jalall. Where the fuck were Rhi and Con?

Inej didn't move. Chanda's lips twisted angrily as she dug her fingers into the sleeve of Inej's coat and whispered something in her ear that he couldn't make out. Inej reluctantly lifted her gaze to him. Her brown eyes shimmered with a weight of what couldn't be undone—and the apology that she couldn't say.

Did he believe her? Could he? Damn, but he found himself doing just that.

"Stop stalling," Chanda said to Inej between clenched teeth. "Remember what I said."

Manu shot Chanda a withering glare, but she wasn't paying him any attention. Inej jerked her arm out of Chanda's grasp and took a small step forward. Manu's gaze followed her as she reluctantly made her way to the handle on the side of the machine.

Chanda moved to stand before him. "What does it feel like to know that you fell for someone who sought to end your life?"

His feet were free. He could kick out his leg and stop Inej from reaching the handle. It wouldn't buy him much time, but it would be something. He engaged his abdominal muscles and started to lift his leg, when a white-hot sting pierced his arm, sharp and sudden like fire slithering across torn skin. He hissed and looked up to find a crescent-shaped push dagger connected to a telescoping pole. The cut from the blade's kiss was shallow, yet pain thrummed like a drumbeat beneath his skin as blood ran down his arm.

Chanda chuckled. "Tiny cuts. Each time you move, another blade will come out and slice you. How many do you think you'll be able to take before you succumb? Or, you can hang there and eventually freeze. Either way, it's going to be a slow death."

"You might kill me. You might even defeat Jalall. But you'll be crushed," he taunted.

"By whom?" Chanda demanded. "You have no idea what's happening. Your supposed friends have left you to deal with things on your own. You have no way to contact them and ask for help. I doubt they would come even if they could. They certainly wouldn't get here in time. Pull the lever, Inej."

Manu slid his gaze to Inej. "You don't have to do anything but get out of here. Run and don't look back."

Chanda sighed loudly. "She won't go anywhere because she knows what I'll do to you if she does."

"You plan on killing me no matter what I do," Inej said as she turned to Chanda. "I came to the mountains looking for revenge. I let my anger and hurt cloud my judgment."

Chanda rolled her eyes. "Stop. I have no wish to hear that you've changed your mind. You made a deal with Gita. There's no getting out of that."

Blood was soaking the sleeve of his tunic. Manu wanted to do something, *anything*. He was used to fixing problems, but this was one scenario he couldn't do anything about. Not for himself or Inej. And that distressed him the most.

"Now, pull the damn lever!" Chanda shouted.

Inej took a defiant step back.

Manu saw Chanda's rage about to explode. "Just do it," he urged Inej.

She shot him a puzzled frown. She didn't want to hurt him. Yet, she needed to. He didn't know what was keeping Rhi and Con, but it was crucial that he buy as much time for them to find him as he could. He dipped his head, telling Inej it was okay.

"Do it," he whispered.

Tears filled her eyes as she lifted her hand and placed shaky fingers on the mechanical lever.

"How sweet," Chanda said sarcastically. Then, in a tight voice, she ordered, "Pull it now."

Manu steeled himself as Inej tugged the switch down. For a heartbeat, nothing happened. The glee on Chanda's face was all the warning he got, right before nine searing lines sliced open the flesh on his back, each tail of the blades from the whip biting deep and dragging pain in jagged arcs.

He attempted to brace for more, but nothing could dull the first strike. His skin felt flayed, his nerves lit like a battlefield. His muscles locked, and a strangled sound he barely recognized as his voice escaped between his clenched teeth as blood welled and heat pulsed through his raw, burning flesh.

Then, the next strike came. He pressed his lips together to keep his agony inside, but his bellow escaped on the third assault. One of the blades hit the bone of his spine and caused him to bow his back. Before he knew what was happening, dozens of blades cut into his arms and legs.

40

Inej was horrified by the scene before her. She rushed to Manu in an attempt to hold his legs and keep him still so he wouldn't be cut again, but she never made it. The elves who'd brought him in were suddenly there, tackling her to the ground. She banged her chin on the floor, sending pain shooting across her face and into her scalp. She tried to look up at Manu, but one of the elves put their hand on the back of her head to hold it down as Chanda's laugh echoed around the room. Manu had gone silent, but she heard the sickening splat of blood as it dripped steadily onto the floor, mixed with the squeak of the chains as he swayed.

She was no match for the two elves, but she couldn't just lie there and do nothing. "Get off me!" Inej yelled in vain.

"What do you think you're going to do, human?" one of them mocked.

Inej saw the spark of black as one elf released a bolt of magic near her cheek. And then, suddenly, they were gone. The moment

Inej was free, she rolled to the side and jumped to her feet. Chanda's eyes were narrowed as she glared at her. The two Dark Elves pulled themselves up from the floor with murderous expressions.

"How did you do that?" Chanda demanded.

Before she could respond, a feminine voice in an accent she didn't recognize whispered in her ear, "If you want to free Manu, do as I say."

Inej tensed, unsure what to make of the woman or her words. But at this point, she needed all the help she could get.

"Answer me," Chanda warned as she took a menacing step toward Inej, her hand out.

The threat of bodily harm was clear, but Inej lifted her chin. It no longer mattered whether she died or not. Someone had come to help Manu, which meant she would do whatever she could to help them succeed.

Inej was breathing heavily, her palms sweating as she met Chanda's furious gaze. "Are you scared? Because you should be."

"Of you?" Chanda snorted. "Not at all."

Shadows moved, and the next thing she knew, two new Dark Elves burst from them. Chaos erupted as everything happened at once. The Dark went after the two females who had held her down. Inej turned away as Chanda directed a bolt of magic at her.

Bronze magic clashed with black as a battle erupted behind her. Inej dove to the side to escape yet another attack from Chanda. She scrambled behind one of the many machines and hastily looked for a way out.

"CHANDA!"

Inej froze at the sound of Manu's voice. She looked to where he had been hanging, but he was no longer there. Inej peered around the side of a contraption for Chanda and saw fear flash over the elf's face before she turned.

"Manu? Can you hear me?"

He fought to hold on to consciousness, and the sound of Rhi's voice gave him the reinforcement he needed. "Aye," he whispered.

"I'm freeing you. Hold on."

The manacles around his wrists released before she finished speaking. He was only a few inches off the floor, but the numerous slashes, as well as the loss of blood, had weakened him. He stayed on his feet by sheer will alone. Every breath moved the skin of his back, sending ripples of misery through him again and again.

But he forgot all of that when he saw Chanda going after Inej and bellowed her name.

"This is a nice attempt, but I expected you to have some help," his ex-friend replied when she finally faced him. "So, I made sure I had some of my own."

At her words, elves poured into the room. Manu spotted Jai and Arya, along with Rhi and a Wood Elf, engaging the new opponents. When Manu looked back at Chanda, he saw her dragging Inej out of the room. He took a step, agony filling him. Each cut felt as raw and vivid as lightning beneath his skin. But it didn't compare to the pain that exploded across his back—bright and unforgiving.

He was the only one who had seen Chanda leave, and he was the only one who could save Inej. He just had to get to her in time. Manu clenched his teeth and ran across the floor in his bare feet, ignoring the blossoming pain. There was a line of Dark standing between him and the doorway he had to get through.

Manu had only taken two steps when Rhi appeared. He watched in amazement as iridescent orbs of magic flew from her hands and struck the Dark, sending them screaming in pain as they collapsed to the ground.

Inej was several inches taller than Chanda, but the elf was stronger than she looked. Chanda had a grip on Inej's arm, her other hand latched onto Inej's hair as she yanked her head back.

"Move," Chanda ordered furiously.

Inej knew the odds of surviving had diminished significantly now that they were out of the room and away from anyone who might help. She fought against Chanda at every opportunity, hoping to give Manu time to come after them. She had seen the line of Dark Elves and knew that, despite his friends' help, it would take time for him to be able to follow. And Shaldorn was a big place with many rooms to hide in.

Chanda half-dragged, half-pushed her toward the stairs. Inej grabbed the railing to keep her feet under her. The moment she did, ice bit painfully into her fingers. She attempted to adjust her grip, but her hand slipped off at the same time Chanda yanked her. Inej lost her balance.

Then the world careened as she tumbled down the hard, granite steps, her shoulder slamming into stone, limbs flailing, and bones jolting with every brutal impact. Until she blessedly reached the bottom. She landed on her front, facing away from the stairs. She lay still, afraid to move, afraid to even breathe.

Above her, the sounds of battle drifted down, along with the occasional grunt and shout of pain. What she didn't hear was Chanda. This might be her only chance to escape. Maybe she could find her way back to Manu, if for nothing more than to beg his forgiveness for her part in everything. But first, she needed to get up.

The plunge had happened so quickly that she had no idea if Chanda had fallen with her or not. Inej lifted her head from the icy floor, and pain promptly stabbed through the base of her skull until her entire head throbbed in time with her heart. Moving cautiously, she got one hand beneath her, then the other, and pushed herself up enough to swivel her head to the staircase. Her gaze landed on Chanda, who lay just a couple of feet away, her eyes closed. She bled from a head wound.

This was it. This was how she would escape. The promise of freedom got her moving. Inej pushed past the aches and pains that seemed to cover every inch of her body. Now wasn't the time to see if any of her injuries were serious. She needed to get to Manu.

Yet as she climbed to her feet and stood unsteadily, she looked at the stairs and worried how she would make it up them again. There had to be another way. She turned, eyes searching desperately. The movement of a shadow had her heart dropping like a stone to her feet. She took a step back as a short, stout Dark Elf emerged.

"Where do you think you're going?" he sneered.

Her hope didn't just fade. It was violently, sadistically ripped out by the roots. She stumbled back a step as a sinister smile curved the Dark's lips.

He held up his hands, white magic bouncing back and forth between his palms. "I think I'll have a little fun with you before I take you to Mortham. Enjoy these last minutes of freedom, human."

The Dark shot his hands out, the magic arcing toward her. He was so quick, she didn't have time to do more than raise her arm in a feeble attempt to shield her face. Suddenly, someone dropped down between them, blocking the attack. Inej lowered her arm to find Manu, his tunic barely hanging on his body. He didn't look at her, didn't acknowledge her, as he and the Dark circled each other.

Manu didn't know if the pain from the torture or the cold hurt worse. It had taken everything he had to launch his body over the railing from the floor above. He knew the landing would be painful, but he forgot all about it when he saw the Dark going after Inej.

He managed not to just block the Dark's attack but also stay on his feet. Out of the corner of his eye, he saw Inej rush behind the stairs. Unfortunately, so did his adversary. Chanda might be down, but he hadn't been able to check to see if she was dead. That meant he had to keep an eye on her, too, in case she woke.

Manu stepped to the side and slid on some blood that ran down his legs onto the floor. He righted himself immediately, but the Dark took the opportunity and delivered a double punch of magic. The first strike got through, but Manu blocked the second. Just as he was about to release a volley of his own, the Dark vanished into the shadows.

Pain exploded through his back as his enemy delivered two more rounds of magic, along with a punch. Manu's legs buckled from the pain. He dropped his right shoulder and rolled to one knee, but when he righted himself, the Dark was gone. Manu clenched his teeth when the Dark delivered yet another strike to his back.

He felt the warm, slick blood flow in thick ribbons into the waist of his trousers. His strength was waning fast. If he didn't get the upper hand soon, he wouldn't. Manu acted as if he were turning to the left. The Dark flashed out of sight. Manu then spun to his right as he stood and reached out his hand into a curtain of shadows, wrapping his fingers around the elf's throat.

The shadows fell away to reveal the Dark's yellow eyes blazing with hatred as he grasped Manu's forearm with both hands in a vain attempt to stop him. But Manu had a hold now, and he wasn't letting go. He squeezed. The Dark's gray skin began to turn purple as Manu constricted his airway. In a last-ditch effort, the Dark struck out wildly with his magic. Several blasts struck Manu, but he didn't stop squeezing until he heard the *snap* of bone, and the elf went limp.

He tossed the Dark aside and turned around to look for Inej. Instead, he found himself facing four Dark Elves, a Moon Elf, and a Mountain Elf. Blood dripped from his arms onto the floor. He would have to be careful not to slip again. He looked at each of the elves, sizing them up. They fanned out to circle him.

Manu had faced off against more elves than this, but he hadn't been wounded then. He called to his magic as he saw the Moon Elf shift to the balls of her feet. She was getting ready to attack when Rhi appeared beside him with the Wood Elf. A second later, Arya and Jai were there.

"Do you mind if we join in?" Rhi asked him with a smile.

Jai lunged forward with a battle yell as the skirmish began.

41

Inej hid behind the staircase to watch Manu and the Dark. Even with his injuries, Manu stood strong and imposing. There was a primal, savage look to him that made her stomach quiver in exhilaration. She had seen him compassionate and patient. Now, she saw the leader.

The warrior.

She was sure Manu would win this fight, but how many more enemies awaited them? Her gaze darted to Chanda. The elf still hadn't moved, but she wasn't going to assume Chanda was dead. Inej was tired of not being able to protect herself. She turned away from Manu's battle and scanned the many bodies around her, looking for a weapon.

Inej kept low as she moved to the closest body. She cringed at the idea of touching the dead, but now wasn't the time to get squeamish. Not when her life hung in the balance. But searching the corpses wasn't easy. Their clothes were frozen, not just to their bodies, but also fabric to fabric. She had to break the ice around a pocket and then carefully slip her fingers inside to work the material free before she could even see if anything was inside. It took entirely too long.

She sat back on her haunches and looked at the next victim. Inej was about to pass him over when her gaze caught the glint of something at his hip. She glanced behind her when she heard Manu grunt, but the stairs hid him from view. She returned her attention to the body and hurried over to it. To her delight, she found the hilt of the dagger and wrapped her hand around it. Getting it free of the sheath, however, was another problem.

Inej worked it back and forth until it finally slipped free. The blade was small and decorated. She tested the edge and found it sharp, despite its ornamental look. She tucked it up the sleeve on her right arm and moved to another body. One weapon wouldn't be enough. She had to find as many as she could.

The cold caused her fingers to stiffen, making everything doubly hard since she couldn't get her hands to work right. Each time she drew in a breath, it burned her lungs. Anxiety drummed through her, pressing her to work faster and faster. She looked at ten more bodies, but none of them had any weapons.

She had moved across the vast expanse of the room toward the second staircase and spotted Manu holding the Dark by his throat. She almost called out to him, but then realized Chanda was no longer where she had been.

That pushed Inej to move quicker. She nearly shouted with joy when she found a second dagger. The hilt was made of bone, and the blade was as long as her forearm. She slipped that one into her left boot. Then she saw a sword attached to a victim's waist and jumped up to go to it. Her foot lost traction, and her arms windmilled until she had no choice but to drop to her knees.

She slid the last few feet to the body, wrapped her fingers around the hilt, and pulled. To her surprise, the sword slid free. She stood and whirled around, only to come face-to-face with Chanda.

"What do you think you're going to do with that?" the elf asked as she wiped some blood away from the side of her face. "You can't really believe you'll get close enough to hurt me with that, do you?"

Inej had wanted a fiend to loathe. Chanda embodied everything that had driven Inej to leave her job and home to travel into this merciless terrain.

Chanda held out her hand. "Give me the sword."

Inej tightened her grip on it and took a step back.

The elf's dark eyes narrowed dangerously. "That was a mistake."

Inej moved a heartbeat before the bronze wisps of magic reached her, twisting as it burned the air around her. Chanda's infuriated shriek bounced off the stone, and fury carved itself into every line of her face.

The elf advanced, bronze magic curling around her clenched fists like smoke. Inej shot a quick glance behind her as she backed up, so as not to trip over any of the corpses. The sounds of battle, louder and nearer, reached them, but Chanda didn't give it a second thought. She wanted Inej's death, and she wouldn't stop until she got it.

Inej didn't shout for help. This was her fight, and though she was at a severe disadvantage, she intended to make a stand.

"For every step you take away from me, I'm going to draw out your death that much longer," Chanda threatened.

Inej grinned. "You don't scare me."

"You'll change your tune shortly."

Inej tried to calculate when Chanda would strike next, but she misjudged badly. Magic surged from the elf's hand as the wisps stretched out in both directions. Inej didn't have time to correct herself since she was already leaning to the side. One of the wisps narrowly missed her cheek, while another burned through the fur of her coat and clothes before searing her flesh.

A shout of pain fell from her lips as she spun away, holding her right arm. Her fingers had almost loosened their hold on the sword, but she managed to keep her grip.

Inej saw a long, wide corridor before her. And at the end, a door. She jogged a few steps before whirling around to face Chanda and walking backward. "You might get away today, but Manu will find you. He and his friends will stop you."

"Half the soldiers at Navara are mine. If I don't return, they will kill the others and wait for my replacement. So, you see, we've thought of everything."

Inej switched the hand holding the sword since she couldn't lift her right arm now. Chanda's magic pulsed, right before she lifted her hand. This time, Inej dropped to her knees and leaned backward. She watched the bronze wisps shoot over her head to land behind her. Then she twisted to the side and found her feet. While she had dodged the strike, Chanda had been able to get close. Inej watched helplessly as Chanda's magic wrenched the blade from her hands. She watched as it clattered to the floor and slid far from reach.

"Where is she?" Manu asked, his foot slipping in more of his blood.

Jai caught him before he fell. "Who?"

"Inej," Rhi said as she watched the last of their enemies fall.

Manu pushed off Jai and stepped over the Sea Elf he had killed. Dread ran like wildfire through his veins when he saw that Chanda was gone. "Chanda has her. We have to find them. Now," he snapped.

"They could be anywhere," Arya said. "This place is massive."

Rhi swung her silver eyes to him. "I'll check the torture room," she said and then vanished.

"I'll head to the left," Arya said.

Jai nodded. "I'll go right."

"I'll go down," the Wood Elf said.

While his three friends could move about quicker than he could, Manu wasn't going to wait around for them. He turned to find the stairs, only to draw up short when he heard a yelp.

"Inej," he whispered, forcing his feet into a run as he headed toward the sound.

With her fingers stinging from the magic lashing her, Inej looked from the sword to Chanda.

"That was a pathetic attempt," the elf sneered.

Inej thought about the two daggers she still had hidden. All she needed was for Chanda to get a little closer. The trick would be to keep away from the elf's magic for long enough to get one of the blades free without Chanda noticing. However, Inej would still have to find a way to plunge the blade into Chanda's chest. The elf's heart would be the best bet, because Inej needed it to be somewhere incapacitating, a place that would stop her instantly. Timing was everything. It was her one and only chance.

"I came to put an end to the kidnappings," Inej said, breathing heavily as she continued to back toward the outside door.

Chanda chuckled and leisurely strolled forward. "That isn't going too well for you, is it?"

Inej shrugged and glanced behind her to see the snow that had piled up from one of the doors being left open. "I'm still alive."

"Not for long."

"You keep saying that, and yet, here I am."

Chanda's smile tightened, ire causing her nostrils to flare. "Let's change that."

Inej spun and started running in a zigzag pattern as she headed toward the door. The air got steadily colder the closer she got.

"Run, little human, run. Though you won't get far," Chanda called.

Magic exploded as it struck the wall a foot from Inej. She stayed on course for another two steps before suddenly darting to the other side. Snow erupted where her foot had been, showering her with ice.

The door was only a few feet ahead. She was nearly there, and while she had counted on the snow, she hadn't thought about the ice. Her foot went out from under her, sending her crashing onto her back. She gasped as her lungs seized, and Chanda's laugh echoed throughout the corridor.

There was no time to hesitate. Inej rolled over and jumped to her feet, letting the small dagger in her right sleeve slip into her palm. Her shoulder still throbbed, but a little discomfort while shoving the blade into Chanda's heart would be worth it.

The elf strode closer. Inej took three steps back, bringing Chanda deeper into the thick snow. The hilt fit into Inej's palm well. She kept her arm still so the elf wouldn't notice the weapon.

"Before I take what's left of your pathetic life, I want you to know that there's nowhere Manu can go that we won't find him. He'll be captured again, and he'll suffer even more. Maybe I'll enslave him."

Inej smirked. "I wonder how you'll explain him getting free to the Masters?"

The jab riled Chanda, just as she wanted. The elf lifted her right hand, tufts of bronze magic moving rapidly as she lunged. Inej knocked Chanda's arm away as she twisted to the right and brought up the blade. Chanda screamed in outrage as the weapon cut into her side in a deep groove, spilling blood onto her coat. Chanda grabbed hold of Inej's right wrist, and they fell in a tangle of limbs.

Manu saw Inej and Chanda at the end of the hallway and raced toward them. Inej needed to hide, but he couldn't tell her that. It would alert Chanda that he was there, and he wanted to use every opportunity he could.

His heart lurched in his chest when he saw Chanda go for Inej. Then, the two were on the ground.

"NAY!" he bellowed as he ran, pumping his legs faster.

Somehow, Chanda managed to dislodge the small blade from Inej's hand. The elf was trying to get on top of her. Inej didn't have to only prevent that. She also had to keep the elf's hands away so the magic Chanda kept discharging wouldn't strike her.

Inej managed to get a knee between them. Chanda was so focused on getting on top of Inej that she didn't seem aware of anything else. Inej grabbed for the second dagger in her boot. Their wrestling dislodged some snow, causing it to tumble into Inej's eyes and mouth as they fought.

Inej jerked the weapon up with all the strength she had. The next time Chanda pushed her onto her back, Inej held the blade still. Chanda's eyes went wide as the knife sank into her chest. For a moment, neither of them moved. Inej dimly heard someone shout.

Chanda looked down at the weapon sticking out of her in bewilderment. Inej swallowed hard as she, too, glanced at it. Chanda slowly sat up, struggling for breath as blood bloomed and spread. Her gaze met Inej's before she listlessly fell to the side. Inej scrambled away and staggered to her feet. Her body trembled as her breath, sharp and shallow, filled her lungs when reality set in. Against all odds, she was alive. But it felt like a mistake.

A flicker out of the corner of her eye drew Inej's attention. She looked, shock mixing with adrenaline as Manu stumbled to a halt, his gaze moving from Chanda to her and back to his friend.

"Help," Chanda whispered, her fingers reaching for him.

A look of disbelief and betrayal contorted Manu's face. Inej squeezed her eyes shut to erase the image, but it would be etched into her mind for eternity. He already held a wealth of animosity toward her for her part in everything. Any hope she had for absolution evaporated because he would never forgive her for hurting Chanda.

Her eyes flew open at the sound of a grunt to find that Manu had fallen to his knees. Inej took a hesitant step forward when she saw the bright red spots of blood in the snow and reached for him. A black-haired woman suddenly appeared beside him. One moment, they were there, and the next, they were gone.

Inej stared at the spot where Manu had been, dazed and unsure of what came next. She had gone up against an elf and miraculously survived. Just because she was alive now didn't mean she would remain that way. Manu, Jalall, and the others would likely demand she be punished. She could argue ignorance, but that wasn't much of a plea. She had come to kill Manu. There was no disputing that.

"Inej?"

At the sound of the familiar voice, she looked over and found Jalall standing with three Dark Elves.

"Are you hurt?" he asked gently as if speaking to someone who had lost their mind.

Inej stared into his dark eyes. Had he come to capture her? Kill her? She was shaking so badly.

Jalall took a step forward. "Inej, let us tend to your wounds."

Inej looked down to see that her coat was splattered in blood. It also covered her hands.

Jalall held out his hands in front of him and took another slow step forward. "You're losing a lot of blood. We need to tend to you."

"It isn't mine," she said.

Jalall froze, his brows snapping together as confusion filled his gaze.

"It's Chanda's. She's right there," Inej said as she swallowed and pointed at the elf.

When no one reacted, Inej turned her head to where Chanda's body had been, but the elf was gone. "She was here. Manu saw her."

"We need to get you back to the city," Jalall stated.

Inej jerked away as he reached for her and took two steps back. "Are you the half who joined Chanda?"

"What?" Jalall asked, his surprise obvious.

The female Dark asked, "Explain, please."

Inej looked between them. She was exhausted from fighting with Chanda, and there was no way she could best four elves. But she didn't know who she could trust, either. If they were with Chanda, her life was over. If they weren't, she had an opportunity to defeat Chanda completely. "Chanda claimed that half the army at Navara was hers to command. She said that if she doesn't return, they will slaughter the others and take control."

"The fuck they will," Jalall said.

"I'm going now," the Dark with facial scars said as shadows immediately closed around him.

Jalall motioned to the two remaining elves. "Inej, this is Arya and Jai. They've been fighting against the Masters, along with Manu and Dain, who just left."

Arya walked over and inspected the spot where Chanda had fallen. "I see Manu's prints here. And it's obvious where Inej and Chanda fought. But there are no other footprints."

"We would've seen someone coming toward us as we walked up," Jai added.

Jalall came to stand in front of Inej. "We need to get you somewhere warm. Your lips are blue."

Inej didn't have time to ask them to let her leave. There was no chance to promise that she would disappear and never return. The moment the words were out of Jalall's mouth, the two Dark were there, their shadows rising to cover them. She had never traveled with a Dark Elf before, and though she tried to focus on them, her thoughts were on Chanda—and the shock that had been carved into Manu's face.

She knew when they reached Navara by the warmth. She had yet to stop shaking. The final dregs of adrenaline were leaving her, and with them, the last of her strength keeping her upright. She reached out for something to hold on to as her knees buckled. She listed to the side as the shadows parted.

"Catch her," Arya called.

Jai swept her up in his arms.

"I'll get some herbs," Jalall said.

Inej let her lids fall shut as she rested her head on his shoulder. "Manu," she whispered.

No one answered. She didn't know if they hadn't heard her or just didn't want to reply. Her body demanded rest, but she could still hear everyone moving about as Jai laid her on a bed. She recognized the sound of Jalall's feet as he ran into the room. Someone helped her sit up, while Jalall put the glass to her lips.

"Let me," said a deep voice she didn't recognize.

The water was taken away, and they laid her back down. Inej attempted in vain to open her eyes and see who was there. Then, someone lightly placed a hand on her arm. A flush of energy darted through her, taking away all the aches, pains, and lethargy. Inej's eyes opened, and she found herself staring up at a human with eyes as black as the night and short, blond hair.

"Hi, lass," the man said with a smile as he straightened. "My name is Con. Do you feel better?"

Inej nodded. "What did you just do to me?"

"I healed you."

She frowned at him and pushed herself into a sitting position. "A human with magic?"

He chuckled softly. "I'm no' human, lass."

The dark-haired woman who had disappeared with Manu moved to stand next to Con. They linked their hands. The woman smiled at Inej before the couple walked out of the room. Jai and Arya followed, leaving her with Jalall.

Inej swung her gaze to him. "What just happened?"

"You were healed."

She cleared her throat. "I got that. Who is Con? And who was the woman?"

"Friends. You'll find out more later."

"Later," she repeated, suddenly worried.

Jalall walked to the door. "I have to go now. The house is locked down, so no one will disturb you. Get some rest. I'll be back soon."

He was out of the room before the last word had left his mouth. A moment later, she heard the front door open and close. Inej blew out a breath and rubbed her temples. The day had been filled with one shocking blow after another. She might not be in prison yet, but that didn't mean they would free her.

She scooted from the bed and threw off the ruined coat before undressing. Thankfully, Jalall hadn't locked her in the room, which meant she could bathe. She found clothes in the bureau and walked to the bathing room.

There was no enjoying the water, not with her future hanging in the balance. She thought about what might happen next as she scrubbed her body. The Mountain Elves did things very differently from the other races. She didn't know their rules or how they punished others. What she knew for sure was that she would have to pay for coming to kill Manu. She hadn't carried it out—or even attempted it. Hopefully, that would count for something.

She had convinced herself that she needed more information from him, but she knew now that she had been searching for an excuse not to hurt him. His stories and the time she'd spent with him had changed her heart. Even if her mind had been slower to catch up, that doubtlessly wouldn't matter. She had been dishonest with everyone from the beginning, and there were consequences for that.

42

Not once had Manu ever thought he would have to battle his own people. He hadn't wanted to believe the information Dain had shared with him, but it hadn't taken long for him to realize just how many had joined Chanda. With Dain's, Jalall's, Con's, Rhi's, Jai's, and Arya's help, he was able to locate and seize those loyal to her. But it had taken hours. Weeding out others would take more time.

His perfect city was no more. Just over half the army and their families were involved. Manu had never thought to mistrust his own people. But the Masters were cunning in how they entrapped individuals to join them. If Chanda hadn't bragged to Inej, the city would be at war with itself. At least, that had been prevented.

But his actions had sent an outcry through the city. He had thought the hardest part had been arresting his people. But that had been nothing compared to gathering the rest and explaining what had happened.

He left out any mention of Con, Rhi, and the others, since he didn't want that information getting back to the Masters. From now on, he would assume there was always at least one spy in his midst.

The only one unaccounted for was Chanda. Someone had gotten her out of Shaldorn. Whether she was alive or not remained to be seen. Regardless of whether Chanda was dead, whoever had taken her had likely seen who helped him and Inej. Their faces would make their way to the Masters.

He told his people about Chanda's involvement with the Masters, her role in Inej's kidnapping and Tahmine's death, as well as the battle at Shaldorn that had resulted in the arrest of dozens of Navarans. The only thing he had omitted were details about Inej being a spy. As he expected, his people had questions. They were scared and nervous and wanted him to calm them. He answered their questions for two straight hours. Surprisingly, no one had asked him to step aside and let someone else lead.

He had expected that.

Now, finally, he was headed to speak with Inej. He was both impatient and nervous.

Jalall fell into step with him as they walked toward his home. "You look like you could fall over."

"We had to fight our own," he murmured. "It never should have happened."

Manu would never forget walking into the barracks and seeing a group of soldiers lined up waiting for him. Had he not known they stood against him, they could've killed him. As it was, a few lives had been lost. It had been a brutal, ugly skirmish, made worse because they were people he had trusted.

Jalall sighed. "That wasn't your fault. None of this is."

Manu grunted and looked to the side. Some had left the assembly, but there was still a large number of citizens who remained behind, talking among themselves. There would be more questions to come. But that was for tomorrow. He'd done his duty to the city and his people. It was time for him now.

"We'll recover from this. We stopped Chanda," Jalall said.

"For now. The Masters will take another run at us."

They drew to a stop as they reached the house. Jalall faced him. "Then we'll take precautions. I've sent messengers to the other tribes to warn them as you asked."

Manu knew it was a stretch, alerting the other tribes. Some might have already fallen to the Masters, but if even one hadn't, it would be worth it. The flipside to that was that he wanted the Masters to know he was aware of their plans. Their attacks would hopefully be more direct now. Either way, he would be prepared.

He looked at the door that separated him from Inej. Con had assured him that she was fine, but Manu wouldn't truly believe it until he saw her for himself. He hadn't wanted Rhi to take him from her, but she hadn't given him a choice. Since he'd passed out right after she touched him, it was probably a good thing. He'd lost a lot of blood.

Arya and Jai would remain in the city for a short time. Arya watched over the house, while Jai used his shadows to move about Navara to see if they could suss out more enemies. The Mountain Elves had lived separately from the other races for too long. If they were to defeat the Masters, things needed to change. It might as well start with him.

Jalall clapped him on the back. "You've been itching to talk to her for hours. What are you still doing out here with me?"

"She might tell me that she wants to leave," Manu admitted.

Jalall shook his head. "That isn't going to happen. But you won't know that until you go inside."

Manu hadn't been afraid of much in his life, but he was scared of losing what he had found with Inej. He had to know that what was between them had been real. Because it had felt very, *very* real.

"Go on," Jalall urged. "You two were meant to be together."

Manu took a breath and grasped the handle, using magic to unlock the door. Then he stepped inside. The house was quiet and still. Maybe she was sleeping. He closed the door behind him, shutting out everything but Inej, him, and the words he had to say.

Manu quietly strode through the house, checking her room and the bathing room before finally finding her in the kitchen. She leaned a hip against the counter, her gaze on the floor as she stared off into space. He wondered what she was thinking. She'd been left alone with no one to answer the many questions she undoubtedly had.

He drank in the sight of her for several moments. Her stunning hair hung freely down her back, while a gown of golden yellow skimmed her curves before falling to her ankles. She was the most beautiful thing he had ever seen. From the moment of her arrival, his world had been turned upside down. And yet, he wouldn't want it any other way. Because he had met her. Known her.

Loved her.

Chanda's words about Inej's purpose in Navara echoed in his head. Inej hadn't denied it, but he needed to hear the truth from her lips. All of it. No matter how painful it might be. He'd already forgiven her, which was something he would tell her soon. She'd had chances to end his life, but she hadn't taken them. Maybe she would have in the future. Maybe she wouldn't have.

Suddenly, Inej blinked and looked up, then froze at the sight of him. Her face tightened, worry clouding her eyes. He wanted to pull her into his arms and kiss away her fears, but he remained in the doorway. If he touched her now, they wouldn't talk. And they needed to clear the air.

"I wondered when you would come," she said.

He leaned his shoulder against the doorjamb. "I've been dealing with those who joined Chanda. If you hadn't shared that information, I'm not sure I'd be standing here now."

"You stopped them, then?"

"The majority of them, I believe. I'm sure there are more. There will always be more."

Inej's gaze darted away for a heartbeat. "You've come for the truth."

"I have." The sooner they got this out in the open and discussed it, the sooner he could learn her wishes. And if she felt anything for him.

"I think I need to sit down for this," she said.

He moved to the side, clearing a path for her to walk. "Of course."

She glided past him, far enough away that they wouldn't touch. It was like a knife in his heart, but he didn't let it show. Manu was surprised when she chose the dining room. Though, it seemed to be their place for discussions. They took their seats and looked across the table at each other.

"I don't know where to start," she admitted.

He rested his hands atop the table. "How about the beginning?"

"All right." She licked her lips and swallowed. "There are some humans who, while not wealthy, make a decent living. That was my family until I was three. I don't remember any of it, but my mother used to tell me about how things were easier. Then my father walked out on us. She could no longer afford the house, so we were kicked out. We stayed with friends for a short while until Mum found work washing dishes at a restaurant. Her hours were long, and the pay barely covered the rent for our little place, but we had a home. She scraped the leftover food from the plates and brought it back for us to eat. Many times, there was only enough for me."

Manu knew Inej wouldn't want his pity, so he remained silent and listened.

Inej shrugged. "We may not have had much, but we had each other. I got my first job when I was eight, and Mum used any free time to teach me. As I got older, she pushed me to find better jobs. That was how I got into cleaning. The pay was marginally better, and with that extra income, we could finally move somewhere better. Then she got sick. Before I realized how serious it was, she was gone."

"I'm sorry," he said.

Her gaze dropped to the table. "She didn't suffer, and I'm thankful for that. We took care of each other. It was us against the world. After she was gone, I had no choice but to continue on. It isn't that I can't make friends. It's more...well, that I never wanted them."

"You didn't want to get close to someone and lose them again."

She looked up at him and nodded. "I didn't know that then, but I see it now. Cleaning allowed me to spend much of my time on my own, even when I was paired with others. Then, Krata came along. If I was rude, she smiled. If I ignored her, she smiled. She was vivacious, as if she had a special kind of light inside her. Everyone loved her. Except me. She didn't seem to care, though. I passed her place every morning on the way to work, and every single morning, she was there waiting. She didn't talk to me, but she spoke to others as we passed. Once we reached work, she always asked which jobs I preferred for that day. I took the best and easiest, and she never once complained. That should tell you a lot about me."

A challenge burned in her eyes, but he wouldn't take it. "When did you stop doing that?"

Her lips parted in shock. "How do you know I did?"

"Because you aren't as abhorrent as you believe you are."

"I was to her."

Manu heard the shame in her voice. "Did you become friends?"

"Krata thought we were. I, however, didn't. She would tell stories as we worked. She had an incredible imagination. Yet I couldn't find it in me to be the kind of friend she deserved."

"What happened to her?"

Inej released a long breath. "One morning, she wasn't there. I didn't wait or check on her. I was happy that I could walk to work in peace. I assumed she was running late, but when she didn't show up, I shrugged it off, thinking she was sick. On the second morning without her there, I began to worry. I checked in on her after work, but no one had seen her. That's when I knew she had been taken."

"And you were working for Gita then?"

Inej nodded. "I had left the agency to find cleaning jobs on my own. I was able to keep more money that way, and I answered an ad. Gita noticed Krata hadn't shown up in a couple of days and asked me about it. That's when she told me that she worked for the DIA. She went on to say that she knew who was responsible for the kidnappings."

Anger simmered in Manu's gut. One day, he'd get his hands on Gita. "Me."

"She gave me a map for how to find your mountain."

"I never saw a map."

Inej shrugged one shoulder. "I lost it right before I fell."

"She knew where Navara was?" If so, then he needed to set up more patrols.

"She knew the approximate location. She told me you'd find me."

Which he had. "I take it she's also the one who gave you the poison?"

Inej shifted uncomfortably in her chair. "Gita told me you would let your guard down around a human."

It seemed Gita knew him pretty well. Damn her.

"I believed every word she told me, down to the fact that it would all end if I stopped you. I'm not trying to make excuses, but I was angry about Krata being abducted."

"And you needed someone to blame. I get it."

She looked away and sighed. "If I had been thinking clearly, I would've seen how outlandish her explanation was. Especially the part about me joining the DIA as an undercover agent if I pulled this off."

"She didn't even give you proper clothing or equipment to travel through the Peaks." And that infuriated him. How many other humans had Gita talked into making the same trip, only for them to fall victim to some tragedy?

"I didn't ask for any either. I don't know why," Inej said with a frown.

"You wanted retribution for your friend."

Inej glanced at the table. "I wanted to erase the shame for how I treated her. But, aye, I did want to exact my vengeance. I thought it would make up for my actions. I honestly thought I could. Me. A human going up against an elf. I didn't stand a chance, and Gita knew it. *I* knew it. Still, I came for you."

"Don't sell yourself short. You fought Chanda and came out victorious."

"It was a fluke."

He raised his brows. "Was it? I don't think so."

Inej swallowed and briefly looked away.

Once more, Manu had to keep himself from going to her. He wanted to wrap her in his arms and shield her from the world. Inej's greatest asset was her fortitude. Life had whittled, bent, and twisted her into the woman she was now. It had tried to break her, but she had stood strong, refusing to crack. She had erected tall, thick walls for protection because no one had been there to shield her.

"Um," Inej said, pressing her lips together. "Gita gave me a box with several vials of poison. All but one was destroyed when I fell off the mountain. I dumped the box and the broken vials into the river."

"And kept the other."

She nodded softly. "I had every intention of taking your life. But...it was harder than I'd thought it would be. Even when I believed you to be the architect of the kidnappings."

"Why didn't you use the poison?" Even as he asked, he knew the answer might not be what he wanted to hear. Either way, he had to know. Otherwise, he'd spend the rest of his life wondering.

"At first, it was because I was too afraid. I had just arrived in the city and knew I was being watched closely. Then the assassin came for you. He told me that I'd done my part and I needed to stand down."

"But you didn't."

"The moment I realized why he was there, I was outraged that someone would take my vengeance from me. The longer I was in Navara, and the more I learned about you, the more I realized that the abductions wouldn't end with you. Someone else would step into your role. I made a quick decision."

One that had saved him. "It nearly cost you your life."

"All I could think about was getting payback for Krata and the countless others. When I woke, I knew my only course was to get close to you."

This was the part Manu had been dreading. He stood and walked to the sideboard to pour two glasses of wine. He set a glass in front of Inej and took a large swallow of his. Then he urged her, "Go on."

"I..." She trailed off, her mouth working as she struggled to find the words.

"The truth. Please."

She brought her glass to her lips, her hand shaking slightly, and took a drink. "I've never hesitated to take lovers, but I had a rule to only share one night. The moment they fell asleep, I left."

Her revelation left him speechless. Those walls of hers had been thicker than he realized. When she said she didn't believe in love, she had meant it. Her soft brown eyes, filled with shame and sorrow, darted to his.

"I never understood why anyone would combine their life with another's. To hand over all that trust, believing the other would never hurt them? I saw firsthand how deeply my father had hurt

Mum and swore I'd never allow anyone close enough to hurt me in that way." She held his gaze for a long moment.

He set aside his wine as she suddenly shoved to her feet. She started to pace with slow, measured steps, her distress evident in the way she repeatedly wrung her hands. As if she were searching for the right words. He could tell her that none of it mattered, that she was free to go. It's what he should say. But the words stuck in his throat. If she left Navara, he'd never see her again. But what was worse? Having her in the city and not being able to touch her? Or letting her go?

Either way he was fucked. She was in his blood now. There was no other for him, but he couldn't force someone to love him.

"I know you have no reason to believe anything I say," Inej said into the silence. "I need you to know that part of the reason I couldn't carry out my mission was because of you. I was suspicious of your kindness. When you got me the baking job, I…" She trailed off and wrinkled her face. "It was my dream. You gave me the one thing I'd always wanted without even knowing it. I was so happy working that I forgot why I was in Navara."

Manu couldn't take his eyes off her, watching her walk from one end of the room to the other. He frowned when she hurriedly swiped at her cheek. His heart missed a beat at the thought of her tears. He stepped toward her, but her words stopped him.

"I was deeply conflicted about my attraction to you. Sharing your bed was easy. Too easy. I broke my rule. I told myself it was because I had to make you trust me, but that was a lie." Inej halted, her gaze on the floor as she dragged in a ragged breath.

Manu tensed, hope unfurling in his chest.

"I wanted to be with you." She slid her gaze to him. "I craved you from a place I didn't know existed."

His lips parted, her name on his tongue when she looked away.

"Then you told me the story about Shaldorn and your part in its downfall—all of which conflicted with what Gita had shared—it only made my confusion about you grow. I could no longer ignore the fact that you could be innocent, but I couldn't exactly lay everything out to you and ask."

"You could have," he insisted.

She started to pace again. "We both know how that would've gone. Besides, I didn't want to chance being imprisoned. I wasn't sure you would be truthful, even if I had gone to you. Nor could I ask Gita. The more I struggled to sort out the truth, the more confused I became. The only thing I knew was that nothing Gita had said about you lined up with what I learned."

She halted by her chair and turned to face him, placing her hands on the back. "When I was attacked here, I was ready to die. I welcomed it because I wouldn't have to make a decision about you then. It would be out of my hands. I was furious when I woke in your bed."

"I should've been there," he told her. He was furious at himself for letting her wake alone. If he had been there, Chanda wouldn't have gotten to her.

Inej shoved her fingers into her hair, raking back the long locks from her face. "I used that time by myself to think. That's when I decided that I was going to tell you everything. If I discovered you were the monster Gita claimed, then that was my fault. If you weren't, then I wouldn't have taken an innocent life. I knew once I laid out the facts of my arrival that you would ask me to leave Navara. I deserved nothing less for my duplicity. I stood at your window, searching for you. That's when I saw you and Jalall enter his home. I suspected you'd be visiting me soon. Instead, it was Chanda who said she was taking me to you."

"She knew I'd track the two of you." He fisted his hands at the reminder of how easily his childhood friend had manipulated everyone. "She knew every move I'd make and planned for it."

Inej picked at one of her fingernails. "I'm so sorry I was involved in any of this."

"You were tricked."

"I should've known. I should've seen through Gita."

Manu shook his head. "You were hurting."

"You almost died. I watched that machine d—"

"But I didn't," he said over her. "I'm standing here because I have friends neither Chanda nor Gita knew about."

Inej's face crumpled. "I began this by coming here."

"Don't carry that. This would've happened without you. You were manipulated. We both were."

She drew in an unsteady breath. "Then let me apologize for stabbing Chanda."

"Why?" he asked, confused.

"She was your friend and I sh—"

Manu took a step toward her, shaking his head. "There's no need. You were fighting for your life."

"I heard you shout."

"Because I thought she was about to kill you and knew I wouldn't get there in time to stop her."

Inej stared at him for a moment before she whispered, "Oh."

"Don't you know? Can't you see how I feel about you?" He'd had a speech planned, laid out with all the reasons she should stay. One where he would offer friendship, and, hopefully, eventually, win her over to show her that love existed. But having her before him, vulnerable and so damn beautiful it hurt to look at her, made him forget every word.

Her gaze searched his as the pulse at her throat beat rapidly.

He was scaring her. He could see it in her eyes and the way she gripped her hands together so tightly her knuckles turned white. But he couldn't stop now. For better or worse, he was going to lay it all out. "I love you."

Her lips trembled before she pressed them together.

"I knew you were hiding something from the beginning. I suspected you were more than you claimed, and while I could've —and probably *should've*—pushed for answers, I didn't. I was drawn to you, and I didn't mean to let that attraction get in the way. No matter what I told myself, no matter how I tried to stay away from you, I couldn't." Manu drew in a breath and slowly released it. "I don't know what will happen with the Masters. They'll retaliate, but I don't know when or how. I offered Navara as a safe place for you. I can't guarantee that anymore. What I can promise is that I'll protect you until my last breath. Please stay."

"You want me to stay?" she asked, so quietly he'd barely heard her.

It was nearly impossible not to reach for her, but he kept his hands to himself. She would have to come to him. "I've never told another woman that I loved her. Why would I say it now and then want you to leave?"

"Because of everything I've done," she began.

He shook his head. "You lied. We've all done that for one reason or another. Regardless of your reasoning, you protected me against the assassin. You even tried to get out of hurting me at Shaldorn. Time and again, you've demonstrated that the last thing you want to do is harm me."

She said nothing as she stared at him.

"I love you, Inej. From your self-perceived rough edges to the walls around your heart. I love your smile, that glorious hair of yours. I love the way my shirts look on you and how you kiss me. You found a place here. I want you to stay. Even if it isn't with me."

A single tear dropped onto her cheek. She dashed it away and sniffed.

He could feel her slipping away from him. Manu tried once more. "I know you don't believe in love. Give me a chance to show you that it does exist."

She turned away, and he dropped his chin to his chest, his eyes closing in defeat. He felt her near and opened his eyes as she came to stand before him.

"I know it exists." She took one of his hands into hers. "You've shown me each time you kissed me, protected me, and fought for me. I see it in your eyes when you look at me. I feel it in your hands when you touch me. I hear it when you say my name."

Manu was almost too afraid to believe what he heard.

She placed her other hand on his chest. "If I hadn't wanted to gain your trust, I never would've given in to the desire to know your body. I was yours from that first kiss. I just didn't realize it until it was almost too late."

"Does that mean you'll stay?"

"Aye, I'm staying."

A big smile spread over his face as he yanked her against him, their lips meeting in a scorching, passionate kiss.

"I love you," he said between kisses.

She cupped his face and looked into his eyes. "I love you."

Manu lifted her into his arms and stalked to the bedroom,

where he intended to spend the next several days undisturbed, loving her.

EPILOGUE

Three days later…

Inej was kneading dough when large hands came around her. A moment later, a hard body molded to her back. Manu's lips found the sensitive spot on her neck, and he moaned into her skin.

"Come back to bed," he urged between hot kisses along the edge of her ear.

"I'm making your favorite tarts."

"I'd rather taste you."

His husky voice sent chills racing across her skin. They had returned to his home after the first night at Jalall's. Their time had been interrupted by Arya and Jai's departure. Neither of them had discovered anything that would lead them to more spies. Inej took that as good news. But Manu and Jalall assumed the spies were good enough not to be detected.

She turned in Manu's arms, careful not to touch him with her hands that were covered in flour. A few of the servants were moving about the kitchen, casting glances their way and smiling. Inej knew it was more about Manu's happiness than her arrival. And that was fine with her. It would take time for her to gain everyone's trust, and that was how it should be.

"I thought you were going out with Jalall this morning," she said.

Manu shrugged and gave her a soft kiss. "I am. I just don't like waking without you beside me."

"If you had slept a little longer, you would've woken to pastries."

He grinned. "I'll stay in bed next time. But you don't need to get up early to bake me anything."

"I wanted to."

"I need to make sure I wear you out more at night to keep you beside me," he murmured before kissing her again.

They broke apart at the sound of giggles nearby. Inej grinned at the trio of younger females as they walked out, casting glances their way.

"I can stay behind. Jalall can handle things."

Inej found a towel and wiped her hands before winding her arms around Manu's neck. "You can't stay beside me all the time. I have the daggers you gave me on my body. They'll always be there now. But you have a city to lead."

"If anything happened to you..." he began.

"I know. I feel the same about you. But we can't live our lives like that. We're standing against a powerful organization. You're the face of that for your people. Go be that for them. I'll be here when you return."

He skimmed his fingers along her braid that fell down her

back. "I know it's too soon to ask, but I want things to be official between us. I want you as my wife. When you're ready, let me know."

"I'm ready."

Manu blinked and pulled his head back. "Are you serious?"

"I am," she replied. "I almost lost you the other day. I don't want to waste any more time without you."

"I'll start the preparations, then." He beamed down at her before sweeping her up in his arms and twirling her around the kitchen.

Reva nervously looked around the dark alley. She had been waiting for days for Sidiq to give her the date and time to meet Arya. She'd held out hope that he would go to Dain, but he had set up the meeting with Arya just as he had promised. That should be enough for Reva. Yet it wasn't. She wanted to see Dain.

She didn't know why Sidiq was so against Dain now, nor would she ask. The look on her boss's face made it clear not to push the subject.

Reva tapped her foot on the ground, trying to rid her body of its anxious energy. It had been easy giving Dain the information since he had come to the pub to retrieve it. She didn't know if Sidiq had nixed that option or if it had been Arya who changed the location. Whatever the reason, Reva now stood in a narrow alley four blocks east of The Crossing.

It was her night off, and she normally spent it in her flat. There were deep shadows everywhere she looked. Humans had poor eyesight at night. For all she knew, each of the shadows was a

Dark Elf. Danger existed everywhere, but at least it was easier to see during the day. The darkness hid all sorts of unpleasantness.

A figure approached from the opposite end of the alleyway. A streetlight caught on long, white hair. The Dark's face was hidden, but Reva could tell by the walk that it was a female. She didn't call out Arya's name. Reva had gotten to know the elf when Jai kidnapped them and held them prisoner aboard his ship for a time.

As the elf moved closer, another light overhead revealed Arya's face. Reva sighed as she flashed a smile at her friend.

"It's good to see you," Arya said, stopping before her.

They shared a quick embrace. "You, too."

Arya looked one way and then the other. "Is everything all right?"

"I have information you need to know."

The Dark Elf's brow furrowed as she studied Reva. "You got free of the Masters. You shouldn't be involved anymore. It's way too dangerous."

"I hear things at the pub. I passed information on to Dain for a little while before he abruptly ended that."

"He did what?" Arya asked in a too-soft voice.

Reva waved away her words. "No one pays attention to me at the pub. I'm merely a server. I pick up on things."

"You need to stop," Arya told her. "I'm serious, Reva. If they learn what you're doing, they'll come for you. And we both know what will happen to you if they do."

Reva held back a shiver of unease. "I know the risks. I also know that what I have for you is too important not to pass on. Dain isn't coming to the pub anymore. I had no way of getting in touch with you. Sidiq was against this, an—"

"Because he knows it puts you in danger. None of us wants to see you hurt."

"Others are getting hurt. And more will if we don't do something." Reva shook her head as she glanced at the sky.

"That's easy for you to say. You aren't in t—"

"They're building another Shaldorn," Reva said over her.

Arya froze, her eyes widening. "Are you sure?"

"I heard those very words at the same time two elves spoke about a human being sent to the Mountain Elves."

"We knew about the human." Arya looked away, obviously troubled. Then, to herself, she said, "Bloody hell. Another Shaldorn. We thought they might."

Reva watched Arya processing everything. "I can find out more."

Arya turned gray eyes to her. "I'm not going to be able to stop you, am I?"

"Nay, you aren't."

Arya released a long sigh. "I won't be able to get into the city every night, and it isn't safe for you to be out like this. Let me sort out a way for us to communicate. I'll be in touch."

Dain followed Reva as she made her way back home. He almost hadn't come when Arya told him that Sidiq had reached out to her because he'd known it had to do with Reva. He had almost called out to her twice. Once, he'd even gotten close enough to touch her but had jerked back just in time. She never knew he was there, and that was how it had to remain. It was how it had to be.

He didn't leave her until she was safely inside her flat. He knew what awaited him. Dain could leave, but he was only putting off the inevitable. He moved unseen through the streets until he reached the rainwood. Once there, he dropped the shadows and leaned against one of the colossal trees. He didn't have to wait long.

Arya emerged from the shadows, indignant, her icy fury something she rarely released. But it was directed at him this time. She stalked to him until they were toe-to-toe. It was Jai who put a hand between them and sought to hold her back.

"How dare you bring her into this?" Arya snapped.

Dain looked at her clenched fists where black magic sparked, waiting to be unleashed. He met her gray eyes. "I didn't bring her into it. Jai did when he kidnapped her."

"You know what I mean," Arya argued, her voice growing louder.

"All right, all right," Jai said, holding his lover back. "Dain's right. I did this."

Arya rolled her eyes. "You didn't ask her to spy for us."

Jai glanced over his shoulder at Dain. Calmly, he said, "I would've done the same in his place."

"Unbelievable," Arya grumbled as she spun away from them and walked a few steps. She halted, her hands on her hips, breathing heavily. Then, she whirled back around. "She has no business being a part of this."

"None of us does, but here we are. Everyone will have to take a stand eventually," Jai said.

Dain watched the couple's exchange. Arya was right. Reva should be as far from them as possible. He wondered if the Dragon Kings would take her in.

"Reva's information was important," Jai argued.

Arya dropped her head back to look up at the night sky through the canopy of trees. "Another Shaldorn." She sighed, calmer now as she looked at Dain. "Why did Sidiq seek me out instead of you? How did he even know?"

Dain had kept so many secrets for so long that it wasn't always easy to release them. "He found out that I asked Reva to work for me. He...took exception to it."

"Why would he care?" Jai asked.

Arya dropped her arms to her sides. "He seems to have taken an interest in her. Maybe he's worried about her. She *was* taken from his place."

Jai's pale gray eyes locked on Dain. "Are Sidiq and Reva romantically involved?"

Arya chuckled but sobered when Dain didn't immediately answer.

"Dain?" she urged.

He dipped his chin. "Sidiq has feelings for her. I don't think anything has developed between them."

"He's the reason you quit working with Reva," Jai guessed.

Dain pushed away from the tree trunk. "Partly. Reva doesn't need to bring any attention to herself, and any connection to us will do just that."

Jai wrinkled his nose. "Her intel is important."

"So is her staying out of the Masters' hands," Arya argued. She shot Dain an apologetic look. "Now, I understand why you stopped working with her."

Jai threw up his hands. "What now? Arya said she'd be in touch."

"We tell Sidiq we're cutting off all communication with her. He'll understand that means not to contact us," Dain said.

Arya shifted her weight to one side. "Are you sure that's wise? We need allies."

"I spent too much time at The Crossing in prior years. They will go there looking for us. We can't go back," Dain said.

Belanore

He stood inside the empty tower apartment and seethed. Gita was gone. She thought she could fool him, but she was wrong. He would find her. Though he wasn't sure if he would haul her to the Masters or kill her himself. He would hold off on notifying the Masters until he found her, but she had played right into his hands earlier than expected. All without even knowing it.

Gita was nothing if not predictable. He knew what she wanted—a return to power. But someone had helped her leave the tower. The fact that she had done it against the Masters' wishes told him plenty.

"Run while you can," he said as he turned on his heel and stalked out. "Because I'm coming for you."

Thank you for reading **MOUNTAIN FIRE**. I hope you enjoyed Inej and Manu's story, because I fell hard for them.

There's a bonus short story featuring Manu and Inej.
Grab it here:

https://mailchi.mp/donnagrant/aftermidnight

If you want more Elven Kingdom stories, I'm pleased to announce that **BURNING SEA** is up next in the series.

BUY BURNING SEA NOW
at www.DonnaGrant.com

* * *

If you love the elves, you'll love the next Dark Universe book set in the Skye Druids series, **KISS OF SKYE**.

BUY KISS OF SKYE NOW
at www.DonnaGrant.com

To find out when new books release
SIGN UP FOR MY NEWSLETTER today at
https://www.tinyurl.com/DonnaGrantNews

Join my Facebook group, Donna Grant Groupies, for exclusive
giveaways and sneak peeks of future books.
https://bit.ly/DGGroupies

Keep reading for a glimpse of
BURNING SEA and KISS OF SKYE ...

GLIMPSE AT BURNING SEA

ELVEN KINGDOMS, BOOK 5

New York Times and *USA Today* best-selling author Donna Grant returns for the next Elven Kingdoms story.

***

BUY BURNING SEA NOW
at www.DonnaGrant.com

SNEAK PEEK AT THE NEXT DARK UNIVERSE BOOK

KISS OF SKYE, SKYE DRUIDS, BOOK 8

Return to Scotland and *New York Times* and *USA Today* best-selling author Donna Grant's Skye Druids, where magic and danger intertwine and a tale of passion, revelations, and new beginnings unfolds.

* * *

BUY KISS OF SKYE NOW
at www.DonnaGrant.com

Keep reading for an excerpt of KISS OF SKYE …

KISS OF SKYE EXCERPT

London

R owen didn't bother to open her umbrella as she walked from the hotel into the drizzle to the waiting cab. She slid into the seat and gave the driver directions before trying to get comfortable in a vehicle that had held dozens of people that day alone.

She looked out the side window and fought against the revulsion that rose. The cobblestone streets, traditional pubs, and medieval architecture impressed her. She didn't care about the city's long history and royal landmarks meant nothing to her. The city was loud, dirty, and crowded.

And if she heard "you're from across the pond" one more time, she was going to scream.

Rowen loosened her fingers that gripped her purse too tight. She only had a little more time in the country before she could get home. She missed her animals. She missed her routine. She missed her life.

The cab slowed as it pulled to the curb. She tightened the belt of her trench coat and adjusted the strap of her purse on her shoulder. She realized as the cab pulled away that she had left her umbrella. That was the second one. Her thoughts shifted away from the vehicle to her surroundings.

There were many similarities between UK and America, but there were just as many differences. For one, parking lots. Or rather car parks. Similar, but different. She sighed and stared at the striking ancient building before her. The white-gray stone matched other prominent architecture around the city. One talkative cab driver had explained it was called Portland stone that was quarried from the Isle of Portland in Dorset. He had gone on—in great detail—about all the different types of Portland stone, but she had tuned him out.

The stone was used as far back as the Roman era, which made it difficult to determine just how old the building was. But she knew. The sun was behind a building as it sank into the horizon. A few rays found their way between structures and struck the windows of a café to her right, blinding her.

Rowen turned her head away as she made for the building. There was a grand entry in the front where others were entering. There were no guards. Druids didn't need them. All she had to do was get through this night, and then she could go home and deliver her report on the London Druids.

From the moment Rowen had read the email invite, she had wanted to ignore it. There had always been open communication between the London Druid and her group, but not once had they ever been summoned. Granted, they had never invited anyone from London to them. Everyone knew the power London had. They were respected but not feared.

Things had changed, though. Small things at first that had been overlooked or explained away. The incidents became larger and more frequent, making everyone sit up and notice. Others had wanted to travel to the UK, but for some reason, she was chosen. Rowen tried to refuse, but here she was. In a city she loathed about to enter a viper's nest.

The heels of her shoes clicked softly on the pavement as she approached the building. She had expected there to be a grand edifice, but the double domed front doors fit in with all the others. There was a fanlight in stained glass above the door. There was an ornate caste iron knocker and handles that held a touch of mysticism in the design.

As she got closer, she was able to see the stained glass was tree of life with its limbs extending outward and upward while its roots mimicked the branches. She stood before the closed door and stared at the raven head protruding from the door holding the knocker in its beak.

Ravens were powerful symbols and messengers to Druids. The birds were particularly linked to wisdom, prophecy, and the connection between the living and the Otherworld. Moreover, ravens were associated with death and transformation.

Her eyes dropped to the handle that resembled a root. If she had any doubts about where she was, they vanished. Rowen grasped the door knocker and struck the door twice.

Almost instantly, both doors swung open and a petite brunette in her early forties greeted her with a toothy smile. "Rowen," the woman said smiling, the corners of her soft brown eyes crinkling.

"We're so excited to have you here finally. Please, come in. I'm Ella, and I'll be showing you around."

For a second, she almost turned and bolted.

***

BUY KISS OF SKYE NOW
at www.DonnaGrant.com

ABOUT THE AUTHOR

New York Times and *USA Today* bestselling author Donna Grant® has been praised for her "totally addictive" and "unique and sensual" stories.

She's written more than one hundred novels spanning multiple genres of romance including the bestselling Dragon Kings® series that features a thrilling combination of Druids, Fae, and immortal Highlanders who are dark, dangerous, and irresistible. She lives in Texas with her dog and a cat.

www.DonnaGrant.com
www.MotherofDragonsBooks.com

facebook.com/AuthorDonnaGrant

instagram.com/dgauthor

tiktok.com/@donnagrant_author

bookbub.com/authors/donna-grant

goodreads.com/donna_grant

pinterest.com/donnagrant1